Double Trouble

Shari Low

All the characters in this book are fictitious and any resemblance to real persons, living or dead, is entirely coincidental.

First published in Great Britain in 2003 by
Judy Piatkus (Publishers) Ltd of
5 Windmill Street, London W1T 2JA
email:info@piatkus.co.uk

The moral right of the author has been asserted

A catalogue record for this book is available from the British Library

ISBN 0 7499 3419 0

Set in Times by
Action Publishing Technology Ltd, Gloucester

Printed and bound in Great Britain by
Mackays of Chatham Ltd, Chatham, Kent

To my own Double Trouble: Callan & Brad,

To Gemma,

And, as always, to John.
Everything, always . . .

Book One

Prologue

Clark Dunhill – Sales Manager – The Deal

'Are you going to give me it in days or weeks?' Nick grinned as Clark deftly manoeuvred into the void that had miraculously appeared next to him at the bar. It took someone special to create a space in the Shaker Bar at 6 p.m. on a Friday. Moses had an easier job parting the Red Sea.

Clark pulled his Samsung s300 from his ear and snapped it shut before tucking it into the inside pocket of his jacket. Armani. And running his fingers through his short and incredibly trendy raven hair. John Frieda. He looked at his watch. Cartier.

He thought for a moment, his pensive expression creating little more than a furrow on his unlined forehead. Botoxed, of course. Although, for a man who spent more every year on ultraviolet sunbed tubes than the entire lighting budget of an NHS hospital, his skin was bearing up remarkably well.

'Two days, three hours and er . . .' He consulted his watch, his brain striving to do a calculation with numbers higher than ten. That usually required the aid of a calculator. 'Forty-three minutes.'

Nick rolled his eyes in resignation and pulled out his wallet. It was a familiar routine. Since the onslaught of puberty, the loss of virginity and their ability to pass for eighteen and therefore gain entry to the finest of drinking establishments (or any alcohol-serving port in a pub-crawl), the first round was always bought by the person who'd had the least recent sex. It was a sadomasochistic thread of their friendship – not only was the loser's sex life crap but he always had to buy more beers than the others and was therefore skint too. Double trouble.

Fortunately, Nick didn't have to worry too much about his financial situation these days, but still it was a shade on the shameful side that he'd opened his wallet first every week for the last year. The last ten years actually. Apart from that one time when he got lucky on a Thursday night and Clark had stayed home due to suspected pleurisy. That was a great week. Historic.

Clark laughed loudly. 'Christ almighty, mate, you're going to have to get your end away soon. You haven't had a good shag since you bent that blonde over the—'

Fiz interrupted them from behind the bar. 'Well here they are – Smarm Man and Noddy. Usual drinks, oh pretentious ones?' she yelled, causing a smirk among all in earshot, including Nick (aka Noddy, according to Fiz, due to the fact that he agreed with everything she said, no matter how rude or controversial) and Clark. They nodded (as anticipated) and Fiz slammed a bottle of Moët on the granite bar top, followed by three glasses placed down a little more gently. One for Clark, one for Nick and one for the presently absent Taylor.

'If you're a good girl we might let you share it with us, straight from the bottle,' Clark offered provocatively. She was in lust with him really, he was sure of it. She was just playing some typical hard-to-get-female mind game.

Fiz snorted. 'Sorry Smarm, I'll pass. I didn't bring in my wire brush and Dettol today – don't know what I'd catch.' She spun on her two-inch cowboy boot heels complete with metal tearing spurs and transferred her wrath to the next unsuspecting customer.

'God, I'm in love.' Nick stared wistfully after her, watching as she served two customers simultaneously with both drinks and insults. It was only the fact that her caustic wit made her amusing and a great talking point for the customers that kept her in a job.

'Hey, Fiz, has Taylor phoned? Do you know what time he'll be here?' he called after her.

Fiz spun back round, her spurs carving a circle on the floor. 'Look, it's chronic enough that I'm reduced to working behind this poncey bar serving overpriced drinks to you lot of twats, but I'm *not* your fecking secretary. Now piss off away from the bar and leave room for nice, paying customers who leave big tips that'll keep me off the breadline.'

'Only if you tell me when he'll be here.' Nick was feeling brave. Besides, she couldn't assault him in the bar – too many witnesses.

Fiz sighed. 'He hasn't called but I was on the same shoot as him today. We finished two hours ago, so the sad case will still be glued to a mirror or trying to chat up another blonde stick insect. Said he was coming down here though, but that's probably only if his ever-intellectual brain can remember the way.' She switched her gaze to a follically challenged chap with an expectant expression next to them. 'Right, baldy, you're next. What can I get you?'

Although they'd rather have an encounter with a sexually transmitted disease than vocalise it, deep down both Clark and Nick harboured more than a modicum of jealousy over their mate Taylor's career. That male modelling lark was the cushiest number in town. How difficult could it be to be surrounded by babes all day, getting every whim catered for (and they did mean *every* whim if Taylor's stories were to be believed)? Lucky bastard. Nick's job as general manager of a Porsche dealership (courtesy of his father who owned the franchise) and Clark's lucrative career in IT sales just didn't quite have the same appeal. Or perks.

Still, they weren't doing too badly, Clark mused as he snapped down the cuff of his Versace shirt and refilled his glass, before shouting to Fiz to pull another bottle from the cooler. As she threw him a look that would render champagne flat in an instant, Clark gave her the thirty-second top-to-toe appraisal. He just couldn't see what Nick's attraction to her was based on. Sure, she was quick with the comments and could be amusing when she tried, but she had a face you could lose in a crowd and hair only usually seen on the victims of electrocution. No class. None. Definitely not in his league. Nick was welcome to her.

He scanned the room seeking out someone more of his elevated calibre. Whoa! Double take. He spotted the blonde walking in the door. Five foot eleven, hair gleaming down to her waist, faded jeans, a white T-shirt, breasts fighting to get out. Now there was his type of woman. He was transfixed, studying every movement of her coltish body. As she cleared the doorway, she stepped to the side and Clark involuntarily rolled his eyes. Bloody Taylor. He should have guessed. As he'd just been thinking, lucky bastard.

Taylor cut a path towards them, holding the hand

of the goddess as she followed him. There was a whooshing noise as the majority of females in the room (Taylor and a gorgeous blonde – there was something for every taste there) who were seated slid off their chairs. Some were even openly staring, chins on cleavage, backs arched, temperatures rising.

Taylor strutted his six-foot-four, V-shaped frame. With his dark blond, shoulder-length hair casually pushed back, Buzz Lightyear jawline and emerald eyes, he was officially (according to the latest survey carried out by *Please!* magazine, the *'provocative must-read for the modern thinking independent woman who is at one with her sexuality'*) the third sexiest guy in the country. Only Jude Law and Sean Bean were ahead of him in the shaggability stakes.

There was a rumour circulating that Liam Gallagher wanted to kick his head in because he reckoned he should have been in the top three. Taylor wasn't worried. The billboard underwear campaign that had emphasised (but not, he swore, exaggerated – it really was that size) his natural asset had elevated him to icon status. He felt he belonged there.

He sailed the sea of surging oestrogen and docked at the bar next to his mates. He checked his watch.

'Twenty-seven minutes. Give or take the odd second,' he gloated.

Nick grinned. It didn't bother him that Taylor had a sex life more frequent than most train services, but he did find the effect that it had on Clark somewhat amusing.

Ego dented, Clark grimaced. Bastard. Lucky. And the dollface didn't even have a hair out of place. They must have done it standing up. So the next round was going on Clark's plastic.

'Nick, Clark, this is Tarissa. We were on the same job today,' he drawled in the standard, nonchalant tone that comes with complete confidence and indifference.

They all murmured greetings and Nick shouted up another glass. It whizzed towards him and missed his ear by an inch. Luckily he was a good catcher.

'So, Tarissa,' Clark endeavoured to make conversation. It wasn't easy to do when he was salivating at the mouth. 'Tell us about today's stint. Perfume, wasn't it?' He remembered Taylor had told him that much last week. 'How did it go?'

'Um, fine. Yeah. It was great,' she smiled, showing teeth straight from a toothpaste ad. Okaaaay, thought Clark, that'll be that conversation-winner then. He was just contemplating whether to have another bash at inducing speech by asking her about, say, world peace or the chemical symbols for all metals when she excused herself to go to the loo.

Clark turned to Taylor. 'Bloody hell, mate, they're getting worse. At least last week's could string together words of more than one syllable.

Taylor grinned lazily and reached for his glass. 'Look, Einstein, I've told you before, who needs conversation when a babe looks like that? If I want to chat I'll call my sister.'

Nick simultaneously tutted and frowned. 'You're a shallow bastard, Taylor. How can you honestly say that you enjoy a night out with a female who has the conversation skills of a lamp-post? Nah, brains. I'd much rather have a bird I could talk to,' he asserted, his gaze never leaving Fiz as she threw a maraschino cherry at a customer who had dared to complain about the lack of fruit adornments on her cocktail.

Clark was listening to all this with amusement. He

could see Taylor's point of view. Going anywhere with Tarissa would stop traffic and the looks of jealousy shooting from every red-blooded male within a hundred yards would be a guaranteed ego boost. But after a while, how boring would that be? And what did it say about you if your girlfriend had an IQ lower than her breast size? After all, he wasn't exactly lacking in the grey matter department, he concluded. He *was* in IT.

'Have to say, guys, I'm somewhere in the middle. Looks are all very well and good, but having a smart female says something about who you are. You know, an intellectual equal, and all that.' The irony of his slang articulation failed to register with him.

Taylor laughed. 'So you want the brains *and* the beauty. Yeh, like that'll happen.'

Clark was mortified. 'Meaning?'

'Well, for a start, mate, what super-brainy chick would put up with you? They all go for academics or serious high-flyers. And they usually look like they've either been smacked by a kipper or eaten a few too many. Nah, females with a seriously high IQ *and* a model bod are in pretty short supply. It's strictly a one or the other deal.'

Clark thought for a moment. Then a slow, maleficent grin crossed his face. 'Granted, mate. So what we're saying then is that *one* woman wouldn't be enough for me.' He was warming to this theory now. 'What I need is *two* women. One with brains, one a physical goddess. One for general knowledge and one for carnal knowledge.' He was quite proud of the last statement. Who said A-level English would be a waste of time?

Nick roared with laughter. 'Yeah, and I'm sure that you could find two females just like that who would agree to accompany you everywhere, one on each arm. Have you got a death wish, mate?'

But Clark wasn't listening. His imagination was leading him onto a parallel plane. He could visualise the scenario. He'd always known that one female wasn't enough to satisfy him; a plethora of two-timed ex-girlfriends could testify to that. The beautiful ones could never hold his attention for long and those lacking in physical perfection were purely a mechanism to pass the time of day (after all, a shag *was* a shag). But this was the perfect solution. Two birds. All he had to do was find them, hook them, reel them in and then keep them apart. He could then pick and choose which one to be with depending on his mood. Shit, why hadn't he thought of this before? Instead of searching for the perfect chick, now he only needed to find two half-perfect ones. It would be a doddle for a man of his stature.

He spotted Tarissa making her way back from the loos. That and the last drop of the second bottle of Moët spurred him to decisiveness. This was a matter of male pride. Even Taylor had never managed to parade two birds in the Shaker on the same night. It would be kudos. It would be retribution. It would put him at the top of the Shag Monster charts where he belonged, once and for all. His chest and other strategic parts were puffing up at the very thought of it.

'Right then. I bet you both a weekend in Marbella that in the not-too-distant future, I'll be in here with two females – one a brain, one a body. And both of them being shagged by the Clark-meister.'

Nick and Taylor grinned conspiratorially at each other. What did they have to lose? The worst that could happen was that they'd have to fork out for half of a weekend for three in the sun. And anyway, Clark's middle name should have been 'procrastination', only he couldn't spell it. Chances are he would have forgotten about this whole conversation by the time his hangover subsided the next day.

They held out their hands and took turns to shake Clark's.

'Deal.'

Chapter One

Cassandra Haven – Financial Director – The Brains

Cassandra clicked on the 'shut down' button of her laptop, prompting the familiar and incessantly irritating tune that it made while powering off, then removed it from the docking station on her desk and slid it into her briefcase. She would need it for the endless hours she planned to work at home that weekend – the annual profit and loss figures were a bugger to do and were due before the board of System Solutions the following Wednesday.

She glanced up at the clock. 11.35 p.m. Christ, she really needed to get a life. Only barmen, bouncers, hookers and taxi drivers were still working in city-centre London at this time on a Friday night. Still, it would be worth it when she achieved her year-end bonus. There was nothing like a five-figure sum to keep the midnight oil burning. She lit a Marlboro Light. Polluting the strictly non-smoking building with one cigarette at the end of every day was her token act of rebellion. Petty, but nonetheless fulfilling. She inhaled deeply as she leaned back in her chair and closed her eyes, trying to ease the tension that had her forehead contorted into peaks and troughs that no amount of collagen injections could disguise. Not that she would ever even attempt cosmetic enhancement of any kind. She didn't even own a make-up bag, for God's sake. She really didn't see the point. Why bother wasting half an hour every morning painting your face, only to take it off again every night? She could put that time to better use in the office doing something far more worthwhile, like making money either for her employers or herself.

Cassandra Haven had been financial director (she explained it to her parents – a school auxiliary and a cleansing department worker from Slough who only ever ventured into the centre of London on Royal occasions – as 'the big cheese in the dosh department') for the last two years. Awarding her the title had been long overdue, as she'd almost single-handedly run the department since joining the company as an accounts graduate thirteen years before. She had risen in the ranks to assistant financial controller after only three years, but then somehow got stuck there while a succession of male financial directors were recruited above her, all of whom realised very quickly that Cass had the department running like a German rail service. They were therefore happy to play golf, take their salaries and long lunches while leaving the very serious Miss Haven to produce the results that they would take the credit for. A prodigious example of delegation.

It was only when the last department figurehead left to assume a prestigious role in the Middle East that Cass finally made her meticulously planned move. She detailed her role, achievements and duties and compiled an in-depth analysis of the future improvements she recommended for the department, and then presented the report to the directors together with a thinly veiled ultimatum.

Fortuitously (and very deliberately) she chose the morning of a media frenzy over a female stockbroker winning millions from her ex-employer in a high-profile sex discrimination case.

Before the week was out Cass had the office overlooking the Thames, the seat on the board, the six-figure salary and the title: Cassandra Haven – Financial Director.

All she'd had to sacrifice was any semblance of a personal life. In her mind it was a no-brainer. It was a case of priorities. She didn't need barbecues and nights at the cinema watching crap movies. She'd rather be at work, reinforcing the sandbags of complete control around her position of success, power and status. That was undoubtedly a far more efficient use of time. Only now that she had achieved career utopia could she even consider enhancing any other area of her life.

Her mobile bleeped to signal an incoming text message. Cass picked up the phone.

'Forgot 2 thnk u for chq. If u r at wk GO HOME. wl call u tmrw. Lv u, Txxx'.

Cassandra smiled. Antonia, aka Toni, was her twenty-year-old sister and mother to her two-year-old nephew Ben. She lived in what was a dilapidated council flat until Cass stood guarantor for the mortgage to allow Toni to purchase it, and then loaned her the money to make it habitable. Now that Antonia was working as a trainee receptionist at System Solutions (a position that she had proudly obtained without any help or influence from Cass), she no longer relied on her sister for financial help. However, every now and then Cass liked to give her a little something – after all, kids were an expensive business.

She smiled half-heartedly to herself as she stubbed her cigarette out on the concrete outside her window and dropped the stub thirty floors to the ground. She hoped that there were no unsuspecting pedestrians underneath. Spending the night in a club with a cigarette end embedded in your highlights was *so* not an attractive look.

She'd lost her train of thought. Oh yes, Antonia, Ben, expenses. How would she know what it really cost to bring up a child? Taking Ben to the park once a fortnight and the odd babysitting shift hardly qualified her as a childcare expert.

Over the last few months, however, she'd realised that it was almost time to change that. Children had always been part of her master plan. First, world domination of the financial markets. Snot, vomit and other body fluids emanating from a small person coming thereafter, when she had the financial security to provide them with the upbringing and lifestyle that even as a child she had aspired to. There would be ponies, there would be private education and most importantly there would be nannies who would allow her to continue to develop her career.

And all of them were starting to feel decidedly imminent. Lately her body clock had become prone to the odd thump every time she picked Ben up and he flashed his gap-toothed grin. She'd stopped minding when he ran his sticky fingers over her new Escada suit or poured yoghurt into her briefcase. OK, so that did still piss her off but not nearly as much as before.

She leaned forward and pulled the *Daily Mail* out of her desk drawer. Cass made a point of speed-reading *The Times*, the *Financial Times*, the *Guardian* and the *Mail* every day. It was crucial that she kept abreast of current affairs, market shifts and global trends. However while flicking through the *Mail* she had stumbled over a headline that had intrigued her: 'Can Women *Really* Have It All?'

Underneath there was a photo of four women all dressed in strikingly similar clothes, smiling as they balanced laptops in one hand, with children of varying ages clutching the other. These were Cass's kind of women: strong, successful, in control. All of them had flourishing careers, salaries that broke the hundred-grand barrier and families that were photo-perfect, excelling at school and fluent in four languages. It was like a snapshot of her future. One that maybe it was time to start planning.

She stood up, flattened out the creases on her skirt, grabbed her briefcase and made for the door knowing that two things were certain: she'd be back behind that desk at six o'clock on Monday morning and sitting in that chair having another sneaky fag at midnight on Monday night. She was nothing if not predictable. For now. But that was about to change.

It must be chucking out time at the Shaker, Cass realised as she fought her way through the deluge of revellers pouring forth from the pub doorway and hogging all the cabs. Although the bar was directly opposite the entrance to her office she'd only been in there once at someone insignificant's leaving do and even then she'd excused herself as quickly as possible and shot back to the office. She didn't do socialising with colleagues. Who knew when their work levels would sink below acceptable and she'd have to fire them? There was simply no point in becoming friends. It was up there with cosmetics on the waste-of-time scale.

Surveying the scene she decided that only violence would prevent the clubbers from nicking every cab she hailed and as she would undoubtedly be outnumbered it would probably be a better idea to walk a few streets to the nearest taxi rank. She pulled her coat around her neck and strode authoritatively through the menagerie. God, these people were sad. Didn't they realise how stupid they looked: loud, clothes now bordering on dishevelled and clearly trying to attract members of the opposite sex? And that was just the cab drivers.

She smiled to herself as she ploughed on through the throng. If she ever began to think that she was missing something in her social life, then chucking-out time at any pub would persuade her otherwise. It brought memories of her university years flooding back like a life-threatening tidal wave. Poor, poor, poor. Her parents hadn't had the money to support her through further education, and since those were the days of meagre government grants, when student loans were just a pound sign in a chancellor's eye, she'd financed herself by working as a cleaner in a nightclub during the day before classes, and as a cashier in the same club four nights a week. There was nothing she hadn't seen there. No form of pond life she hadn't encountered or physical act she hadn't witnessed. Much as the absurdity of those saturated with alcohol had often made her laugh, the whole experience had put her off bars and nightclubs for life. She'd rather have a spreadsheet than a Singapore Sling any day of the week.

She was so immersed in thought that she didn't realise until it was too late that her briefcase was caught on something. She simultaneously gave it a tug and turned round to see what the obstruction was, just in time to see a fully-grown male completely lose his footing and sprawl face down across the pavement. Shit! This was all she needed – a drunken tosser with a balance problem.

She considered just marching on but the strap on her briefcase (exhibit A) was firmly tangled around his ankle.

'Excuse me, but if I could just have that back,' she snapped curtly as she bent down to retrieve the errant strip of leather. A loud groan emanated from under the hair on the ground. She unwound the leather from his leg, just as a stunning baby beige blonde, the type that were usually only seen in shampoo adverts and draped across the bonnet of the latest Jaguar, came rushing over and swept down to the injured man.

'Taylor, Taylor babe, are you OK?' she shrieked, while somehow managing to slur at the same time. It was like the mating call of a parrot after a bottle of Jack Daniels. Cass rolled her eyes. This was getting worse. Now she had a deranged drama queen to contend with too. She made a bid for escape, deciding that absence makes the guilt go quicker.

'Hey, you!' She didn't even need to turn back to know that the furious voice was coming from under the thick mop of hair spread across the pavement.

She considered breaking into a run, but realised it would be futile. Speed had never been her thing. Better to stay in a crowded place than run the risk of an irate albeit injured man pursuing her through the streets of London. She turned slowly to see a tall and perfectly formed guy with messy hair holding two hands in front of his face, the inebriated blonde clutching on to his arm either *in* support or *for* support, she wasn't sure which.

'For fuck's sake! I think you've broken my nose!' he yelled at her from behind his palms. Were those nails French-manicured? Uuuurgh, what a dickhead.

She raised both eyebrows in a sardonic stare. 'Then you should have been watching where you were going,' she countered, in what she pitched as a semi-aggressive tone. She hoped that in his incapacitated state this would dissuade him from further argument. That and the worry that she might deliberately attack him this time and do him horrendous damage – like breaking a nail.

She was right. Taylor settled for blatant insults instead and emitted a stream of expletives that included lots of 'stupid cow's, 'fucking blind's and finishing with a 'should be fucking locked up'. Meanwhile Heidi Klum's doppelgänger wandered off, calling for a cab. Presumably to take them in the direction of the nearest A & E department.

Cass could feel the eyes of at least twenty pub evictees boring into her. She took a deep breath, threw her head up into her most arrogant posture and strode off. Sod it. If they remembered this little altercation in the morning it wouldn't matter – she was probably a drunken blur to them anyway.

She reached the taxi rank in the record time of five and a half minutes, to find that the queue was longer than the one outside a post office on pension day. She checked her watch. Midnight. As she pulled her sleeve back down, she was surprised to see that her hand was trembling slightly – a result of being thrust onto centre stage of pub-crowd hell, she thought. She perused the queue again and realised that only the very drunk and those who had lost the power of their legs, due to short-skirt-induced hypothermia or paralysis caused by four-inch Jimmy Choos, could withstand these temperatures without the aid of brandy and a St Bernard.

'Bollocks,' she muttered to no one in particular, which was just as well as due to the fact that she was obviously sober, probably an aloof cow and definitely not on the pull, her fellow queuers were completely oblivious to her. Besides, they were too busy trying not to die of cold.

She made a mental calculation: stay here for ever waiting for a cab or a snowplough (whatever came by first), or walk the short distance to the Romp Room, one of London's hippest clubs. It was everything Cass despised. It was a magnet for pissed page-three models, dickheads wearing Versace and thick gold chains, coked-up premier-league football players, and slappers on the prowl for their next tabloid kiss and tell. And the other five hundred or so customers were just nobodies in various states of undress or overdress, who spent the whole evening throwing cocktails they couldn't even spell down their throats while looking for their next shag. Not her thing. Never.

She wouldn't be seen within spitting distance of the place were it not for the fact that her mate Paul was the manager and he'd feed her coffee and gossip until her feet thawed out. Her brain didn't get the chance to make the decision – her feet took over and she was at the door of the club in ten minutes.

There were six bouncers (or CCTs as they liked to be known – Crowd Control Technicians) at the door, all subtly moving from foot to foot trying to keep warm. It was still obscenely early in clubland. In another hour their adrenalin would be flowing and acting as a natural insulator as they herded the inevitable hordes of revellers in and out of the venue.

One of the six bouncers at the door stepped

forward to greet her. He was wearing one of those earpiece-with-microphone contraptions that made him look like a cross between a drive-thru server at McDonald's and Kylie Minogue. She was sure that wasn't the image he was striving for. She'd seen him before and he instantly recognised her as one of the boss's friends. It never hurt to give a little chat to those with the guvnor's ear.

'Go right on up there, darling.' He winked at her while gesticulating to the semi-concealed stairs behind the doorway that led to Paul's office. 'And just let me know if there's anything else I can do for you,' he added suggestively, to the amusement of his colleagues, as she made her way up the stairs.

Cass briefly turned back. 'You can take your eyes off my ass and organise a coffee for me, there's a good boy. Do you think you'll remember all that or shall I write it down?'

She resumed her climb to howls of derision from the other stewards. To them, the only thing better than seeing a colleague shot down in flames by a member of the opposite sex was . . . well, actually there was nothing better than that. Their chests all puffed out a centimetre in the misguided belief that if *they* had issued a chat-up line Miss Frosty Tits Boss's Pal would have leapt into their arms and be offering sexual favours within the hour.

Cass knocked briefly on Paul's door and entered without waiting for an acknowledgement. She scanned the room. Empty. Fab. Not. The choices were to go down into the main club and look for Paul or sit down, put her feet up and wait for him to come back. He was probably just down doing a final briefing to the staff or setting up the tills, she decided. She'd wait.

Creak. She involuntarily jumped. Christ, this was turning out to be a strange night. First she'd assaulted a stranger on the street, then she'd subjected a doorman to a ritual humiliation and now she could have sworn that the office desk had just moved two inches sideways. She put her hand to her temple and made slow circular motions. She definitely needed a couple of days off. Creak. Her eyes flew wide open again. That desk had definitely bloody moved. She was sure of it. She tentatively raised her heels and tiptoed towards it. Either this was a poltergeist's night out or the desk had termites that were practising formation dancing.

She crept over and swung her head round the side of the desk ready to face a character from a Harry Potter book (no, *of course* she didn't own one, she'd just been reading one to Ben). She shrieked in surprise at the sight of the two grown men crouching underneath it, before dissolving into gales of laughter when she realised who they were.

'Well, well, well,' she spluttered as the two bodies disentangled themselves from their hiding place and started to stretch up. 'After all these years, the truth comes out. And here was me thinking you two were just good friends. So the rumours all those years ago were true, Paul, you dark horse. And Jeff, I'd never have guessed this. Now I know why we didn't work out.'

She had to stop. She was laughing so hard that talking at the same time ran the risk of inducing lockjaw.

Paul and Jeff stood up and brushed themselves down. 'Very funny, Cass. Hugely funny in fact,' Jeff retorted somewhat ironically, 'but it's not how it looks.'

That set her off again. 'I know, I know,' she splut-tered. 'You were just inspecting the floorboards.'

The fact that she was the only one in the room laughing had no dampening effect on her whatsoever. She just couldn't believe that her two best friends (in fact, her two *only* friends), one of them an ex-boyfriend, were obviously tampering with each other's anatomy and she had never realised it. God, she was dim sometimes. She'd come expecting some salacious titillation to amuse her while she waited for a cab, but she hadn't anticipated that she'd get an actual physical demonstration. She was so glad she hadn't gone straight home – she wouldn't have missed this for the world.

Paul raised his right hand and swung an innocuous metal box about an inch long that had wires sprout-ing from every side at her.

'Em, I give up. No, wait . . . A new range in chrome condoms, perhaps?' she asked, finding herself intoxicatingly amusing.

Paul rolled his eyes. 'No, you daft cow. It's a concealed listening device. A bug. Jeff was just helping me fit it to the underside of the desktop. What did you think we were doing? No, don't tell me.'

Cassandra's face fell in disappointment. Discovering that her two best friends were gay was the most interesting thing that had happened to her outside the office in months and now it seemed that she'd misinterpreted the whole situation. Ho hum. Still . . . a bug? What was going on? She pulled up a chair and kicked of her sodden shoes. May as well get comfortable for this.

Paul pre-empted her question. 'I think one of my assistant managers is extorting money on my nights off, so I'm rigging the office in the hope of getting evidence. Jeff is helping me set it up. We've already put a camera in the plant behind you.'

Cass resisted turning round. Despite her misconception about the situation, she was still intrigued. And astounded. Paul had been the manager and shareholder in the Romp Room for five years. He was a well-known figure in the nightclub world. There weren't many bouncers who'd made the transition to owner/manager, but Paul had. She was amazed that anyone would be brave or stupid enough to cross him.

'Damn! I thought I'd stumbled into the middle of an illicit affair. But I suppose grand theft and subterfuge will have to do. Tell me more.'

Jeff spoke. 'That's about it. Takings always drop by about fifteen per cent when Paul's not here, so he wanted it investigated. That amount of cash would be impossible to steal from a till without it being obvious, so it must be happening at a higher level. Thus Inspector Gadget here was called in to help.'

She watched as Jeff took a dramatic bow and this time they all laughed. His James Bond obsession with all things geeky, boy-toy and with code numbers instead of names was a big plus in his role as a bean counter – due to his surveillance talents his employers had the lowest pilferage levels in the industry.

When he straightened back up, he pulled her out of her chair and enveloped her in a hug. 'So how're you doing, Miss Haven? Long time no see.'

Cass playfully brushed him off. 'Jeff, I had dinner with you a month ago and you know I hate all that touchy-feely shite so stop cuddling me.'

He made a hopeless, what-can-you-do, a-man-tries-his-best, gesture at Paul, who smiled knowingly in return. This was the way it had always been with them.

They'd all been friends since the three of them met in their first month at uni. Jeff was on the same accounts course as Cass, but had never plucked up the courage to attempt to penetrate the 'piss off, I'm not interested in making friends' vibes that she emanated. He would frequently psych himself up to approach her then decide to leave it to another day. Should he try? Maybe? Maybe not? Decisiveness had never been his strong point. He thought that was his biggest weakness, but he wasn't sure. It might be. Then again . . .

It was only when he got a part-time job as a barman in the nightclub she worked in that he began to make tentative conversational approaches to her.

Paul already worked on the door, courtesy of the fact that he was six foot four and as wide as a standard pool table. Clubbers thought he was scary. In reality, had there been a war he'd have been firmly categorised as a conscientious objector, such was his aversion to and fear of any form of violence, but the sheer intimidation value of his appearance assured that this was never put to the test. Even the drunkest man wasn't foolish enough to take on the massive black guy on the door.

After closing time, it was normal for all the staff to stay behind for a few drinks and then go on to a party in someone's flat or digs. Most of the staff were students so the offer of free alcohol was never refused. Jeff's weekend wasn't complete if he didn't wake up in the morning on a strange carpet surrounded by the rest of the club staff. Most of them became like family: they worked together, by virtue of the nocturnal hours socialised together, and invariably a few of them slept together.

Except that is, the blonde (dark blonde, natural, no highlights), surly girl from uni who worked as the cashier. Despite repeated invitations from various people in the staff room, Cassandra never joined them, never participated in any of their all-night drinking sessions or pre-work coffees.

It aroused Jeff's curiosity. In class he would stare at her when he was sure she couldn't see him. She was intriguing; so focused and solemn. He'd never once seen her smile or, God forbid, laugh. He'd never heard her make a glib comment or even groan when they were given weighty assignments on a Friday afternoon.

Instead, she listened intently to every lecture and made reams of notes, while Jeff struggled just to stay awake. However, something in him was drawn to her. He put his intense curiosity down to the fact that he felt sorry for her because she was always alone. Cass put it down to the fact that he was a mad stalker with a twisted fixation with the back of her head.

Unbeknownst to Jeff, she had noticed him too. How could she fail to? Everywhere she went, there he was three feet behind her. It had to be more than coincidence. The guy was a nutter. And he was irritating the life out of her.

Eventually, she could stand it no more. It was four o'clock on a Saturday morning and the staff were queuing outside the manager's office for their cash-in-hand earnings. Jeff found himself standing behind Cass.

As sodding usual, she thought.

He took a deep breath and puffed out his chest as he'd seen the doormen do when they were going in for the kill with a female. Jeff may have been sociable and popular, but he was also a virgin who was massively inexperienced on the girl-pulling front. He was just about to speak when he changed his mind. Chest deflated. Bottle crashed. He would leave it to another night.

He mentally wrestled with himself. No, he wouldn't leave it. He wanted to speak to her. He was going for it. He could do this.

'Em, hi. We're all going to a party at Paul the bouncer's house. Do you want to come?' he blurted to the back of her unstyled, short fair hair. She obviously didn't do trends.

She ignored him at first. So he tapped her on the shoulder of her brown duffel coat and repeated the question. She slowly turned round to face him.

'No.'

'Are you sure? We're, em, all going. All of us. The staff that is. To Paul's place. Should be a laugh.'

'No.'

'Well, if you decide you want to . . .'

Cass exploded so violently he feared for her toggles. 'Look, I said no! Did you not get that? You're a mad git! Every time I turn round you are there. Why would I want to go somewhere else that you'll be? Do you think I want to give you even more time to stare at the back of my head? God, you're sick. Why the hell would you want me to go anyway? To make your life as a sicko stalker a bit easier?' She hissed the whole outburst into his face, without stopping for breath. Every other member of staff within earshot suddenly found their shoes to be the most fascinating objects on the planet.

Jeff was stunned. Just for a change, he wasn't sure how to react to this. Should he apologise? Or should he be furious? Or sympathetic that she had obviously undergone a social skills bypass operation?

It took him a few moments to regain his power of speech. When he eventually did, his voice was thick with equal amounts of shock, anger and uncertainty, causing him to stutter through his sentences. He tapped her on the shoulder again and heard her exasperated sigh as she turned to face him again. The fear of violence made him get his speech in quickly.

'Because you're always alone and you, em, look so serious and I thought, well, maybe you could do with a laugh. And I kind of thought that maybe you were, well, nice, underneath, maybe. But well, I guess I was pretty far off the mark.' A nervous laugh. Then he decided to go for the mature approach. 'But I was obviously wrong, so you can fuck off, you rude bitch.'

He turned and strode off, shouting to one of the others to collect his wages for him. Raising his voice was unnecessary; a shocked silence had descended in the corridor, although it was all his fellow staffers could do not to burst into a round of applause. It was about time someone tore a strip off that stroppy cow. But they couldn't believe Jeff had done it – he was the most mild-mannered guy you could meet.

Cass was stunned. What was that guy all about? His words resonated in her head. Could do with a laugh? Serious? Nice? How dare he! Her personality was nothing to do with him. How dare he cast aspersions as to what she needed in her life. Witless tosser! Her face was burning as she collected her £12 wages and grabbed her coat. I mean, what makes him think he can speak to me like that? *Rude?* What was he *talking* about? He was the rude one. Not to mention a complete dickhead.

She pulled her coat around her and pushed her hands into her gloves and her unruly mop into a hat that bore a close and unfortunate resemblance to a tea cosy. Her teeth would have been chattering if they weren't clenched together in fury. Prick, prick, prick! And he'd almost sounded like he felt *sorry* for her. That was all she needed. A post-pubescent male with acne and a stalking habit feeling pity for her. Urgh!

There was a commotion behind her as a group of the waitresses poured out the door. They eyed the stuck-up cow from the cash desk with a complete lack of interest, the Jeff incident already gone as they focused their minds on which members of the opposite sex they intended to make a beeline for at the party.

Cass could see that they'd all reapplied their make-up, obviously in anticipation of the night ahead. She wondered at their energy. It had been a long, busy, exhausting shift, it was nearly three o'clock in the morning, and yet these girls were laughing uproariously and overflowing with enthusiasm. Maybe that's what a social life did for you, she pondered. Maybe the ... no, forget it, she wasn't even going to go there. Oh crap, she couldn't help herself. The train of thought refused to be derailed. Maybe the schizoid stalker was right. Perhaps she *was* too serious.

'Excuse me.' Cass looked to see who had spoken, then realised that it was her. The gaggle of girlies in front of her turned round with more than a hint of incredulity on their cosmetically enhanced faces. 'Are you all going to the party at Paul's place?'

The waitresses gave each other quick glances of confusion before slowly nodding.

Cass took a deep breath. 'Do you think I could tag along?'

Their lips touched for the first time that night. The moon was bright, the stars were out and there was the smell of jasmine in the air. When romance consumed them they were carried away on a sea of emotion to a clinch of intimacy that . . . Actually, it didn't happen like that at all.

After Jeff recovered from the shock of Cass's arrival and the even bigger shock of her apology (albeit a brief and curt one said in a grudging tone), they settled into a free space at the top of the stairs, with a packet of cigarettes and two two-litre bottles of Diamond White cider. Cass, not wanting to admit that she'd only ever had the odd glass of Asti at relatives' weddings, knocked the cider back glass for glass with her newfound friend. The conversation was tentative at first, but worked its way up to full disclosure after they gradually realised just how much they had in common: working-class backgrounds, fairly isolated childhoods, a fascination for logic and figures, a deep-rooted appreciation of Carol Vorderman . . . it was almost like fate had conspired to throw them together. Only they didn't believe in fate, it being non-tangible and not supported by any scientific evidence.

It was getting light outside when Cass decided to make a move – luckily it was Sunday so her cleaning shift was late afternoon as opposed to the early mornings of the rest of the week. However, she did have a chronic need to pee after sitting in the same spot for the last four hours.

She put her hand on Jeff's shoulder to give her leverage to get to a standing position. Wow. Head rush. The cider coursed through her bloodstream like lava. She took a few steps, then crash! Performing a series of moves only before witnessed being performed by an Eastern European gymnast at the Olympic Games, she tumbled down the stairs sending plastic bottles, tinfoil ashtrays and an assortment of sleeping and semi-conscious bodies flying in every direction.

The avalanche finally stopped when she landed with a thud in the lower hallway. Jeff dived to help her but was slowed by the fact that he was on cider-delayed-reaction-time. He slid down the stairs on his front like a body surfer. He would have carpet burns for many weeks as a memento of the occasion.

When he reached the bottom he realised Cass's eyes were closed and, oh God, she wasn't breathing. He felt for a pulse. None. Panic rose in his chest. This was all his fault. He'd been so horrible to her and that had made her show up there in an attempt to prove him wrong. And then he'd realised how nice she was and she was just like him really and now she was dead and *he'd killed her*!

He started sweating and crying and shouting to what was left of the party crowd to help him, call 999, do anything, but even the noise of two fully formed teenagers toppling down a flight of death-trap stairs hadn't roused any of the others.

His heart thundered and his mind screamed. First aid! Oh, God, it was so long since he'd done first aid as part of his Boy Scout lifesaving proficiency badge. He plumbed the depths of his mind. Recovery position! That was it – the recovery position. Nope, no use. She was dead. There was no recovering from that. Fuck, fuck, what should he do?

Just as he was slipping into a panic-induced faint,

he remembered: mouth-to-mouth resuscitation. He leaned forward, tilted Cass's head back as far as it would go and lurched towards her mouth like a jet-propelled sink plunger. He suctioned on. Suck or blow? Oh, fuck, he couldn't remember. It was suck. No it wasn't. Blow. Definitely blow.

He was on his third gust of wind when he felt a hand thrust at his shoulder with such a force that it caused bruising that would last even longer than the carpet burns. 'What . . .?' he stuttered in astonishment.

'Don't you ever, *ever* touch me without permission.'

He stared down. This was just too surreal. Cass was dead. Yet she was *talking*. Shouting actually.

And now she was smiling.

'OK, you have my permission. Carry on.' So he did.

Two things happened in the following year.

The first was that Paul's housemates moved out and he asked Jeff and Cass if they wanted to move in (not, he would admit later, because he loved their company – more because he thought they were fully paid-up members of Geeks Anonymous and would therefore be unlikely to renege on the rent, trash the place, or use it for illegal or immoral purposes).

The second thing was that Cass and Jeff decided they made better friends than lovers. Or rather, better study partners, as that took up 90 per cent of their spare time. It wasn't that they were averse to a romantic entanglement, but in their list of priorities earning money to support themselves and immersing themselves in the joyful intricacies of the British tax system ranked much higher. And anyway, quite frankly Cass couldn't see what all the fuss was about. Sure, a good snog was mildly pleasing, but then so was bacon on toast with a cheese topping and at least that fulfilled several dietary requirements. All snogging did was pass the time of day and give you a chin rash that made you look like a serial glue sniffer. And as for sex . . . Well, it was pleasurable, also passed the time of day and it did burn off 550 calories an hour, but all that body fluid – yuck! No, far better to follow the great British trend for DIY. Only not the kind that the *Changing Rooms* team performed in your front room. There was no big explosive combustion of their relationship. It just kind of drifted off until they reached the point where they realised that they hadn't locked lips (or anything else) for over a month. Plus Jeff had begun to feel a stirring in the nethers whenever a new, petite, and delectably shy barmaid called Cindy brushed past him. Virgin to ladykiller in one swift relationship. He was born to lurve. Kind of. Maybe. He wasn't sure.

He broached the subject with Cass when they took a ten-minute coffee break while preparing for their end-of-year exams the following May.

Naturally, when talking about anything resembling emotions, physical activity or commitment he suffered from the typical male reaction, inbred through the centuries: he started to sweat profusely, stammer nervously and he had to fight to control his eyeballs which were darting around the room checking that the exits weren't blocked. Cassandra spotted it immediately and before he had uttered his first sentence had predicted the whole conversation, analysed it and formed a suitable reaction and reply.

'Cass, I wondered, em, what you thought about, em, our . . .'

She put her hand over his. Better to put him out of his misery quickly. She wanted to get back to work. 'Jeff, you don't have to say anything. I completely agree. Friends?'

He nodded, mentally thanking the Male God of Chuckers for making his first dumping of a female an easy one. He smiled. 'Thanks, Cass.'

Cassandra shrugged. It was nothing. Now if they could just get the next ten chapters done they could call it a day. And then maybe there'd be time for a spot of DIY.

It took about three weeks for Paul to broach the subject of his lodger's failed romance with Cass. In fact, it had taken him that long to notice, since they were never exactly wrapped in a tornado of passion and shagging like porn stars on Viagra in the first place. He'd only discovered that their flame of lust had been extinguished like a bonfire in a monsoon when Jeff had suggested they have a party in order that he could corner Cindy the barmaid and potentially seduce the life out of her. Only he couldn't decide what to say or when to do it. That guy was destined to live a life of solitude, thought Paul. But then, he wasn't doing much better.

It was an age-old incongruity that you could take the ugliest of men, put him in a white shirt, a black tie and a badge marked SECURITY, stand him on the front door of a nightclub and immediately he'd become irresistible to 90 per cent of the nightclub-going females of the world (or at least he would *think* he was). And in Paul's experience those statistics weren't far off the mark.

On an average night girl after girl would proposition him, and not just the slappers either. No, some of them were genuinely gorgeous. On a few occasions he'd arranged to meet them after work, gone for coffee and even occasionally had partaken of recreational under-duvet indoor sport. But he couldn't remember the last girl that he'd been even slightly inclined to see for a second date. He had to face facts: he was never going to meet the love of his life standing in the doorway of The Vibe. There was more chance of him catching pneumonia than a partner.

However, since the rest of his day was spent either sleeping or at the gym (unfortunately he went in the afternoons when the majority of young, single females were at work), he was beginning to despair of ever achieving 'partner' status with a member of the opposite sex. He'd even started alternating which side of his double bed he slept on so that the mattress wouldn't dip on one side. Muscle was so much heavier than fat.

He didn't get it: he was decent-looking in a Lennox-Lewis-body-but-with-a-shaved-head kind of way. He was articulate. He liked to laugh. Hell, he even had his own house, left to him by his father who'd died on Paul's eighteenth birthday four years before.

But hey, it could have been worse. He could have joined the rest of the doormen in the Premier Fuckability League, the long-running competition to establish who shagged most girls in a year. The results were declared every Christmas, with the winner taking home a Santa Claus G-string complete with flashing sack. If sex was a recognised sport, his work colleagues would qualify for Lottery funding, such was their dedication to the cause.

It wasn't Paul's thing. To the acute annoyance of the rest of the door crew, he refused to divulge any details of his sex life whatsoever. Which in their book only meant one thing: not that Paul had morals, integrity and an aversion to one-night stands because he wanted to build a solid relationship with a partner of like mind.

Nope, the bloke was gay.

Unknown to Paul, they were currently running a sweepstake on which month of the year he would 'come out'. The prize fund was a hundred quid and a blowjob from Kirsty the club nymphomaniac. Such was her altruistic nature, she had even offered to give a consolation prize to the runner-up. She was a saint, that girl.

Paul put his feet up on the table and returned to the book he'd been reading just as Cassandra came storming into the kitchen, flicked on the kettle and grabbed a packet of chocolate Hobnobs from her food cupboard, interrupting his thoughts. Paul smiled. Cass amused him. She wasn't capable of doing any less than three things at once. She was a woman on a perpetual mission. He liked her but she definitely wasn't his type. He liked girls with a feminine side – who were happy just to take things easy and enjoy life. Cassandra was more driven than a Skoda.

'Hey Cass, how's things?'

She returned his smile and then, to his surprise pulled out a chair and sat down. This was unheard-of. Paul had already worked out that, nice as she was, Cass considered casual conversation completely superfluous to requirements. She must be ill.

'Are you OK?' she asked, concern faintly detectable. It struck her that although she and Paul worked together and lived together (in a strictly 'pay rental' kind of way), due to the fact that she was at uni all day and then they were surrounded by the other club staff at night, she could count the number of actual conversations they'd had on her fingers. She had no idea why she had an urge to have one now. Must have been Paul's dejected expression arousing the tiny and usually well-hidden humanitarian streak that she harboured. That and the fact that she'd sat her last exam that day and the Hobnobs were the closest she was going to get to a celebration. Might as well go the whole hog and throw in a deep and meaningful conversation as well.

Cass knew all about the sweepstake at work. Her position at the cash desk by the front door meant that she heard every word of every conversation that the doormen uttered. She had noticed that Paul was the quiet one. She'd also come to realise that, unlike the others, he wasn't put on this earth to demand sexual favours from as many members of the female species as possible. After months of working there she considered all doormen to be over-testosteroned megalomaniacs with crap chat-up lines.

Paul was perplexed at Cass's concern. 'Yeah, why?'

'Because this is your only night off and you're sitting in the kitchen reading a Jackie Collins novel.'

Paul gave a wry smile. 'One of my sisters left it here.'

'You're an only child.'

'OK, OK, I give up, Sherlock,' he laughed.

He has such a nice smile, Cass thought. For a bouncer.

'It's my reading policy – I read whatever is number one on the *Sunday Times* fiction bestseller list every week. This week it's Jackie Collins. Who knows what it'll be next week? It's one of life's little adventures.'

Cass smiled back. Nice smile *and* literate *and* obviously in touch with his feminine side. She mentally reminded herself to put a tenner on August in the sweep. If he was now reading Jackie Collins in public (well, his kitchen was semi-public) then he was just about ready to leap out of that closet. And God knows she could do with the cash.

'Sorry to hear about you and Jeff splitting up,' he continued tentatively, still waiting for some invisible bungee rope to ping her back to a study position in her bedroom.

Cass shrugged her shoulders. 'We weren't exactly Kylie and Jason anyway. It's no big deal.' She rapidly changed the subject. Talking about herself made her as uncomfortable as a Buddhist at a bullfight.

'What about you? How's your life going? How come you're not out gallivanting on a hot date then?' May as well pry a little, just to check her imminent ten-pound investment.

'Couldn't be bothered, to be honest. I'm having a bit of a dating drought these days.' He shrugged.

Cass felt genuinely sympathetic. It must be difficult for him to meet like-minded guys when he was surrounded by those big sexist lumps of meat every night.

'To be honest, I can't remember the last time I met an intelligent, interesting, not to mention hugely attractive girl.'

He saw the surprise on Cassandra's face and misunderstood its source.

'Present company excepted, of course,' he blurted, hoping against hope that he hadn't mortally offended her. He didn't want her moving out and leaving him with an empty room to fill.

But she was laughing. 'A *girl*? You mean you're not . . . you know?'

'I know what? Into older women?' he replied, confused. He certainly was not a granny-grabber. He left that to Dave, the ex-head bouncer. Dave had bragged for weeks about the gorgeous, if slightly mature (*'she don't half know what she's doing that one – a right terrier'*) bit of stuff he was banging only to be crushed and humiliated when the female lost her handbag. One of the contents she listed to the investigating police officer was her pension book. Another victory for the cosmetic surgery industry. Dave couldn't handle the humiliation and was now working as a brickie in Dulwich.

Cassandra hesitated, waiting until she'd stopped giggling to speak. It was a nice sight. He hadn't realised that she could do giggling.

'Em, no. What I mean is . . . you're not *gay*?'

Paul paused. Was that what she thought? Was that what everyone thought? No wonder his love life was further down the toilet than a U-bend.

'No, I'm not gay. Just hopeless with women.' He was laughing now. Bloody hell. One Jackie Collins novel and the whole world decides that you swing the other way.

Cass shook her head and held out the packet of biscuits. 'Yep, you and the rest of the male species. Here, have a Hobnob.'

Just as well she hadn't put her money in the sweepstake after all.

Cass shrugged off her wet coat as Paul sat down behind his desk and Jeff perched on the corner of it.

When the three of them were together like this it still felt strange to her sometimes. It was like they were still kids, not the successful adults they'd turned out to be.

They'd all managed to fulfil their ambitions. Cass was a director. Jeff was the financial controller of a hotel chain and Paul had taken out a mortgage on his house to go into business with the owner of The Vibe, the club they'd worked in all those years before. The result was the Romp Room and he'd recouped his investment tenfold. But he *still* didn't have a girlfriend.

'Anyway, Miss Haven, to what do we owe the pleasure of your company? Aren't you normally still slaving over a hot laptop at this time of night?' Paul asked.

God, even her friends thought she was a complete sad cow with no life, Cass realised. Was she that predictable? Obviously she was. This had to change. Life Plan A had been a success – she was top of the money tree at System Solutions. It was definitely time to move on to Plan B.

'Oh, nothing special. I was just passing and missing the company of my friends. Can't a girl just pay a spontaneous visit once in a while?'

'No.' It was simultaneous and it was definite.

Then Paul spoke. 'Come on, Cass, spill the beans, otherwise we'll have to torture you. We could . . . oh I don't know – Jeff, what will we do to her?'

'Snog the face off her and whisper sweet nothings.'

'Eeurgh! Torture indeed. The very thought makes me want to heave,' Cass retorted, making vomiting actions.

The boys laughed and then both took a step towards her, tongues out and at the ready.

'OK, OK, you win.' She held both hands up to halt them then changed her tone to one of playfulness. 'I just thought I'd let you in on my latest news,' she said, trying to be as coy and mysterious as possible. It was an effort. She normally only did pragmatic and direct. Paul and Jeff glanced at each other, intrigued. This was a whole new side to Cass.

'Well . . .?' Jeff prompted after her dramatic pause. 'Don't tell us – you're taking a career break and you're going to backpack around the world in search of your inner being?' He was being ironic. He knew that Cass didn't do career breaks. Or 'inner beings' for that matter. She thought spiritualism was something to do with vodka and Bacardi.

'Nope, not quite, but I am going to take a career break.'

Their eyes rose in surprise and a touch of alarm. Cass's career was her life; if she was taking a break from it then something must be wrong – seriously wrong.

'You see, I'm going to have a baby.'

There was a stunned silence. You could have heard a bug drop.

Chapter Two

Polly Kent – Marketing Assistant – The Body

'I bloody hate hold-ups – my thighs hang over the top of them making my legs look like two mushrooms on heels,' Zoë wailed.

Polly and Chloe laughed, but offered no sympathy. The hold-up moan was one that Zoë repeated every Friday night and they'd long ago realised that no amount of contradiction would convince Zoë of the truth: that she had legs that Pretty Polly would put on billboards. Best just to ignore her and let her get it out of her system. A couple of glasses of champagne on her always-empty, flat-as-floorboards stomach would soon diminish her recurring bout of self-criticism.

The three of them made final checks in the mirror; Zoë and Chloe's were long lingering studies, Polly's a fleeting glance. They looked like office-professional versions of a girl band, sporting as they did the official designer look for babes employed in London marketing roles: black suits (Polly in trousers, Zoë and Chloe in pelmet-sized skirts), black shoes or boots and tight ribbed tops stretched over perfect size eight-to-ten bodies. Only their long, straight, centre-parted hair had any measure of individuality: Zoë and Chloe sported Jennifer Aniston-Pitt sun-kissed streaks while Polly's perfect golden skin was exquisitely framed by a mane of jet-black gloss. Completely devoid of split ends, of course. Weekly lunch-hour treatments at Daniel Galvin had seen to that. She looked like Pocahontas in trousers.

Polly gathered up her stuff and checked her watch. 'Ten minutes to clock off, girls. Better get back to our desks before Miles thinks we've buggered off and deserted him.'

Miles Conway was director of marketing at System Solutions (or SySol for short). Miles's marketing genius had spearheaded the meteoric growth of SySol over the previous ten years and if there was one thing he was sure of it was that image was everything. On his advice the company had offices with the 'right' Soho address: trendy, happening, in the buzz area of the city but not too pretentious. It was Miles who positioned SySol with both manufacturers and customers as a company that was synonymous with cutting-edge technology and had the service and support levels to back it up. And it was Miles who employed only beautiful, female marketing graduates from wealthy backgrounds, who had cut-glass accents and more connections than Heathrow. After all, image *was* everything.

He watched as Polly, Zoë and Chloe trooped back to their desks and made a show of shuffling papers until their official down-tools time of six o'clock (an obscene hour to finish but born of the fact that the girls were incapable of getting to their desks before ten o'clock in the mornings).

Miles pretended not to notice that a copy of *Heat* was sticking out from under the paperwork in front of Zoë. Or that there was a distinct whiff of nail varnish wafting from Chloe's direction where her hands were obviously busy decorating each other under her desk. It amazed him that every week she painted her nails without actually being able to see them, yet the Revlon Red wasn't up to her knuckles. That was definitely a talent, albeit not one that he paid her to practise.

His gaze switched to Polly, as usual the only one of the three who was genuinely justifying her salary. He could forgive her the Friday-afternoon sojourn to the Ladies to prepare for after-work drinks, as she was diligent, conscientious and obscenely bloody beautiful the rest of the week.

God, he was definitely in lust. Sweet, kind, unspoilt Polly. He didn't care that she wasn't the most ambitious, creative employee he'd ever had. It didn't even bother him that he knew she was only here biding her time until she decided whether to travel the world, get married to some upper-class nob or devote her time to volunteer work while living off her Dad's millions. All that mattered was that he got to glance up from his desk and have her face in front of him.

He'd never met anyone like her. She totally captivated him and sent him into a daze of daydreaming, imagining what it would be like to hold her, to nuzzle into her neck, to make rampant . . .

'Goodnight, Miles, see you Monday.'

He snapped out of his reverie instantly. Jesus, that was close. He'd been so immersed in a Polly fantasy that he hadn't realised that she was now standing in front of him.

'Right! Bye then. Have a great weekend.' He smiled.

Polly gave him a curious look. It always amazed

her that a guy who spent most of his time in a catatonic trance could be so brilliant and successful. Weird. Must be an eccentric, creative genius thing, she decided. She liked Miles. In the two years she'd worked for him she'd never seen him lose his temper (and Zoë and Chloe gave him plenty of reason to), raise his voice or be arrogant. That was quite unusual for someone of his level of success, especially in marketing. Her chosen field tended to breed eccentrics and volatile characters who ended up either seriously rich or seriously burnt out.

She wondered if Miles was so subdued outside work. She'd suggested inviting him to join them on their Friday-night drinking sessions, but the others had always vetoed that idea. The last person they wanted to see in the pub was their boss. They spent enough time avoiding him during working hours.

The girls tottered over to the Shaker, exuding that Friday feeling from every pore, except the ones on their feet that were screaming in agony at being manipulated into four-inch heels without the benefit of anaesthetic. Still, fashion was worth it. And it did give them great calf shape.

They fought their way to the bar. The place was bordering on intolerably busy now, warm, sticky bodies in suits they'd had on since the morning, all pressed up against each other. It was like the Piccadilly Line at rush hour. The slate floors, glass tables and leather seats were invisible under the mass of briefcases, feet and the odd body that had been there since lunchtime and was now slumped in a corner.

Zoë and Chloe waded through the throng, lapping up the salacious glances of the suits they had to squeeze past. Polly as always was totally unaware of them.

'Christ, it's Atomic bloody Kitten,' Fiz declared drily as they reached her.

Polly laughed. 'Whatever you say, dear. Now make yourself useful and rack up the cocktails. And make it snappy.'

For the first time that evening there was a dip in the level of noise at the bar as a nervous incredulity fell over everyone within earshot. Someone had actually answered back the caustic bitch behind the bar. Good grief! The beautiful girl in the black suit was either insanely brave or just, well, *insane*. They waited for the ritual annihilation that was sure to follow. They only hoped the poor girl was wearing a bulletproof vest. The pause was interminable. Then, just as they were about to dive for cover, the unbelievable happened. Miss Caustic Gob's face broke into a smile and she leaned over and kissed the black-suited girl on the cheek.

'How's it going, my sweet? You look fecking gorgeous as ever. What can I get you tonight then?'

The collective sighs of relief caused a breeze.

'Three Cosmopolitans please, Fiz. What time do you get off?'

Christmas 1985: annual party for the children of the employees of the Kent chain of hotels.

Santa had just distributed presents to the two hundred overexcited small people in the Kent Plaza Hotel ballroom and a mini-riot was breaking out at the table nearest the windows. An eight-year-old girl with a tangle of auburn curls was repeatedly slamming her just-unwrapped My Little Pony onto the desk, accompanied by a shrill mantra of, 'I hate My Little poxy Pony. I want He Man,' spat over and over with ascending volume.

Santa's not-so-little (unsuccessful diet again) helper, who'd had the misfortune to be appointed to look after that table, raced around to her side.

'Now, now, there. I'm sure My Little Pony is a great toy to have. Why don't you drink your orange juice and have some cake with all your new friends.'

The helper's face was burning with embarrassment. Trust her pigging luck to get this table. It was bad enough that she had to dress in this stupid, pathetic pixie outfit that made her look like snot with legs, but now the whole room was watching her. She knew what everyone was thinking: if she couldn't control a table of ten kids, how could she control her cleaning squad in Kent Towers? This little shit could ruin her promotion chances.

A can of Fanta flew across the table, drenching two unsuspecting 'new-found friends' and inciting floods of tears and a cacophony of 'I want my mum' from both. A square of Christmas cake followed rapidly in its wake.

'Feck off! I want He Man! This is a *girl's* toy.' Felicity couldn't help herself. It wasn't that she meant to swear, but Mammy always did when she was upset with her, which was quite a lot. Sometimes it felt like 'feck' was Mammy's favourite word, as she said it all the time. That and 'Sweet blessed Mary, what terrible things did I ever do to deserve a child like this?'

Santa's not-so-little-and-now-severely-pissed-off helper read the brat's name badge then leaned over and whispered in her ear.

'Listen, Felicity, I hate to point out the obvious, but you are indeed a girl. Now take the toy, shut your mouth and don't dare throw another thing or I'll dangle you by the ankles from that window. Understand?'

Felicity took a deep breath and gave the pixie her most evil glare. Then screamed at the top of her lungs. 'I HATE YOU! And that Santa is a fake! The *real* Santa knows I want a He Man. I hate that Santa!'

The pixie gritted her teeth so hard that her molars wobbled. Her decision to remain childless (forced due to the fact that she hadn't had sex in twenty years) had now been vindicated. They were all little bastards. She was about to surreptitiously grab Felicity brat-face by the armpits and attempt to squeeze her ribcage hard enough to prohibit speech while forcibly removing her from the room when a beautiful little angel (literally – she was wearing a tutu and wings) appeared at her side.

'Here you are. There was an extra one left over. I think Santa must have left it for you.'

She placed a He Man in the hands of the wailing child, who immediately shut up and stared down at it.

'Th-th-thank you. It's my very best present ever. I was so scared that I wouldn't get one. Thank you, Santa,' she shouted to the fat man in red making a hasty retreat from the room followed by an incandescent pixie, her face so purple it now clashed with her outfit.

The angel smiled. 'That's OK. I'm Polly, how do you do?'

The brat looked down with incomprehension at the outstretched hand. 'I'm Fiz. Do you want a My Little Pony?'

Of course it was a cliché that Polly Kent and Felicity (Fiz) O'Connor were well aware of as they grew up together – the boss's daughter being best friends with the cook's child – but they cared not a jot. It didn't matter to them in the least that one had money and one didn't. Or that one of them had privileges the other could only have dreamed of were it not for the fact that Polly's parents encouraged her to share everything. She didn't need any prompting. As far as they were both concerned, what was Polly's was also Fiz's, and what was Fiz's was usually, well, stolen.

Kenneth Kent was also aware that his whole life had been a cliché. He had built up his hotel chain from humble beginnings as the landlord of a block of bedsits in the East End. A few master strokes of inspired property development together with a couple of deals that were just on the right side of shady had conspired to fuel his meteoric success in the hospitality industry.

Now he owned three four-star properties with five-star aspirations and names: the Kent Towers, the Kent Plaza and the Kent Continental. He had become the major player that he had always intended to be but he was under no illusions; he knew where he had come from and never lost his working-class values.

He was also smart enough to know that when Jilly Droughton, the beautiful daughter of Lord Droughton, agreed to marry him she wasn't doing it for his stunning good looks and breeding. It was amazing what his money could buy. In this case, a wife. In return he provided the cash and expertise required to renovate and maintain the crumbling Droughton pile on the Cumbrian border.

It wasn't that Jilly was a ruthless gold-digger, intent on stripping him of his assets, then discarding him. More that she had been brought up in an aristocratic if impoverished family, where marriage was not necessarily synonymous with fidelity and everlasting adoration. She actually really did like Kenneth Kent. He was certainly more interesting than any of the other men she met during her debutante season (financed by opening the gardens of Droughton House to the public for two consecutive summers). The bottom line was that her family were counting on her to marry well, marry soon, and marry rich. And in her opinion, she did all three. Especially when the strangest thing happened. After a few years of marriage, Jilly Droughton had realised that she was genuinely in love with this ambitious, ruthless businessman who adored her. As much as he was dictatorial in the extreme in his professional life, he was the epitome of tenderness and compassion to his wife.

By the dawn of their fifth wedding anniversary, when the reconstruction of Droughton House was finally complete and she could have walked away without disappointing her family, she realised that Kenneth Kent was her family now. She returned every ounce of his love with equal measure.

They had been together for ten years when Polly was born and from that moment onwards she was the centre of their universe. Kenneth's priorities changed instantly and he went from being an obsessive workaholic to a family man with a bordering-on-balanced professional life. He still ruled his empire with a tyrannical demand for perfection, but he now often did it by telephone from the centre of his daughter's ball crawl.

When Polly came home from that Christmas party in 1985 with her new best friend Felicity, Kenneth was horrified – not by Fiz, but because he established that her mother hadn't shown up to collect her because her shift in the kitchens at Kent Continental had overrun. After a few phone calls, he discovered that the woman, Patricia O'Connor, was a commis chef serving under a head chef whose role model was Attila the Hun. To Ken's disgust, it transpired that she'd been threatened with the sack if she had left the kitchen before her tardy replacement arrived.

Patricia O'Connor was a single mother who needed her job just to live and provide for her daughter. She'd fled Dublin when her husband of two years disappeared with the widow O'Donnell from the house next door. The humiliation wasn't half as worrying as the thought that he might return – he was a foul-mouthed bully who regularly staggered home from the pub with an empty wallet, a raging head and make-up on his shirt. Patricia lay every night and said ten Hail Marys and four Our Fathers (she concentrated more on Mary, her being a woman and therefore having the ability to nag God on her behalf) that the Good Lord would intervene and put an end to her misery. The day Ted O'Connor didn't come home, she upped it to twelve of each prayer in thanks.

But some worries did remain, feeding her daughter and keeping a roof over their head being the biggest ones. She needed her job; so on the day of the party, Patricia had had no choice but to stay at work. She called a friend whom she knew was working at the party in the sister hotel and asked her to collect Felicity, but by that time Felicity and Polly were already ensconced in Polly's chauffeur-driven limousine.

Kenneth was outraged that someone who worked for him could be put under that much pressure and treated so badly. The head chef was given a severe bollocking (he didn't fire him – he knew how difficult good chefs were to find and, after all, business was business) and Patricia was transferred to the live-in cook's position at Kent Castle, their baronial family home. It was the most profitable tantrum that Fiz had ever thrown and Patricia thanked God every day (and twice at Mass on Sundays) for it.

Polly and Fiz had been inseparable thereafter. Except, of course, when Polly was sent to St George's while Fiz attended the local state school in Windsor. But they didn't care. Their friendship had survived everything, the diversity of their personalities complementing each other. Where Polly was prone to naivety and hopelessly optimistic and positive, Fiz grounded her with a pessimistic predilection to violent outbursts that could render a grown man impotent. And often did.

The only time their relationship was severely tested was many years later, when Polly became engaged to the Honourable Giles McAdam.

Their fateful meeting occurred at a UNICEF charity ball at the Kent Towers. Both of them were seated at the same VIP table, courtesy of the McAdam family's large tax-deductible donation and Polly's family being the hosts.

Eighteen-year-old Polly, as always, looked effortlessly exquisite. Her hair was twisted into a high chignon, held in place by a tiara with dewdrop pearls – a Droughton family heirloom. She wore a cream silk Balenciaga sheath, the boned corset accentuating every one of her curves and crevices, complete with elbow-length silk gloves. If the event were a beauty competition she would have won first prize even if she said she couldn't give a toss about healing the world and didn't like children or old people.

But she did, of course. Polly liked everyone. By virtue of her sheltered life, where everyone treated Ken Kent's daughter as if she were minor royalty, Polly had a view of the world that was born of extreme cosseting. Everyone was nice to her. Since she was a toddler all those she encountered had treated her with unfailing respect. Even those whose speciality was irreverence to anyone with money couldn't help but be nice to the sweet little girl with the perfect manners. The blatant obsequiousness because the Kents were loaded pissed Fiz off, but she understood it was just a fact of life. And anyway, if anyone was ever nasty to Polly then she'd have to defend her and that would get her into trouble. And she was always in enough trouble already, thank you very much.

Polly's stomach bubbled with excitement. She'd been looking forward to tonight for ages. She nudged Fiz, who was sitting beside her, stunning in a navy satin bias-cut dress with shoestring straps that crossed over her back and a skirt that fell to the floor over her diamanté Manolo Blahniks. She thought it was so great that she and Fiz were exactly the same size and could share their clothes.

'Who's the guy on your left – he's gorgeous,' Polly whispered.

'He's a fecking prick,' Fiz replied out of the corner of her mouth, so the prick wouldn't hear her. 'He's so smooth it's a wonder he's not slid right under the table and landed on his arse. If he leers at me one more time I'm going to have to bat him in the mouth with that flower arrangement,' she spat, gesturing to the table centrepiece.

Polly laughed. She didn't believe a word of it. She was used to these outbursts and knew that they were just Fiz's harmless way of expressing herself. Fiz disliked the whole world on principle. Although she wasn't sure what principle that was. But it definitely involved a lot of four-letter words beginning with f.

The prick, it transpired, was twenty-one-year-old Giles McAdam, future Laird of Dreghorn and heir to a family whisky distillery that churned out a prestigious single malt and raked in millions in export revenues.

Giles McAdam zeroed in on Polly like a nuclear warhead on missile lock. By the time the band struck the first chord, his partner for the night (the rather jolly daughter of a member of the shadow cabinet) had been unceremoniously dumped. By the time the auctioneer slammed down his mallet on the first sale of the charity auction (a week at a health farm promising spiritual enlightenment, weight loss, facial rejuvenation – bought by Giles's jolly, suddenly *ex*-girlfriend, in a desperate bout of comfort spending), he was focusing all his attention on Polly, much to Fiz's disgust. And by the time the cabs drew up at the door to collect the benevolent crowd, he had persuaded Polly to join him for dinner the following evening. Polly was entranced. Giles was just *gorgeous*. And funny and interesting. And damned sexy. In fact, Polly thought he was the most charming man she'd ever encountered. Fiz wanted to retch.

Their courtship had lasted for three years, during which the girls became increasingly distant. Polly's time was taken up with studying for her marketing degree at Bristol University and Giles, who had a job courtesy of nepotism at company HQ in the city, a yellow TVR and a predilection for hedonistic pleasures.

He swept Polly off to Paris three months after

meeting her, wooed her with fine wines, sublime food and long walks, and introduced her to Parisian culture. When he proposed, Polly cried. Giles was the most perfect man she had ever met. Except for her father, of course.

From Giles's perspective, Polly was the most flawless specimen of femininity he had ever set eyes on and he couldn't imagine ever meeting a more suitable female to be the mother of his children and carry on the McAdam name. It was just a pity that he'd met her so soon – he wasn't quite at the Volvo and monogamy stage yet (he felt that one thing went with the other; his TVR had pulled more birds than he had). Still, she was in Bristol all week while he was in Party Central, so he could have his cake *and* the gorgeous little Australian with the tight arse and the massive tits who worked in the patisserie beside his office.

Meanwhile, the only culture Fiz encountered was in the yoghurt she had for breakfast. To her utter joy, she had managed to secure a place at St Martin's, studying fashion and design. She was ecstatic and didn't care (OK, she did just a bit – that and unfortunate genes were what made her prone to the occasional outburst) that despite a contribution to her education from Mr Kent, she had to work most evenings and weekends in a variety of ever-changing bar and waitressing jobs. She was fired so often that her P45 had been in more bars than Budweiser.

The girls' relationship therefore faded from togetherness of Siamese proportions to brief irregular encounters in coffee shops, chatty e-mails and long telephone calls where Polly would extol the virtues of her fiancé, Giles the Great, and Fiz would attempt to conceal her utter contempt of him. She couldn't explain why she had detested him on sight and she didn't even try to. After all, if he made Polly happy . . .

She did occasionally see Giles in her various places of work. He didn't recognise her as Polly's friend and that suited her fine: at least she didn't have to make polite conversation with him for Polly's sake but she could just dole out her ritual abuse and in this case really *mean* it. She once encountered him slumped semi-conscious in Bar B52, with a sprinkling of white powder around his nostrils, an empty vodka bottle between his legs and so much lipstick smeared on his face that it looked like he'd been shot at speed into a Max Factor counter. She contemplated calling Polly, then decided to do the decent thing – after all he was her erstwhile best friend's fiancé. So she shopped him to the police. Let the prick explain that one to his family.

Unfortunately, they never got to find out. A night in the cells, followed by the engagement of a law company with more big guns than an artillery corps saw the case of drunk and disorderly dismissed as a misunderstanding – Mr McAdam had in fact been suffering from a particularly debilitating bout of food poisoning. Sure, Fiz thought. He'd obviously caught it from not washing his hands before sniffing his coke. Urgh! She hated him more than periods *and* Sloane Rangers. And she really hated those.

It was in Fiz's final year, as she prepared for her final exams, that Polly inadvertently fired up an emergency flare. During Fiz's weekly call to her mother from the communal phone in her King's Road bedsit, Patricia let slip that Polly had returned home and looked ghastly. Fiz's brow furrowed. The words 'ghastly' and 'Polly' were as alien to each other as

'Giles' and 'morals'. She had a bad feeling about this. Something told her that she and Giles the prick were about to have a disagreement.

Polly leaned over the toilet and threw up with such force that her throat made a pain-filled strangulation sound. She felt wretched. She hadn't been this sick since her GSCEs. Nervous tummy, the doctor had said that time. And every time before that. She'd been plagued by the same ailment since childhood. Whenever she experienced any form of excitement, fear or apprehension, her stomach immediately rejected its contents.

But what would he say this time? Devastated tummy? Utterly betrayed tummy? Can't believe I was taken in by such a, as Fiz would say, *wanker* tummy? Fiz. God, she wished she were here now. It would be worth any amounts of 'I told you so's' just for her to walk in the bathroom door.

She clutched the porcelain and tried to heave herself up into a standing position, but just as she almost got to vertical her knees buckled and gave way. She was back down where she started.

'Polly, darling, are you OK?' It was her mother at the door, her voice edged with concern. 'Shall I call for Dr George?' It struck Polly how infantile that sounded. Her mother had always called the family doctor by his first name in order to make him sound less intimidating. It worked when Polly was a child, but the effect had worn off now. And she really didn't want a man within a hundred metres of her. Ever again.

Polly forced some strength into her voice. 'No, Mum, really. I just need some sleep and I'll be right as rain. It's just something I've eaten.'

Wasn't that the truth! The irony struck her and she retched again, the memories of her last night with Giles flooding back. Was it only three days ago? God, it seemed like a lifetime.

Giles had collected her from her last lecture on the previous Friday and whisked her back into London. They'd had a quick change, a quick wash and an even quicker copulation (when *was* the last time they'd made slow, tender love, she wondered), before heading out to Teatro to meet a crowd of Giles's workmates.

When they walked in, everyone at the table turned to look. Polly had met them all many times over the years but still never quite felt she was one of the crowd. It was difficult to put her finger on why. She just always got a strange feeling when she was with them, like there was an undercurrent or unspoken agenda that she wasn't party to. Kind of like they were all watching a movie, but it was in Cantonese and only the others could see the subtitles. Still, a healthy self-esteem and politeness compelled her to be gracious and she shrugged off her reservations. She was just tired and being oversensitive, she decided. Too much studying and not enough pampering had made her a bit touchy.

As the night progressed, though, touchiness developed into distinct uneasiness. Giles was getting louder and louder and his frequent jaunts to the toilets told her that he was back partying with his friend Charlie again. He'd promised her he'd quit that muck. She really didn't understand the appeal. Still, he was under a lot of pressure at work and with her being away all week she supposed that he needed to let off a little steam now and then. He'd told her tens of times that he only did it to make their separations more bearable. She supposed in a weird way that it was a testament to how much he adored her. And no one was perfect. She could put up with the odd misdemeanour in the man she was going to marry, especially when he was so wonderful in every other respect. It would be different later in the year when she moved back to London and they could start house-hunting and planning the wedding. There'd be no need for the Colombian talcum powder then.

Polly drove home. Giles wanted to go on to China White or Attica, but she was exhausted and he'd finally capitulated when she said she didn't mind him going back out as long as he saw her home safely first. She was secretly hoping that when they got back to his flat she could persuade him just to climb into bed, but she had her doubts – he and Charlie were wide awake and ready to party.

She switched off the alarm as they entered the duplex in Belsize Park. It was a gorgeous apartment but too masculine for her taste – all chrome and black leather with the mandatory bachelor's bar in one corner. Polly couldn't see herself there at all. No, a town house in Richmond or Chelsea was more her style . . . oak floors, white walls, an eclectic mix of glass and wood furniture. Mmm, contemporary and eclectic, that was the look she would go for. She must remember to consult her mother for the names of interior designers who were hot at the moment. Yes, she'd call her tomorrow morning . . .

'Hey, babe, bring your gorgeous little ass in here, darling.' Giles snapped her out of her reverie. He'd gone straight through to the bedroom and the tone of his voice made it clear he didn't want her for conversational purposes. She gave a small shrug. If she were honest, the last thing she felt like doing was having sex for the second time that day. All she wanted was to curl up next to him and kiss him until she fell asleep. Which wouldn't be long, judging by the way she was feeling. Still, at least if he wanted sex then he wouldn't be going back out again, so she'd get to snuggle in for the night. That would be just heavenly.

She fixed a smile on her face and went into the bedroom, but as soon as she saw him the smile froze in astonishment. He was lying on his back on the bed, hands behind his neck, still fully dressed except for his fly, which was open to allow his penis to stand ramrod straight and ready for action. Polly's eyebrows narrowed as she absorbed the sight. She didn't quite understand. What was that on his . . . Oh no. Clarity struck her like a criminal in a hit and run. His penis looked oddly white not just because it had limited exposure to the sun's rays, but because it was coated in a grainy white powder. He was giving a whole new meaning to the expression 'coke-head'.

Polly hesitated. She hated to seem prudish or strait-laced. This was the nineties and Giles was her future husband . . . behind closed doors and all that. But anger started to rise. She drew the line at this. And he would just bloody well have to accept that and respect her feelings. Still, she didn't want to upset him too much. She went over to where he was lying, swiftly took a tissue from the bedside table and started to wipe off the coke.

'Hey!' Giles yelled in fury. But Polly worked quickly. She had the powder wiped off in seconds and her lips replaced it. His fury subsided instantly and he started to groan. 'Yes, babe. Oh, yes. Oh that's it. Oh, yes. Yes. Yes. Oh, Candy . . .'

Polly's head snapped up. What? Had he just called

her by another name? Or had some of that mind-altering stuff remained on his privates and affected her hearing?

'*Pardon?*' she whispered tersely.

It took Giles a few seconds to realise that his job was no longer being blown. He stared down at her. 'Darling, darling, why have you stopped?' he asked in incomprehension.

Polly paused for a second, still unsure if she had heard correctly. 'Giles, did you just call me Candy?'

Giles. Startled expression. Rabbit. Headlights.

'Eh, eh, yes, sweetie. But it's just a term of endearment. You know, like sweetie, honey, my little chocolate drop . . .'

She'd never heard that last one before but on the whole his explanation seemed fairly plausible. Obviously she'd misunderstood the whole thing. God, she felt such a fool. And he looked so adorable with his big brown eyes etched with concern at upsetting her. Back to the job in hand . . .

The *Mission Impossible* theme cut through her thoughts like a hedge cutter through Playdo. Since she was already in the right vicinity, she reached into his trouser pocket and pulled out his mobile phone. She flicked it on, expecting it to be the guys they'd just left wanting to know what time Giles was coming back out to play. She was right. Partially.

'Hello?' she said loudly, hearing the din of a night-club or loud bar coming through the earpiece.

'Hi, I think actually I have the wrong number,' a puzzled voice replied. 'I was looking for Giles.'

Must be one of the secretaries or one of Giles's colleagues' girlfriends who'd been sent to make the call. What *were* that lot like? Nothing would drag them away from their champers.

'No, you've got the right number. Who's calling?' Polly asked in a singsong tone.

There was a pause as she listened to the caller's reply. She handed the phone to Giles. 'It's Candy.'

There was a knock at the bathroom door. Polly sighed. She didn't have the energy to attempt to clamber up again from her position on the floor.

'I'll be out in a minute, Mum.'

Behind her she heard the door opening. For goodness' sake, couldn't her mother leave her alone? But then, Mum *was* still under the impression that she was suffering from a particularly rare strain of botulism, not her heart being broken by a fiancé who was addicted to coke and hedonism. The very thought made her stomach lurch again and she quickly leaned over the loo.

She felt hands gather up her hair and hold it back while she concentrated hard on expelling what was left of the contents of her stomach. If this episode reinforced nothing else, it confirmed that she just didn't do trauma.

'Thanks, Mum,' she murmured, wiping her mouth with a tissue.

'It's me, Pol. So,' she said softly, 'what's caused this then? What's that fecking prick done to you?'

Polly smiled, despite the tears that were welling up in her eyes. Fiz.

It took three hours, two bowls of chicken soup, three more nauseous visits to the bathroom induced by relaying the details of the fateful night, and sixteen requests that Fiz stop swearing so loudly lest her mother overhear and wonder what was going on. Fiz was apoplectic. And full of remorse. She should have spilled the beans on that wanker the second that she'd had proof of his habits. But then, she just hadn't wanted to be the one to break Polly's heart. Ironic. Now she'd allowed that specimen of crap to stomp it to pieces.

'Pol, have you still got keys to his place?'

'Yes, why?'

'I'm just going to go and collect the rest of your stuff,' Fiz assured her in an innocent tone.

Polly wasn't convinced. She knew her friend better. But, hey, so what if Fiz poured ketchup on the carpets or cut the sleeves off his suits. Giles bloody deserved that and a lot more for what he'd done.

She raked in her bag then handed over a key ring with a mortise key and a Yale. 'The alarm code is 999.'

'Should be 666, the bastard,' Fiz replied, as she took the keys and kissed Polly on the cheek.

Don't worry, my love. Mr McfeckingAdam will pay for this and then some, she thought, but didn't verbalise. Polly had enough to trouble her. Instead she simply said, 'Back soon, Pol. Now give me a list of what's there so that I don't miss anything.'

Polly wrote down everything she could think of.

An hour later at the flat, Fiz was meticulous in the collection of the property. Three black bin liners later she'd removed all traces of her friend from the prick's apartment. And she'd also somehow managed to jimmy the lock on his desk drawer and remove both his address book and cheque book.

Soon friends and acquaintances of Giles McAdam the length and breadth of the country (including a grandmother with an ever-changing will, several high-ranking politicians and a junior member of the royal family) were regularly receiving the most explicit-bordering-on-illegal pornographic material in print, delivered to their addresses for Giles's attention and paid for by cheques drawn from Mr McAdam's account.

Much to Giles's embarrassment and humiliation, it went on for months. Or rather, until all the cheques in the book were used up. His phone rang with one confused and frankly shocked friend after another until, well, the phone just stopped ringing altogether.

There was no point going to the police. Some horrid friend of Polly's had called him to say that if he took that course of action or cancelled any as-yet-unused cheques from the stolen book, she would go to the papers with photographs of him stoned into a stupor in some bar months before. How the fuck had she managed to get those? He was sure no such pictures existed. Well, almost sure. And how did his sweet little Polly know someone as degenerate as that? But he knew he couldn't call the bluff. He couldn't bring the family name into disrepute (any more than the current barrage of porn winging its way from the back gutters of several European cities was already doing). His father would never forgive him for it, and neither for that matter would Granny. She'd be off to the lawyers to amend her last will and testament before you could say 'chop up that line for me, doll-face'.

In time, despite his protestations of innocence, that old adage 'there's no smoke without fire' began to surface. It would be years, if ever, before Giles McAdam would be reinstated on London's top guest lists, until people stopped washing their hands immediately after they'd shaken his, or until the sound of the whispers following him everywhere subsided. Fiz O'Connor had damaged his reputation indelibly and indefinitely. And that was just what she'd intended. Fiz, one. The wanker with the coke habit, nil.

The Shaker was starting to quieten down now, with most of the after-work revellers having been summoned home via mobile phone by irate spouses in the suburbs. Some of their places had been taken by a new crowd – people who were just popping in for a few lubrications before making their way to a nightclub. Having spent the last two hours getting ready with meticulous care, they eyed the remnants of the after-work crowd with distaste. The suits were too pissed to care.

Chloe and Zoë were doing that dance thing. The one that single girls on the pull did where they simultaneously moved their shoulders in time to the music, played provocatively with their hair, cased the room for talent and tried to lock eyes with anyone who displayed the shaggability criteria, all the time pretending they were having a hilarious conversation with each other.

Fiz was on her break and had joined them on the drinking side of the bar. The speakers blared out an old version of 'Papa Was a Rolling Stone' to a crowd that thought this was a reference to an ageing rock band.

Polly could see Fiz's lips moving and leaned closer to hear what she was saying to her.

'Oh feck, Dumb and Dumber are penis-hunting again,' she yelled in Polly's ear, while gesticulating at Chloe and Zoë. 'Would you look at them! They're fecking shameless. Is it any wonder men think blondes are bimbos when those two are living proof? They make swizzle-sticks look intelligent.'

Polly laughed. 'Having a bad night, Fiz?' Then,

without waiting for a reply, 'You know, maybe we should be a bit more like them. After all, I haven't had a relationship lasting more than a month since Giles and you, well . . .' She trailed off, not wanting to state the obvious, that Fiz hadn't *ever* had a relationship lasting more than a month. Or a week. OK, so she'd never had more than one-night stands, but that had been her choice. As far as Fiz was concerned, men were an inconvenience only to be called on in times of heavy luggage or car problems.

Fiz just rolled her eyes. The day she started to act like Dumb and Dumber would be the day that she certified herself as insane and climbed into a strait-jacket, shouting 'Feck off you tarts – don't contaminate me!' at the top of her voice.

Polly wasn't convinced though. It had taken her months to get over Giles. Not that she had ever wanted him back after what turned out to be his litany of transgressions and infidelities, but she did miss being part of a couple. She missed the love and the cuddling, the teddies and the planning for the future. She longed to snuggle up in bed with her perfect man, his hands stroking her hair while they debated names for their future children.

In fact, if Polly were entirely honest with herself, she didn't hold much with the current trend of women having careers first, then babies in their thirties while doing yoga and interviewing nannies to cover for their return to the workplace.

No, she'd always wanted children while she was young. She'd always imagined she'd be happily married just like her mum and dad, and onto her second child by the time she was twenty-five. And here she was, twenty-three and not even a boyfriend. What was wrong with her?

It was true that Fiz did act as a slight deterrent by intercepting all males who came within a thirty-metre radius of them and threatening death, but that surely couldn't be the only reason. No, she must be giving off the wrong vibes. She pursed her lips, deep in thought. The next guy who caught her eye was going to get a smile. She wasn't going to react in her usual way of diverting her gaze to the floor and pretending she hadn't noticed. She threw her head up high. She was available. On the lookout. Open to offers. Actively seeking a partner of the opposite . . .

'Hi.'

The male voice only centimetres away from her ear made her jump. She'd been so deep in thought that she hadn't noticed Fiz going back to work and her place being taken by a guy. And a gorgeous one at that. Out of the corner of her eyes she could see Chloe and Zoë spinning so quickly they were in danger of hunk-inflicted whiplash, while grinning from ear to ear and arching their backs to throw their breasts into attack positions.

The guy standing next to Polly didn't so much as glance in their direction. He couldn't take his eyes from her. She was without a doubt the most gorgeous female he'd ever seen in his life. And he'd seen a few . . . hundred. But this bird was stunning. Yep, in light of the bet he'd made earlier with his mates, he couldn't believe his luck. Barely a couple of hours after he'd promised them beauty and brains, here was the first lucky candidate for the position of stunning arm-adornment. He wondered if she realised that it was about to be her lucky night.

He switched on his eye-twinkle; the one that gave him George Clooney-esque crinkles. On a female they would have been called crow's feet and regimentally attacked with a never-ending supply of creams and probes. On a guy they were crinkles. Cute ones that he knew made the babes swoon.

What line to use? He had so many and prided himself in his ability always to select the right one at the right time.

'Get your coat, you've pulled?' Nope, too brash.

'How do you like your eggs? Fertilised?' Nope, just a tad on the too-cheeky side for this one – she looked a bit upmarket.

He made a lightning decision. He'd play it straight. No chat-ups. No gimmicks. Straight.

'I'm Clark.' He flashed his most captivating grin, the one that showed off his veneers (Harley Street, a thousand quid each – those cosmetic dentists should be wearing masks and *not* the surgical kind!).

'Polly,' she replied, automatically returning his smile and at the same time thinking what gorgeous teeth he had. 'Pleased to meet you,' she continued.

As their eyes met, their peripheral vision and all other contact with the world around them momentarily crashed as they absorbed each other.

Lucky. Or they would have seen and heard the barmaid clocking their meeting, slapping a hand to her forehead and shouting, 'Ho, twit-face, get away from my mate if you want to leave here with your bollocks.'

Chapter Three

Clark – The Pull

Clark performed his favourite task of the day – checking himself out in the floor-to-ceiling mirrors of his bedroom, before whistling approval at his reflection and making for the door. Tonight he lingered just a little longer than usual. From the bottom: shoes, polished, Versace, class; suit, Armani, black, stunning; shirt, Austin Reed, grey silk, style; tie, present from Polly, not his taste but Hugo Boss so therefore sufficiently expensive; face and hair – he grinned at his image – bloody gorgeous, mate, bloody gorgeous.

He climbed into his navy Porsche (his gratitude that one of his best mates was the director of a Porsche dealership and had given him an obscene discount in return for a new IT infrastructure was never-ending) and roared off. He was feeling good tonight. This was going to be the big one. The night that all his hard work and patience with Polly paid off. He had specifically chosen that night because the next day he was off to a sales conference in Cannes (all those gorgeous French females with the massive tits and that accent and, oh God, he was getting a hard-on just thinking about it) and he wanted to test out the whole 'absence makes the heart grow fonder' theory. Polly's heart, of course.

Anyway, it wasn't a moment too soon. He was bloody sick of all this 'being the perfect gentleman' crap. Who the fuck had invented all that nonsense? Wining, dining, flowers, presents, all the 'I respect you too much to take this to the next level until you're entirely sure' . . . God, he was making *himself* nauseous. But instinct had told him that it was the right way to play it. OK, instinct, Polly's personal minder and an implied death threat, that is. If he'd have known that first night in the Shaker how much he'd have to work at this one, he might not have bothered.

'Can I buy you a drink?' Clark asked loudly, trying to make himself heard over the din of the Shaker. Polly nodded, as he'd known she would. They just couldn't resist him, could they? And anyway, even if the unthinkable had happened and she'd said no, her two pals looked like they'd be up for a pull and they were no slouches either. Not quite in this Polly's league, but he wouldn't kick them out of bed for farting. 'Champagne? Only I'm getting a bottle for my mates and me anyway. Why don't I get two and you can all join us?' he said making eye contact with Pol, but gesturing to Zoë and Chloe. May as well line up a couple of substitutions and if he didn't need them (and he was sure he wouldn't), then maybe Nick could have a bash at one of them. It was about time he had something to take his mind off the bitch behind the bar. Zoë and Chloe gave a chorus of 'Ya, great, love to's'.

'Two bottles of Moët and three glasses please, wench,' he called to Fiz, keen to demonstrate that he had a sense of humour as well as a knowledge of historical terms. Unfortunately, it also gave him an excuse to demonstrate that he had a knowledge of first aid, as a beer mat flew across the bar like a Frisbee and caught him right in the eye. He folded like a Z-bed. Polly screamed in horror and lunged towards him, turning her head to scream at the barmaid as she did so.

'For Christ's sake, Fiz, you're a maniac. What did this poor guy ever do to you?'

Fiz was too busy being proud of her aim to be fazed by any pain she'd inflicted. 'He breathes,' she replied, staring at Clark. 'Watch yourself there, Smarm Man,' she warned.

Polly shook her head. Sometimes Fiz went too far. She was out of control this time and she'd tell her so later. But first, the lovely guy clutching his face on the floor in front of her . . .

Clark bit his bottom lip. Shit, he thought. He'd been trying to impress the chick and now here he was on the floor like a complete wuss. He berated himself for his reaction. He should just have shrugged the pain off and continued talking but it had come as such a shock that his reactions had been instinctive and like a hostage in a siege situation he'd fallen to the floor instantly. If truth be told, it didn't even hurt now that the initial shock had subsided.

He squinted his eyes open, expecting to see an audience of faces laughing at his performance and holding up cards giving scores for artistic impression, but as his pupils focused all he saw was the concerned expression on the face of the vision in front of him.

'I'm really sorry, I don't know what comes over her sometimes. Are you OK? Can you see?'

It took him a few moments to absorb the situation. She almost sounded like she knew the assassin behind the bar. His confusion must have been obvious.

'It's just that she's a bit overprotective sometimes. Not to mention an aggressive sadist,' Polly continued in a voice loud enough for Fiz to hear every word and roll her eyes in contempt.

'You, you *know* her?' Clark stuttered, still clutching one side of his face while he decided whether to play the incident down and look super-cool, or exaggerate it and go for the sympathy vote.

'Unfortunately!' Polly asserted, looking straight at Fiz. She didn't mean it but she just wanted to convey how annoyed she was. Fiz rolled her eyes again. 'Actually, she's my best friend. Or *used* to be, before tonight.'

Clark groaned. Oh, crap. Wonder if it's too late to dump this one and just go for her pals instead? But he'd already made his move – he couldn't backtrack now. She'd better be worth it.

She was. During the next couple of hours, Clark almost forgot that he was doing this for a bet, as his well-practised charm offensive took over and he smothered Polly in all the right words and actions. It was his standard act – kind of like being on automatic pilot. And it invariably ended in a landing that was a bumpy ride. Literally. A career in sales was a great training ground for picking up women. It taught all sorts of invaluable skills and Clark was expert in deploying every one of them. Probing questions, listening to the replies, assessing the client's true needs and tailoring the proposal to fit the criteria. And overcoming objections, of course.

There would be none of those with this Polly bird though. This was a guaranteed sale. Another few features and benefits of the product (i.e. him) then he'd go for the close. He congratulated himself on his choice. Yes, the shagmeister radar was on fine form tonight. Not only was this chick absolutely fit, but she seemed like a genuinely nice person too.

The only drawback was that they worked for the same company. He'd always adhered to the code of not shitting on your own doorstep, but he decided to make this an exception. It wasn't as if they were in contact with each other at work. System Solutions was such a huge organisation, and he spent so much of his time out of the office, that they'd never even met (although he did vaguely know her boss), so he wasn't worried about any professional conflict.

The pros definitely outweighed the cons. Polly was gorgeous, sweet and, going by her accent and the looks of her clothes, obviously not skint. Bingo, he thought as she excused herself and nipped to the loo. He'd be taking her home to meet his parents next. Not.

He smiled at the thought as he slugged his champagne straight from the bottle and waited for Polly to return (Zoë and Chloe had long ago been pulled and swept off to some party by blokes with surnames as first names – Dalton and Dexter or something else in his opinion just as wankish).

For a fleeting moment he wondered what his parents would think of this one. So far he congratulated himself on an unbroken record – he'd taken home several girlfriends over the years and so far his parents had liked exactly, well, *none* of them.

No, that wasn't strictly true, he corrected himself. His father had approved of them all as potential trophy girlfriends for *him*. Clark knew that his old man hated the fact that his son was pulling better birds than he was. After all, weren't females supposed to be attracted to money and power? Sam Dunhill had both in abundance.

The Dunhills had lived a relatively impoverished existence until the late eighties, when Clark had hit puberty and Sam had hit on a gap in the market. The mass shift of emphasis in the City from technical and engineering trades to financial and IT careers had caused a massive void in toilets. Not in a white porcelain literal sense, but in plumbing. And Sam Dunhill had filled that gap. It was easier to get a parking space than a plumber in London, and that was nigh-on impossible (although just as expensive).

Thus Plumb the Depths was born: a company of over a hundred CORGI-registered plumbers, available 24/7 at rates guaranteed to plunge the householder towards bankruptcy. But at least their loos wouldn't be blocked.

There had been one slight blip a few years before. For a fleeting moment Clark had thought that his days of unlimited allowances and trips to the family's weekend house in Brighton were over when one of those sanctimonious investigative documentaries on the telly had set their investigation team on Plumb the Depths. They'd exposed a litany of cons. Their plumbers were charging 500 per cent mark-ups on parts, or billing for the time it took to nip to the nearest plumbers' merchants and deciding to pop in for a pie and a pint while they were at it. Some were even deliberately damaging the boilers so that the man-hours, parts and repair bill would be higher.

What they also discovered was that the plumbers were all subcontracted to Plumb the Depths instead of being directly employed by them, in order to create a loophole that the payment in income tax could easily fall through. However, since Plumb the Depths took a percentage of the bill, they were still deemed as being liable for the plumbers' actions.

That had been a nervous night for the whole family as they contemplated the downfall of their drain-clearing empire. Thankfully it was only a matter of hours before the next call from a desperate customer came in. What they'd failed to realise was that there was a much-anticipated death scene on *EastEnders* that night and nobody except a couple of security guards on the night shift and a few old grannies who didn't know how to change the channels on their remote controls had actually watched *Expose the Crooks*. Profits had continued to soar and so had Clark's monthly allowance from the old man.

Clark loved his dad. And who cared that he liked the odd extramarital dalliance – that's what all men did, wasn't it? Further proof that one woman just wasn't enough for a guy. It was genetic programming.

That wasn't to say that he didn't love his mum too. Sheila Dunhill was a corker. But she did – what was the expression Dad liked to use – oh yes, 'bump her gums' just a bit too much. Sheila had an opinion on everything and if she didn't she would make one up. They'd even had to get rid of their parrot as the vet's bills for treating the parrot's earache were swallowing company profits. Plus the bird (in the feathered sense) had started screaming for mercy every time Sheila entered the room. They had replaced the pet parrot with a Dictaphone so that Sheila still had something to talk to all day and Clark assured her that he listened faithfully to the little tapes that dropped in the post through his door every morning. Most of them averred that he needed the love of a good woman, while at the same time saying that he was to be careful not to get 'trapped' by some harlot after her precious boy. After all, no one was good enough for her son. Even royalty would have to go through a strict vetting process.

No, Clark decided as he watched Polly weave her way back from the Ladies, it would probably be safer to keep her away from his folks for now. And anyway, he just wanted to shag her, not live happily ever after.

'You look miles away,' Polly commented as she retrieved her glass from the podium in front of her. As she did so, the lights came up to signal chucking-out time.

'Just thinking that my parents would love you,' Clark replied. Polly blushed. God, this guy was so sweet. I mean, how many guys thought about their parents these days? Most of them were more concerned about her trust fund or getting into her knickers. Clark had spent the night making really interesting conversation and finding out all about *her*. She hoped he would ask to see her again. Despite Fiz's antics (which he'd so generously forgiven) she'd definitely say yes.

'So, would you like to have dinner with me tomorrow night?' Clark went for the hard-sell direct close. She didn't look the type to play coy and evasive so he was feeling confident of the answer.

'That would be great,' Polly replied with a smile. Then suddenly her face fell. 'Only, I promised my friend that I'd go out with her tomorrow night and I couldn't let her down at such short notice.'

Crap. Clark saw his cat jump back out of the bag. He didn't want to let this one go cold – there was no telling who would snap her up if he didn't seal the deal now. He was thinking on his feet. This could actually be a good thing. Her *and* her pal. There was nothing like pulling two birds with one stone. Shit, he was brilliant.

'Tell you what, why not bring your friend and I'll bring my mate Nick. You never know, it might be the start of a beautiful relationship.' He grinned. Females loved that 'relationship' stuff – made him sound all David Beckham, into commitment and monogamy.

'Are you sure that would be OK?' Polly checked. 'It's just that it's her only night off and I'd hate to desert her.'

'No problem at all,' Clark reassured her, at the same time wondering what her mate did for a living that meant her working night shifts. He hoped she was a nurse. They were wild when they got going. 'What does your friend do?' he asked casually.

Polly looked at him with a perplexed expression. 'But you know what she does.' She gesticulated towards the bar. 'Fiz works here.'

Oh fuck, *that* friend. Anyone but her.

He scanned the room for Nick or Taylor. He had to give one of them the signal that meant he needed to talk to them urgently. Surely one of them would be able to make it the following night. Nick was his best bet. He already had the hots for the psycho bitch behind the bar so he'd be up for it. Yes, he definitely would. In fact, he'd love him for this. He might even wangle a free upgrade of his Porsche CD system out of it.

He couldn't see either of them so they started to make their way outside. He cursed himself for having drunk so much. If he'd stayed sober he could have had the shag machine parked outside and she'd have been begging him for it all the way back to his flat. Fuck oysters, Porsches rocked when it came to getting females hot and ready. As it stood, he'd have to act the gentleman and find Polly a cab, before escorting her home and kissing her chastely on the cheek so as not to incur the slagging of a London cabbie. It was bad enough that he'd have to incur the cost of a London cab. He hoped she didn't live far away. Anywhere within a two-mile radius would be dandy – that way he could see her home and make it back to meet the guys in a club later. He might even get a start on the second stage of Operation Double Shag and hook up with a plain bird with brains. Where did they hang out then?

But at the door, Polly put her hand on his arm. 'So, here's my mobile number. I'll be at my parents' house tomorrow, but we can arrange where to meet when you call me.'

'Don't you want me to call you a cab and see you home?'

'No, that's OK. I'll wait for Fiz. We usually go for something to eat before we go home on a Friday. I'll break the news to her gently about tomorrow night.' She smiled ruefully. 'It might not be a pretty sight.'

Wasn't that the truth, Clark thought. The psycho bitch would have a stroke when she heard about their plans. He only hoped that she didn't force Polly to cancel. But then he'd heard Polly stand up to her earlier, so she obviously wasn't a complete pushover. Except where he was concerned of course.

Clark impulsively reached over and ran his fingers through the hair at the side of her face. 'See you tomorrow night,' he said in his softest tones. That was the way to do it. Tender. Caring. Reel them in.

Polly nodded and smiled. 'See you then.'

He turned to leave, joining the throng outside just as Taylor did a triple back somersault with pike over the handbag of some bird in a mac. Clark heard the thud as he landed. He went to intercede then thought better of it. Taylor was now yelling at the back of his attacker and it wouldn't do his image any good to be seen anywhere near a street fracas. You never knew who might be watching. Next week's crumpet could be just round the corner and it wouldn't do for her to witness him in anything less than a state of complete control and cool.

He waited till Taylor's attacker had cleared the scene and Tarissa had helped him up from his horizontal position then disappeared, before he rushed over.

'Taylor, mate, are you OK?'

A stream of blood was pouring from Taylor's nose and it was already starting to swell. That, together with the muck smeared across his face and clothes from landing sprawled on the pavement, and the water streaming from his eyes caused by the pain and shock of the injury, combined to make Taylor the 'ugly pal' for the first time in living history. Clark struggled to summon any sympathy or suppress a grin. Tonight was getting better by the minute.

'Fhucking bith athaulted mhe. Ah'm gnoing hnome,' Taylor spat out, along with several fluid ounces of blood and snot. 'Tharitha's away thoo find uth a cab.'

'Nah mate, don't be mental, we're going clubbing. Come on, honestly you look great.'

Taylor visibly perked up at this and raised his eyebrows inquisitively. His ego loved a good stroke. 'Do I?' he asked uncertainly.

Clark continued. 'Honestly, mate. Ditch the skinny one and we'll head over to the Romp Room.

It's always chockers with talent on a Friday night.'

Taylor looked around. Tarissa was nowhere in sight. And the Romp Room *was* always great on a Friday – the manager, Paul, always let him in free and showed him straight to the VIP bar where there were loads of totty from the glamour mags. He knew how to treat a celebrity, did Paul. But then he was already onto a sure thing with Tarissa . . . he debated, just as a cab shot past with Tarissa slumped in the back of it clutching a Marlboro to her lips. Daft cow was so pissed that she forgot to stop and collect him. Oh well. In that state she'd have been useless anyway. The Romp Room it was.

'What the hell happened to you?' Nick gasped as he joined them. He'd been in deep conversation all night with an old classmate whom he'd bumped into for the first time in ten years. He'd missed Taylor's grievous bodily harm, Tarissa's defection and Clark's successful pull.

Clark kicked him on the ankles. 'Just a minor bump, but he's fine now, aren't you, mate?'

He slapped Taylor on the back causing a blood clot to shoot out and hit the back of a girl in a white suit. Served her right. White suits were *so* ten minutes ago.

Nick cagily nodded. Clark was obviously underplaying this to make Taylor feel better. He could go along with that.

They started walking in the direction of the Romp Room.

'So anyway, Nick, where you been all night? And more importantly, what are you up to tomorrow night?' He didn't wait for an answer. 'Because have I got good news for you . . .'

*

Clark decided on dinner at the esteemed curry house, Mahatma Gloves, for the double date. Normally he'd have taken a female to somewhere a bit more exclusive on a first date – The Atlantic, Nobu, The Ivy – but he was having to cough up for four this time and anyway, he knew Polly was already seriously impressed with him. There was no point in spending needless cash and over-egging the pudding. Or over-creaming the chick.

Besides, he'd be damned if he'd spend any more of his hard-earned cash than absolutely necessary on that bitch mate of hers. His eye was still bloodshot and he'd developed a nervous twitch in the presence of beer mats.

The days after they'd met, despite her protestations, he'd insisted on picking up Polly at her parents' home. Always paid to put in a bit of extra effort on the first date – might as well build up his shag credits early on. Although he hadn't realised that would necessitate a drive to what was practically the countryside.

Following her directions, he'd driven out to the west of the city, then through Richmond Park and exited on the Ham side. He whistled to himself as he drove through the village. Every house was bigger than the one before. And that was only the ones he could see. Half of them were hidden behind ten-foot walls, penetrable only by three passwords or an SAS crack team.

He checked his directions again. *Half a mile after leaving village, Kent Lane on left-hand side*. It struck him that he was sure Polly had said her surname was Kent the night before. What a coincidence. He found the opening and turned into it. There was nowhere to go but straight ahead. Five hundred yards later, he stopped in front of two gates. There was a gold-leafed plaque on one of them. Kent Castle.

He let out a low whistle. He'd thought she came from a bit of dosh, but this was astrofuckingnomical. He rolled down the car window and pressed the buzzer on the post next to him. A camera on top of the right-hand gate automatically swung in his direction. He smiled at it. Fantastic! Somewhere right now he was on the telly. He hoped they had his best side. What was he thinking? *Both* sides were perfection.

A voice came over a speaker on the post. 'Good evening. How can I help you?'

'Good evening. I'm here to collect Polly. Polly Kent, that is. She's expecting me.'

After a few moments the gates swung open. He drove up the driveway lined with thirty-foot beech trees that bordered the manicured lawns, to a house that was more like a rambling stately home. He gave another involuntary whistle.

Holy shit, she was seriously loaded.

He rang the doorbell and a guy in a black suit answered the door. A butler! Thank Christ he'd worn his new Prada suit or else he'd be feeling seriously intimidated here. As it was, he decided with a raise of one eyebrow, he looked like he fitted right in. Yes, he was born to this life. You've cracked it, my old mate, he thought to himself.

'Miss Polly will be right with you, sir. If you'd just like to wait in the garden room.'

He showed Clark through to a room overlooking the back garden. That didn't even begin to describe the scene before him. It was more of a work of art–cum–tourist attraction. It even had a maze. A butler *and* a maze. This was getting better by the minute.

He took another sip of the mineral water that the butler had offered before he'd discreetly disappeared. Back off downstairs, Clark imagined, to sit with the cook, the maids and the chauffeur until they were needed again. Did servants still sit round a big table in the basement waiting to be called? Or was that just in old BBC dramas?

'Hi there. So you found us, then.' Polly stated the obvious.

Clark spun round. For the third time that night, his breath stuck in his throat. Jesus Christ, his lungs would be wondering what was going on.

Polly stood in front of him, a vision in brown leather trousers that moulded to every bend and curve of her body, a white off-the-shoulder top (Dolce and Gabbana – he'd noticed the same one on Claudia Schiffer in *OK!* the week before), and camel leather boots. God, she was ravishing. He could grab her right now and bend her over that sofa. There would be a first. He'd never fucked anyone in the presence of a maze before.

'You're beautiful,' he said, maintaining eye contact and smiling, sales techniques coming to the fore again.

Polly grinned. 'Thank you.'

He marvelled at her. She didn't have an ounce of arrogance about her. For someone who had probably been told that she was gorgeous on a regular basis since childhood, she didn't seem to have a vain bone in her body.

Outside, he opened the door of the Porsche and held it as she climbed in.

'Nice car,' she offered, but not in the hysterical *oh my God I'm going to come and can we please drive somewhere that there'll be lots of people I know* way that previous pick-ups had done. But then, Polly was hardly just a pick-up, he thought. She was a bit of class. They were well suited.

'Some house,' he commented as they headed back up the driveway. It was so long he half expected to see a Cessna making a landing in front of him. 'I have to ask, Pol, are you, like, royalty or something? Is your old man, like, a duke or a lord?'

He cursed himself. He knew he was sounding uncool, that he should just be taking all this in his stride, but he was just too dazzled to conceal his curiosity.

'No, he robs banks and operates car-theft gangs.'

The Porsche swerved off the road, nearly bursting a tyre on a grass verge.

'*What?*' Shit, this was all he needed – to get in tow with the daughter of a master criminal. He didn't fancy ending up with sawdust where his kneecaps used to be.

Polly laughed. 'I'm kidding. He's in hotels.'

Clark was relieved but still in a state of astonishment. 'Who is he? Conrad fucking Hilton?'

Polly was still laughing. 'Close. Uncle Conrad is a friend of the family. But no, my dad's name is Kenneth. Kenneth Kent.'

Well, fuck me dead in a master suite with a Jacuzzi and room service. The daughter of Kenneth Kent. One of the true self-made millionaires and icon to every up-and-coming entrepreneur who dreamed of emulating his level of success. Clark included. He smiled a grin that was wider than the dashboard.

'Polly, my love, fasten your seat belt. You're in for a great ride.'

He came down to earth with a thud that shook the

building to its very core when he entered Mahatma Gloves. The Anti-Christ, Daughter of Satan, was already sitting there. In his enthusiasm he'd forgotten all about their two dining companions. He wondered how much it would take to bribe Nick to feign illness. Surely if that happened, Fiz wouldn't want to hang around and play gooseberry. On second thoughts, that wouldn't surprise him. She was evil incarnate.

The first words were spat out of her mouth like dental rinse. 'Did he pick you up at the mansion?'

Polly nodded.

'Faaaantastic,' Fiz drawled. 'But of course, you wont be impressed by that level of dosh, will you? I mean, you're not at all shallow – are you, Mr Puddle?'

The hairs on the back of Clark's neck stood up. What was the penalty for assault of a mouthy cow these days? Whatever it was, he would happily do the time. It would be worth it.

Polly laughed. 'Ignore her, Clark. Honestly, it's the best thing. If she gets out of hand we'll request that they make room in their storage freezer and just bung her in there for the rest of the night.'

Fiz adopted a petulant expression. But she hadn't completely run out of steam. 'So which of your dead-beat mates have you dragged along in the pretence of a cosy curry love-fest then? Please God don't make it be that big prat, Taylor. Nah, he wouldn't be seen dead in here, no mirrors. So it must be the other one. Noddy. Whassisname? Dick? Sick? Prick?'

'Nick. But you can just call me Noddy. It's got an endearing ring to it.'

The three of them turned to see that Nick had arrived and was busy giving his jacket to the waiter while listening to the disparagement. Remarkably, his face showed not a trace of irritation.

Fiz, however, at least had the decency to look just a little embarrassed. Grumbles of apology almost escaped her gob – after all, Noddy Nick was probably the least offensive of the three. He was actually quite personable.

The main thing he had going for him, as far as Fiz was concerned, was that he didn't look manufactured like his plastic Ken-doll pals. Nick probably went to a normal barber, as opposed to a *salon*. He didn't work out, so his slender frame was unenhanced by protein drinks, weight repetitions or circuit training. His eyes were blue. Not stunning. Not piercing. Not the colour of the deepest oceans. Just blue. And he definitely didn't pull Taylor's favourite stunt, which was to leave on his mascara after a photo shoot. She had a feeling Nick wouldn't even know what to do with a mascara brush. Nick was just . . . normal. But definitely not her type. She didn't want normal. She wanted maverick. Maybe. Possibly. Oh feck, who knew what she wanted? She certainly didn't. Right now all she wanted was to keep Smarm Man away from Polly. But first, she'd better say sorry.

'Em . . .' she started. But couldn't continue. She didn't *do* apologies. Thankfully Nick put his hand up.

'No need. I know that the minute it was out your mouth you regretted saying it and the only reason you did was to cover up for the fact that you've secretly been adoring me from afar and lusting after my finely tuned body for months. Admit it, Fiz, you want me.'

Coming from Taylor or Clark, this would have been a statement that they honestly believed, born of arrogance, complacency and the utter belief that they were to women what Botox was to ageing actresses – utterly irresistible and ultimately desirable. But coming from Nick, with his floppy – but not in a cheesy, Hugh Grant way – brown waves, his crooked nose and his cute smile, and in a self-deprecating tone with an accompanying shrug of the shoulders, it just served to endear him to all within earshot. Including, although she'd die rather than admit it, Fiz.

The meal passed without further event or drama, right up until the last remnants of naan bread and chicken jalfrezi were being cleared from the table. In fact, casual observers might even have taken the group to be two long-established couples having a great night out.

Fiz and Nick were getting on like a house on fire (one that hadn't been started by Fiz in an insane arson attempt). For every verbal bomb that she presented, Nick had the right comment to defuse it and render it harmless. Fiz loved it although she did find it a bit strange that she was having a great time with this guy whom she'd been abusing from the other side of the bar for months.

Shame about his friend. No amount of dodgy Indian beer could alter the fact that she thought Clark was a prime-time dickhead. Worryingly, Polly seemed to like him. She'd spotted them doing a fair amount of hand-touching and toe-tapping under the table.

Polly was so naive. She was so busy looking for the good in everyone that she couldn't see when people were out to use her, abuse her or just generally be horrible. That's why she needed protection.

Fiz had a sudden sense of déjà vu. She'd just realised who Clark reminded her of.

'So Polly, how's Giles doing these days? Have you heard from him lately?'

Polly's head snapped up. Clark sensed her annoyance. Who the fuck was Giles?

'He's her ex.' Fiz answered his unsaid question. 'Turned out to be a complete bastard. Still, he won't treat anyone like that again in a hurry, will he?'

Clark shifted uneasily. He knew tonight had been too good to last. Polly closed her eyes in resignation and put her head in her hands. She was about to order Fiz to shut her mouth when Clark jumped in. He couldn't contain his curiosity.

'Why, what happened to him?'

Fiz raised her eyebrows and adopted her most innocent expression and tone of voice. It wasn't one that came naturally to her.

'Oh, something about importing porn . . . but I think he got let off with just a police caution. It was a shame about the two broken legs though. They never did catch that hit-and-run driver.'

Clark could feel the lamb bhoona churning in his stomach. Fuck, fuck, fuck. He knew that Kenneth Kent had a reputation for being something of a hard nut in his early days in the East End, but surely . . . not in this day and age? No one would be *that* over protective of their offspring, would they? Nah, it was surely a freak coincidence. He turned to Polly but she didn't return his gaze as she was frantically signalling the waiter.

'Excuse me,' she yelled when the waiter caught her eye. 'Could you do something for me?'

The waiter nodded. Polly was the most beautiful female he'd ever seen. He'd do anything that didn't involve live insects, emptying his bank account or donating organs.

'Could you check in the kitchen and see how much room there is in the storage freezer?'

Weeks later, as he added a final lick of gel to his already perfect hair, he told himself that the threat of permanent disability or possible loss of life had no bearing whatsoever on the development of his relationship with Polly. Nor did the fact that he'd frequently found he liked being with Polly so much he almost forgot why he was there. Almost, but not quite.

No, he was still doing it for the prize of a weekend in Marbella and the look on the guys' faces when he strolled into the shaker with Polly on one arm and Miss Brains on the other. But first things first. Polly hadn't quite signed on the dotted line yet. It was now two months since that first date in Mahatma Gloves and the Costa del Sol was Costa del Calling him. He smiled at his own joke. He must remember to drop that line next time he was with the boys.

After the somewhat eventful first date, when he'd limited his alcohol consumption to just two beers (a mistake in hindsight – perhaps another eight or nine would have numbed him to the terror he experienced when Fiz gave the description of Polly's ex's time on the life support machine), he had taken her home and kissed her on the doorstep. Not a chaste kiss on the cheek – he was trying to be a gentleman, not a Catholic priest. It was a full-on snog that did include tongues where appropriate.

He and Polly had slipped seamlessly into being a couple. He'd put his master seduction plan into operation and if he did say so himself, it was working a treat. He'd called her every day, sometimes twice, just to say he was thinking about her. Chicks loved all that crap. Truth was he thought about Arsenal, sex (not necessarily with Polly – that's why females like Jordan were invented) and his commission plan more than he thought about Polly, but hey, she didn't need to know that.

He also texted her daily with amusing little one-liners that were guaranteed to put a smile on her face. He could tell that Polly was falling for every ruse he came up with. Her expectant tone, her looks of excitement, the way she laughed so easily at his (undeniably witty) line in chat. Shit, he was good. And Polly was falling for him too, hook, line and sinker. He just knew it. And the Shagmeister was never wrong.

As for their time together, well, he pushed the boat out. Literally.

He realised that a bird with Polly's class must be used to lavish dates, so he trawled the Internet seeking out big, romantic gestures. He now worshipped at the click of Lastminute.com. So far they'd had, among others, a candlelit boat ride on the Thames, a picnic in Hyde Park complete with Fortnum and Mason hamper, Bollinger and a butler, a day at the zoo where he'd sponsored a chimpanzee in her name and a tandem parachute jump. Not only did that one knock a major dent in his bank balance, but it had also scared the crap out of him. They'd also eaten out at least twice every week in the best restaurants in London. City-centre maître d's would be able to have a group week away in Benidorm on the money he'd bunged them in the last two months.

But it was going to be worth it. It was an integral part of the plan to get Polly to the stage where she absolutely could *not* live without him. Where her very existence and happiness depended on him. That way, he reasoned, he could eventually ease off the gas with Polly while he spent some time working on Plan B. B for Brains, that is. It was a tough job, but he was up to it. He *was* the Shagmeister, he reminded himself. And when he won this bet his reputation as a ladykiller would be cast in stone. He'd be an icon. He'd make sure of it.

Not that any aspect of the mission had been too tough, though. Polly was actually a great girl. In fact, he'd enjoyed himself more with her than he had with any other chick in recent memory. OK, apart from sex with Angie in the toilets at Chinawhite and that blow job from the Bruce Springsteen groupie at the after-concert party that Taylor had blagged them into. Mmm. Those were memorable occasions indeed. However, in the strictly clothes-on category, Polly rated pretty highly. Indeed every time they were together he realised that he was actually having a great time. So at least all that dosh wasn't completely wasted.

Although he'd deny it in open court, sometimes the unthinkable happened and his mind would wander to the prospect of a long-term relationship with her. Long-term? Clark Dunhill? No way, matey.

He told himself that it must be the lack of sex – it was affecting his judgement. Long-term relationships were for old geezers and those who were grateful just to pull one female.

No, it would be criminal to limit himself to one chick for any length of time – life was too short and there were too many unexplored anatomies. And he was a modern-day pioneer.

His Porsche roared to a stop outside the Notting Hill flat that Polly shared with Beelzebub, when she wasn't out at her parents' house in the country. He crossed his fingers that the barmaid from hell was already away to her night shift in whatever pub or cemetery she was currently haunting. Shit, he hated her.

Polly constantly made excuses that she was actually lovely and just misunderstood, or that she was simply being protective of her, but Clark knew the truth: she was one of those evil feminist things who hated men. She was sick. Very sick.

Polly had been ever-diplomatic and managed to keep them apart most of the time. He hoped tonight was one of those times. After all, he didn't want the big seduction ruined by having to kill his girlfriend's flatmate. That would be a passion killer – not to mention a bit messy.

Polly buzzed him up as soon as she heard his voice. He kissed her as she opened the door, gently nudging her back so that she was against the wall in the hallway, her hands running through his hair and stroking the side of his face. He had to have a serious word with his anatomy. Down boy. It's not quite the time yet. This has to be perfect.

He playfully bit the end of her tongue with his teeth.

'Feed me now, my babe, or I might have to go for more than just your lasagne.'

Polly laughed as she pushed him back and took his hand. 'Right this way, oh hungry one. But I warn you, I cooked it myself so there's no refund if it's inedible. Which it probably is.'

He liked the way she could make fun of herself. Too many females these days took themselves entirely too seriously. One little cheeky comment and they would lambaste you, threaten a claim for emotional distress and speed-dial their therapists. But not Pol. She liked a laugh, even if it was directed at her.

He listened for the sounds of any other inhabitants but there was none. Fiz was out. Great. Operation Big Shag could commence.

Polly dished out the food. A tray of lasagne so big that ten prisoners coming off a month-long hunger strike would struggle with it, a garlic loaf and a Caesar salad. On the centre of the table was a bottle of Shiraz, already opened. He poured two glasses and handed one to Polly.

'To us,' he said with a smile. Then he put his arms round her waist and kissed her slowly, ignoring the Pyrex dish that was threatening to lift the skin from her hands as he did so. Polly swatted him away and rapidly threw the Pyrex onto the table, trying to ignore her throbbing fingers. Clark tried to ignore the throbbing of a different part of his anatomy. Steady, boy, steady.

They were onto a dessert of Häagen-Dazs when Clark launched the first offensive. It was time. Operation Big Shag had lift-off.

'I forgot to tell you, babe, I'm going away tomorrow for a couple of days.'

He watched her face fall. She was disappointed. Fantastic.

'It's a work thing,' he continued. 'An international sales conference in Cannes. All the European offices are sending their top guys.'

He couldn't resist that small token of self-gratification. In truth he was only getting to go because Steve Copeland, his sales director, was nursing two broken legs after an unfortunate incident involving three bottles of Krug, a Swiss chalet maid and a ski lift. But hey, one man's misfortune . . .

Polly smiled and nodded her head.

Come on, he thought, come on. Ask me how long I'll be away for, there's a good girl. Show how much you'll miss Clarky boy.

'How long will you be gone?'

It was all he could do not to punch the air in triumph. And she even looked devastated. Fucking brilliant!

'Until Friday, babe.'

Polly said nothing. But her forlorn expression spoke volumes. Clark reached over and took her hand. 'You know, Polly, I'm going to miss you so much.'

She raised her eyes to meet his. Time for the big one, he told himself. She's primed, she's ready and she's going down. Literally, hopefully.

'In fact.' He glanced down in mock embarrassment (that expression was a crucial accompaniment to the speech he was about to make and he'd practised it in the mirror every day for the last week – it had to seem like this was an emotional life-defining moment). 'Polly, I don't know how to say this. The thing is, I've never felt this way before. I think . . .' He paused. Mental drum roll. Deep breath. Go for it. 'I think I'm in love with you, Pol.'

He stared into her eyes. For a split second he thought he'd blown it, that she was going to shake her head and tell him to get over himself. Surely not. He'd worked this to perfection – there was no way it was going to blow out now and yet . . . nothing.

She was just staring at him. Don't say a word, he told himself. Golden rule of sales: never speak when the target is considering the proposition.

The pause seemed to last for minutes but it was probably only twenty seconds. He had to clamp his teeth together to stop himself from uttering a sound. Then, just when he thought he was going to have to regroup and come back with a different pitch, he noticed it. It was a glistening. Yes, there was moisture, he was sure of it.

Suddenly, a big fat tear appeared in her left eye and wobbled, then silently rolled down her cheek. Senfuckingsational.

'You do?' she whispered, joyful trepidation in every word. He nodded, fixing his face into the same expression that Tom Cruise wore in the big love scene in *Jerry Maguire*. Great film that. A job in sport *and* nooky with that blonde bird – that guy had it made.

'Because . . .'

He snapped back to the moment. Christ, his mind had wandered there.

'Because, I love you too,' she whispered.

Keching! Sold! Done deal! Now for the commission. Or rather, the big bonus cheque. He stood up and gently pulled her towards him. He leaned down and softly touched her face. (Richard Gere in *Pretty Woman* – about to have sex with the hooker. How great would *that* be – she'd know every trick in the book.)

He kissed her softly, gently, and then pulled back. Without saying a word, he turned and led her to the bedroom, his anatomical compass pointing north and leading the way.

Time for delivery of the product. And she wouldn't be disappointed.

'I'll just be a minute . . . I need to go to the bathroom.'

Surprised, he turned round to see Polly looking deathly pale.

OK, so that wasn't what he'd expected and her sprint to the toilet did kind of spoil the moment. But hey, the poor girl was probably just caught unawares by his announcement and now wanted to go spray some perfume around her bits or whatever it was that the shy ones did before sex.

Well, it must be a shock for her, he supposed. She's just overwhelmed, poor mare. Understandably, he thought with a grin and a quick check in the hall mirror. Looking *good*. The lights were definitely staying on tonight.

He was distracted from his reflection by the sound of the toilet flushing. Four times. Come on, love, he prompted silently to the bathroom door. Any longer and I'll have to start without you.

Chapter Four

Cassandra – The Entrapment

As the British Airways jet made its descent to Nice airport, Cass had a thought that almost induced a rueful smile. Almost. A fully-fledged grin was likely to leave permanent damage in her fragile state. She realised that she'd managed to absolutely astound her two lifelong friends by acting completely out of character twice in as many months. Once was the previous night's indulgence which had resulted in this killer of a hangover. The other was that night in Paul's office when she'd announced her plans.

'You see, I'm going to have a baby.'

Silence. Nothing. Not even a sharp intake of breath from either of them. It was like they'd been told a joke and they were now waiting for the punchline.

A full minute passed, then it was as if Jeff had a sudden moment of clarity. He jumped up from his position on the edge of the desk and rushed over to her.

'Oh my God, Cass, congratulations. When's it due? When did you find out? And oh shite, I don't believe I'm going to say this, but who's the lucky guy? You're taking secrecy to a new level, my love

– I didn't even know you were seeing anyone.'

She quickly disentangled herself for the second time that night. God, she hated all that huggy stuff. Personally, she blamed Americans. Brits had been borderline phobic about physical affection until American touchy-feely culture had invaded the screens. It was a downward spiral. They'd be high-bloody-fiving and wearing baseball caps and jeans with the crotch at the knees before the year was out. It was an outrage.

'Jeff, for goodness' sake. Don't go all emotional on me. I'm not seeing anyone and I'm not pregnant. Yet. I'm simply making you aware that I intend to be in the very near future.'

They both resumed their expressions of incomprehension crossed with concern that their friend had indeed worked herself into a deranged mental state. All work and no play makes Cassandra a candidate for Prozac and a natty line in straitjackets.

She glanced from one to another. 'And don't look at me like I've just announced that I've grown a penis. Although now that I think about it that would solve my immediate problem, i.e. the lack of a male organ.

'Anyway, the situation is that I've now reached the position I aspired to on the corporate ladder. Therefore I've decided to turn my attention to my personal life. So I'm going to have a baby. Preferably soon.'

Paul finally found his voice. He was visibly grappling to come to terms with this. 'Eh, Cass, what about the small issue of male participation? Or are you going along the sperm donor line? Or adoption? I mean, I take it you do have a plan.'

He realised what he'd just said and who he'd said

it to. It was Cass; of course she had a plan. She didn't make a cup of tea without thinking through the kettle strategy first.

'One-night stand. No ties, no involvement, and none of that "I'll respect you in the morning" crap.'

'I can't believe I'm hearing this,' Jeff declared somewhat irately. 'Haven't you heard of AIDS? Or of other sexually transmitted diseases? For Christ's sake Cass, you've taken leave of your senses.'

'Actually, I was going to ask one of you two to oblige.'

They both looked at each other, trying to work out which of them would have a stroke first.

'I'm *kidding*,' Cass laughed.

The same thought ran through both Jeff and Paul's minds. They were now acting as one. They both gave an uncertain laugh, before Paul became official spokesperson.

'Jesus, Cass, I thought you meant it. Shit, you really had me worried. You with a baby! Should have known you were winding us up; you've never been in the least bit maternal.'

She shook her head. 'No, I mean I'm kidding about asking one of you two. I'm deadly serious about the rest of it. Do you want to hear the action plan?'

The guys nodded, at a loss for words. They were still hoping that this was a mad joke brought about by chronic stress-related overwork.

Their hopes were soon blighted.

Cass explained how she was going to ensure a suitable candidate filled the position of egg fertiliser.

'System Solutions has just introduced a healthcare plan for its employees. This necessitated full medical examinations involving testing for all of the aforementioned afflictions. Those took place this week. So now is my window. SySol has a workforce of over a thousand in London, eighty per cent of whom are male. An outrageous statistic, incidentally – no wonder it takes a fortnight to get anything bloody done. Anyway, that's eight hundred potential sperm donors. I just have to select one of them. It *is* unfortunate that the candidate will therefore work for the same company as me – I'd much prefer it to be a stranger but, as you so rightly say, you have to be careful these days.'

They stared at her, aghast. It was like watching a reality TV show – an incomprehensible event was unfolding in front of them yet they couldn't quite believe that it was for real.

'So are there, like, criteria for this poor, unsuspecting guy?' Jeff asked, still dazed by the whole concept.

'Oh, don't give me that "poor, defenceless, male person" crap, Jeff. Guys have been shagging around with impunity for years, picking up females and discarding them as soon as the line on the pregnancy test turns blue.'

She thought about Antonia, but didn't mention her – she never discussed her sister's life with anyone.

'So this time, it's me who'll have the control. The guy will get his rocks off – one happy man. And I'll be left with the baby – one happy lady. It's a win-win situation. The morning after, I'll wave bye-bye to my very own sperm donor and never see him again. Of course, there's no guarantee that it'll work first time so I may have to keep him around for just a little while.'

The whole scene was getting more bizarre by the minute. It was the most ludicrous, not to mention the most immoral, callous and calculated thing the guys had ever heard.

Cass read the situation and absorbed their reactions. Suddenly, she gave a sad smile. 'Come on guys, go with me on this one. You know I've never met anyone I've wanted to settle down with – neither have either of you. But the difference is that you two have plenty of time to meet someone younger and start a family. I haven't. This is it for me. Am I to be penalised by a life empty of children just because I didn't meet the right guy in time? You must admit that there's a certain injustice there. So I'm righting a wrong. Going for a child while I still can. And I really want both of you to be on my side.'

It was suddenly hugely important to her that they support her, but if they didn't she'd do this alone. They knew her well enough to realise that.

The guys shrugged their shoulders. They had to admit, what she said did have logic. Of a sort.

Paul looked at Jeff for a consensus. He almost indiscernibly nodded.

'OK, Cass. When it all ends in tears we'll be here. But you are definitely a few decimal points short of an equation, my love.'

Cass laughed. If she weren't so averse to the notion, she'd hug them.

'Thanks, guys. Now are you sure neither of you want to volunteer for the job? It would save me a whole lot of hassle.'

Cassandra mentally ran through her checklist as she surveyed the methodically packed Samsonite on the bed in front of her. Three lightweight suits, four cocktail outfits, one casual for any free time, one formal for the corporate ball, underwear and sleepwear. Accessories and footwear for all.

She contemplated packing one more casual ensemble but discarded the idea. She was going to work, not to play, although she guessed that SySol's American parent company would probably have arranged some inane team-building excursion on at least one of the days or evenings. Bloody waste of time.

She couldn't believe that she'd drawn the short straw and been selected along with Miles Conway, the marketing director, to represent the UK board. Excuse for a jolly, that's all these stupid conferences were. After all, the majority of the communication could have been done via conference call or at a push, video streaming.

At least marketing had a direct relationship with the sales function so the trip might be of some value to Miles. The only connection Cass had to the sales team was that she consistently tried to get the bastards fired for fiddling their expenses. I mean, since when was a night at the Spearment Rhino lap-dancing club appropriate entertainment for a client? They were a bunch of chancers, the lot of them.

She had tried to veto the whole jaunt, but she had been outvoted. The sales director had insisted that it was a vital component of his motivation strategy for his team and that the rewards in sales upturn after the conference would more than justify the cost. Mmmm. Somehow she doubted it. She was just glad that it was coming out of the Americans' budget and not hers.

Anyway, divine retribution for going up against her on this at the last board meeting had been foisted on the head of sales – he was now in a hospital bed with both legs encased in plaster of Paris after a fall while skiing. Served him right. He was worse than useless anyway – cut about like he was the proverbial dog's bollocks, just like the rest of the sales team. God, she hated them almost as much as she hated witless night-clubbers.

She perused the suitcase again. There was plenty of room left. Should she pack a couple more options for eveningwear? All the outfits she'd included were geared towards warm temperatures, but maybe she should pack one rainy-day trouser suit just in case. After all, even Cannes had the odd summer shower.

The intercom buzzed and she automatically frowned. She wasn't expecting anyone. Unless it was her cleaner, Margaret Mary (no prizes for guessing that she was of Irish descent), calling round to collect her wages. She wasn't due them until next week but perhaps she'd realised that Cass was going to be away on pay day and was pre-empting the situation. Well, too bad. She was getting a post-dated cheque, if that was the case. No matter how small the amount, the money was better collecting interest in Cass's account until the very last moment possible. As far as she knew she wasn't a registered charity and she didn't intend to act like one.

She went over to the intercom phone and looked at the video screen. A tall, beautiful blonde was waving enthusiastically into the camera, the huge smile on her face and the sparkling eyes making her seem even younger than her twenty years. In her left hand she carried six suit bags.

Her right hand momentarily stopped waving and returned to the speech button.

'Sis, hurry up and let me in – my arm's about to fall off here.'

Cass pressed the button and Antonia bounded up the stairs like a gazelle released back into the wild. A gazelle carrying Gucci, that is.

She thrust the suit bags into Cassandra's arms and gave her a hug at the same time.

'Hey, Cass. Thought you might need these back since you're going away on your jolly tomorrow.'

Cass melted and hugged her back. 'Thanks, Tone.'

She didn't want to say that she had at least a dozen designer suits and hadn't missed the ones that she'd loaned to Toni when her sister had started in her new position as receptionist at System Solutions.

Toni gushed on, hands on hips. 'As of last pay day I officially own my own smart professional clothes and am a cosmopolitan woman of the working world.'

Cass laughed. It was great to see her sister so happy. She'd had such a rough time over the last few years, after she'd stupidly believed everything that her childhood boyfriend had told her about all that love and happy-ever-after crap. Where had she ended up? Bloody seventeen, pregnant, in a council flat with a boyfriend noteable only by his absence. She'd love to punch his lights out, but then she supposed he wasn't much more than a kid himself. One with skid marks on his trainers from when he'd bolted after Toni got pregnant.

'Aaaaaand, here's a cheque.' Toni put her hand up quickly to stop the objection that Cass was about to spit out. 'No Cass, I want to. You've lent me a fortune over the last couple of years and I can start paying you back now. I *want* to pay you back. And I'm not listening to any arguments. And you'd better cash the cheque, otherwise I'm going to have to start passing you brown envelopes full of cash at work and people might think you're involved in some fiddle of the tea bag fund.'

Cass took the cheque. She really didn't want to but

she knew that, like her, Toni had a hefty dose of pride and loved the fact that she was now paying her own way. It was the same pride that prohibited Toni from telling anyone at work that they even *knew* each other, never mind had originated in the same womb. She wanted to be appreciated on her own merits and not on the basis that her sister was one of the company bigwigs.

Cass gave her another hug. Just one. There was no need to go all American just because it was a moment of emotional happiness.

'Well done, sis. I'm really proud of you. So where's my gorgeous nephew tonight then?'

'He's sleeping over at Mum's. Since I'm working and Ben's at childminder's every day we don't pop in for afternoon coffee like we used to. I think she misses him. So she's taken him overnight tonight and I'll bring him home tomorrow afternoon. Just this once though – she wouldn't like to miss her nights down the bingo more than once in a blue moon.'

'So what are you doing tonight then?' Cass asked.

'No plans. Ben's night with Mum was only arranged this morning so I didn't have time to call Brad Pitt and tell him that I'm available for wining, dining and sexual favours. That's why I'm over here. You're the only other person I know who's so sad that they sit in on their tod on a Saturday night. I bet you even know the telly schedule off by heart,' she joked.

A shoe flew in Toni's direction.

'I do so have a life, madam! Christ, sometimes I wish Mum and Dad had done the normal thing and stopped having sex after I was born. You're a pain in the arse sometimes, Tone.'

Toni laughed and returned the shoe. 'Aw sis, come

on. You don't mean that.' She gave her sister a playful nudge. 'You can act the big shot tough lady at work but I know you're a softie underneath.' She put her arm round Cass's shoulders. 'Now stop being a grumpy cow and let me buy you a chicken chow mein. Who says the Haven sisters don't know how to have a good time!'

'OK. But it's only because I feel sorry for you, you being a single mother statistic and all that.'

Antonia chuckled again. Cass's digs were purely in jest and she didn't mind in the least. It had been a different story up to a few months ago when she'd been stuck in a disgusting flat with no job, no money and no life. But thanks to Cass and seriously hard work on her part she'd managed to turn things around and now her life had never been better. She loved her work, she had an income (albeit most of it went on childcare fees and clearing her debts, including the one to Cass) and best of all she had Ben. She adored her boy. If she could do it all again she wouldn't change a thing, but she was glad the worst was over.

Superstitiously, she reached for Cass's bedside table to touch wood, and screamed as the phone on top of it rang at exactly the same time. She grabbed the receiver.

'Hello, this is the Haven bordello, how can I help you?'

Another shoe flew in her direction and she dodged to avoid it.

'Cass?' the voice on the other end said tentatively.

'No, this is her sister. Who's calling?'

'Hey Antonia, it's Jeff. How are you? Long time no see.'

He racked his brains to remember when he'd last

seen her. Must have been at Cass's graduation when Toni was about, oh, six or seven. He wasn't sure. He was crap at guessing children's ages. And Cass rarely mentioned her, although he vaguely remembered something about her having boyfriend troubles a few years before. Cass didn't give the details but she seemed upset about it. Still, boyfriend problems often happened to teenagers when they hit puberty. Look at the disaster he'd been at that age. In fact, he grudgingly acknowledged, he wasn't much better now.

'I'm great, Jeff. How're you?' she said in her sweetest voice. She'd always wondered if he and Cass were an item. Amazingly, although she would say they were quite close now, they'd never discussed Cass's love life. Or any aspect of her life for that matter. Cass was a closed book and liked to keep everything close to her chest. One that Toni reckoned had not been touched by a member of the opposite sex for a long time. A mental image of Cass snogging came into her head. Yuck! No, she decided, Cass wasn't the smoochy type. She'd far rather get intimate with a calculator.

She passed the phone to Cass but stayed in the room, watching her sister's expression get more indignant and irritated as she spoke. She wished she could hear both sides of the conversation instead of just one.

'Hey, Jeff. What's up?'

'For Christ's sake, you're the second person that's said that to me tonight. Do you all think I'm some sad, lonely cow who sits alone every night waiting for a phone call?'

Short pause. Despairing tone.

'Oh sod off, Jeff. Now, the point of this call was what?'

Silence, then, 'And you think *I'm* sad? I'd never have fallen for that excuse. She's had a better offer.'

Toni was intrigued. Cassandra's face was now intensely studious as she listened.

'No, she's definitely had a better offer, mate. You'll get over it. OK, you can wallow for five minutes, but that's it. Any longer than that and you verge on pathetic.'

Another pause.

'Nothing. We were just going to get some Chinese food and a video.'

'Sure you can. OK, see you soon'.

Twenty minutes later, the intercom buzzed again. This time Antonia released the button and opened the door. She heard Jeff slowly plodding up the stairs and smiled as he rounded the corner. He stopped dead in his tracks.

'Antonia?' he stuttered incredulously.

She nodded. Why did he look so shocked?

'But, but you're an *adult*. I thought you were still a kid. I got you these.'

The three of them shrieked with laughter as he held out a can of Tango and a bumper-sized box of M&Ms. For an intelligent guy, he never was the smartest.

They'd finished their sixth bottle of red wine, eaten five different Chinese dishes, shouted at the cringingly clichéd answers the contestants on *Blind Date* gave to the obviously pre-rehearsed questions, then watched hours of *Friends* reruns on an obscure digital channel. Pretty much a perfect Saturday night.

'Holy crap, it's almost one o'clock,' Toni slurred, trying to focus on her watch. 'Or else it's five past twelve and the night has just dragged 'cos you two are really boring company,' she giggled.

The other two joined in her laughter. After spending all night with them, Jeff was now used to the way Antonia teased her sister mercilessly and he had given her goddess status because of it. It was a brave woman who took on Cassandra, even in jest.

After all the years he had known her he was seeing a different side to Cass tonight and he was sure it wasn't just the alcohol affecting his judgement. No, Antonia definitely had a softening effect on Cass that made her somehow more, well, *human*. He'd never have believed it was possible. It was a bit like discovering Margaret Thatcher cried at Disney films.

'So, what are we doing now then?' Toni clambered to her feet.

'We're going to bed, Toni. I've got an early flight in the morning. You can sleep with me and, Jeff, you can have the couch.'

Toni was outraged. 'No way! This is the first night in three years that I've been drunk, young, single and unencumbered by a small person. I'm not going to bed now.'

She paused for a moment trying to focus her thoughts.

'Don't you two have a mate who runs a nightclub?'

Jeff nodded before Cass could stop him.

'Well then,' Toni continued as she grabbed Jeff's hands and pulled him to his feet. 'Why are we still sitting here? Let's go find the party.'

Bing bong. 'Ladies and gentlemen, welcome to Nice. We would ask that you stay seated until . . .'

Cassandra rubbed the bridge of her nose without

removing the dark glasses that straddled it. The Chanel specs weren't there for effect. They were the only things preventing her body from spontaneously combusting, leaving only a puddle of wine as evidence of her existence.

God, her head hurt. What the hell had possessed her to go along with Toni the night before? Actually, she corrected herself, it wasn't strictly speaking the night before, more earlier that morning.

After Toni's announcement that she wanted to go out, they'd called a taxi and were at the Romp Room within half an hour. Paul had been delighted to see them and after demonstrating the same reaction as Jeff when he realised that Toni was now a fully paid-up member of the adult female species, he'd ushered them into the VIP section. It was full of B-list celebrities, members of boy bands and models. She was so drunk that she was seeing double, but one guy did catch her eye: he was tall, with long blond hair, square jaw, quite good-looking really. Had a bit of an evil stare though. She couldn't think how she knew him. Someone said he was a model, Taylor someone or other, so she must have seen him in a magazine ad or on the telly. Whatever.

She'd shrugged it off and had another glass of free champagne supplied courtesy of the management. Her last recollection in the club had been of her dancing in the style of Kylie Minogue (gyrating hips, lots of pouting, while talking in an Australian accent) to pop records sung by people half her age. What was she thinking? She didn't do dancing, she didn't do drinking and she didn't do Kylie bloody Minogue. Wasn't it supposed to be older siblings who were a bad influence on the younger ones? Well, she and Liam Gallagher were blowing that theory.

When the club closed, they'd all returned to Paul's house. It was an exercise in nostalgia, as he still owned the same home that they'd all shared when she and Jeff were students. They'd all sat round the kitchen table, bottles of beer now replacing wine as the drink of choice. It went down much better with the kebabs they were devouring at the same time.

The combination of fresh air, conversation and food had a slightly sobering effect. Thankfully, Cassandra's world stopped spinning round-round-baby-round-round. Or, at least, it slowed down to a less nauseous speed.

'So come on then, what's wrong with you lot?' Antonia teased. 'I want to know what the story is. Have you all got a permanent aversion to relationships or what?'

She sat back, intensely proud of herself. It was no mean feat to have pronounced 'permanent' and 'aversion' in her condition.

The others looked baffled. Why was Toni asking them if they had a 'terminal conversion to relationships'? Was that some modern lingo that they weren't up to speed with yet, they being bordering on geriatric as she repeatedly reminded them?

Eventually they worked it out.

Paul spoke first. He was the most sober so his brain was reacting slightly quicker than the others. Cass was still wondering what she was doing there. She hadn't been this drunk since she was, em . . . ever. She'd officially never been this drunk in her life.

'Jeff is still single because he takes so long to decide whether he likes someone that they're already married, engaged or in the process of emigrating by the time he asks them out.'

The others shrieked at this assessment. Even Jeff had to acknowledge that it was perceptively accurate. 'It's a God-given talent,' he said with a shrug.

'Cass is still single because she's intent on world domination. Even if she does intend to do it with a baby strapped to her back.'

Toni didn't understand this last comment, but was too drunk to care. Was Cass going to put Ben in a papoose and take him hiking? She hadn't said. Anyway, next! She wanted to hear what the story was on Paul. There must be a good reason why he wasn't living in happy coupledom. Was he gay? What a waste.

'And I, despite years of trying, just haven't met the right girl.'

'When are you going to learn?' Cass hollered. The beer was making her giddy, but she was intent on articulating her point. 'You have to stop hanging around nightclubs, Paul.'

'I hate to point out the obvious, Cass, but I *work* in a nightclub.'

'Good point. So you do. But you have to realise, Paul, and I'm only telling you this because I love you . . .'

Jeff and Paul nearly fell off their chairs at this statement – Cass admitted to loving no one and nothing. She must be having some kind of alcohol-induced breakdown.

'. . . that if a female gives you her telephone number written on a G-string, then she's hardly likely to be the kind of girl who wants to take you to a poetry recital. You're fishing in the wrong pond, Paul. And only catching trouts.'

The others resembled goldfish as they listened dumbfounded to Cass's bizarre analogy. What was she on about? Did she have a secret subscription to *Anglers' Weekly*, or what?

He knew that her underlying message was right, though. He *was* constantly surrounded by the wrong kind of women.

Or at least he used to be, he thought, surveying the two women sitting in front of him. It hit him like a ton of bricks (which of course, due to his size and shape, made no dent whatsoever). Shit, he'd been blind. The answer was staring him in the face and he'd been too blind to see it.

Until now, that is.

Cassandra dressed carefully for the first morning of the conference. Mercifully, her hangover had now subsided to just a life-threatening case of dehydration.

She slipped on the jacket of an Escada suit over a white silk blouse, and adjusted the pearls around her neck and in her ears. As she quickly checked her reflection, the right adjectives flew into her brain: efficient, smart, calculated, measured, thirsty. She did for a second contemplate adding a slick of the lip gloss that she'd picked up at the Boots counter in the departure lounge the previous morning in a moment of residual-alcohol-in-the-bloodstream insanity. She decided against it. Adjectives: frivolous, girly and pink. Action: lip gloss fired at speed into waste bin.

She made her way through the delegates to her seat without stopping to speak to anyone. There was only one person senior to her at the conference and she'd be sitting next to him at lunch, so there was no immediate demand to interact. Plenty of time for networking later at the buffet.

She opened her mobile phone and called the

London office for an update on the stock-market values (New York and Tokyo had closed up overnight) and the current sales figures for the week. She always liked to have the most up-to-date figures immediately to hand.

While she waited for her assistant to access the data, she surveyed the crowd. She hadn't seen so many designer suits in one place since the last state funeral. It was an Armani-fest. With more than a few Versaces thrown in for good flash effect. Typical sales people, she mused. All flash and no substance. Verrucas had more appeal than a week stuck in a room with this lot.

She jotted down the new figures and snapped her mobile shut. Bad idea. One of the brown-nosing twats might approach and try to have a conversation. Perish the thought.

She opened her phone back up and held it to her ear, furrowing her brow to give the impression that she was deep in conversation with someone hugely important. That would stop any of the plebs in their tracks. There was nothing these guys wouldn't do to get in with someone on the board in the hope of furthering their careers.

Now *there* was a thought. She scanned the room. Could one of these vacuous, Versace-clad minions be useful to her in a strictly sperm-donor sense? She mentally checked off the criteria. Tall, attractive . . . Actually, that was it. Tall and attractive. After all, she was blessed with an IQ higher than most MENSA members, so she already had the brain. All she needed now was the brawn. And the sperm.

The first speaker took the podium and called the seminar to order. He introduced himself as Jack Sinclair, the director of sales for EMEA (Europe,

Middle East and Africa) and gave an overview of the agenda and objectives for the week.

'... and build a consolidated framework to take SySol into the new millen ...'

Cass zoned out. This was like watching paint dry. It was nothing more than a platform for employees with huge egos to strut their stuff and act important. And she had absolutely no desire to fan the flames of anyone's ego. It was going to be a long week. Thank God she'd had the foresight to bring along the next year's budget framework – she could sit quietly and get on with that for the next five days.

A round of applause broke her concentration, and she glanced up from her paperwork to see a new speaker taking the podium. Now there was a man who fitted the criteria, she decided instantly. Over six feet tall, jet-black hair groomed to perfection, skin that had seen more than a facial or two, great shape, great bone structure ...

She stopped herself. He probably belonged to the Hungarian or Romanian delegation, had more than likely left a wife and six children at home, and didn't speak a word of English.

'Good morning, everyone. First, I'd like to introduce myself. My name is Clark Dunhill and I'm here representing the London sales team, in place of our sales director, Steve Collins, who is unfortunately indisposed. The theme of my presentation today is "Strategies to Guarantee Surpassing This Year's Sales Targets".'

He stopped to take in the crowd, making eye contact with the key players from the States, before continuing. She had to give it to him. This guy had confidence in spades and he definitely knew how to work a room.

He continued with a smug smile. 'To adapt a saying from a British icon, "Can we reach them? YES WE CAN!"'

Silence. Not a sound in the room. The joke had sunk like a supergrass wearing cement boots. The other delegates were shifting nervously in their seats, aware that they were supposed to be giving some reaction but not quite sure what it should be.

A smile played on her lips as she switched her gaze back to the podium. Mr Dunhill was still beaming at the crowd wearing an expression that was a cross between that of a president schmoozing on the campaign trail and a door-to-door sales guy trying to flog a housewife some dusters. He was pure treacle. And he thought he was fantastic. He misread the embarrassed silence as undiluted awe at his charismatic opening pitch. Oh, good grief, this was worse than *Blind Date*. Even her toes were curling.

Cass was transfixed as Clark oozed through the rest of his presentation, littering it with clichés, innuendo, and naff company rah-rah-rah sycophancy. This guy was unbelievable. He was gorgeous, he was vain, he was cheesy and he was so smooth you could ice-skate on him. He was also, if the content of his presentation was anything to go by, bordering on thick. He was, Cass realised with celebration bells dinging in her ears, the future father of her child.

It had been easy. Insanely easy. A salesman and his sperm are soon parted, thought Cass, as she lit a Marlboro and took a deep puff, careful not to move into an upright position for fear of reducing the chances of the mini-Clark sperm squad reaching their targets. If they had the intelligence of their producer then chances were they were lost and stopping to ask her cervix for directions.

She had thought her plan through while she was sitting in the hotel's beauty salon immediately after the conference closed for the day. Her previous opinion that booking the conference at the Carlton Hotel, the glorious white-fronted luxury establishment on the main drag in Cannes, was an absurd extravagance had now altered somewhat as she sat being pampered by her own personal beautician and hairstylist.

Why had she never tried any of this stuff before, she wondered, as Jacques practised his expert head-massage skills on her scalp? Oh, it was glorious. She'd never again disparage 'women who lunched'. OK, she would, but she wouldn't really mean it in future.

When they'd finished she almost didn't recognise herself. For the first time she could see her cheekbones, her pout and her resemblance to her sister. If anyone had told her she'd scrub up this well she'd never have believed it. Whatever Eve and Jacques were charging it wasn't enough – they should definitely get a bonus for the miracle they'd just performed.

At dinner that night she had positioned herself so that she was on the next table to him and in his eyeline. She deliberately lingered when she caught his eye, doing what she hoped was an 'I-like-what-I-see' expression as opposed to an 'I'm-a-mad-stalker-and-I've-got-an-axe-under-the-table' one. She reckoned it was working when the frequency of his stare increased as the night went on and a glimmer of a smile developed into a full exhibition of his veneers by the time coffee was served.

She made her way to the bar as soon as the tables were cleared and took a cigarette from her bag. It had no sooner touched her lips than a lighter appeared from behind her and lit the end of it. Christ, that was close, she thought. If she'd been unfortunate enough to have tossed her hair at that moment she'd now be standing there looking like Yul Brynner. She knew whose arm the lighter was attached to before she even turned round.

'Hi there.' He sounded like a DJ from the days of mobile discos that came complete with record collections and one strip of green and red flashing lights. The ones who used to succumb to pressure from aunties at family functions and play 'Hi-Ho Silver Lining' so that all the women could line up and do the Slosh. She shuddered at the memory of her working-class upbringing. The day she decided to do the Slosh was the day she started campaigning for the legalisation of euthanasia.

She smiled back. 'Hi.'

Pause. Oh crap, what was supposed to happen next? She hated this mind-games nonsense. This was exactly why she was still single – she couldn't be arsed with all this flirtatious stuff. And besides, Eve had plastered her eyelashes with so much mascara that if she batted them she was likely to give herself whiplash.

'I noticed you at the conference today, busy scribbling away. Were you taking notes for your boss?' he said in a husky voice. He'd obviously been practising that one to maximise his appeal. It didn't work.

She was momentarily startled. 'Pardon?'

'What I want to know is . . .' He leaned closer to her ear. 'What do *I* have to do to get a PA as gorgeous as you?'

A *PA*? The arrogant bastard! Cass struggled not to spit a retort that would have him careering towards the wall behind him at speed. A fucking PA! Not that there was anything wrong with being a PA, but she bloody wasn't one and she hated his presumption that because she was in a skirt and at the conference she was there in a strictly subservient capacity. She'd check the payroll when she got back to her office, but she was pretty sure she earned at least three times the salary of this cocky little shit.

Still, there was a bigger picture here, she reminded herself with a deep breath. There was no point wiping the floor with this guy until he'd served his purpose. She conjured up every ounce of self-discipline she possessed and adopted her most provocative stance and tone.

'Oh, I don't know. Maybe you could ask me nicely and I'll take down some, er, *notes* for you.'

She even coyly twiddled her fingers around her hair as she said it. He thought he was a smooth operator? She'd show him what smooth really looked like, the arrogant tosser.

He bought her a drink. She made a split-second decision to act the part and ordered a Malibu and pineapple instead of her preferred Scotch on the rocks. She'd read somewhere that it was a popular drink among the glamour-girl set. She tried not to grimace as it slid down her throat. It tasted like suntan lotion, but it was an essential part of the performance: tonight she wasn't Cassandra Haven, financial controller, boot-your-bollocks-in-a-heart-beat-if-you-step-out-of-line. She was Cassandra Haven, PA, easily impressed. And apparently horny.

She wondered how long it would take him to make his move.

He'd been boring her senseless with brags about his life for the last hour. So far she'd heard about his Porsche, his male supermodel best mate, his designer wardrobe, his weekly manicure and the size of his last commission cheque. She knew that he excelled at all team sports, was a black belt in two different martial arts (chow mein and origami, she reckoned) and had been headhunted by every major IT company in the City of London.

He droned on further, his chest expanding with every boast. She began to fear for the buttons on his shirt. If they popped off due to the pressure of his inflating pecs they'd take her eye out. He was, she mentally summed up for him, actually a demigod and she should thank the Universe that the cosmic fates had conspired to place him in her vicinity.

She glanced quickly at the group that he'd abandoned to take up residence at her side. She vaguely recognised a couple of them as being from the American sales team. Fabulous. He'd obviously decided that the possibility of getting into her underwear was more important than networking the room. Or maybe he intended to do both. Maybe she was just to be a quick shag and then he could return to his mates and brag about pulling the secretary chick. Well, there was nothing she liked more than efficiency. She decided to help him out there.

She experienced a moment of hesitation but slapped it aside. It'll be worth it, she mantra-ed silently. This was all just a small hurdle to be jumped (or perhaps straddled) in order to achieve her life plan. And besides, she might not have another chance to do this with someone who had just been certified free of any medical ailments. No, it had to be him and it had to be now.

'Clark, I've just realised that my shoes are hurting my little, bitsy toes. I think I'll have to go up to my room and change them. Would you come and . . . keep me company?' There was no mistaking the suggestion in her voice or in the wording.

He raised an eyebrow in reply before slowly smiling and subtly placing his hand under her elbow. 'Lead the way. Sorry, what was your name?'

'Sandra.' She wasn't sure why she'd automatically used her nickname from the days at a Slough primary school. The teasing she'd taken for having a 'posh' name had been relentess, so she'd used the abbreviated version until she reached puberty, decided that people could sod off if they didn't like it, and reverted to her full name.

'Well, lead the way, Sandra. I'm right behind you.'

I bet you are, she thought.

They entered the lift with two Japanese tourists and an overweight tanned guy in his fifties who had his long hair (apart from the bit on the top that had the surface of a golf ball) pulled back in a ponytail, and what appeared to be eighteen-year-old models on each arm. It was a snapshot of the future. That's exactly what Clark Dunhill would look like in twenty years, she thought. If he lived that long. The Porsche, the origami, or an irate husband might kill him first.

She pushed the room key into the door and waited for the green light to flash. She nudged the door open and entered the room. Behind her, she heard him close the door and walk towards her.

As she kicked off her shoes, she felt the hands encircle her waist. She slowly turned, allowing him to pull down the straps on her black Ben de Lisi cocktail dress as she did so. She pushed him back against the wall, almost miscalculating and thrusting him into the en-suite. But like a true smarmy bastard he recovered well from that one and adjusted his position to eliminate any danger of the bathroom door hinges damaging his suit. Class.

They deep-tongued for at least a few full minutes, their breathing getting heavier and speeding up with every tongue thrust. Cass kept her eyes closed tight. Despite herself she was actually beginning to enjoy this. It was a bit of a shock adjusting from fake anatomical devices that required batteries, but she was beginning to get used to it.

He pulled back. 'Oh baby . . .'

She latched back onto his gums at such speed that she almost chipped his veneers. But it was necessary. She couldn't let him speak now. He'd only come out with some inane banalities and she'd lose her arousal quicker than a dropped wallet on Oxford Street. And anyway, there was no need for him to utter another word. He'd pulled. What more could there possibly be to say?

He swooped down to lick her neck, then up to her ears. Mmmm. Good God, that felt fantastic. His hands slid up her arms, onto her shoulders, he pushed gently downwards, then slightly harder, then . . .

Whoa! She realised what was going on. He wanted her to fall to her knees and perform a service. She almost laughed out loud. That definitely wasn't on the agenda. This was to be strictly a full cappuccino experience, not a quick espresso with a squirt of cream on top.

She resisted his urge and found his lips again with hers, while pulling him back onto the bed. He fell on top of her, putting one arm out to stop himself from crushing her, and pulling down the bodice of her dress with the other. He lowered his head and started to nuzzle at her nipples, slowly circling them with his tongue, then playfully biting each one in turn.

Oh for fuck's sake, what was he doing now, she thought as he moved even further down the bed, his tongue slipping across her hip bones. Crap. He'd obviously decided that if he made the first move in the oral sex department then she'd reciprocate. One good blow deserves another.

Cass was starting to get irritated. How arrogant was this guy that he could just assume he was in charge here? And for the record, she couldn't be bothered with oral sex. It just gave the guys who performed it a reason to think that they were the greatest shag in living history, when the truth was that she spent the whole time contemplating her year-end report or the state of the financial markets. It was the ultimate inefficient, superfluous act.

She felt a fumbling between her legs and looked down to see his head disappearing. Nope, this was a complete waste of her time. Evasive action required. She sat up and reached down to cup her hand under his chin, then pulled it towards her face. His expression was one of surprise – he obviously wasn't used to the female running the show. Well, there was a first time for everything.

When his head reached the level of hers, she deftly slipped her hand down to his crotch and undid his fly. A flick of the wrist and he was inside her.

Her muscles contracted to a vice-like grip and his breathing now sounded like he spent his days in a dark room making dodgy phone calls.

He tried to manoeuvre her again. He obviously

wanted her to roll over and go on top. She quickly considered and dismissed it – not the prime sperm-gathering position, some of the little buggers might succumb to gravity – so it was therefore a no-goer. She shifted her weight so that he couldn't flip her over. This was getting more like a wrestling bout than a passionate encounter. And it had gone on quite long enough, she decided. She wanted it over and quickly.

She tilted her hips and pulled him even further inside. 'Now. Come NOW!' she demanded.

He was obviously a man who responded efficiently to requests as his back arched and he let out a string of 'Yes, yes, oh baby, yes!' before collapsing on top of her. She silently congratulated herself on her assertiveness and the result. They all liked a bit of domination, these suave types.

There was a full thirty seconds of silence before he rolled off and smiled at her, his expression one of anticipation.

What? Was he expecting her to tell him how wonderful he was? Ha! He'd be waiting a long time then. In Cass's opinion, praise and ego-boosting were as productive a use of time as cunnilingus.

She leaned down to the floor at the side of the bed and with one hand slid her cigarettes and lighter out and lifted them to her mouth, all the while careful not to tilt or move her hips in any direction that would cause the loss of the essential body fluids. She lit a cigarette. All by herself, this time. The snappy manners obviously only came into force before a good rogering.

Clark shifted uneasily. It was almost like he was at a loss as to what to say and do now that she was disrupting his well-practised routine. She saw him furtively glance at his watch. He was obviously starting the stopwatch. She was sure that he probably had a personal time limit for how long he had to stick around after sex, even though every instinct was telling him that he'd bought the goods, tried them on and now it was time to go look for a newer model.

'You can go now.'

His face snapped round to hers. 'What?'

'That was great, but you can go now. I like to be alone after sex. Just a little quirk of mine. I believe a lot of secretaries feel the same. Must be something to do with the job.'

How dim was he that he didn't even get the sarcasm? Instead, his reaction was one of barely concealed delight, mixed with a modicum of petulance at being the dismissee. Cass could tell that had never happened to him before. Right now she should probably be clutching on to his ankle and begging him not to leave. Yeah, right.

'Em, so I'll . . .'

For the second time that night Cass stopped him from speaking, this time by putting her finger up to her mouth in a shushing gesture.

'Don't say a word,' she whispered in her best sultry voice. 'I don't want anything to disrupt my karma.'

That would get rid of him. There was nothing lads hated more than females who warbled on about new-age spirituality. She was right. He was in the elevator before her aura even had a chance to glow. The only glow came from her cigarette as she took another deep drag.

God, she realised, the ciggies would have to go if she had indeed managed to fertilise an egg.

How difficult could it be, she pondered? Millions

of sperm, one egg ... surely the odds were in her favour. And it *was* right in the middle of her cycle, when her bits were at their most receptive. She said a silent prayer that she'd been successful. She didn't want to go through this palaver again in a hurry. She crossed her fingers. Then her legs. Might as well try to keep the little buggers in there for as long as possible.

Chapter Five

Polly Kent – The Result

'So what time is Smarm Man, the superstud getting back from the airport then?' Fiz asked with just a hint of contempt.

Polly grimaced at her. 'Six o'clock. I'm going to collect him at Heathrow.'

Polly's stomach lurched at the thought. She was *so* excited. She had missed him so much. She understood now why her relationship with Giles had ended in heartache: it was because she was meant to be with Clark.

She could hardly believe they'd only been together for two short months. In that time they'd grown closer than she'd ever felt to a guy. Time didn't matter. He was the man of her dreams, her soulmate. How many other guys these days still believed in old-fashioned courtship? He'd been so respectful, wanting to get to know her as a person before they pushed their relationship to a deeper level. He was just the most special guy she'd ever known. Every ounce of her was rapt in anticipation of his arrival. It was also covered in Ysatis body lotion – she wanted to smell gorgeous for him.

He'd called her every day since he'd left. At least

twice. In fact, he'd only been gone a few hours when he'd called her the first time, to tell her that his keynote speech had been a triumph. He'd been the star of the show that day and there was talk of promotion within minutes of him leaving the podium.

Of course, she'd had to cajole all this information out of him. That was one of the things she loved about him: he was just so modest and self-effacing. He *hated* to talk about himself and she always had to prise out any details. It had been the same later that evening when he'd called to say goodnight. He'd been pretty vague about the evening's activities but he'd eventually revealed that he'd been locked in conference with one of the other representatives – the vice president of global sales – discussing the strategic sales plan with him.

God, he was *so* smart. He was definitely going places. And she hoped that she was going with him. Her face erupted into a grin. Yes, she was sure of it.

The night before he left, he'd told her he was in love with her. It had been one of the best and most emotional moments of her life. The way that it had just spilled out, so spontaneous, like he just couldn't contain himself any longer.

'And I don't suppose this time apart has made you realise what a complete wanker he is, has it?'

Polly spun round, her face a picture of exasperation and irritation. Fiz immediately raised both her arms, palms forward.

'OK, OK, don't bite my head off. I was only asking. Well, hoping actually.'

Polly shook her head. 'Why do you hate him so much, Fiz? You can be so bloody spiteful sometimes. He's a gorgeous guy, I'm happy, he's happy. Live with it.'

'Even if the thought of sex with him makes you vomit?' Fiz countered.

Polly gave a yell of exasperation. 'It does not make me vomit! It only did the first time because I was nervous and you know that nerves always make my stomach turn. For your information, he was bloody brilliant in bed: he was tender, and caring, and—'

'Oh for feck's sake, stop. You're making *me* want to heave now.'

Fiz put her head back into the book she was reading while Polly stormed into the kitchen and flicked on the kettle. Cup of tea, that's what she needed. It would serve two purposes: it would calm her stomach, which was beginning to gurgle in excitement at the prospect of seeing Clark, and it would take he mind off wanting to murder her best friend. Almost.

She grabbed a digestive and started to munch. Fiz could be an official nightmare sometimes, she pondered. But then, they'd been together through thick and thin and she knew that Fiz was also her biggest protector. Apart from Mum and Dad, of course. She knew how lucky she was. Since childhood, she'd been wrapped in a metaphorical blanket of love and security. Her parents were still happily married after thirty years together. They still held hands when they walked, and her father's face still lit up when her mother entered the room. As far as Polly was concerned, that was normality. Love, security, honesty: they were all the components of everyday life that she'd grown up with and anything outwith that was alien to her. Even Fiz lived by those morals, although she tried to disguise it. But Pol knew that Fiz would always be there for her and vice versa. Even if she did want to kill her sometimes.

The phone rang and she dived for it. It might be Clark – maybe his flight was arriving early.

'Hello.'

'Hi, Polly, it's Nick. Is Fiz there?'

Polly's shoulders dropped. Here we go again, she thought. A repeat performance of the act that had taken place the week before. And the week before that. In fact, every week since that first night at Mahatma Gloves.

'Hi Nick, I'm, em, just in, so I'm not sure,' she lied. But it was only a white lie, she told herself – just one to spare the poor guy's feelings. 'Just hold on and I'll go check.'

She took the cordless into the living room where Fiz was still spreadeagled on the sofa with her nose in a Danielle Steel novel. The irony of it. The girl who thought that romance was an evil fallacy, propagated by a coalition consisting of the entertainment industry, florists and greeting card manufacturers, was reading the latest offering from the Queen of Slush. Fiz was one big contradiction in terms.

Polly held her hand over the mouthpiece. 'It's Nick for you again. Talk to him, Fiz, *please*,' she whispered.

Fiz shook her head violently. 'No way. He's a twat. Tell him I'm not here.'

'But you got on really well with him! You liked him, Fiz, you know you did!'

But Fiz was still insistent. 'Tell. Noddy. I'm. Not. Here. Pol,' she hissed. 'I'm not interested.'

Polly despaired. Sometimes, actually most of the time, she struggled to comprehend her friend's actions. She knew that the bravado and aggression masked a vulnerable person. She knew that that person had a perennial mistrust of men stemming back to when her father had 'buggered off with some tart' as she put it. But surely she couldn't keep this up forever.

'Eh, sorry, Nick. I've checked everywhere and Fiz isn't in. Can I give her a message?'

'Polly, if I ask you something will you be honest with me?'

'Mmmm.' Bugger, she thought. The last thing she wanted was to get caught in one of Fiz's man- (or woman-) made nightmares, especially when she was standing less than five feet away from the woman herself.

'Fiz is sitting right in front of you at the moment, telling you to say that she's out, isn't she?' Polly looked at Fiz, who was returning her gaze with a quizzical expression.

She hesitated, then, 'Eh, yes, Nick, that's correct. She's probably working late or something.' Good grief, she could have been a spy in the last war – she was handling this subterfuge brilliantly. But then, she did like Nick and according to Clark he was seriously besotted with her friend, so this was for Fiz's own good. Fiz just didn't know it yet.

'And every time I've called in the last two months, she's been there and just didn't want to speak to me?'

'Yes, Nick, that's right, I'm looking forward to seeing him,' Polly answered.

Fiz now rolled her eyes and went back to her book, satisfied that the twat had ended today's stalking episode.

'You know I'm not going to give up, Polly. I really like her,' Nick continued.

'Of course you shouldn't, em, give up going to the pub just because Clark's been away.' Polly was starting to sweat now. Maybe she wasn't cut out for this after all.

'So I'll call again next week then, Pol. And do me a favour. Try and work on her a bit for me. If I could just get her to go out with me once then I think it could be the start of something. Physical violence probably,' he added with a laugh.

'No problem, Nick. I'll give Clark that message. I'm sure he'll love the idea.'

She clicked off the phone with a sigh of relief. Persuading Fiz to change her mind about something? It would take alcohol, drugs or hypnosis and Fiz didn't subscribe to any of those. All she could hope for was that the Danielle Steel books would start to rub off on her.

'So what idea of Nick's is Clark going to love then?' So she had been listening.

Polly shrugged her shoulders. 'Oh, he didn't go into details – he just said he was looking to inject a bit of excitement into life so he was thinking of taking up some kind of extreme sport . . .'

'Fecking twat,' was the reply.

Polly pulled the MG into a space in the Terminal 1 Departures car park – it was always less crowded than the one for arrivals, a trade secret passed on from one of her father's chauffeurs. That reminded her, she hadn't called her mother for two days. She'd give her a quick ring on the mobile while she waited for Clark.

Clark. God, she couldn't wait to see him. She struggled to remember what she'd thought about, what had filled her day, before she met him. It was almost unbearable to think that during all the heartache after Giles, and while she despaired of ever meeting the right guy, Clark was right under her nose. Well, actually, seven floors under her nose if she were being pedantic. It was a wonder they'd never bumped into each other in the lifts, or in one of the three staff restaurants. Maybe he'd held a door open for her. Perhaps they'd been in the same line-up area after the last fire drill.

Imagine if she hadn't gone to the Shaker that night. She might never have met him. She shuddered at the thought. No, that wasn't possible. They were destined to meet. They belonged together. And the best thing was that he felt the same way. God, she was lucky, she reflected. She had a great family, a fulfilling job (albeit a stopgap until she took a career break to bring up her children) and an amazing boyfriend who adored her. If she weren't such an optimist she'd think it was all too good to be true.

She made a call to the Castle and heard her mother's voice on the line. They made quick plans for a celebration dinner before Polly spotted Clark in the distance and rang off. 'Have to go now, Mum. So, see you then if not before. No, I'm sure it'll be fine with Clark – he's dying to meet you both. Love you. 'Bye.'

She snapped it shut and waited for Clark to get nearer to her. There was a sea of people between them and she didn't want to bound towards him, surrounded as he was by important-looking executives in suits.

She recognised a couple of faces among the mêlée from the corporate photograph portraits that she'd organised for the shareholders' report the year before. There was Jack Sinclair, director of sales for EMEA, who worked out of their Milan office, but who spent two weeks of every month in London.

And wasn't that Cassandra Haven, director of finance? That was strange – she was sure that Clark had said this was a sales conference, not finance. She dismissed the question. Maybe Miss Haven was travelling back from a holiday and it was pure coincidence that she was there at the same time; after all, there were hundreds of people disembarking from at least three or four flights which all seemed to have landed at the same time. Maybe she had some exotic European boyfriend and had nipped over to visit him.

She briefly wondered what Miss Haven was like. She always seemed so aloof and austere. On the day of the photo shoot she'd refused to wear make-up or let the stylist touch her hair or clothes. She'd also told the photographer that he had ten minutes to get the shot and then she was going back to her office. This had made Polly laugh, as it was the opposite stance from that of the men involved. The chairman had insisted on so many shots in so many different poses that they'd had to send out for more film. And some Grecian 2000, but that was another story.

Clark spotted her and his face crinkled into a grin. Her heart surged and her stomach spun. God, he was gorgeous. She couldn't believe her luck.

She watched as he shook hands with the suits nearest to him and walked towards her. She was dying to jump into his arms, but Clark would be so embarrassed if she did. He was quite shy really. He didn't seem to do public demonstrations of affection – he said what they had was so private that he didn't want to share it with the world. That's why they didn't seek each other out at work or make their relationship common knowledge. Clark said that he wanted people to look at her purely for herself and her achievements, not just as someone's girlfriend. He was so wonderful. He always wanted the best for her, was always thinking about her welfare. She couldn't love him more.

He reached her and leaned down to kiss her. 'Hey you. I missed you, babe,' he whispered in her ear. 'I thought about you every moment I was away. It felt like a lifetime.'

'Oh, I'm sure that's an exaggeration! You were far to busy working to think about me,' Polly teased.

'Let me prove it then. Come on, let's get out of here.' He grabbed her hand and pulled her towards the doors.

'This way,' she countered, leading him towards the lifts that would take them to the correct car park.

When the lift doors closed he dropped his briefcase and cupped her face in his hands. His tongue was just reaching the back of her throat and his hips pressing hers against the mirrored walls when the doors pinged open. They sprinted towards the car park.

He checked out the area, puzzled. 'Where's your car, Pol?' he asked, searching for her blue Volkswagen Golf.

She shrugged her shoulders, trying not to act too embarrassed by what she was about to say. As she'd been thinking earlier, she had a charmed life.

'It's gone.'

'You mean it was stolen?' Clark exclaimed. 'Oh, Polly, babe, I can believe it – when did it happen?'

'No, it wasn't stolen. It's actually back at my parents' home – they've given it to the housekeeper. That's my car over there.' She pointed at the brand-new black MG gleaming in the corner. 'Dad bought it for me a couple of days ago. It was meant to be a surprise for my birthday, but he couldn't wait until then to give it to me. He's a bit like a big kid that way,' she concluded.

Clark seemed momentarily startled. Maybe he didn't like the car. 'Birthday? When's your birthday, honey?'

'A week on Saturday. And I hope you don't mind, but I've said we'll have dinner with my parents. They're dying to meet you.'

There was a momentary pause. Polly looked at him searchingly. She so hoped he would be OK with her plans – after all, hopefully one day they'd all be one big happy family.

Polly turned to Clark as they trotted up the steps of the mansion. 'You're very quiet tonight, honey. You're not nervous are you, darling?'

Clark cleared his throat. 'Of course not. I'm really looking forward to meeting your parents.'

She had her doubts. Clark had barely said a word since he'd picked her up at the flat. He was probably a little apprehensive, and who could blame him? She was sure she'd feel the same way when she met Clark's family. She hoped that would happen sooner rather than later. She must remember to mention it to him again.

She stole another glance at him. Yep, he was definitely not his usual carefree self. How typical of him. He was obviously uncomfortable and nervous, yet he was putting a brave face on it for her sake. He always put her first. And she loved him so much for it.

She'd barely seen him since he'd returned from Cannes. He'd been under so much pressure at work, poor love, because he was earmarked as the company's rising star and was in such demand.

It wasn't even as if she could sneak into his office to give him a quick hug and a dose of moral support because the nature of his role meant that he was usually at meetings in clients' offices or entertaining them in the evenings.

It was torture having little or no contact other than a few text messages throughout the day. Zoë and Chloe had both remarked how she never let her mobile phone out of her sight these days and wondered why she seemed preoccupied. She didn't tell them of course. No, Clark was right. What they had was private and between them and she wasn't going to subject their relationship to any form of office gossip. There would be plenty of time for that later. When things progressed to being more, well, *official*.

Henry, the butler, opened the door. She would normally have just let herself in with her keys, but the only bag she had which matched her floor-length silver beaded gown (Ungaro – three weeks' wages but so worth it – it was practically an heirloom) was a tiny silver Gucci clutch and it was only big enough for a lipstick, an atomiser and her mobile phone.

'Good evening, Miss Polly. Mr Dunhill.'

Good. He'd remembered Clark's name from his last brief visit. Hopefully that would make him feel more at ease. She turned to give Clark one more smile of reassurance before they stepped inside.

'Good evening, Henry. How are you tonight? You look very handsome.'

She stood up on her tiptoes and gave Henry a peck on the cheek. He returned the gesture with a modest smile. He had a massive soft spot for Polly. He'd been with the Kents since she was a toddler and watched her grow into a beautiful young woman – both inside and out. He'd hate to see her hurt again like she'd been by that last one. A good leathering that Giles deserved for what he did to that girl. And he'd heard through the grapevine that he'd got one. Car accident? A bit unlikely in his opinion, but then he wasn't paid to give opinions. The important thing was that Miss Polly was smiling again.

He cast his eyes towards Mr Dunhill. Very smart young man. Well groomed. They made a lovely looking couple. In fact they could almost be related, what with the two of them having hair that was black as coal and the same colouring. Yes, they could almost be brother and sister, by God. But then it often happened that people were attracted to partners who resembled them; he'd seen that many times over the years as he'd answered this same door to thousands of visitors.

Maybe that was where he was going wrong; why he was still single at his time of life. He should be searching for someone who resembled him! So where would he find a short, bald lady with a slightly protruding paunch, and one leg that was half an inch shorter than the other?

He laughed silently to himself. That would be a scary picture! Maybe he'd be better staying a bachelor after all. He stood back to let Polly and her young gentleman pass. He wondered if Mr Kent would like him. He'd soon hear about it if he didn't.

Polly led the way into the drawing room, holding Clark's hand as she went. Her parents were already there, sitting on a window seat, Kenneth Kent's arm draped casually round his wife's neck as she leaned against him. It was the kind of intimate situation that Polly had lived with her whole life. She loved the fact that her parents still cuddled on the couch. Fiz thought it should be punishable by twenty lashes and community service. But then, she would.

'Mum, Dad, this is Clark.'

They both stood and then her dad strode towards them, her mother right behind them. She kissed them both on each cheek, and then watched as Clark put out his hand and her dad shook it with a warm grin.

'Pleased to meet you, Clark. Please call me Ken. And this is Jilly.'

'Pleased to meet you, Ken, and you, Jilly. I can see now why Polly's so beautiful,' he added, looking at her mum.

'Yes, she does take after me in the looks department, doesn't she?' her dad retorted.

Clark was momentarily speechless – that compliment was directed at Polly's mum, but her dad ... then he caught the twinkle in Kenneth's eye and laughed. As did the others.

Yes, it was going to be a wonderful evening, Polly decided. This was without a doubt her best birthday ever.

Dinner was fantastic, although Clark did seem slightly surprised as the courses were served. Big thick slices of cold melon to start, sausages and mash with onion gravy to follow and hot apple crumble with custard for pudding. All finished off with hot tea and a box of After Eights. The cuisine didn't exactly match the surroundings or the dress code. Eventually, as she scoffed the last chocolate, she enlightened him.

'All my favourite things.' She smiled.

'Sorry?' he replied, obviously confused.

'Dinner, tonight. It's all my favourite things. It's a family tradition. We always have dinner on our birthdays and we get to eat all our favourites. Ever since I was a child these have been mine. Although I think I've eaten a bit too many of the mints – I'm starting to feel decidedly queasy,' she added with a laugh.

It was true. She was starting to get that familiar bubbling sensation in the pit of her stomach. It must be overindulgence, she decided. After all, tonight she'd had absolutely nothing to be worried, upset, or nervous about. Clark had been an absolute star.

Over dinner the conversation had flowed. It was fantastic to hear her father and Clark discuss so many different subjects – from cars to politics, it seemed like they both had a viewpoint on everything and quite often those viewpoints were the same. Clark was exactly the way he'd been that first night they'd met: asking loads of questions, being interested in their answers, so witty and smart at the same time. If it were possible, she fell more in love with him as every hour passed. He was so charming and unaffected.

She'd caught her mother giving her a wink when the men weren't looking. So Mum approved. But then, Mum would love anyone who made her happy.

At midnight she suggested to Clark that they should make for home and was delighted to see his crestfallen expression. It confirmed what she suspected: he liked her parents as much as they obviously liked him. As they were leaving, her father folded her into his arms.

'Happy birthday, my darling.'

'Thanks, Dad. And thanks again for the present. I love you. Sorry to dash away so early, but I really am feeling a bit out of sorts. But please tell Patricia that the food was sublime as always.'

She turned to Clark. It had suddenly struck her that she'd never told him how she and Fiz met.

'Patricia is Fiz's mum – she's a lovely lady and has been the cook here since I was a child.'

She could see that Clark was sceptical. Given his opinion of Fiz and hers of him, it was no wonder really. She did wish that they would at least try to call a truce, but Fiz was bloody impossible sometimes.

'And how have you been getting along with Fiz, then, Clark – she's a bit of a handful, isn't she?'

Polly laughed. 'Mum, don't be cruel. You know what Fiz is like with any boyfriend I've ever had. She makes poor Clark's life a misery. But he's so understanding . . .' She glanced back at Clark, her adoration obvious.

'I can imagine. Well, it was a pleasure to meet you, Clark. And I do hope we'll see you again soon.'

'I think you can count on that, Jilly. And I look forward to it.'

He shook Ken's hand and kissed Jilly on the cheek before turning and placing his arm round Polly's waist as they crossed the driveway to the MG.

Jilly slipped her hand into her husband's. 'Well, love, what do you think of him?'

Kenneth Kent inhaled slowly. 'I think we might be in for a bumpy ride with this one, Jill. I just hope our Polly is up to it.'

Clark barely said a word as they travelled back into the city. As they drew up outside her flat, Polly started to get concerned.

'You're very quiet, darling. You did enjoy yourself, didn't you?'

Clark turned to face her, his expression serious. 'Your parents are great, Pol.'

Silence.

'Pol, are you really sure that you're in love with me?'

She was shocked by the question but didn't hesitate for a second before she replied in the fiercest tone, 'Of course I am! How can you even question that? Why are you doubting me, Clark?'

His voice was soft. Apologetic even. 'I'm not doubting you, maybe just looking for some reassurance. Meeting your parents tonight gave me a bit of a jolt. As I watched them tonight, all I kept thinking was that I hope that'll be us in twenty years' time, Pol. Married, with a family, and still happy.'

He reached out and brushed her hair back from her face. A big fat tear ran down her cheek as she took his hand from her head and kissed each finger one by one, her eyes never leaving his.

'That'll be us, Clark,' she whispered. 'I promise.'

The following Sunday, Polly lay in bed at four o'clock in the afternoon. Fiz bounced in the door. Thank goodness, Polly had started to worry about her.

'Where've you been? I've been worried sick about you. I expected you home straight after work last night.'

'Out.'

'Out where?'

'Just out.'

'God, Fiz, have you regressed back to puberty? You're acting like you're fourteen again and I'm your mother.'

'Which you are not, so stop interrogating me. I'm taking the Fifth Amendment on where I was last night. It's a long boring story and I'll save it for a rainy day. Anyway, why are you still in bed? Did our budgie die or something. Only I didn't realise we had a budgie.'

Polly laughed. Bloody Fiz – she was impossible and incorrigible and she could make her laugh like no one else.

'No, I'm sick.'

'Don't tell me. You're suffering a reaction to your boyfriend – you're allergic to smarm.'

'Shut up, Fiz, I don't want to hear it. I've been throwing up all day again. I definitely ate something earlier in the week that didn't agree with me.'

'I'll be sure to tell my mother that. You've been ill since the day you ate her hand-prepared birthday meal.'

'Don't you dare!' Polly yelped. 'She'd be horrified.'

'Yes, but at least she'd be round here pronto with some chicken soup and we'd get a decent meal,' she replied as she slammed shut the door of the empty fridge. 'Pol, we're a domestic nightmare. Thank feck you occasionally live a life where servants are included in the package and thank feck again that I can live on fast food, otherwise we'd starve.'

The mention of chicken soup sent Polly diving to the basin at the side of her bed. She retched for what seemed like ages. There was nothing left in her stomach to bring up. She slumped back on the pillows. She suddenly wondered if Dr George would travel to the city to do a house call. Whatever he charged, she'd pay it. If she wasn't dead by the time he got there. She'd never felt as bad as this in her life. Wasn't food poisoning meant to work its way out of your system in a couple of days?

Fiz read her mind. 'Hey, Pol, if this was food poisoning wouldn't you be over it by now?'

'I was just thinking the very same thing,' Polly groaned. 'What do you think is wrong with me, Fiz? I feel so awful.'

Fiz looked perplexed.

'No idea, honey, I'm a barmaid and stylist – I'm only good in emergencies that involve alcohol, split fabric, laddered tights and cocaine-overdosed models. I'm useless in the real world.

'The last time I saw anyone this ill was when a French chick in a bikini, with so much collagen in her lips that she looked like Daffy Duck's uglier cousin, vomited in a bucket that was a prop on the beach set we were using for a suntan lotion shoot. At first we thought she was just having a reaction to the photographer's unfortunate personal hygiene issues – he smelled like a marathon runner's shoe after twenty-six miles. Anyway, turns out that the poor cow was pregnant. Stupid woman. I mean, in this day and age . . .'

She was interrupted by the sound of Polly retching again. She turned to see her lift her head from the basin, a big fat tear rolling down her cheek.

Fiz dived over to her and put her arm round her. 'C'mon, Pol, it's not that bad. It'll just be some kind of seven-day bug. Or a life-threatening form of dysentery. Have you visited any Third-World environments lately? I mean, except Clark's armpits, that is.'

Polly shook her head and then exploded in a heart-wrenching sob as more tears gushed down her cheeks.

Fiz sensed immediately that she was missing something. Unfortunately Polly had just realised that she was missing something too. Her period.

'Oh, Fiz. I think . . . oh no. Fiz, could I be pregnant?' Polly resembled a little girl who was beseeching her parents to reassure her that Santa really did exist.

Fiz was astounded. 'No, Pol. Shite, God couldn't be that cruel. There's no way he'd make you pregnant to that twat.' She was in denial. This couldn't be true. She'd fecking kill him. 'And anyway, you never forget to take your pill. And the only things that affect the reliability of that are antibiotics and . . .' She stopped. Oh. Feck. This was like watching a car crash in slow motion. It couldn't be happening. But it was. 'Vomiting,' she finished weakly.

Polly's head fell into her hands. Fiz wanted to join her under the duvet and cry too. This was the worst news she'd heard in years. It couldn't be true. It just couldn't.

'Polly, stay there, I'll be back in ten minutes.'

'Don't leave me now,' Polly wailed to Fiz's disappearing back. 'Fiz, where are you going?'

She was back in five, brandishing a pregnancy test from the all-night chemist four streets away. She must have flown there and back on the broomstick that Clark claimed she owned.

'Let's do this, Pol. It'll put you out of your misery. It'll be negative, I'm sure of it.' She was trying to project a confidence that she didn't feel. Tonight's whole situation had an air of doom only previously witnessed in bad B-movies where the good guys were lined up against big baddies in dark shades brandishing AK-47s.

She sat on the edge of the bath while Polly peed on the stick. They both watched the watermark cross the two square boxes, then the blue line appear on the second box. It was the longest minute of their lives. One that ended with another blue line and two simultaneous wails.

Pol sat silently now, arms wrapped tightly round herself, staring into space. Fiz embraced her. She'd obviously slipped into shock. For a long time, and totally contrary to usual form, Fiz said nothing. This was one of those moments when her reaction would be remembered for the rest of their lives and although she wanted to kick the bath until it resembled the mosaic tiles on the floor, she knew such an act wouldn't help her friend.

And it was Polly who mattered here, not her.

Eventually, Fiz excused herself and returned a few minutes later with hot tea. Polly sipped it, still silent. Finally she spoke, at first so quietly that Fiz had to strain to hear her.

'You know this is going to be great. It was meant to happen, Fiz.'

The whole time that she was speaking she was slowly nodding her head. It was almost as if she were convincing herself of something and developing a new resolve.

'Er, what did you say?' Fiz couldn't believe her ears. Polly had lost it. She was definitely a couple of chants short of a Hare Krishna.

A smile crept across Polly's face and as it did her chin lifted, her back straightened and her shoulders stretched back. She looked like she'd just shrugged an anvil off the top of her head.

Polly's grin was all over her face now.

'Honestly, Fiz. I mean, it's a bit sooner than I expected, but in a way I'm really, well, *pleased*. And Clark will be too – he was just talking the other night about what our children would be like.'

Now Fiz wanted to vomit. She'd had a sudden mental picture of a Smarm Man, junior version, dressed in Baby Armani and trying to impress little girls at the nursery with his designer haircut and battery-operated Porsche. Like father, like son. Puke.

The excitement in Polly was visibly starting to bubble over now. 'I have to tell him now! Tonight! Quick shower then I'll nip over to his place.'

After another spontaneous retch, she stripped off her clothes and climbed into the shower.

'It'll be fine, Fiz. I know you hate him, but let's face it, Fiz, you hate everyone. Except me . . . And I know you don't like it, but Clark loves me, honestly,' she shouted over the noise of the water. 'As I said, he was just talking the other night about how he could see our future together and there were children in that picture. He's *so* romantic sometimes.'

'Your *future*? What, was it a marriage proposal then? Does he want to waltz you up the aisle? Well he'd better bloody hurry up otherwise you're going to need a fecking crèche at the back of the church. Marriage my buttocks, Pol. I'll believe it when I see it.'

Polly was getting exasperated. Fiz could be so bitter and twisted sometimes. Why couldn't she see that this was destiny? Polly had always known that she wanted two things in life: marriage to a gorgeous man who adored her and a brood of beautiful children. She admired females who were driven and successful in their careers, but she'd always known that wasn't her path. No, this was exactly what she should be doing.

She ran her hand over her stomach. No sign of a bulge yet. Maternity clothes! She'd need a whole new wardrobe. She must ask Mum tomorrow. Oh my God, Mum and Dad! She'd have to tell them. She felt a small pang of apprehension. They'd be shocked. A little disappointed at first, maybe. But then her confidence started to surge again. They had liked Clark so much. And they'd grow to love him. Especially when they saw how happy he made her. And they'd be great with grandchildren. And Mum would help her decorate the nursery and prepare the layette and . . .

Through the steam, she caught sight of Fiz. She had a feeling that this was going to be her biggest challenge.

'Fiz, it'll be OK. Don't look so cynical,' she asserted with an indulgent smile. She knew that Fiz was just worried for her. It had been the same way their whole lives.

Fiz tried to rearrange her features into another expression but couldn't do it. Outrage and scepticism remained. Polly ignored it.

'I can see his reaction now – I mean, he might be a bit shocked at first, but he'll be thrilled, he really will.'

A loud buzzing noise came from the hallway.

Fiz left the room and went to the intercom. She just wished she shared Polly's optimism, but she suspected that Smarm Man would rather have piles than a pregnant girlfriend.

She pressed the external door release button. She hoped that she'd done the right thing. Texting the prick from Polly's phone while she was in the kitchen making tea had been a bit sneaky. Especially when the message read HORNY WOMAN IN NEED OF SERVICE. GET HERE NOW!

It was the only thing she could think of that was guaranteed to have him rushing up the stairs like his arse was on fire. She reckoned that in view of Polly's recent decline into insanity, it was probably better that she break the news on home ground – at least then the men in white coats would know where to find her.

She opened the flat door and heard his footsteps pounding up the stairs. Right on cue . . .

His expression as he rounded the corner and saw Fiz standing there was priceless: confusion mixed with shock and horror. If Fiz didn't feel so awful it would have warmed her heart. He approached her cautiously, sensing trouble.

'Fiz?'

Fiz threw her weight forward onto her left foot, then followed through with a right jab that sent him reeling across the hall, stopping only when he thudded against the opposite wall then slid down it, holding his jaw and screaming in pain.

'Polly's in the bathroom, you prick,' she spat as she stepped over him and started down the stairs. 'And she's pregnant.'

Book Two

Chapter Six

Clark – The Juggle

Clark raised his arms high above his head and stretched like a panther in the sun. Which, let's face it, was close to the truth, he thought.

This was the life. The rest of the delegates were off on some excursion to a vineyard, but he'd pleaded off with a dodgy stomach. What was the point of plodding round a field of trees with a bunch of blokes he'd never see again in his life? He'd much rather be lying here drinking the stuff than seeing it get made.

If the boys back home could see him now they'd be well pissed off: lying on a sunlounger on a private hotel beach in Cannes, drinking champagne by the bottle, watching a bevy of half-naked women sun themselves and splash around in the sea, and the best part of all was that he was getting paid for it!

God bless Steve Copeland for getting frisky on the ski slopes, maiming himself and having to drop out of this jolly. He must remember to buy him a drink when he got back to London. And he'd have to fill him in on the week's activities. Well, most of them. He took another slug of Krug and stared at the buttocks of a passing female. His libido took over, sending frantic signals to his brain. No cellulite on those, love.

No, he wouldn't divulge *all* the details of this week, not by a long shot. He would of course elaborate on his opening speech. That was a corker. And that opening joke went down a storm. Stunned into silence by his brilliance, they were. Yes, Steve would hear all about that.

He checked his watch. Four-thirty. Another five minutes and then he'd get back to his room for a shower. He'd arranged to see Sandra at five and he didn't want to be late – she was a feisty one, that, and he didn't want to rattle her cage, not when the going was this good.

His mind wandered back to that first night together. A fling hadn't been on his agenda at all during this trip – he'd planned for it to be a solid session of networking, drinking and positioning himself for greater things – but when sex is offered on a plate, well, what kind of man would say no to that, eh? He didn't get to be the Shagmeister he was without regular training.

But bloody hell, she was stroppy. Wouldn't let him do any of the usual moves. And he'd thought birds loved that whole 'going down on them' thing. He'd had them crying out for more when he'd done that in the past. Not that he liked it much, but it did make them eternally grateful. And the things a female would do when she was grateful . . .

The way she'd kicked him out straight afterwards with all that karma crap, though, was bang out of order. If he hadn't seen her at the conference earlier that day he'd have sworn she was either a nutter or a hooker, the way she wanted it over with so quickly.

The next morning, he'd half expected her to do the

shy, coy, chase-me act that most birds pulled after the first wham-bam, but no, not her.

He thought his luck was up on the second day of the conference when the speaker announced that they would be splitting into several different focus groups for the rest of the week. He was disappointed that Sandra was in a different one from him – lessened the chances to pull her for a rematch. After all, she might not have been much of a looker, and definitely not in a bird like Polly's class, but a shag was a shag and he was already well in there. And if the bird liked it quick and quiet that was fine by him – left more time down the bar for drinking and hobnobbing with those in the know. He'd cracked it: best of both worlds.

As she passed him en route to the room designated for her group, she slipped a note into his hand. He'd opened it later in the bogs. 'Same room, same script, 10 p.m.'

He punched the air and then looked down at his hips as he swung them from side to side, doing his bloody brilliant rendition of Robert Palmer's 'Addicted to Love'.

'They can't get enough of you, mate,' he told his groin with a laugh after his final chorus. 'You're bloody irresistible.'

The Shagmeister was here and he was happening.

Ding, ding, ding, ding. The vice president rattled the side of his glass as he stood up behind the top table. Clark broke off from the conversation he was having with the sales director from Milan. Always good to keep in with those blokes – meant he had somewhere to stay when he nipped over to Italy to top up his wardrobe. The gear there was half the price.

'Ladies and gentlemen. I'd just like to take this opportunity to thank you all for your contributions to this week. I'm sure you'll all agree . . .' Clark tuned out. His gaze had shifted to the end of the top table where Sandra was sitting. He briefly wondered how she'd got a place up there – must be taking notes on the speeches or something. Shame there was a cover around the front of the table because he wouldn't mind a quick leer at those legs. The ones that had been wrapped round his ears only a couple of hours before.

He definitely wouldn't mind seeing her when they got home. Not in public, or anything like that, but to continue the contact just the way it had been all week: in, out (literally), no chat, no commitment and no fuss.

He doubted it would happen, though. He'd decided that she was almost certainly married. Why else would she be so desperately into quick, emotionless, cold sex? Or rather, hot sex but without the chat. The longest conversation they'd had all week was, 'Yes, yes, oh, my God, yes, goodbye.' She was his idea of the perfect woman!

As far as he was concerned, females didn't do that. It was a fundamental flaw in the female species that they went all clingy and needy after the first bang. Or maybe that was just the effect he had on them, he pondered. No, she was definitely married and just looking for a bit of a thrill and some wicked nooky. And he'd been the very man to provide it. Every single night of the seminar. He'd be glad to get home for the rest. OK, that was a lie.

Still, he was quite looking forward to going home. Home. Polly. He had to admit: to his surprise he had missed her. Not that he'd sat in his room pining every night (obviously), but every now and then he had wondered what she was up to or found himself making a metal note to tell her something. This must be what being in a couple felt like, he thought. Even if it was just a temporary measure designed to get him a damn good time, a legendary reputation among the guys, and a weekend in Marbella.

That reminded him, it was time to start on the second part of that mission – finding the ultimate brainy bird. He'd do that as soon as they got back. He'd heard one of the guys bragging the night before about some MENSA meeting he'd been at. What a prick the guy had been in his Burton suit and his Barratt shoes. He hadn't made *half* the commission that Clark had last year, so it just showed you where logic got you – high street bloody shopping, that's where.

'Show off to me when you're in Gucci, mate,' had been Clark's parting comment before sloping off for a tête-à-tête with the delectable Sandra.

However, it did give him an idea of where to start looking for bird number two. After all, he was hardly going to find her in the Shaker.

A round of applause spread through the room. 'Fuck a duck,' Clark whispered with a bored sigh to no one in particular. This closing speech was lasting longer than a session with Sandra (who was still sitting at the top table looking good enough to eat – well, not physically, as she'd demonstrated she wasn't into that). He doubted there was anyone in the whole town of Cannes whom the speaker hadn't thanked. He would be mentioning the pool cleaner and the road sweepers next.

'And finally, ladies and gentlemen, I'd like to thank the representatives of the UK board of directors, who generously gave their time to be here this week. I'm sure you'll agree that their presence demonstrates the commitment of the SySol board to the integration of all departments. Remember colleagues, "Together We Can Conquer",' he vowed with passion, regurgitating the seminar slogan.

The delegates made weak hand-clapping motions. They wanted to act willing and enthusiastic, but then again they didn't want to give the speaker an iota of encouragement to stay up there any longer. They were losing the will to live. And the ice was melting at the bar.

He was off again. 'So, on that note, sincere thanks to the UK director of marketing, Miles Conway . . .' At the top table, Miles stood up. There was another round of applause. Louder this time. No one wanted to get on the wrong side of Miles Conway – the man was a legend in the silicon world. Clark was particularly vociferous. Although they'd never met, he knew that Miles Conway was Polly's boss. Polly rated him highly so he must be a good guy. She was a great judge of character, his Pol. She was going out with him, wasn't she? He couldn't resist a grin at the thought.

'. . . and director of finance, Miss Cassandra Haven.' The applause was riotous this time. No one, but *no one*, wanted to be seen to be dissing the holder of the purse strings. If she'd held out her feet they'd have kissed them.

Clark paid particular attention to the top table now. He wanted to see the tart who had knocked back his last expenses claim for the night he took the Japanese directors of a software company to the Spearmint Rhino. Bloody expensive night, that was. Just as well they'd signed on the dotted line the next day. It was a one-million-pound deal for the company and a nice four-figure sum for him. He had been well fucked off though when he realised that he'd have to foot the expenses bill out of his own pocket. Honestly, these prats in finance had no idea what it took to get sales out there.

Where was this bint then? He had a good mind to chin her later. Even if she did have a reputation as a total ball-breaker.

His eyes ran the length of the top table. Strange. There were only a couple of other females up there and he was sure they were foreigners. Probably shagging the European big cheeses.

The applause continued. Nope, the only female up there was . . . Sandra! Why the fuck was Sandra standing up and taking a bow? She was only a fucking secretary.

He didn't understand.

'Thank you, Miss Haven. Your support this week has been much appreciated,' the speaker concluded.

Miss Haven? Clark's eyebrows furrowed into a perplexed expression. Miss Haven? Cassandra Haven? Ball-breaker extraordinaire? *Sandra*? Oh fucking hell.

His eyes closed as he knocked back what was left of his after-dinner liqueur in one gulp, causing a choking fit that almost drove the MENSA twat to attempt the Heimlich manoeuvre. After he'd swatted him away and his eyes had cleared of choking-induced tears, he realised that Sandra, or rather Cassandra, was staring at him. Was that the glimmer of a smile on her lips? He felt the anger rise. This bitch had played him for a complete tosser. And to think he was going to put the drinks he'd bought her that first night on expenses. Better get those off the claim form pronto.

He cornered her in the bar immediately after the seminar had been officially closed, leaning close to her ear so that they couldn't be overheard.

'Cassandra Haven?' he hissed, his voice thick with contempt. 'I thought you said you were a fucking secretary?'

'No, *you* said I was a secretary, Mr Dunhill. Anyway, what's the problem? Feeling threatened?'

Clark blustered. She had a point. What *was* his problem? Self-analysis wasn't his strong point – that was just a bit too deep for a man of his calibre – but he supposed if he really thought about it what was bothering him was that he'd thought he was banging some insignificant female all week when in fact he'd been with someone who could in theory make or break his career. Cassandra Haven was on the board of directors, for Christ's sake. That was just all too dangerous territory.

And come to think of it, *she* had been pulling the shots all week. She'd totally manipulated him. His brain was racing now. She'd just snapped her fingers and expected him to come running. And he had, because he thought that she was only some married tart looking for a quickie and grateful that he was supplying it. Not some high-flying ball-breaker who'd obviously just wanted someone to service her while she was away from home. That was all he'd been to her.

The thought horrified him. He'd been her plaything. The bitch had *used* him. His blood was boiling now. How dare she? This was sexual harassment. What was that film? The one with Bruce Willis's missus, where she wrecked Michael Douglas's career because he stopped giving her one? *Disclosure*. That was it. So was that what was going to happen here?

Was he going to get home to find his promotion chances ruined if he didn't jump to attention? Or rather, if a vital piece of his anatomy didn't? This was a nightmare. A bloody nightmare. She was still waiting for an answer. Best not to be too aggressive. Didn't want his P45 waiting for him when he got back.

'Em, no. That is, I don't. Feel threatened, that is. Just think you should have been upfront with me, that's all,' he back-pedalled furiously.

She smiled lazily. 'Yeah, and I suppose you're a paragon of honesty with every female you screw,' she replied. He was starting to seriously dislike this chick. She was brutal.

His mind automatically went to Polly. He'd been totally honest with her! Most of the time. Well, OK, some of the stuff he said was a bit of an exaggeration, but that was all just for effect. Part of the plan. The plan!

His mind started whirring again. Oh, Christ, he'd just had an amazing thought. He'd been shagging what was allegedly one of the smartest chicks in London. He'd heard that she was rated as one of the top ten females in finance. And he'd seen her naked! He suddenly started to laugh. He'd done it. He'd found his female with brains! He was laughing louder now. He couldn't believe his own skill. He should have, of course, as he *was* the Shagmeister. He'd achieved the second part of his mission without even realising it, *that's* how bloody brilliant he was!

'Share the joke,' Cass demanded.

It would be the last thing she demanded of him. From now on, he would be calling the shots. Now that he knew what he was dealing with, or rather *whom* he was dealing with, he just had to manipulate the situation a little.

He had to get her into the Shaker Bar the first night the boys were there. He'd get Cassandra on one arm and Polly on the other, and he'd be packing his Ambre Solaire for that weekend in Marbella before he could say, 'Clarky-boy's the Shagmeister.'

He hadn't quite worked out the logistics of how he was going to pull it all off. He'd have to get rid of one (or both) of them afterwards, before they realised what was going on. He'd give that some thought, but it would come to him. Didn't everything? Sometimes without him even realising it. Wicked!

It was all he could do not to give his prick a little shake of congratulations. That would come later, he decided. Actually, he might let Sandra take care of that.

He gave Sandra, sorry, Cassandra, his most 'fuck me now' expression.

'No joke. I was just thinking how glad I am that I came here. It's been truly unforgettable. And the best thing of all has been you. The way you ...'

Cass put her hand up to stop him. 'Look, Clark, no offence, but save the crap. I'm not interested in the act, the flattery or your conversational skills. Which I'm sure are fantastic, by the way.'

Did he detect just a note of sarcasm there, he wondered. No, he was sure it was simply her unfortunate way of phrasing things.

'It's not necessary. In case you hadn't noticed, I'm a guaranteed lay. For now. So, my room, fifteen minutes ...' She glanced around the bar at the rest of the delegates enjoying their final night booze-up. 'And you'll be back down here in thirty. Deal?'

He visualised the expressions on Taylor and Nick's faces when they met this lady (if you could call her that) – they'd be awestruck.

'Deal.'

'You are kidding me,' Taylor laughed incredulously. 'Put it there, mate, you're a demon!'

Clark reached over and shook the outstretched hand, bending at the waist in a mock bow as he did so.

'Thank you, thank you. You can all line up now and I'll be giving autographs, interviews and tips on being fanfuckingtastic for the rest of the evening.'

Taylor was still highly amused. This was the first night that Clark had met the guys since his return from Cannes two weeks before and he had just finished recounting the details of his French experience. He lapped up the acclaim. Until he realised that it was only coming from one source in the group. He turned to Nick.

'So what do you reckon, mate? Deadly or what?' he asked with a grin.

Nick was still silent, his expression pensive.

'Deadly could be the right word. What about Polly? Have you given a thought as to how she'll feel about this if she finds out?'

Clark couldn't have been more stunned if Nick had ripped open his suit to reveal items straight out of the Victoria's Secret catalogue.

'What are you on about, mate? How will Polly find out anyway? And if she does, well them's the breaks – I'll bluff my way out of it somehow.'

Nick shook his head and returned his gaze to the bottle of Bud in his hand. Taylor and Clark looked at each other and both shrugged their shoulders and had a silent, 'I don't know what the fuck's up with him,' 'Neither do I,' conversation.

'What's the problem, Nick? It's all part of the game, remember? A weekend in the sun on the Costa del Shag. Or is that what's pissing you off? You know I'm getting close and your wallet's beginning to get nervous? Well, so it should mate, 'cause I'm about to empty it and channel the cash in the direction of the next flight into Malaga airport.'

Clark said all of this in a 'slap on the back, that's my boy' tone. Nick was now even less impressed.

'The bet's off, Clark.'

Clark paused. Had he heard right? Taylor shrugged his shoulders again – he didn't have a clue what was going on but he didn't like the undercurrents he was picking up. He had no intention of getting into the middle of anything, especially if there was any possibility of it getting physical. His nose was only just returning to its perfect profile after his altercation with that mad bitch in the mac. If he ever met her again he'd . . . He wasn't sure. But he'd definitely do something.

'Off? Why? What's up with you, Nick? Been taking wuss pills, or what?' He still expected Nick to break into a laugh at any minute and confess that he'd only been winding him up. He'd be waiting a long time.

Nick was seriously agitated now. For a man who raised his voice only when it involved twenty-two men and a rubber ball, who was generally more chilled than Häagen-Dazs, his decibel level was rising to previously unwitnessed levels.

'Piss off, Clark. I just want nothing to do with this whole thing. How can you do this to Polly?'

Clark was matching Nick's level of irritation now. 'What are you, her minder?'

Nick emitted a short sarcastic snort. 'No mate, just someone who doesn't want to see the poor girl get trampled on. I mean, for Christ's sake, Clark, how can you do this to her? She really likes you. In fact, the poor cow thinks she's in love with you because you've been filling her head with a whole load of crap about strolling off into the sunset. You've even been to meet her parents. How sick is that? Good evening, Mr and Mrs Kent, I'm just here with your daughter for some fucked-up bet and I'll maybe see you again sometime after I've shafted her and moved on to someone else. Way to fucking go, Clark. You're such a big guy. My fucking hero. Not.'

He grabbed his jacket and made for the door, pushing Clark out of the way with his shoulder as he did so.

'See you later, Taylor.'

'Yeah, em, shee oo lair.' His voice was unclear as his hand was covering his face. For protection. Just in case. They watched Nick's back storm out of the doorway.

Clark was incandescent. 'What the fuck was that all about? Has he lost the plot or what? Been watching too much fucking *Oprah*, that boy. Gone all female on us. Fucking "what about Polly". What's it got to do with him, anyway? I mean . . .'

'Back in a minute, mate. Just going for a quick one.'

Taylor darted off to the loo. There was no way he was staying around Clark when he was on a rant – it would only encourage him. Best to let him cool down on his own for ten minutes. Then he'd suggest heading over to the Romp Room later – that would soon have him out of his pissed-off mood.

Anyway, if he were truthful, much as he'd never admit it to Clark, he could see Nick's point. Clarky was being a bit of a bastard. Not that he was an angel himself, he admitted (as he entered a cubicle and smiled to see a pile of *Loaded*, *FHM* and *Esquires* piled by the side of the toilet – that was why he loved this bar, it catered for every need), but at least he was upfront with the chicks. He never promised them undying love and devotion. Oh no, not him. There was no way he was going to get into that whole relationship nonsense. What was the point when there was so much variety out there? It would be like living in a supermarket but eating the same thing for dinner every night. Mental.

Back at the bar, Clark was seething. Who the fuck did Nick think he was, talking to him like that? He had a good mind to go after him and have it out. Later. He had enough on his plate without having to deal with a mate who'd turned into a premenstrual mood-swinging woman over night.

Just how would Polly find out anyway? That wasn't part of the plan. In fact, after he'd got them both into the Shaker on the same night and won the bet, he'd decided that he was going to keep on seeing her. For a while anyway. Until either he got bored or she got clingy, whichever came first. His heart rate began to calm back down at the thought. Fuck Nick. He was just suffering from a case of jealousy. And who could blame him? Polly and Cassandra – it was enough to make any man jealous.

His pulse rate had now slowed to almost normal as he thought of his two conquests. Or rather, one and a half. He wasn't entirely sure that he'd actually conquered Cassandra. She wasn't exactly responding as anticipated. If he were entirely honest with the guys (which of course he'd rather amputate a limb than be), he was struggling severely on that front. But it was only a temporary hitch. It had to be. Clark Dunhill didn't *do* failure.

Ever since they'd touched down at Heathrow, Sandra had been more elusive than his expenses receipts.

That had been a close one.

As he'd come through Arrivals that night he'd been so busy looking at Sandra's (he still couldn't get used to her proper name – she'd always be Sandra to him) arse that he hadn't seen Polly until he was almost upon her. He'd thought for a minute that Pol was going to pounce on him. That would have been a bastard to explain to Sandra. Not that she'd ever even asked him if he had a girlfriend, but he was sure she wouldn't like it. After all, it was only normal that a chick would want him all to herself. But no, Pol had played it cool. Although not as cool as Sandra, who'd marched off without so much as a goodbye in his direction – she obviously didn't want to give the game away to their colleagues and that suited him fine.

It was all just a bit close for his liking, seeing as they all worked for the same company. But hey, SySol was a big place, and this whole situation was nothing that he couldn't handle. He'd just got Polly out of there pronto before Sandra had seen their big reunion.

A smile curved his lips as he replayed the rest of that night in his head. Polly had definitely missed him, all right. She'd rushed back to his place in her new fuck-off MG and demanded a servicing that lasted until morning. He'd had to go along with it – after all, he was supposed to have been shag-deprived for a week. He'd just thrown her a few classic one-liners, let her climb on top and lain back and thought of . . . thought of what to get her for her birthday actually. That was a bit of crap timing. As if he hadn't spent enough on her already. And how the hell could he match up to a sports car? In the end he'd solved the problem brilliantly. His cousin Tam had a sideline melting down knocked-off jewellery and recycling it or moulding it into the most ingenious forms to aid smuggling. His best job ever had been when he'd implanted a rod of pure 24-carat into the centre of some Asian carrier's wooden leg. Anyway, a quick call to Tam the next morning and he'd ordered up a gold bangle set with diamonds.

'How many sparklers you looking for, mate?' Tam had asked.

Clark had thought for a moment. He had to get this just right. Not enough and it would look like he was cheap, too many and it would look like the bracelet was a fake.

'Go for ten, mate. Set at even spaces. How much will that skin me?'

There was a whooshing noise at the other end as Tam noisily inhaled, then 'Since it's you I'll do it on the cheap. Five hundred OK?'

Clark nearly choked. Five hundred! That was a fucking fortnight in Majorca. There was no way he was shelling that out.

Tam heard the muffled utterances of shock. 'Tell you what, mate, I could use cubic zirconias. That would bring it down to under a hundred.'

'Tubit zer what?'

'Cubic . . . never mind,' Tam said in exasperation. His mother, Molly, always banged on about how her sister's son Clark was the big high-flyer, making millions in the City in some flash job, yet here he was choking at the thought of five hundred quid and acting dumb as shit. Still, didn't surprise him. He'd never been the sharpest tool and Tam had never been particularly partial to him.

'They look like diamonds, they last like diamonds and she'll never know the difference. I've got a big job on just now for an Arab with an aversion to export tax, so I won't be able to do it for a couple of weeks. That OK?'

There was no way he was going out of his way for this one – not for a measly hundred quid.

Clark agreed. He'd just bluff to Polly that he was going to such effort to get the perfect thing made for her that it wouldn't be ready dead on her birthday. She wouldn't mind. In fact, the thought that he was going to so much trouble to have something so personal made for her would have her loving him even more. As if that were possible, he thought smugly as he hung up the phone. Good guy, that Tam. He'd always liked him.

That was one problem solved, he congratulated himself as he unpacked his suitcase the next morning. He wanted to get it done before Pol got out of the shower, so that she could drop his laundry at the dry-cleaner's. He turned his mind to the other pressing matter. Sandra. It would prove to be a lot more difficult to sort that one out.

He called her on the internal phone system the minute he got into the office. She answered immediately. 'Cassandra Haven.' Crisp. Efficient. He liked that. Another few sentences of her dulcet tones and he'd get a hard-on.

'Hey, babe, it's your favourite sex machine here,' he said in a voice thick with laughter and promise. Silence. He felt his phone start to ice in his hands. Still silence. Getting even frostier. Then eventually she spoke in a quiet, scarily calm, but nonetheless terrifying tone.

'Don't ever, ever, call me at work again. I thought I'd made it clear to you that I wanted no further contact after our return. Now be a good boy and pay heed to that, OK?'

The phone went down. Clark stared open-mouthed at his receiver. What? How dare that bitch speak to him like that? Who did she think she was? And didn't she know who *he* was?

Then it dawned on him and he cracked up into a chuckle. Bloody hard to get! She was playing the old hard-to-get act! He'd known it would kick in eventually. After all, she *was* human. Chicks always did this when they were seriously into you, just to make you want them more. And to think he'd nearly fallen for that 'no contact' shit. It would have served her right if he had. OK, so she hadn't let him practise the old Clark speciality, oral pleasure, that would have induced everlasting gratitude. But then she wasn't exactly Kate Moss, so she must be creaming herself to have bagged someone who looked like him. That's obviously why she was resorting to the mind games, just to keep him interested. And if she was so insecure that she had to go down that route, it was fine by him. He liked a good challenge. She'd soon be eating out of his hands. Just like all the rest of them.

The following two weeks were an exercise in human mating strategy, as Sandra blocked every attempt he made to see her. He had to admit she was good at the whole coy act. He called, the phone got slammed down. He sent flowers. Anonymously, of course. He didn't want anyone else in the company to rumble them. Not, as it turned out, that that would be a problem unless they decided to pick the blooms out of the skip in the alley at the side of the building where he'd spotted her assistant dumping them. He'd been bloody furious that she'd done that. Forty quid they'd cost him. He had a good mind to charge them to expenses.

He'd e-mailed her, only to receive a standard memo in return, threatening disciplinary action for the misuse of the company's property and time.

Christ, she was good. She'd even amended the message on her personal mobile (he'd got the number by tapping into the human resources private files – the fact that he was an IT specialist came in handy sometimes) to 'This is Cassandra Haven. I'm unable to take your call. Please leave a message, except if you know for sure that I don't wish to speak to you, in which case please lose this number. You know who you are. Goodbye.'

She must really want him to go to this much effort, he decided.

By the end of the second week, though, he was getting thoroughly bored with the whole thing. The golden rule of romantic mind games was not to push things too far and that's exactly what she was doing. Only the fact that she perfectly fitted half of his Marbella duo had kept him interested for this long.

Well, that and the fact that if he was honest he was beginning to have doubts over whether or not she actually *was* at all interested in him and instead of making him back off, the very concept that she didn't want him was making him more intent on pulling her. No one had ever knocked back Clark Dunhill and he didn't want to set a new precedent. He was sure if that were the case it was only because they had never conversed enough for her to really get to know him. Although normally his under-duvet action would have been enough to keep her returning like a jet-fuelled boomerang.

The whole affair began to seriously bug his happiness and fill far too large a space in his head. Several times he'd even blown off Polly because he just wasn't in the mood for her. Polly was guaranteed love and adoration. Sandra was something different. She was a mission.

It came to a head the night before Polly's birthday dinner. He'd popped into the office to register the sale that he'd just achieved while dining with a team of guys who were launching a new lad's mag from their recently acquired offices in Docklands. They'd ordered nearly three hundred grand's worth of kit (courtesy of their backer, a venture capitalist on the wrong side of leery who wanted a ringside seat at every photo shoot as part of the deal). Since it was the last day of the month, Clark had until midnight to register the sale if he was to get the commission in the following month's salary.

At two minutes to twelve he pressed the 'enter' key on his system. It was weird being in the offices alone at that time of night. He kept waiting to be assaulted by a nervous cleaner brandishing a Dyson.

If he were a woman, he reckoned, he'd take this opportunity to have a rummage through other people's desk drawers. That was the kind of stuff that fascinated females. He briefly wondered what Polly kept in her desk, seven floors above him (assorted stationery, a picture of him, a bridal magazine and three packets of Revels was the answer).

And what about Cassandra? He was sure her office was on the second floor from the top, the thirtieth. The thirty-first, being the closest to God, was the sole preserve of the MD and anyone wanting to top themselves after a bad quarter by launching their bodies from an extreme height.

Not that he was particularly interested in Cassandra's drawers, he thought with a shrug. At least, not the wooden variety. And, he told himself, he didn't much care what that mad cow had in her other ones either. An AK-47, a vibrator and a whip if her current performance was anything to go by.

He entered the lift and pressed 'ground'. Or at least he tried to. He was astounded when his finger somehow slipped upwards and hit the '30' button instead. Shit. He had the willpower of a fat alcoholic with a compulsive spending habit.

The doors pinged open and he tentatively stepped out onto the lush, thick, monogrammed navy carpet. Bloody typical. They only had cheap beige carpet tiles on the sales floor.

He scanned the corridor, checking to see if there were any security cameras. How would he explain this? He was creeping about like an SAS hit squad. It was one thing 'accidentally' pressing the wrong button on the lift, but what excuse could he give for creeping down the corridor checking the names on the doors? He should turn right back, he decided. He should. Definitely. But his feet were compelling him in the direction of the door at the end of the corridor with the faint glimmer of light glowing from under it. Someone was home.

Strange, he thought as he stealthily approached it, he was sure he could smell cigarette smoke. He kept moving towards it as if drawn by some invisible force. It was like a really crap sci-fi film and the mothership was calling him in.

He knew what it would say on the door before he reached it. Cassandra Haven. Correct.

It was slightly ajar and he pushed it open. He had to give her credit – she didn't even jump. If he'd been there on his own and the door had suddenly opened, he'd have shit himself. Metaphorically.

'Oh for crying out loud, are you stalking me or what? Only I don't remember ordering a shag delivery tonight.'

She took a long puff on her cigarette and waited for him to reply.

He was torn as to what his response should be. He was actually beginning to believe that she seriously did not want to see him. This was exactly the way he'd treated females in the past – the ones who just couldn't walk away and accept that it was over. He almost felt sorry for some of them in the end.

Is that what she was feeling for him now? Pity? And why the fuck did he care? It wasn't even as if he particularly liked her anyway. She'd been nothing but an easy lay and a shortcut to a weekend in the sun.

Still, he couldn't believe that she was giving him the brush-off. Not him. That just didn't happen.

This all flashed through his brain in an instant. He'd show her. He'd deliver a killer line that would have her begging for it again. It was a movie moment. A dramatic scene. The dialogue had to be brilliant. Think Tom Cruise. Think James Dean. Think Mel Gibson.

'Em, I thought these offices were non-smoking.'

Think Health and Safety official.

Where the fuck had that come from? He couldn't believe that his legendary suavity, his cutting wit, his ruthless charm had deserted him.

This was a nightmare.

'Did you come up here to give me a lecture? Fine. My hand is slapped. I'm feeling suitably chastised. I'll never touch another cigarette and I'll say four Hail Marys and an Our Father before I go to bed tonight. Happy now? Close the door on your way out.'

She bowed her head, her gaze returning to the screen in front of her.

'Is that it? We spend a week together and then you think that you can just snap your fingers and I'll disappear? You're a ruthless bitch.'

Clark couldn't believe that the words were coming out of his mouth, but he was powerless to stop them. He'd never been so mortified and at the same time bloody furious in his life. The whole situation was like a massive scab that he couldn't stop picking.

Cassandra rolled her eyes. 'OK, Clark, stop. I'm feeling your pain,' she replied drily, her tone making it clear that she was anything but. She stood up and made her way over to him. Suddenly her head listed to one side and as she started to speak her tone softened.

'Look, I'm sorry. I know that you'd hoped we could carry this on further, but relationships just aren't my thing. I'm in a place right now where I only want to concentrate on my career and that leaves no time for anything or anyone else. It wouldn't be fair to you. You're a great guy. You deserve much more.'

It was that line that did it. Clark suddenly realised that he'd doled out that same speech almost verbatim many times before and he hadn't meant a single word of it. It snapped him into action.

'Save it, Cassandra. I couldn't be less interested.'

He spun round and charged back out the door. OK, so it wasn't exactly a killer line, but it would do.

As he strutted down the corridor, pride and dignity wrestled with insecurity and rejection. The former emotions won. He would not let her walk all over him. She'd see how much she missed him when he wasn't calling her every day. She'd soon come running back. He'd bet his Gucci leather three-quarter length coat with the red satin lining and the unique stitching detail on it.

His head was still absorbed in the whole scenario as he drove Pol home from her parents' the following evening. It had been a really good night, he had to concede. He'd actually been disappointed when Pol had said it was time to leave because he reckoned he was on the verge of getting invited for a round of golf at Stoke Park. He'd been dying to play there for years, ever since he discovered that it was the course used in the movie *Goldfinger*, where James Bond (Sean Connery of course, the rest were crap up until Pierce Brosnan – in fact some people said he bore a close resemblance to Pierce. When Pierce was younger, naturally) first encountered Oddjob. Kenneth had mentioned in passing that he was a member there and Clark had dropped several hints. Another half-hour and he reckoned he'd have been looking out his clubs. Still, there was plenty of time.

Kenneth Kent, to his surprise, was great company and not in the least scary. His years of success had obviously rubbed off his rough edges. Although, Clark had to admit, he still wouldn't like to get on the wrong side of him. He made a mental note that when he dumped Pol he would have to let her down gently.

Maybe he could call it a day and with a bit of clever manipulation manage to keep in with her old man. Ken would be a great contact to have in the future. The big golf events, the Grand Prix circuit, the international footie fixtures – he bet Kenneth Kent patronised all these. Yep, he'd definitely try to keep in with him.

Polly was a lucky girl. She had great parents and she had him. Not to mention an inheritance that could buy Bond Street and still have change left over for a Big Mac. No wonder she was always happy. Still, he'd decided to hit her with some faff on the way home just to keep her sweet. He didn't want to lose two ladies in two days – it didn't bear thinking about. He decided to blow her away with some 'man of the nineties, I'm just feeling sensitive and need to know you'll always love me' crap. It did the trick. She welled up and smothered him with love, adoration and promises of eternal worship.

Yep, that maniac Sandra just hadn't realised it yet, but he *was* still the Shagmeister.

Taylor returned from the toilet three *FHM*'s and two *Loaded*'s later. Which wasn't actually that long, as he didn't read the magazines, he just scanned the pictures looking for his lovely face in the advertisements.

He counted one car brand, two fashion labels, and one health-club chain all fronted by his gorgeous bod. He was particularly proud of one of the fashion ones: a new range in skin-cling boxers. He'd made that Calvin Klein model Travis look only moderately gifted. He'd even managed to demonstrate his assets to the gorgeous female photographer in the studio dark room after the shoot. What was her name? It was, uh, it was . . . oh, who cared? She was up for it, he was up for it, the job was done. Everyone was happy.

He made a mental note to have a word with his agent. Four major campaigns in the same month was great for the bank balance, but he didn't want to get overexposed. In that sense anyway.

'Has Nick come back yet?' he asked Clark, scanning the room at the same time. He was sure Nick's tantrum was just a temporary aberration induced by dodgy beer or something. He'd never seen Nick take the hump about anything. It wasn't in his nature.

Clark was still as gobsmacked by it as Taylor.

'Nah, mate, no sign of him. Don't know what the fuck that was all about. I'll give him a buzz tomorrow.'

Just at that moment the beep that signalled an incoming text message came from the direction of Clark's torso. He fished into his inside pocket and pulled out his Samsung.

'Bet this is him now saying, "Sorry I was an arse, I'm on my way back for a piss-up", Clark laughed. Taylor shrugged his shoulders. Somehow he doubted it.

Clark checked the screen. HORNY WOMAN IN NEED OF SERVICE. GET HERE NOW!

He slammed his beer onto the bar. Polly was a fucking star! This was just what he needed to make him feel back on top again. Literally.

'Sorry, Taylor, have to run. Woman needing to be shagged, you know how it is.' He slapped Taylor on the arm. Not too hard. He knew how paranoid he was about bruising.

Taylor smiled back. Yes, he did indeed know how it was. In fact there was a gorgeous brunette in the corner who had been giving him the eye all night.

Lights, camera, action, strut. He had a feeling he'd be overexposed again before the night was out.

Clark watched in a daze as Fiz stepped over him and gave him a kick with the back of her heel as she did. The spurs on the back of her boots ripped through the leather of his Gaultier jacket and the Diesel jumper underneath. He didn't feel a thing. The pain in his jaw caused by Fizz's fist and the pain in his head caused by her accompanying words were overloading his system to such an extent that every other function shut down. He couldn't even clamber back to his feet. If it were a cartoon, there would be a little ring of stars circling his head and his eyes would be rolling in their sockets. He barely, only just, found his voice.

'*What?*' he stuttered uncomprehendingly at her back as it moved at speed down the stairs.

At the half-landing she spun round. 'I said she's pregnant, you prick. Only the fact that she loves you is stopping me from killing you where you lie, you piece of crap. And it was me who texted you, not Polly. She's in the shower so she doesn't know you're here and she doesn't know that I've just imparted the good news to the future dad. Now get in there, act surprised when she tells you and make her happy or God help you.'

If her words had been bullets, his insides would now be decorating the fifty-quid-a-roll wallpaper that lined the stairway and dripping onto the lush plum carpet. At least the colour would blend.

Clark closed his eyes. A feeling he had never experienced in his life was creating a devastating physical reaction. His stomach was contracting and pressing downwards, like he'd eaten the most rancid curry imaginable. His lungs were pushing violently against his ribcage, cutting off all available breath and causing a crushing sensation that was forcing him to double over in pain. His heart was racing so fast and beating so loudly he could actually hear it. It sounded like a techno CD being played at maximum volume and ten times the normal speed. He was dying. He was going to die like a dog on the stairs after being kicked by a passer-by. This is what the approach to hell felt like.

He tried to swallow but the combination of his undoubtedly fractured jaw and the fact that he had less saliva than a three-day-old corpse in the desert made that impossible.

Pregnant. Pregnant. Pregnant. Baby. His. Pregnant. Polly. Baby. His brain was a tumble-dryer and the words were going round and round, falling over each other and leaving no room for any other rational thought.

After what seemed like a fortnight he managed to struggle to his feet. The effort almost caused his chest to explode. His stomach threatened to collapse at any moment. He stared at the open door. He could faintly hear the sound of the running water in the shower. Pol had been in there for ages. She insisted on having a shower every morning and every night. It was one of the things he would tease her about. Not that it annoyed him. He actually found it quite endearing. He loved the smell of her coconut shampoo as she nuzzled into him in bed.

'Oh God,' he groaned audibly. What the fuck was he going to do?

He heard the water snap off and Polly shouting for Fiz. She obviously didn't know that Fiz was currently out negotiating with an underworld arms supplier to buy enough ammunition to wipe him off the face of the planet.

He heard the sound of the hairdryer being switched on. His brain slowly began to function again. Hairdrying would buy him at least half an hour. Thank Christ Polly hadn't succumbed to fashion and gone for an elfin cut.

He reached over and gently closed the door, then turned and bounded back down the stairs. He needed to get out of here. He needed to think. He bolted out of the door and ran round the corner to where he'd abandoned the Porsche. Was it really only ten minutes before that he'd slammed it into the parking space and leapt out like a man possessed, merrily making his way to his girlfriend's house for the promise of a good seeing to?

He climbed into the driver's seat and put the key in the ignition. He was about to turn it when he slumped back in the seat. He had no idea where he wanted to go. None.

He grabbed his phone out of his pocket and pressed the speed-dial key for Taylor. It rang out. He was probably still in the Shaker and couldn't hear his phone ringing. He pressed another button for Nick. It rang. Thank God. And rang. Come on Nick, pick up the phone. And rang. Eventually, it clicked onto an answering machine. Clark disconnected. There was no one else. He was having the biggest crisis of his life and there wasn't a fucking soul he could speak to.

Just when he thought that it couldn't get any worse for the first time since he caught his penis in his zip when he was fourteen, he felt the tears well up in his eyes. The panic that had barely subsided from life-threatening levels bubbled over again and he thudded his head onto the steering wheel.

This just could not be happening to him. But it was. Think, Clarky boy, think, he told himself. He took a few deep breaths trying to restore a modicum of calm. He had to work out what to do. He was in sales (and bloody brilliant at it, he automatically added to that thought), so he was trained to think on his feet. To make snap decisions. Cut and thrust. Cut and thrust.

A vision of Polly flitted into his mind. How the fuck had she let this happen? She wasn't some stupid teenager like his cousin Kylie, who got up the duff so that she could jump the queue on the council housing list. A maisonette in Hackney, she'd ended up with.

No, surely Polly hadn't done this deliberately, had she? What possible reason would she have for doing that? She was loaded, she was gorgeous, she had everything a girl could want.

It struck him that he'd never even asked her if she was on the Pill. He thumped his head back onto the steering wheel.

'How. Fucking. Stupid. Could. I. Be?' he spat out loud in time to the thud of his head being repeatedly banged on the wheel. Another deep breath. And a rub of his forehead. It was now every bit as painful as his jaw.

Maybe it wasn't his. Maybe Polly had been seeing other guys behind his back. Maybe she was shagging, em, shagging who? Her boss! She was always banging on about how fantastic Mike, or Morris, or what was his name? His mind had gone completely blank. He'd met him in Cannes only a month or so before. Miles! That was it. Yep, she was always saying how great he was. They were at it! Banging like bunnies!

Elation started to affect his thought process. It was Miles's baby she was pregnant with! Of course it was! She'd been doing the dirty on him all this time. Fantastic! Snap. Crash. Elation evaporated. Who was he kidding? Polly would never cheat on him. She didn't have it in her. She didn't even exaggerate on her expenses claims.

Think. Think. He glanced at his watch. Another few moments and she'd be switching off the hairdryer. Should he go back up? Fleeing the scene seemed like a far better idea.

Pregnant. Baby. Family. Oh fuck, family. Polly's family. Kenneth Kent. Polly's ex. Broken legs. Fuck. Her dad would have him in cement for this.

The last thought was just too much for him. He opened the car door just in time and vomited the contents of his stomach onto the road. A passing lady with a Yorkshire terrier in a sheepskin doggy jacket tutted out loud.

Think. Think. He had to decide what to do. He was running out of time. Immediate options. Short-term solutions. Brainstorm. You can't brainstorm with only one person. Fuck, he'd try it anyway.

Options.

Run. No use. Her dad would track him down and he'd be claiming disability for the rest of his natural life. Assuming that he had a life afterwards.

Go up there and face the music. Tell Poll he'd be there for her. And he would. By fax. From his hideout in the Afghan hills. At least then she might live in hope that he'd return and persuade her father to give him a stay of execution.

There was one other option that kept popping up and being swiftly hammered back into the ground. Mmmmaar . . . Shite, he couldn't even *think* the whole word, never mind say it.. Mmm ... Mmmm. He clenched his eyes tightly closed and took a deep breath. Mmmm ... Marry her! Mother of God, the ground shook. Clark Dunhill said the M-word. And not even in jest. It was an option. A shite one, but it was an option. Short-term. Immediate reaction. Life-saving.

He threw the concept around a bit more. He could ask her to marry him. Get engaged. He didn't actually have to go through with it. It was a short-term solution. A way to get through the immediate situation without seeming like a complete bastard. And losing his legs.

The more he thought about it, the more it appealed. It would buy him time. He could work out how to extricate himself later. There would be a way. He'd think of something. He always did. He was Clarky boy. But first things first.

He picked his phone up from the passenger seat and scrolled though the numbers. When he found what he was searching for, he pressed 'call'.

'Tam? Clark here, how's it goin', matey?' Pause.

'Strange? Do I? Nah, I'm fine, mate. Just a bit of a sore throat?' Pause.

'Listen, that job I asked you to do – have you started on it yet?' Pause.

'No, no, I'm not rushing you, mate. In fact, that's bloody brilliant. You see, there's been a slight change of plan. I need you to run me up a ring.' Pause.

'No, not a gent's ring. It's for my girlfriend.' Pause.

'I need an engagement ring.'

Chapter Seven

Cassandra – The Revelation

Cassandra sat on the toilet staring at the white box perched on top of the beech vanity unit across from her. She'd been sitting there so long that the shape of the toilet seat was now imprinted on her buttocks.

She wondered if she should call someone to provide moral support, but couldn't decide if that would make this whole task harder or easier.

Harder, she eventually concluded. It would definitely be hugely uncomfortable if someone else were there anxiously monitoring her reaction. No, she wanted to be alone when she found out. Besides, nothing on earth would let her allow someone else to either see, hear or even have a mental picture of her peeing. The indignity of it.

She lifted up the box and then swiftly placed it back down. She wasn't quite ready yet.

She couldn't believe she was having this reaction. It had taken her a while to identify the emotion she was experiencing and she was shocked when she realised that she was actually nervous. Scared, even. And she wasn't even sure what she was apprehensive about.

What if it was positive? That was what she'd

planned, what she wanted. Wasn't it? Only now that it could possibly be coming close to a reality, it didn't seem quite so straightforward any more. Especially since lover boy had transformed from Jack the Lad, fuck 'em and chuck 'em, into the serial stalker from hell. Jesus, men were so predictable – the minute they thought they couldn't have something, attaining it became like an obsession to them.

She mentally totted up the number of attempts that he'd made to contact her. Between the texts, the calls, the e-mails, the gifts (I mean, a silk cami set from Janet Reger hand-delivered to her office – was the guy on drugs? Or just living in the seventies when gifts pretty much ensured full capitulation on the female's part and a blow job on the next date?) and the visits, it was veering into treble figures.

And that night in her office ... She'd almost felt sorry for him. Until she reminded herself that he hadn't been quite so emotional when he was trying to get into her knickers.

It did cross her mind, briefly, that she had used him for her own purposes but ultimately the same was true of the reverse: he had used her for a quickie (and he hadn't even broached the subject of birth control!) and she had taken advantage of the resulting biological effect. Several nights in a row. She reasoned that the more muck she threw (or rather, *he* did) at the cervix, the more chance there was of some sticking. Anyway, it wasn't as if this was going to have any effect on Dunhill's life at all. She had absolutely no intention of telling him. No, this was going to be her baby. Hers. No one else's. None of this Sunday father crap. The last thing she wanted or needed was Clark Dunhill around weekly for the rest of her life. She'd sooner remain childless. Or emigrate.

She picked up the box containing the two sticks again and slowly started to unravel the cellophane. It was just like opening a cigarette packet. The familiar sound and image catapulted a craving straight to her brain. A ciggy. She'd have one of those first before she did the test. It might be her last. She'd have to chuck them immediately if the line went blue. She knew the blue line was the confirmation of a positive result, having read the back of the box more than twenty times. Shit, she was getting as compulsive as he was.

Childless. What would she do if it were negative? Would she have another try? There was a gorgeous-looking guy in the production office who always smiled at her when they met. Glen? Greg? Graham? She couldn't remember. Not that it mattered. How much did you need to know about a person to have a quick exchange of body fluids?

She immediately dismissed the idea. Good God, if this didn't work and she went down that route she'd have a reputation as the office slapper before the year was out. That's if she did decide to try again. Maybe if this was negative she should just resign herself to the fact that she wasn't meant to be a mother and move on. It wasn't as if she didn't have plenty of other fulfilling areas in her life. She had her career. She had Toni. She had, em, her *career*. Crap. Who was she kidding? She didn't want to be sixty and still putting in eighteen-hour days in a concrete tower with a no-smoking policy. She took another drag on her cigarette. No, she wanted this test to be positive. She did. Really.

She tossed the cigarette into the sink (she could almost hear Margaret Mary tutting as she fished that out later – let her earn her salary for a change) and quickly tore the rest of the wrapper off before wrenching the box open. She grabbed one of the foil-encased tubes and tore it open. She pulled the two halves apart, stripped and soaked.

When she'd finished she sat back down on the loo and realised that she'd completed the whole exercise so quickly that she still had two lungs full of smoke. She slowly exhaled as she checked her watch, then returned her stare to the white stick. Sixty. Fifty-nine. Fifty-eight ... Twenty-six. Tenty-five ...

There was no need to wait any longer. The result was already obvious. There was one stick. There were two numb buttocks. There were two windows. There were two blue lines.

There was a baby.

Cass picked out her clothes carefully, as she had done every day for the last four weeks. It was the morning of the SySol board's quarterly review meeting and it was imperative that her outfit conceal her slightly thickening waist and swollen breasts. She didn't want anyone to think that she'd suddenly hit the biscuit cupboard. She had long maintained the view that weight problems were a drawback in business: the unspoken consensus was that if an employee couldn't even control what he or she put in their mouth, then how could they maintain discipline and motivation in other areas of their life – i.e. work? A pathetic generalisation but one that she had to admit she was prone to making herself – the first sign of a large gut or arse on a member of staff and she immediately checked their expenses for signs of too many long lunches on the company account.

The most important aim of her attire that day was to ensure that nobody would have even a glimmer of suspicion that she might be pregnant. Not that the thought would ever cross anyone's mind. She was sure that lot believed she'd taken a vow of celibacy when she joined SySol and committed to dedicating her whole life to the cause. Which, come to think of it, wasn't too far off the truth.

She checked her appearance in the mirror. Her red Escada suit screamed authority and power. It said notice me, fear me, and don't dare even *think* about crossing me. Just the desired message. The long-line tailored jacket skimmed her shape without clinging. She turned to the side. Nope, not a sign of a bump. But great breasts.

She threw a silk vest and a pair of strappy L.K. Bennett kitten mules into a tote bag. She was meeting Paul and Jeff after work and wouldn't have time to change the whole outfit so a quick variation on the accessories would have to do.

She wondered if they would notice any change. She'd barely seen them over the previous couple of months – just a couple of quick dinners – but that was nothing new. They'd never had an 'in your face' friendship and she liked it that way. It prevented the embarrassing confrontations which would have been inevitable if it all got too claustrophobic. Much as she adored both of them in her own way, intimacy just wasn't her thing.

Paul had been on the phone a lot though. She didn't know what had got into him. He wasn't quite at Dunhill stalker level but he certainly made contact at least once every couple of days as opposed to the fortnightly schedule of old. Maybe he was just going through a lonely phase, she pondered; some kind of mid-life I-shouldn't-be-spending-every-night-in-a-nightclub-because-oh-good-Lord-no-I-might-start

-to-resemble-Peter-Stringfellow crisis. She laughed at the thought. She couldn't imagine Paul's glorious bald, black head with a mullet.

During every conversation she'd had with both Paul and Jeff since she returned from Cannes, she'd waited for them to mention the pregnancy plan, but they'd solicitously avoided it. They were obviously adopting the mindset that it was just some bizarre rash idea that she'd now realised the folly of and gaily abandoned.

They should know her better. She didn't do bizarre and she didn't do rash. And she certainly didn't do gay abandon – that was just a vicious rumour started by her underlings, who were intrigued by the fact that she never seemed to have a man in her life. Those same underlings were now lining up every Tuesday at the dole office. They obviously weren't doing their jobs properly if they had time to gossip about her all day.

She'd surprised herself over the previous few weeks by her reasoned calm. It helped that she'd had not even a glimmer of nausea or discomfort. She didn't really understand what women were on about when they complained about the hardship of pregnancy – it was a breeze. Those overreacting, dramatic, hysterical women who wailed about it like it was a terminal illness gave the rest of the female species a bad name. It was all down to those bloody American chat shows again. They were just playing to an audience and fishing for sympathy and attention.

Thankfully Clark Dunhill had at last taken the hint and pushed off, although it had made her smile to see that in a last token of petulance he'd charged three bouquets of flowers, all of which had arrived at her office, on his last expenses form. She'd authorised them for payment. It was the least she could do. She figured that the company could afford it, she was worth it, and after all it was a small price to pay for what she'd received in return. Although somehow she didn't think that the board of directors was ever going to find out about that little transaction. She had to have some small token of rebellion now that she'd quit smoking.

No one could be an angel all of the time.

'Hey, sis, where are you off to looking all deadly and vamp-like?' Toni grinned from behind her marble desk on the ground floor of the SySol building.

Cass scanned the foyer to check that nobody was around. They were both still paranoid about anyone discovering their connection, so most days Cassandra just marched straight past Toni with a slight wink being the only discernible sign of any recognition.

'It's OK.' Toni knew what Cass was thinking. 'Hilary had a dentist's appointment so I've been on my own for the last hour. Phoned every sex line I could find.'

Cass's eyes automatically widened and she was about to spit a rebuke when she caught Toni's expression.

'Kidding. Keep your designer accountant knickers on,' Toni laughed.

Cass flicked her the V sign, at which Toni immediately switched her gaze over Cass's shoulder, visibly paled and stuttered, 'Goodnight, Mr Copeland. Have a good evening.'

Cass's stomach flipped. Shit! Had Stephen Copeland, director of sales and fellow board member, just seen her making a violent rude gesture to a receptionist? He still hadn't got over her attempts to block the Cannes conference. Or the one he was trying to plan for the following quarter in Glasgow. At least she'd managed to get that one scaled down – Steve had planned for it to be in Venice. He was so pissed off with her that he'd have her up in human resources on a charge of misconduct in a heartbeat for what he'd just witnessed.

She slowly turned round, desperately calculating the appropriate way to professionally phrase, 'if you even attempt to make trouble for me I'll have your bollocks for lunch, you little shit.'

The foyer was empty. Toni let out a squeal of laughter.

'God, you're slow tonight, sis. You'd never have fallen for that one before.'

Cass slowly shook her head, irritated but at the same time relieved. She'd had enough battles at the quarterly review that afternoon, trying to get the others to recognise that some cost-cutting was going to have to be implemented if they were to stay on track to hit their profit targets. Trouble was that most of the board were still stuck in the nineties' mindset that if it involved a computer then it must be profitable, and continued to spend recklessly on that basis. They were so wrong. If SySol was to continue to track in the top three UK IT re-sellers, they were all going to have to tighten their belts.

Except her, of course. She couldn't get hers any tighter. Her skirt was bloody killing her. It had been fine first thing this morning but now for some reason it was leaving welts on her skin around the waistband. The last thing she felt like doing was going out, but she didn't want to cancel so late in the day.

Antonia was still laughing. Cass looked at her

wearily. 'OK, Tone, my sides are splitting. You should be on a stage, you're so funny,' she said drily.

'Ooooooh, who's got the arse-ache tonight then?'

Cass managed a smile. 'Sorry, love. Anyway, I'm going to meet Paul and Jeff for dinner.'

She didn't ask what Toni was doing. She hated to rub in the fact that Toni stayed home every night of her life because she couldn't afford a babysitter and their mum refused to give up her bingo to watch her grandson more than once a year.

Cass had offered to arrange childcare many times to let them go out, but Toni refused. She was such a bloody typical Leo. Proud.

'Fantastic! Do you mind if I come? Only I've got a free night. Ben's staying at his friend Abby's house tonight and I'm having them both next week. Do you think I should let them sleep together? Only I think Ben's a bit young for a committed, monogamous relationship just yet.'

Cass chuckled. 'I agree. He's far too young to limit his options. And yes, it would be great if you could join us.'

'Fantastic!' Antonia replied, bringing one leg out from under her workstation, pulling up her trouser leg and slapping her foot on top of her desk. 'Because I got these new fuck-off boots and I'm just dying to show them off.'

Cass checked them out. Leopardskin. Three-inch heels. Outrageous. And definitely not suitable for a work environment, even if Toni's feet were hidden all day. Still, she decided as she registered the huge grin on her sister's face, they obviously made her happy. The fuck-off boots could be Toni's little rebellion.

'They're gorgeous, Tone. We're obviously paying you far too much. Now get your coat and let's get out of here before someone spots them.'

She didn't have to say it twice.

'Piccadilly Piccadilly, please,' she shouted to the cab driver, hoping that he realised she wanted to go to the restaurant of that name and wasn't just a tourist with a repetitive speech impediment.

Jeff and Paul were both there when they arrived and were thrilled to see Toni. She got a bear-hug from each of them. Cass tutted in disgust.

'Oh for Christ's sake, you lot, will you stop that? You're putting people off their meals.'

The others just laughed. 'Ignore Mrs Frosty Tits there.' Toni gesticulated in Cass's direction.

Cass was outraged. '*What did you call me?*'

'Don't you know? That's your nickname at work, Cass. But don't worry; if they knew you they'd see what a wonderful warm human being you really are. I mean, look at the way you're smothering us all with affection. I feel quite overcome,' she mocked.

Cass just shook her head. She wasn't in the mood. She wanted to go home and get this skirt off and get into a pair of her comfiest pyjamas.

She struggled through the next couple of hours, feeling so progressively dreadful that she struggled not to put her head on the table and groan. Insultingly, the others didn't even seem to notice. She wanted to skip dessert and go straight for the bill but Toni wouldn't hear of it and ordered banoffee pies all round. Cass's insides flipped over.

Conversation had been great all night. Jeff was a bit stressed at first – something about his boss being in a bastard of a mood because he'd just found out his daughter was up the duff (Cass maintained a noncommittal, innocent expression throughout that one). She'd never met his boss, Ken Kent, but it was on her list of aspirations. Now there was a man she'd love to spend some time with – in a purely conversational, professional way. He was fascinating to her and she avidly read anything that concerned the building and growth of his empire. From a working-class man to an entrepreneurial icon: definitely her kind of guy.

Jeff started to lighten up when he revealed his big news: the Kent hotel chain was expanding and had bought properties in Madrid, Barcelona and Florence. The others gave a rousing cheer. Cheap weekend breaks on the horizon!

By the time the banoffee pies arrived, they were gossiping about the coupling Paul had witnessed in a Romp Room fire exit between an allegedly gay member of a boy band and a Botox-paralysed, collagen-enhanced soap star who wasn't far off her bus pass.

Toni screamed with mirth and Cass gave a vague smile. Not long to go. Another half an hour and she could reasonably excuse herself on the grounds that it had been a hard week at the office, and make her way home without being accused of being a party-pooper.

She picked up her spoon and scooped up the top layer of toffee and cream. It looked delicious. She raised it to her mouth and had just inserted it when the aroma of it hit her nostrils. A cataclysmic explosion erupted in her stomach and her hand flew to her mouth. She tried to stand but her legs had the solidity of the banana that was still slushing on her tongue. She tried to swallow, but it was refusing to budge. And everything she'd eaten so far was coming up to join it.

She looked around in panic and then grabbed the first thing that came to hand. Just in time she got it to the vicinity of her mouth. In what seemed like slow motion, the others realised what was going on and turned in horror, just in time to see Cassandra Haven vomit into her Louis Vuitton briefcase.

Silence. Cass closed her eyes. Then her head fell into her hands. Still silence. Every head in the immediate vicinity was now turned to face them, aghast expressions on the faces of all of them.

Jeff, Paul and Antonia were frozen to the spot, shocked beyond belief at what had just happened.

Eventually Toni found a weak and incredulous voice. 'And you said *we'd* put people off their meals?'

Cass raised her head sheepishly as the restaurant manager flew to her side, the threat of a potential lawsuit crashing in his head. He should never have hired that new chef – he'd had a bad feeling about him from the start. And this woman looked like a professional – she'd have Health and Safety crawling all over the kitchen like locusts. Bollocks, he wished he'd taken the weekend off and gone with the wife to her mother's in Skegness like she'd asked.

'Madam, madam, are you all right? Can I get you a glass of water, a cab, some fresh air?' A lawyer? he thought, but he didn't vocalise that one.

It did strike Cass that he was the only person in the room who was actually showing an iota of concern. The rest of the diners, especially the ones around her table, were still stunned into paralysis.

'No, no, I'm fine, really. I'm dreadfully sorry.'

She felt for the poor man's reputation. She knew how these things worked. It would be all round London diners by the end of the night and he'd be staring at empty tables for the next month until it had blown over. She couldn't do that to him. Business was business. She'd never sabotage someone else's livelihood. Unless it was to the benefit of her own, of course.

'It wasn't the meal that caused this.' She raised her voice to save the straining necks of the other diners who were desperate to hear what was going on. 'It was actually due to the fact that I'm pregnant.'

There were several noises all at once. There was the sigh of relief from the restaurant manager. There was a rumble of discomfort from the men in the room who were totally grossed out by the whole incident but didn't want to appear unsympathetic and draconian to their female companions. There was the soft 'aaah' of empathy from every female in the room who'd ever given birth. Except one. From Toni there was just a gut reaction and an expression of astonishment.

'Holy crap,' she whispered to no one in particular. 'My mother will have a heart attack.'

Cass gingerly placed the black bin liner (generously supplied by the restaurant and now containing one soiled briefcase) into her bath. She'd sort it out later. When she could think about it without vomiting again. She'd had to stop the cab seven times on the way home. So much for a painless pregnancy. She was sure the vomiting was supposed to stop around now, not bloody start. She intended to have a serious word with this child.

A smile flickered at the very thought. A child. Her child. And his, but she didn't need to dwell on that. She gave her stomach a rub. OK, emotional moment over. Time to face Bill, Ben and Weed.

She went into the lounge, where Paul, Jeff and Toni were sitting next to each other on the sofa, and prepared herself for the interrogation. They'd fired random questions at her in the taxi in between vomits but she'd managed to placate them with the promise that she'd reveal all in the comfort of her pyjamas and her own home.

To give them their due, once the shock had worn off their concern for her had kicked in and they'd smothered her with affection. It had only made her heave even more.

She crossed the room and sat on her black leather lounger. It had the facility to recline to give added comfort when chilling out, kicking back, having a beer and watching the telly. Unsurprisingly, Cass had never used that function. Maybe it was time to start.

Antonia slid off the couch and sat down at Cass's feet. She rubbed Cass's thigh.

'Sorry, sis, that I was crap in there. It was just a bit of a shock. Are you OK? About everything, I mean. About being pregnant? You must be devastated. I know how much your career means to you. Oh, Cass, I can't believe it. But don't worry, Sometimes accidents are just meant to be. We'll get through it. After all, we've done it before.'

She turned to face Paul and Jeff. 'So which of you two heroes is the father of my niece or nephew?'

Two blank faces stared back at her. Then their gaze shifted to Cass in a gesture of defiant expectation. Neither of them could believe she'd actually gone through with this. They thought the whole pregnancy concept was like a restlessness for a new house or a car upgrade, and that it would just fizzle out after a while when its impracticality had sunk in.

Cass put her hand on top of Toni's. 'Honey, it's neither of the guys. It's someone else's baby. And it wasn't an accident.'

'You mean you've got a *boyfriend*?' Toni gasped, astounded. 'How can you have a boyfriend when you have absolutely no life? No offence intended,' she added as an afterthought.

It crossed Cass's mind to be annoyed and affronted. Why was it so unlikely that she would actually have a relationship? But there was no point in challenging this point now – there was enough emotion flying around for the moment.

She motioned to speak, when a wave of nausea returned. While she waited for it to pass, she examined the guys' faces. Jeff was obviously totally confused, like he couldn't make his mind up how he felt or what his reaction should be. No change there then.

Paul? She tried to analyse his face but she couldn't interpret his expression. It could have been disgust. Or it could have been anger. Or maybe it was just worry. He did take other people's woes to heart and have sleepless nights over them. That was why he was the unlikeliest nightclub manager in the world. He was far too nice a person.

When the nausea finally passed, she gave her captive audience an edited version of events: as the guys knew, it was pre-planned ('You both knew? And you didn't tell me? How could you, you hopeless gits?' Toni had gasped), it was a one-night stand, she knew the father briefly, but wasn't prepared to divulge who it was. No, he didn't know that she was pregnant. No, she wasn't going to tell him. And yes, she was happy about it. Delighted in fact. And she hoped they'd be happy for her too.

Antonia was silent. Cass noticed she was chewing her bottom lip. She'd done that ever since she was a child when she was really angry or really scared. Cass didn't relish either of those options.

'What are you thinking, Toni?' she asked gently, aware that this was a fairly monumental turn of events for her sister to absorb in five minutes.

Toni just slowly shook her head, staring at some space in the middle distance.

'Toni?' Cass prompted again.

'I'm thinking that you have no idea what you've got yourself into. You're crazy Cass.' The volume of her dialogue was rising. 'You did this deliberately? You actually *chose* to become a single mother?'

Cass nodded.

Toni was getting seriously worked up now and Cass had no idea how to defuse her ire. She gesticulated to Paul and Jeff, who were sitting mute on the sofa, but they just shrugged. They were men. Without a death wish. They knew better than to get in the middle of two females having a strop. Especially sisters.

'Do you have any *idea* what you've got yourself into? Have you even *contemplated* how hard it's going to be? Oh, I know you're financially stable, Cass, but that's not the issue – it's the responsibility. It's lying in bed at night, knowing that the little guy next door depends on you for everything, materially and emotionally . . .'

Her voice was beginning to crack now and the tears were welling in her eyes. Cass thought of and dismissed several lines of mitigating arguments. It wouldn't have mattered even if she had known what the best thing to say was, because Toni was on a roll and no one was getting a word in edgeways.

'And what about the baby? Are you going to give up work?'

Cass shook her head.

'So! You're going to palm it off to a nanny at seven o'clock every morning then look in on it sleeping soundly when you get home at midnight? The poor little thing. Have you even thought about that, Cass? Have you thought about how the baby is going to feel? You haven't, have you? You're a selfish bitch, Cass, you really are.'

Antonia stomped up onto her feet. Cass was dumbstruck. She had never, ever seen her sister lose her temper before. She didn't even know she had a temper. Toni was the most sweet-natured, mild-mannered girl Cass had ever met. Where the hell was all this coming from? She didn't have a chance to ask. Toni, tears now streaming down her cheeks, turned and stormed out of the door, slamming it behind her. It was like the big exit scene from a movie.

Cass stared at Paul and Jeff for several seconds, at a loss for words. Then Paul quickly dived to his feet.

'I'll go after her, Cass. I'll call you later.' He still looked pissed off, Cass decided.

'Make sure she gets home OK, Paul,' she shouted to his departing form.

The door slammed for the second time in under a minute. So out of three people in the room with her, two had now left in an obvious state of irritation to say the least.

Cass raised her eyebrows searchingly at Jeff. 'Well? Are you going to bollock me and then follow them too?'

He stood up and walked towards her, then lowered himself onto his knees next to her. He took her hand.

Emotion alert, emotion alert, her brain screamed. Difficult as it was though, she didn't pull it away. She didn't even flinch. She was running out of allies, and although she knew she was more than capable of travelling this road on her own, it would be much better to have someone by her side. As long as they weren't actually touching her, of course.

Jeff still hadn't spoken. They could be here all night. Cass was more than familiar with Jeff's time-frames on decisions, opinions and action plans. He could grow a beard in the time he'd take to ponder something this big.

'I'm here for you, Cass. You know I always will be. And I want you to listen to what I'm going to say and think about it before you answer. I've got a proposition for you . . .'

Cass woke with a groan and quickly flipped her upper body out of the bed so that it was above the basin on the floor beside her.

That was close. She'd almost missed that time. Margaret Mary was in danger of actually having to earn her wages again – she was still twittering on about the time she'd had to fish a cigarette butt out of the sink.

Cass flopped back down on her pillows. God, she felt awful. And not just because it was Monday morning. This was like the worst case of Gandhi's revenge ever. Why the hell were women cursed with periods *and* pregnancy? Not to mention childbirth. She didn't even want to contemplate that one yet.

In fact, she had come to realise, there was a lot about this whole thing that she hadn't thought through properly. The effect it would have on those around her for a start. She still hadn't spoken to Toni since she'd departed with sparks flying from her heels the Friday before. Or Paul for that matter. They'd obviously decided that her course of action wasn't something they could associate with.

To her surprise, she was genuinely upset. Must be her hormones.

The Cassandra of old would have thought, Stuff them, and carried on regardless. The new Cass, in between pebble-dashing various surfaces in her flat, was definitely feeling a touch saddened by it. OK, she was actually devastated by their abandonment and kept discovering tears falling down her face. It was definitely hormones. She hadn't cried since she heard that Elvis had died in 1977 and even then it was only because Mrs McDonald from next door had a Pekinese called Elvis which Cass was particularly fond of and mistakenly thought had met his demise. It was one of the happiest moments in her life when she realised that Elvis the mutt was actually alive and well (although he was in mourning for the icon he was named after – he was off his Pedigree Chum for days).

Oh no. She grabbed a tissue. The very thought was making her gush again. Christ Almighty, she was turning into a wreck both physically and emotionally. She was actually beginning to feel empathy for the women on the telly who needed a hug in times of crisis.

She reprimanded herself severely. She had to pull herself together. After all, it was (she checked her watch) . . . SHIT. It was half past nine. She hadn't slept this late in years. In fact, ever. She should have been at work hours ago. She'd better call and . . . She realised what day it was. Relief all round. She'd booked the day off.

Her first scan was scheduled for two o'clock that afternoon. At this rate it would take her until then to get up and dressed, bearing in mind she had to factor sick time into her day.

She pushed herself upright. She had to get to the bathroom to brush her teeth. Her mouth felt like a family of skunks were living in it.

As she passed her floor-to-ceiling mirrors, she inspected her profile. Still no bump. Not that she expected one to have miraculously appeared since the last time she checked the Friday before.

She wobbled into her pristine white-tiled bathroom, ignoring the black bin liner that still had residency in the bath. That would have to go straight to the skip now – there was no way it would be salvageable. She had considered dealing with it and retrieving the documents inside before having the briefcase professionally cleaned, but instead she'd just attacked it with the shower hose until it was unsoiled but drenched. She'd get copies of the paperwork and, as for the case, she'd claim it on her personal effects policy that was linked to her house insurance. She'd just say she'd been mugged. They'd never believe it if she put 'used as a vomit receptacle'.

She brushed her teeth then climbed into the shower, just as the phone started to ring. Stuff it.

It would only be Jeff, checking up on her for the fortieth time in two days. He really was taking the whole care and support thing a bit too far. Actually he was taking *everything* a bit to far. Or was he?

She shuddered. No, she wasn't even going to think about that today. She'd spent most of her waking hours since Friday considering his proposition and she was still no closer to making a decision. Shit, she was getting more like him by the day. He was infecting her with his legendary powers of indecision. Or maybe he wasn't, maybe it was the hormones. Hell. She couldn't even make her bloody mind up about that!

One person his idea would please was her mother. She'd made the journey to Slough to see her parents the day before. She figured she'd better break the news to them before Antonia did.

When she let herself in, her dad was in his usual position in front of the telly watching the Austrian or Bavarian (or somewhere in that general direction) Grand Prix. Her mother was in her usual spot watching the *EastEnders* omnibus on the telly in the kitchen. Cass was at a loss to understand why. Her mother never missed a soap opera of a weekday evening, so why was it necessary to watch them again at the weekend? It wasn't as if something was suddenly going to change. It was sad really. How empty must her life be that she had to live it vicariously through a box on the kitchen worktop?

She briefly wondered if her parents ever actually communicated these days. Not that they ever were the type to have profound political conversations around the dinner table, but she was sure they did occasionally have a real conversation when she was younger.

'Want to meet me after bingo and we'll go up to the King's Arms for a drink?' her mother would ask on a Friday night. Her father would nod. Then twenty minutes before he left she'd hear him in the bathroom shaving and showering. She'd always thought that was quite romantic, her father making an effort with his appearance just to go out with the woman he'd been married to for thirty years. It kind of made up a little for the fact that they barely gave each other a glance the rest of the week.

'Hi Dad, how're you doing?'

He turned from the telly, automatically smiling. 'Hello, love. You're looking well. Your mother's in the kitchen.'

She briefly wondered why it never crossed his mind that she might have come to see *him*. It was the same when she telephoned – if her dad answered the phone it was passed straight over to her mum after just a cursory greeting.

She supposed it was all part and parcel of his upbringing. He was of the old school, her dad. It wasn't that he didn't love her but he'd sooner chew his own shoe than give her a hug and a kiss when she walked in the door. It was obviously an inherited trait.

She went on through into the kitchen, an explosion of Formica that was straight out of the seventies and should have stayed there. Her parents would never dream of replacing it though. The whole concept of DIY had completely by-passed them. They lived more by the ethos of 'if it isn't broken don't get down to B&Q to buy a new one'. Cass despaired.

She worked up gradually to breaking the news. She was shocked to realise that she was actually a bit nervous of their reaction. For God's sake, she was a 35-year-old woman! It was bit late in life to start worrying about what her parents thought.

She hated to disappoint them though. They were so proud of her – the first in her family to go to university, buy her own house, own a brand-new car . . .

She was so clever, her mother was forever telling her bingo buddies.

'Don't know where that one got her brains from,' she'd prattle, before continuing, 'Of course, our Antonia, she got the looks.'

In the end Cass adopted her most calm, pragmatic tone. The one that said, 'This is the way it is – deal with it.' The one she used on the board when she had to deliver bad news like their company cars were getting downgraded from ostentatious Jaguars to mere Mercedes. They had been distraught. She struggled to understand men – they'd trade a vital organ for an Aston Martin.

'Mum, I've got something to tell you. I'm pregnant. Four months. I'm not in a relationship with the father. He knows nothing about it and I intend to keep it that way. It wasn't an accident; I did it deliberately because I don't want to go through the rest of my life without a child.'

She took a deep breath. Her mother was just staring at her. Speechless. Cass briefly checked for a visible sign that her mother was still breathing. Yes, that was a blink. She hadn't killed her. She could proceed.

'I'm not giving up work. The baby is due in March and I'll have a nanny who will look after it so that I can continue to support us and develop my career. I'm not moving house. My flat has three bedrooms so it's big enough, and there's a park nearby for the little one to run about in so it's all perfect.'

There. That covered everything. 'Oh, and I hope you're happy about it.'

That was definitely everything.

There was a long, long pause. Peggy Mitchell had thrown at least three people out of the Queen Vic before her mother showed any sign of a reaction. Eventually, she shook her head sadly.

'I don't suppose there's any point in me arguing or disagreeing with you. There never was. Not only have you decided what you wanted, but you've already gone ahead and done it. You'll never change, Cassandra Hilda, so there's no point expecting you to.'

Her mother had deployed the big guns: it was how Cass knew that she was seriously pissed off – the middle name was vocalised.

Cass cringed internally. It wasn't exactly a rapturous response but then it wasn't 'never darken my door again' either. She hadn't been disowned, merely disapproved of. That was becoming pretty much a recurring theme for her.

Her mother pressed her for more details (more so that she could pass on the correct information to her bingo posse in an act of martyrdom – 'I don't know where I went wrong with her – after the education she had . . .') and told her just to ask if she needed anything.

Of course, her mother knew she wouldn't. Cassandra had been entirely independent since she was twelve and got her first job at Slough market, so she wasn't about to start now. Still, Cass couldn't say she hadn't offered.

Cass left feeling just a fraction depressed. Antonia had stormed out and never been heard of since. Her mother had been saddened and pissed off and she hadn't even told her father – her mum said she'd better leave that to her: he hated to be interrupted during what she called the 'Grand *Pricks*'.

But then it could be worse. She could be married to a dickhead like Clark Dunhill and instead of feeling a trifle down she'd be feeling a trifle suicidal.

The thought cheered her.

The door intercom was buzzing furiously as Cass emerged from the shower. She grabbed a bath towel. She'd have to upgrade to jumbo-size ones soon.

She started to feel queasy again. Bloody brilliant! Just when she'd started to think she might go a whole hour without throwing up.

The entryphone was still buzzing. Cass couldn't decide what to do: run for the door and risk damaging the lounge carpet with a sudden eruption of stomach contents, or ignore the phone, merrily throw up and then let the perpetual buzzing noise induce a migraine. Hmmm. She'd much preferred it when her major choices in life were Armani or Versace.

She went for the door. If it was Margaret Mary and she'd forgotten her keys again she'd bloody sack her.

Cass checked the screen and saw the top of a head. Light ash blonde. Antonia.

She pressed the door release and watched the mane of hair disappear, then listened to the thuds as three-inch heels bounded up the stairs.

She opened the door and Antonia flew at her.

'Thank God!!!!!! Why didn't you answer the phone? Or the door? I've been ringing all bloody morning.' She stopped to gasp for breath, then continued. 'I've been so worried! I had visions of you lying up here in a pool of blood fighting for life and then you'd die and I wouldn't have been able to say sorry and I'd feel terrible and have to sit on your grave every Saturday for the rest of my life apologising to your headstone for deserting you.'

Antonia stopped short. 'What?' she asked a puzzled-looking Cass.

Cass shook her head. 'Nothing. I just have huge difficulty in believing that we came from the same womb. I'm sure you must have emerged from somewhere a lot more dramatic than Imelda Haven from Slough. Joan Collins perhaps?'

Antonia grinned and enveloped her sister in a bear-hug. Cass just grimaced.

'I am sorry, Cass. For my reaction. I think I just couldn't believe that you'd voluntarily put yourself through everything that's happened to me over the last three years. All the tears and the heartache.

'But then last night I was lying with Ben and I realised that if you didn't have this baby you might never know what it's like to cuddle up to a little gorgeous bundle and smell the shampoo in his hair and strawberry yoghurt on his breath. You wouldn't know how fantastic it is to hear someone saying "I love you, Mum", and feel them giving you big, sloppy kisses.'

'Antonia, stop! I'm going to be sick.'

Toni gave an exasperated yelp. 'Oh, for God's sake, Cass. There's got to be *some* emotion in your life. I mean, I know the very thought of it turns your stomach, but . . .' The sight and sound of Cass throwing up into the pot plant beside her stopped her in her tracks. 'Oh. You mean literally. Sorry Cass,' she said weakly.

Cass returned to the bathroom and got out the Colgate for the second time.

'Don't worry about it, Tone,' she replied as she ran her toothbrush under the tap. 'I should have told you before. It was really insensitive of me to announce it in the middle of a restaurant. I just didn't think. I'm sorry. Sensitivity has never been my strong point. Truce?'

'Truce.' Antonia smiled. 'As long as you promise not to throw up anywhere near my new leopardskin fuck-off boots.'

'Miss Haven, please.' The rather overefficientlooking nurse summoned Cassandra through to the examination room. Antonia went with her.

Cass had tried to persuade her to go back to work, but Toni was having none of it – she'd heard from her mother that Cass had her first scan that day so she'd already called in sick, pleading a severely upset stomach. Well, it was the truth. The fact that the stomach didn't actually belong to *her* was a mere technicality.

The doctor examined Cass and ran through a checklist of questions. For a man who charged more per hour than a high-class hooker, he was remarkably brief and curt. If you've seen one you've seen them all, Cass decided.

He then spread a jelly on Cass's stomach and landed a probe on top of it. He wiggled it about for a few seconds and then suddenly stopped. The room was filled with a sound that resembled the 9.42 city express train to Euston.

Tears streamed down Toni's face as a blurred shape appeared on the screen.

'That's my niece,' she choked, 'she's beautiful.'

'Or nephew.' The doctor smiled at her indulgently.

Bloody typical, Cass thought. I'm paying this man more than the cost of a new kidney and he treats me with disinterested indifference. Antonia utters one sentence and he's suddenly empathetic conversationalist of the year.

'Isn't it gorgeous, Cass?' she said, still crying. 'That's your baby.'

'Are you sure?' Cass replied, perplexed. 'Only I think you might be at the wrong bit, doctor. That looks like a kidney stone.'

'I don't believe you said that!' Antonia replied as she

helped Cass back on with her coat. 'You'd better watch out, Cass, 'cause the baby will soon be able to hear what you're saying – it's going to come out as bitchy as you if you keep that up!'

Cass turned to utter a quick and witty reply (she was sure one would come to her in a minute). If she were honest, though, much as she'd concealed it well, the first sight of her baby had actually moved her. A little. There was a definite stirring. Along with a definite confidence that she was doing the right thing. She was meant to have this little one and she was starting to feel something approaching excitement at the thought. Her life was going to be complete. Whole. It would be perfect.

'Oh, hello! How are you doing?'

Antonia was off to the left, talking to a dark-haired female at the waiting area.

'Great, thanks. Just here for a check-up and a scan today. God, I'm SO excited – I haven't slept a wink.'

Her excitement obviously hadn't rubbed off on the redhead sitting next to her. She had a face like fizz.

'Well, good luck and let me know how you get on.' Antonia's voice dropped. 'Oh, and please don't mention to anyone that you saw me here – I called in sick today to come with my sister. Between you and me, OK?'

The girl turned and glanced at Cass. There was a flicker of recognition, but Cass ignored it. The last thing she needed was a 'baby buddy' – all that chatting about nappies and sterilising. No thank you.

'No problem,' the girl replied. 'I'll see you in the morning.'

Antonia followed Cass into the foyer.

'Who was that girl, Tone? I vaguely recognise her. Was she at school with you or something?'

Toni snorted. 'I wish! She probably went to school in Geneva or somewhere like that. That's Polly Kent, from marketing.'

Ah, so that's where I remember her from, Cass thought – she organised some photo shoot for the board the year before. Nice girl, from what she could remember. She really hadn't paid her that much attention.

'She's lovely, Polly. Always stops for a chat on her way in and out of the building. Actually, this is her twelve-week scan today as well so she must be due about the same time as you. Different circumstances though, I have to say.' Antonia grinned cockily to Cass. 'Polly has actually shared the news of her baby with its father. In fact, they got engaged a couple of weeks ago. Huge surprise, because no one even knew they were seeing each other.'

Cass started to tune out. Antonia's powers of gossip were astounding, and of no interest to her whatsoever.

'Mmm. What's his name, now? He works in sales. A bit gorgeous. Drives a Porsche. Dunhill. Yep, that's it. Clark Dunhill.'

She only just caught Cass as she fainted to the floor.

Chapter Eight

Polly Kent – The Shotgun

'Look on the bright side – it's the child of Smarm Man so the birth will be a doddle. It'll just slide out in a bubble of hair gel and Aramis. Then it'll lie back and have a fag to reward itself for all the effort.'

'Another word, Fiz, and I'm going to make you wait outside. You're only here because Clark is swamped and Mum and Dad are having lunch with the PM at Downing Street. Although Mum did want to cancel. But how could I let her? Cherie would have been so disappointed.'

'Oh, I know,' Fiz concurred. 'Last time I stood Cherie up she was gutted. She had the hump for weeks. I nearly didn't get invited to her next Ann Summers party.'

Polly hit her with her bag. But she couldn't help giggling. 'Nothing personal, Fiz, but I do wish Clark was here. He's gutted that we've had to reschedule this twice to fit around his meetings and *still* something came up at the last minute. He just works so hard.'

She had absolutely never, ever, in her whole fantastic life felt as happy as she did now. She rubbed her rounded stomach. She was thirty-five weeks pregnant and already straying into size fourteen jeans. She didn't care, though. What did her appearance matter? Clark adored her no matter whether her posterior could fit comfortably into the seats of his Porsche or not.

How could she even think of such trivialities when she was carrying their gorgeous child? Thirty-five weeks. Even if, God forbid, the baby decided to come early, it should be fine now. It would be wonderful. Her life was perfect. And it had been since she'd broken the news to Clark.

Polly jumped as she saw the reflection behind her in the mirror. She snapped off the hairdryer.

'Clark! What are you doing here? Oh my God. I can't believe this. I was just on my way over to your place.'

'Why?' he replied, then continued impatiently, 'No, don't tell me. Polly, I have to talk to you and I couldn't wait any longer. I've been thinking about us all weekend and I've come to some conclusions, so I needed to see you tonight. Sit down. Please,' he implored.

Polly's stomach started to rumble. Oh, no. He looked so serious. He looked so strained. He looked like he had the weight of the world on his shoulders.

Polly's mind went into overdrive. The panic button was pressed. The one that made her so terrified that she wanted to cry and throw up at the same time.

He's here to finish it, her brain screamed. Here I am, standing with his child inside me, and he's met someone else. He wants to be alone. He needs space. He's bought a yacht and decided to spend a year sailing the South China Seas. Then she remembered the candlelit cruise on the Thames when he'd thrown up all the way from Chelsea Harbour to London Bridge – she crossed that one off the list.

But still, he was here to call off their relationship and she was pregnant!

God, she needed to call Mum. And where had Fiz disappeared to? She didn't want to be alone when he left. She'd say nothing. When he said goodbye, she wasn't going to tell him about the baby. She'd never want to keep a man that way. She'd tell him later, of course. After the pain had healed. Not that it ever would – she loved this man more than anything else on earth. Life would be unbearable without him. And she was pregnant!

Clark was unfolding her fingers one by one from the hairdryer. She hadn't realised that shock – the second one of the night – had rendered her paralysed. He steered her gently over to her bed and sat her down. God, he was so caring, so tender. How would she ever live without him? Especially in her pregnant state? Pregnant, pregnant, pregnant. The word was firing around in her brain like a deflating balloon.

'Pol, honey, babe. I don't know how to say this . . .'

He was sweating. She could see the tiny bubbles of perspiration forming on his forehead. He took another deep breath. She was still holding hers. Here it comes, she thought. Only the sure knowledge that bending over would induce severe vomiting stopped her from assuming the crash position. Besides it might be uncomfortable for the baby – her being pregnant and all!

'Pol. Honey. I know we've only been together for a few months. And I know this might seem a bit out of the blue . . .'

She clenched her eyes tight shut and prepared

herself for the 'going too fast need some space' speech. The one that Fiz used on a guy after the first date. Fiz, the one that wasn't pregnant, that is.

'But Polly, the thing is, I love you very much and I, em . . .'

Polly was tempted to open one eye, but was too busy being in turmoil to give the command to the optic nerve. Why was he telling her he loved her when he was about to call their whole relationship off? Dump his pregnant girlfriend!

'Polly. Pol. Babe. Will you marry me?'

'And of course, you said, "Piss off, you smarmy twat, I wouldn't be seen dead within a hundred yards of a registry office with you."'

Polly grinned. 'Shut up, Fiz. You're just jealous.'

Fiz was deadpan. 'Oh I am. Green.'

Polly ignored her. Nothing could bug her happiness tonight. Or rather, this morning. It was three o'clock and Clark had just left. She had so wanted him to stay the night and he'd been desperate to too, but he had to get home to get fresh clothes etc. for work. Letting him walk out the door had been so difficult. The only consolation was that she had heard Fiz come in an hour before and was desperate to go and wake her to tell her the news. Fiz wasn't quite as excited, naturally.

Polly recounted every single detail of the night's events. Stopping regularly to mop up the floods of tears that were pouring down her face. Tears of joy.

'And then, I said, "But Clark, I have to tell you something first, something that might change everything." And so I told him. That I was pregnant, that is. That I'd just found out. Oh and Fiz, guess what he said? Even you can't criticise him for this . . .'

'Try me.'

'Well, he looked really shocked but, and this is how I know it was his gut reaction, he immediately grabbed me and held me so tightly and said, "Pol, it was just meant to be. It's fate. I come here to ask you to marry me on the very night you discover you're pregnant. A baby! We're going to be married and we're going to have a baby. I love you, Pol – you've made my life amazing."'

Fiz had to hand it to him – he got ten out of ten for artistic impression. Wanker. He was *such* a fecking wanker.

She still felt ill at the very thought of the direction Polly's life had now taken. If only she'd followed her instinct and many urges to kill the prick then this would never have happened. What were the chances of them tracing strychnine back to her? She'd have got away with it, no problem. But then, she thought with a sigh, even killing him wouldn't make her feel better after the latest events: only a long drawn-out torture and *then* death would be adequate retribution for this fiasco.

The worst thing was that it broke her heart to see Polly so happy when she knew that he was a lying toad. She did have a stirring of guilt at having interfered, but the only reason she'd done so was that she couldn't bear to see Polly hurt – not on top of the latest development. She'd do everything she could to ensure that Clark Smarm Man Dunhill didn't trash her friend. Even if it did stick in her throat like a chicken bone from Big Bird.

Still, she couldn't resist the odd dig.

'So, let me see the ring then?' she prompted.

Polly harrumphed. 'I don't have one yet.'

'Why not? Surely a man proposing to the love of

his life should have come prepared with a ring? That way if it's only a little chip of a stone you can tell him to bog off and get a bigger one before committing yourself to a miserable git.'

Polly was getting exasperated now. As usual.

'I told you, he hadn't planned to come over tonight. He is just so spontaneous sometimes. He had planned to ask me in a couple of weeks' time but couldn't wait any longer. He said he had to know that I'd spend the rest of my life with him. God, he's so romantic. Anyway, he's having my ring made. He designed it himself – said he wanted it to be far more personal than just picking one out of a shop window. He's gone to some exclusive jewellery designer and the ring will be ready in a couple of days. I can't wait to see it, Fiz. I can't help thinking that this is all such a miracle.'

'Neither can I, Pol. It's definitely fecking miraculous.'

Telling her parents had been a lot more difficult than telling Fiz. Polly knew that they had such preconceptions of how her life would turn out and this didn't quite fit that plan.

Mum and Dad fully expected her to be in a relationship for at least a couple of years before making a commitment. And then they would expect a formal engagement (announcement in *The Times* and the *Guardian*), followed by a fantastic wedding in one of Dad's hotels with possibly a full feature spread over ten pages in *OK!*, *Hello!*, or at the very least, *The Hotel & Caterer Magazine*.

Then, a couple of years after that, they'd anticipated being proud grandparents and all spending summers together in the villa in Marbella, Dad teaching his grandsons to play cricket and box while Mum read Enid Blyton to the girls.

The latter events would still happen, of course, only they'd come much sooner than expected. About four years sooner.

As always, Clark had been so thoughtful and sensitive about how they would feel. It was incredibly important to him that they stress he had proposed to her *before* he had found out she was pregnant. Which was true of course. By about ten minutes. But they just exaggerated the time differential slightly when they broke the news. Clark didn't want them thinking that he wanted to spend the rest of his life with her for any reason other than the fact that he adored her. Which was true. But other people could be such cynics. Even ones who loved you and had your best interests at heart. She thought of Fiz. *Especially* ones who loved you and had your best interests at heart.

They travelled up to Kent Castle the following Sunday. Had it really only been two weeks since she'd been there for her birthday dinner? When she'd blown out the candles on her cake and wished that she and Clark would be together always?

And now look at her! Travelling with the man she was going to marry and pregnant with their child. It was magical.

Clark was understandably nervous. In fact, they'd had to stop at every service station on the way there for either her all-day morning sickness or for Clark to get a bit of fresh air. She totally understood it. Dad could be a bit daunting sometimes, until you got to know him.

She glanced at Clark. He was so handsome (although he was worryingly pale). She could just picture him striding along the golf course in ten years' time with Dad on one side and their young son on the other. Of course, they'd have at least another one or two by then. Being an only child she'd always fantasised about having brothers and sisters and she was determined to deliver that dream to her offspring. She must ask Clark how many children he would like. She glanced sideways at him. He looked so tense. Perhaps she'd wait a while on that question; let him see how wonderful it was with one child first before planning the next.

And besides, there were so many other things to discuss. The wedding, for instance. As usual, Clark had put what was best for her before his own feelings. He was dying to get married as soon as possible, but he'd said that he didn't want her wedding day marred by the violent all-day sickness she was suffering from. Since there was no way of predicting when that would abate, and since by the time it did she would probably be the size of a wardrobe, he'd suggested that they wait until after the baby was born before settling on a date for the ceremony. He was just so considerate. But that didn't mean they couldn't discuss options for their big day. Clark got so excited when they did that – she could tell just by looking at him that his heart was racing. Bless.

Henry opened the door (forgotten her keys again) and directed them through to the garden room. Ken and Jilly were already there, sitting on a white jacquard love seat by the French doors, which were wide open despite the autumn breeze. That must explain why Clark was covered in goosebumps from head to toe. His skin bore an uncanny resemblance to a turkey leg.

The customary kisses, hugs and hand-shakes were traded. Then events overtook preparation and planning. Clark and Polly had planned to wait until after dinner to break the news, but before they'd even moved through to the dining room, Jilly commented on her daughter's demeanour. There was something going on. Polly had always worn every emotion on her face and, unless she was very much mistaken, this one was unadulterated bliss. No matter what her husband's (and if she were completely honest she did somewhat concur) reservations about this chap were, he certainly seemed to be making her daughter happy. She had to know more.

'You're positively glowing, my darling,' she complimented Polly, as the men delved into a conversation about the forthcoming Ryder Cup. As far as she was concerned woods, drivers and irons belonged in the countryside, automobiles and laundries. In that order. The very mention of a putter plunged her into a catatonic trance. Far better to divert her attention to her daughter and leave the men to it.

'Is this some new cosmetic product that I should know about?' she teased, knowing full well that a glow of that magnitude could only be attained by sheer happiness. But then, Polly had always been a very positive and contented child. Since the moment of Polly's birth, Jilly had felt truly blessed. It was almost as if God, by way of apology that she and Ken had never produced the brood of children they longed for, had attempted to make it up to her by giving her the closest thing to perfection he had on the shelves. Polly.

'God, Mum, I can't wait a minute longer. Mum, Dad ...' she interrupted her father. Clark swung towards her, his expression one of a bungee jumper right before they took the plunge.

Polly reached over and took his hand.

'Clark and I have something to tell you. Well, two things actually.'

Kenneth Kent wasn't looking at his daughter. Years of conducting negotiations and deals had taught him to study not the mouthpiece, but the big picture. And if he wasn't mistaken, the big picture was sweating profusely.

Oh no. He couldn't have . . .

The one obvious thing, the event that every father dreads the most (apart from a serious crack cocaine addiction, joining of weird religious cults and a predilection to hormonal mood swings) flew to the forefront of his mind. If this bastard had got his Polly in the club he'd . . .

Polly nudged Clark. He leapt off the platform, heart thundering, stomach collapsing, elastic firmly tied to his ankles.

'Em, Mr and Mrs Kent,' he started nervously. God, Polly thought, it was so sweet. He was so nervous yet he still found the courage to give her hand a reassuring squeeze. Only, if she were honest, it *was* starting to hurt. A lot.

'Kenneth and Jilly,' he continued weakly, changing his tack. Kenneth and Jilly returned his gaze with quizzical (and in Kenneth's case borderline homicidal) expressions.

'We came here tonight because we wanted to, or rather, em, I wanted to, that is, we wanted to tell you . . .'

Kenneth Kent's fists were involuntarily clenching. He knew it was the year 2000. He knew his Pol was a big girl now. He knew that girls these days didn't wait until they married before, well . . . He couldn't even bear to finish the thought. He still considered

Pol his little girl and had no wish or intention to change his perception of her. He'd therefore convinced himself that she would limit herself to holding hands and the occasional peck on the cheek before marriage.

So this wise-arse (he'd already decided that was an apt description of Polly's boyfriend) couldn't possibly, possibly be going to say what he feared most. His Polly couldn't be pregnant. It wasn't possible. He'd fucking k—

'I love your daughter very much.' Clark turned and smiled at Polly. Nervously but convincingly. 'And I hope you don't mind, but I've taken the liberty of asking her to marry me. And we'd like your blessing.'

Silence. Then the sound of two prolonged exhalations. One was Clark's, understandably. He'd done it and he was still alive! The relief at having bungeed back up without watching his vital organs splatter across the tarmac was considerable.

The other sigh was emitted from the lungs of Kenneth Kent. Thank God, he raised a silent prayer of gratitude. They only wanted to get engaged. Well, this Dunhill boy wasn't perhaps what he would have chosen for his beloved, but then he was aware that his expectations did run a tad high in that area. Prince William was still a bit young to be settling down.

No, engagements he could handle. After all, they were like Greek plates and informers' legs – made to be broken. That reminded him, he wondered if that insidious prick Giles was still using a Zimmer to get around. Must remember to check that one out. He'd known he was trouble from the start. He didn't get quite such an ominous feeling from this wise-arse, but he had plenty of time to investigate him. He'd push for a long engagement. In the meantime, he resolved to make the boy feel welcome – it was the least he could do for his Pol. He grabbed Clark's hand and pumped it.

'Congratulations, my boy. Great news.'

His other hand was clapping Clark's opposite shoulder. He didn't quite go as far as hugging him. There were some things that his East End upbringing just altogether ruled out. Now what was the name of that private investigator he'd used to track down Giles after he'd trashed Polly? He'd get on to that first thing Monday morning – there was no way he was waiting until after Polly had been hurt this time. If this boy wasn't what he seemed, he wanted to know about it pronto.

'Welcome to the family. We're delighted, Clark. I know we haven't got to know each other so well yet, but we'll soon rectify that.' Bloody right, he thought. I'll know everything but your inside leg measurement soon, lad.

He turned to Polly, who was being squeezed tightly by his missus. It was a beautiful picture. There were tears streaming down both their faces. Planning their daughter's wedding was something he knew his wife had anticipated with delight for many years.

Jilly released Polly and turned to Clark. 'Congratulations, Clark. I know it's probably not my place to say it, but you're a very lucky man.'

'Oh, Mum, that's enough,' Polly light-heartedly rebuked her while wiping away the tears. 'You're biased. *I'm* the one who's lucky. Clark is wonderful.' She gazed at him adoringly, her eyes conveying every ounce of her love, before her father pulled her towards him and crushed her to his chest.

'Congratulations, love. We're so pleased for you.'

Jilly hugged Clark and kissed him warmly on the cheek. When she stood back, she held onto his hand. 'So have you thought about a date yet then? There's just so much to organise!' she exclaimed gleefully, mentally rattling through the numbers of her events organiser, florist, caterer, Philip Treacey and what was the name of that divine little bijou boutique who did those hand-painted silk shoes that were to die for?

Calm down there, Jill, don't go pushing them just yet, Ken thought, as Polly disentangled herself from his bear-hug. Have to make sure that this one's the right one while there's still time to reverse the situation. No point in getting carried away just yet – after all, what was the hurry?

Polly smiled and clasped Clark's hand again. Strange, Ken thought, his suspicious antennae popping up like two periscopes. The boy still looks nervous. He's definitely hiding something. He wondered if it was a criminal record.

'Well, Mum, Dad, the thing is, we thought we'd wait until next year to tie the knot . . .'

That's what we like to hear, Ken thought. He loved it when something went to plan.

But Polly was still talking.

'Because, well, actually, we're going to have a baby.'

The gleam from her face could have lit London. The steam from Kenneth Kent's face could have heated it. He was a lava bucket short of volcanic. He saw stars. His heart thundered. His rage rushed from the feet that were desperate to lash out, to the fists that were fighting to assume a position around Clark Dunhill's neck.

Even Jilly couldn't hide her astonishment. But her superior breeding overcame her shock.

'Oh, Polly,' she cried, 'that's wonderful. Truly wonderful. I'm going to be a grandmother! Kenneth, I think this calls for champagne.' She turned to her husband and her heart sank. She'd only seen that look a couple of times before in their whole lives, and both times it directly preceded incidents that were major news stories but somehow didn't quite make it into the press. She prayed that he wouldn't cause a scene. For Polly's sake.

'Oh, it certainly calls for something,' Kenneth replied, through gritted teeth encased in an expression that crossed a forced smile with a now-definite homicidal grimace.

It was like a scene from *The Godfather* (or any other Martin Scorsese movie for that matter). The big cheese was eating spaghetti with the skinny guy who'd just been pinpointed as a traitor but didn't realise yet that he'd been rumbled (although he was sitting a bit uncomfortably in his seat and had a visible personal hygiene problem around the armpits due to being shit-scared of even sitting in the same room as the Boss).

Anyway, over dinner the Boss tells the sweaty one all the reasons why he's a good guy and important to the organisation, so just as the after-dinner cigars are burning down to their last puff, Sweaty Pits is beginning to relax and think that he's the dog's bollocks: the Boss loves him *and* he's getting a wedge for imparting information to a rival family. He's starting to puff up around the pectoral area and plan a double session with Sylvia Mary Frances, the hooker who has a day job conducting the choir at Our Lady of the Misconceptions when a guy (or, more accurately, a brick shithouse in pinstripes) bangs open the door and riddles him so full of bullets he could double as a colander.

Kenneth Kent was the boss. Clark Dunhill was the colander.

Kenneth turned to his wife. 'You're right, my love, I'll just arrange it'.

He pressed a buzzer and heard the voice of his own personal brick shithouse. He gave the order.

'I'll bring it right up, Mr Kent,' Henry replied.

Miles Conway stretched up from his desk. A glass partition separated his office from the rest of the department. It was, he contemplated as his eyes followed Polly getting up from her desk and gliding over to the coffee machine, like having a window to perfection. Miles attributed his success to his ability to play movie-like scenes in his head. Unlike those in more cerebral professions he didn't think in words, figures or equations: he thought in pictures. The latest slogan – he visualised it splashed across a billboard. The artwork for the new magazine campaign – he imagined how it would look on the page before it was even printed. His lunch – a visual premonition of it was on a plate in front of him before he'd even ordered it.

However this gift could also, he acknowledged, be a curse. How cruel that he could close his eyes and see in full Technicolor how amazing life with the stunning Polly would be. He slipped into the familiar scene that played out in his head at least once every twenty-four hours (it could rise to double figures on a slow day), the one where Polly came towards him, her eyes twinkling with lust and laughter. She leaned over his desk and placed a coffee just out of his reach to that he had to stretch out to pick it up. When he did so, Polly bent down so that her lips brushed his ear. 'Photocopy room, NOW,' she hissed, 'I can't wait a minute longer to have you.' He rose and followed her (walking with a decidedly odd John Wayne-type limp, it had to be said), and as they reached their destination she turned and pulled him, slamming the door behind him with her leather-encased foot. Did he mention that she was wearing thigh-high black boots? Whatever. Her chest was against his now, rising and falling rapidly . . .

'Miles?'

For Christ's sake! His feet slipped off the desk and his hands immediately flopped to his groin area to cover the cause of the John Wayne limp.

'Are you OK?' Polly asked hesitantly. Miles was definitely working too much – sometimes she thought he just wasn't on this planet at all. But then, probably that's why he was such a genius.

'Yeah, er, sorry, Pol. Just giving some headspace to the new campaign for next spring. Er, fantasi— I mean, thinking it through. And that. Of course. Yes. That's exactly what I was doing.'

He really needed to take a holiday. The poor man was working so hard he was bordering on delirious.

'Sorry, then. To disturb you, I mean, but can I have a word?'

He nodded, his face still a subtle shade of cherry.

She walked towards him and as she approached his desk she leaned over. Her hand, the one holding a steaming mug of coffee, moved towards him as she placed it gently down on the corner of his . . . oh, good God, he could feel himself slipping away again. It was like an action replay.

Then she sat down. 'Thought you might like a

drink,' she said as she gestured towards the cup.

'Yeah, er, thanks. Great. Absolutely.' He knew he was warbling. Get it together, man. Concentrate. He ordered his subconscious to take the rest of the day off. He couldn't have it hijacking any more of his working day – he'd either get fired, slapped or arrested.

'So,' he announced in his most professional voice. 'What can I do for you, Polly?'

'Well, actually, I have something to tell you.' She beamed.

Oh no. She's leaving. She's here to resign. Pictures flew through his brain like a VHS tape on fast-forward. Polly sitting under a banner for a rival company, being offered a position with double the salary. Polly walking up the aisle to stand with a poncey-looking guy in a morning suit in front of a vicar who stumbled over the ponce's triple-barrelled name. Polly, naked . . . No, that was the photocopier room again.

'I just wanted to let you know that I'm pregnant.' Silence. Even the photocopier was still. He was confused now. Had she actually said that or had that been in his head? Only usually when she told him that she was pregnant with his child they were wrapped up together in front of a roaring open fire in a snow-bound cabin in Aspen drinking Krug and eating chocolate-dipped strawberries.

'Pardon?'

'Pregnant. I am. Sorry Miles, I know that it'll cause you some inconvenience. But I intend to keep working. As long as I can, that is. And I'll make up any time I take off for hospital appointments or anything like that.'

'Of course, yes, well . . .' He was aware that he

should be saying something here, but in his befuddlement he couldn't quite put his finger on it. It was difficult to concentrate when the fantasy on which your every future plan was based was sitting in front of you telling you she was up the duff.

Oh, yes.

'Congratulations.'

'Thank you. We're so excited.' She grinned.

'We?' It was out of his mouth before you could say, 'Heart trashed and in the gutter, leaving a life of desperation, anguish and alcoholism as the only possible future.' Of course there must be a 'we'. He despised him already.

She wrinkled up her nose as she gave an embarrassed shrug.

'My fiancé.'

Miles was astounded. From the general office chit-chat he had long ascertained that, quite inexplicably as far as he was concerned, Polly was single. Where the hell did the fiancé come from? Could you get those in Harvey Nicks now?

Polly registered his surprised reaction.

'That's a familiar response,' she laughed. 'We've kind of kept this relationship under wraps, because, actually, he works here at SySol.'

'Whe ... whe ... *where*?' Miles stuttered, aghast.

If he'd thought for a minute that Pol would have entertained a relationship with a mere IT employee, he'd definitely have asked her out long ago. OK, he wouldn't have, but he'd have thought about it. Really hard. And he'd have tried desperately to pluck up the courage to do something about it. Only the presumption that she wouldn't contemplate a fling with anyone sporting less than their third million and a private jet had stopped him. Look at Giles McAdam – his family were worth more than some Middle Eastern countries.

'In the sales department, actually.' Was it Polly's imagination or was Miles reacting really weirdly to this? She'd never had him pegged as the dramatic type, yet he was acting like this was the biggest news he'd heard all year.

This conclusion might have had something to do with Miles's chin hitting his desk at speed. Sales! That bunch of cocky bastards. It must be Steve shag-a-knot-in-a-tree Copeland. So it was Polly who'd put him in traction, making him miss the Cannes conference. The lucky bastard. He'd have done anything to have got those broken legs during a ski trip with Polly. He was gutted, but he made a weak attempt to be professional and courteous. He'd just give Copeland's shins an accidental kick next time their paths crossed. With a bit of luck the legs would re-fracture. He knew he was being petty but it was making him feel marginally better. Only marginally. He stood up and leaned over the desk, hand outstretched.

'Congratulations again, Polly, and thanks for letting me know. If you need anything at all just say.' He wondered if she realised that full body massage, the moon, the stars and a lifetime of adoration were included in that offer. 'And I hope that you and Steve are very happy together.'

'Steve? No, it's Clark. We've been together for quite a while now but we haven't said anything so that it wouldn't affect our careers. But yes, we will be. Happy. Very.'

She shook Miles's hand and returned to her desk, smiling. Miles had been so lovely, as she'd known he would be. He was always so understanding.

Strange that he thought she'd meant Steve, though.

Steve Copeland's infidelities and indiscretions were legendary – he was a serial seducer. She wouldn't touch a chap like that with a bargepole. Dishonesty was the biggest turn-off in a man. That's why she was so lucky to have found her Clark. He was so straight, so open, so truthful about his feelings.

Back in his office, Miles was reeling. This was catastrophic. Clark? As far as he knew there was only one Clark in sales and that was the guy who'd replaced Steve in Cannes. What was his surname? Fags. Clark Benson ... nope. Clark Hedges ... urgh, what was it? Dunhill! Clark Dunhill. The image immediately evoked a memory.

The Carlton Hotel. The fourth floor. Sometime before midnight. Miles returning to his room to make some calls to the American marketing team in LA. A room door opens. A man exits, stuffing his shirt into his open trousers. His hair is tousled; his eyes try desperately to focus in the light. Miles slips his keycard into his room door and enters before the man spots him. But not before he hears him say:

'Night then, doll-face. Same time, same place, same position tomorrow night, eh?'

The man was Clark Dunhill. And Miles was pretty sure that the woman wasn't his beloved Polly.

Fiz brought Polly a cup of tea and a sticky toffee cream-filled ring, then squeezed onto the sofa beside her. It wasn't easy. It was only a three-seater and Polly was taking up two and a half of those as she lay flat on her back with her legs stretching up the wall behind them, feet pointing at the ceiling, her 35-week bump visibly bobbing up and down. Her face was a mask of concentration.

'If you're doing those bloody pelvic floor thingies again then fecking stop right now – the mental picture will put me right off my cream bun.'

Polly laughed as she struggled to a position more conducive to indulgence.

'God, Fiz, I'm going to miss you so much. Who's going to make me laugh when I'm feeling rotten?'

'Ask Smarm Man an intelligent question and then watch as he flounders for the answer. That always does it for me.'

Polly sighed. Her best friend's borderline psychotic hatred of Clark aside, she felt a real sadness when she contemplated her impending move. True, it was mixed with incredible excitement at the prospect of building a home for her new family in the gorgeous little bijou mews house in Belgravia that Dad was so kindly letting them have (what an absolute stroke of luck that the tenants were repatriating to Washington that month).

There was just so much to do. The house was to be decorated, the nursery was to be planned. Thank goodness she would be stopping for what was ostensibly supposed to be her maternity leave soon. She thought about that for a second. That was quite sad too, actually. Especially when, in truth, she knew that she definitely wouldn't be returning to work. She had tried to tell Miles that she'd be better just resigning and being done with it, but he'd objected profusely. In the end they'd agreed that she'd stop on maternity break and then let him know what she wanted to do for sure when it was time for her to return. He was such a sweetie.

She surveyed the stacks of boxes piled around the room, ready for the movers who were due to arrive the next morning. It was just clothes, CDs and personal stuff really. The Belgravia house was already furnished so she was leaving the contents of this flat for Fiz and her new housemate.

'Have you found anyone to share with you yet, Fiz?'

'Yeah, Cameron Diaz and Drew Barrymore are moving in next Friday. It's going to be great, all that karate and shit. By the end of the month I'll be thinking "Polly who" and never off the phone to Charlie.'

Polly leaned over and cuddled her. 'I'll miss you, babe.'

A loud sniff emanated from beneath the auburn tangle.

'Likewise.' Fiz gave Pol a squeeze. Not too hard though – she didn't want all that waters and gushing and ruined carpets drama to happen when she was around. That was one scenario she'd happily leave to Smarm Man.

'So you haven't then, found someone to share with yet?' The thought of Fiz living alone really bothered her. For all her bravado, she knew that Fiz never went to sleep at night without checking the door, the windows and the meat cleaver under her bed.

'I'm working on it. Oops, time for a sharp exit, here comes father of the year.'

The sound of the Porsche pulling into a parking space under the window alerted her to the arrival of her nemesis. She put her head upside down and shook her hair, then stood back up, wiped the ring of toffee and cream from her mouth (she should actually have done that first – her hair now came in three flavours) and grabbed her bag.

She gave Polly a quick kiss. 'Don't wait up for me – I'm not sure when I'll be home.'

'Again, Fiz? That's the third time this week. If

I didn't know better I'd think you were avoiding me,' Polly joked, knowing that Fiz was living in terror of her going into premature labour in their kitchen.

'Of course I am – you keep eating all the cakes. I'd be anorexic if I sat in with you every night. Oh, hello, Smarm.'

Clark nodded in her direction as he passed her. 'Ugly cow. How's your day been?'

Polly rolled her eyes. She was getting used to these exchanges between the two of them. She liked to kid herself that it was all in jest; the stress of the truth would be too much. Especially in her condition.

'Oh, fine. We went to see your baby on its belated 35-week scan performance. It's cooking away nicely. Said to say hi. Actually, that's a lie. It said, where the fuck is my dad and why does my Auntie Fiz have to take my mum to all her appointments?'

Clark rounded to Polly. 'Honey, you know—'

Pol put her hand up. 'Clark, ignore her. I totally understand and you know that I don't mind. She's just trying to irritate you.'

Fiz gave a beaming smile. 'Mission accomplished.'

'And we saw the woman from work again today,' Polly continued. 'She's looking great – you would hardly believe that we're at exactly the same stage. She's so tiny compared to my big Space-hopper here.' She unconsciously rubbed her stomach. 'Anyway, we've arranged to meet for a decaf and compare notes next week.'

'What woman?' Clark replied, picking up the bottle of Evian at Pol's feet and taking a slug.

'You know, I told you last time I met her. After the twelve-week scan ... God, what's her name? Honestly, I think my brain cells are transferring directly to the baby – I can't remember anything these days.'

Clark grinned indulgently. 'You didn't tell me you met anyone before. Don't worry, baby, it's not important. It'll come back to you eventually.'

Polly sighed in exasperation. This was ridiculous. Her brain was mush. Only that morning she'd found her toothbrush in the oven. And she hadn't even realised that she *had* an oven. Twice this week she'd forgotten Mum's phone number even though she called it every day of her life. Repeatedly. She concentrated furiously.

'You know, the finance department. The director. Miss Haven. Of course, that's it! Cassandra Haven!'

Squelch! Confused, Polly looked down at the damp patch spreading on the front of her hot pink low-slung Juicy Couture dance pants. Either her waters had broken and squirted upwards or Clark had just splurted a mouthful of Evian water all over her.

'Clark . . .?'

Chapter Nine

Clark Dunhill – The Truth

Clark entered the classroom.

'Ah, Mr Dunhill,' the middle-aged teacher with the unfortunate perm greeted him. 'Lovely to see you. You're just in time – we've just finished for the day.'

He smiled and nodded his affirmation. If they were really quick they might even get to Burger King for a quick snack before going home to Polly's organic, non-genetically modified, perfect balance of protein, fat and carbohydrate meal. He couldn't believe how well she cooked now, considering that when they met she thought a microwave was a brief goodbye.

Clark turned to face a sea of expectant faces. Home time was always the best part of the day for the kids.

'Right then, let's be off,' he said.

In the back left-hand corner, an impossibly cute little boy stood up. He was the image of his father. Jet-black hair, long black eyelashes, and already the beginnings of a jaw line that could crack granite. Clark's heart swelled. The boy lifted his Louis Vuitton backpack and started to walk towards him.

'Coming, Dad.' He grinned. That was Polly's smile. His gorgeous Pol.

Just then there was another bang as another seat folded up and a blonde vision in pink threw her calculator, palm pilot and logarithms manual into her briefcase. Clark smiled again.

'Coming, Dad,' she announced. Another indulgent smile from Clark.

A few seconds later, another bang. Then another. Then another. One by one, like some bizarre human version of a domino-dropping world record attempt, every seat in the room folded up and the six-year-old who had been sitting on it gathered their belongings and marched towards him.

'Coming, Dad.'

'Coming, Dad.'

'Coming, Dad.'

'Coming, Dad.'

Clark catapulted to a bolt upright position and clawed at his chest in an attempt to remove whatever was crushing it so hard that his ribs were cracking. His breathing now came in short, shallow rasps, like a diver who'd run out of oxygen a hundred feet below the surface and had shot back up, breaking through the surface the very instant before his lungs exploded.

The dream again. With trembling hands he wiped the sweat from his face with the sheet. It was saturated.

The dream. He was tortured. In the semi-darkness he reached out for Polly, but the other side of the bed was empty. His heart raced. In the semi-darkness his eyes frantically searched around the room looking for some sign of familiarity.

With a crashing pain, he realised everything. He knew where he was. He knew why Polly wasn't there. And he knew why he'd had the dream again.

The one that was coming almost every night now.

The one that started on the day she came home from her 35-week scan.

Only that morning, Clark had congratulated himself on his handling of the whole situation. It was a frequently used saying in his profession that 'problems were opportunities to shine', and if he did say so himself, such was his glow that he could deflect ships away from the entire south-east coast. Yes, life wasn't bad. It wasn't too bad at all, he thought smugly.

OK, so he was in a relationship with a woman who was going to have his child. And yes, that was the last thing on earth he could possibly have wanted just a few months before. But in the weeks since Fiz had broken the news with an accompanying right jab, his world hadn't quite crashed into the pit of despair that he'd anticipated.

In the days after he and Pol had made the announcement to her parents, he'd experienced a major paradigm shift. Somewhere in among his sleepless nights, panic attacks and overindulgence in every mind-altering substance he could legally get his hands on (he'd soon given that up when he realised he was beginning to suffer from acute paranoia – he could have sworn someone was following him and it had started to freak him out), it had slowly but very definitely dawned on him that this whole turn of events was actually an opportunity for advancement. It was a master stroke – a veritable jackpot.

From a professional perspective, a business relationship with Kenneth Kent would get him further up the corporate ladder than another dozen deals at SySol. The connection combined with his natural skills and talents (vast as they were) would put him into the big leagues. The stratosphere of the corporate world. The guys would be so jealous. Even Taylor with his never-ending supply of bucks and babes would be put firmly into second position on the success grid.

And as if that weren't enough, there were some other definite bonuses. The biggest one being that he was now officially trendy. Wasn't a baby the latest status symbol? Wasn't it fashionable to be in a relationship and be family-orientated? He allowed himself a satisfied grin. Two words. David. Beckham. He leaned over the bathroom sink and pulled his toothbrush from the cabinet. When he closed it, he checked his reflection in the mirror. Actually, if it wasn't for the different hair colour he and Becks could be brothers. He practised his simultaneous eyebrow raise and devilish grin. He kissed the mirror – oh baby, he still had it.

Anyway, yeah, a baby. Admittedly it had taken him a while to get used to the idea, but he was well into it now. How cool was this babe going to be? Pol's and his looks, his charm, the Kent fortune to inherit when he (it was definitely male, he'd decided) was twenty-one. The boy had it made. And so had he.

Yup, this whole situation had a few definite plusses (apart from the fact that he was now more than ever a style icon). There was the fuck-off pad in Belgravia that daddy Kent had given them. Now that *was* impressive. How many other guys of his age had managed to achieve that, eh? Apart from Becks.

Then there was the entry to the most exclusive golf clubs, hospitality boxes at every major football ground, the permanent availability of the best tables at the top restaurants, the free weekend breaks in the Kent hotels throughout Europe . . . the list of perks that being associated with that family could bring was never-ending.

And, of course, he had a gorgeous girlfriend, who, granted, was now on the wrong side of chunky, but had been a complete revelation. He had expected Polly to turn into a demanding, mood-swinging jailer, but to his surprise she had actually been more laid-back than ever. It was almost as if having a child was taking up so much of her head space that she didn't have time to start making demands on him.

Thus, as many nights out with the blokes (or should he say 'bloke' – where *was* Nick anyway? He still hadn't seen or heard from him since that night in the Shaker when he'd done a bunk in a strop) as he wanted. There was no harm at all if he occasionally, all right regularly, said that he'd be late home due to 'working' and instead popped out for a beer. Polly wasn't exactly going to waddle in and check on him, was she?

To his surprise, though, he'd discovered that he wasn't interested in any of the usual chicks who threw themselves at him. His shag-alert must have moved upmarket now that he was almost one of the Kent family.

And anyway, it all balanced out. Some nights, he'd actually caught himself bunking off early to get home and check on how she was doing. What was that all about? It was the Beckham syndrome; it was rubbing off on him. He'd be writing Pol's name in Swahili on his forearm next. Or was it Cantonese? He could do it in bubble writing and Pol would be thrilled – she thought everything he did was awesome. Who could blame her?

He had played the attentive prospective father to a T, lying on the sofa at night, her head in his lap, discussing names for their baby. Rubbing that anti-stretch-mark gunk into her belly. And letting her go on top when they indulged in some prenuptials (who knew that you could still shag when you were up the duff?). Oh the depravation. The things he did for her . . .

Admittedly, he did keep an eye on the amount of Jelly Babies she was knocking back (he didn't want to end up with a girlfriend whose arse resembled conjoined Lilos), but that was for her sake. Birds were so self-conscious about their appearance. He couldn't understand all that vanity himself.

He replaced the toothbrush and prepared the floss, mouthwash, tweezers (nothing worse than shaggy brows) his facial scrub, moisturiser, cologne and hair gel.

All in all, he knew he'd handled the whole situation brilliantly.

The first challenge had been the engagement. They'd decided on a low-key celebration (he was thrilled about that piece of masterly organisation – didn't make so much as a dent in his wallet) due to the fact that Pol was still chucking up like something out of *The Exorcist*. Uuurgh. He made himself scarce whenever that was going on and let that trollop Fiz handle it – that was what women were for.

In the end, they'd settled on dinner at Mahatma Gloves, in tribute to the fact that they'd had their first date there. Pol's folks had been a bit perturbed at that one but she'd soon talked them round when she explained their reasons – it was all for her sake, she'd insisted, and wasn't it so romantic? They'd capitulated in the end, albeit he wasn't sure that they were completely happy with onion bhajis being the first course at their only daughter's engagement celebration. Still, they got over it for their beloved Polly's sake.

It had been a bit tricky explaining to his folks that they were being invited to his engagement meal to meet his pregnant fiancée when they hadn't even been aware that he was seeing anyone. But the look on their faces when he'd told them who it was! Polly Kent! His dad nearly cried with pride. 'You've learned well, son. Looks, money and a fine pair of knockers; aye you've learned well.'

Even his mother eventually got over her initial reaction of 'Oh my God, I knew some tart would trap you into marriage some day by flushing her pills down the toilet!' It had taken about three seconds. 'Who is the slapper?' One. 'Polly who? Kent?' Two. 'Kenneth Kent? *The Kent Plaza*?' Three. Full recovery.

'Oh my word, I'll just nip in to Jean next door and tell her the good news. Then I'd better call Isa from the bridge club. And your Auntie Molly, of course. She'll be thrilled to know. Shame that boy of hers has never amounted to anything. Molly would never admit it, but I heard he sells shady jewellery for a living.'

By the time the vindaloos were served the old folks were getting on in great style. His dad and Kenneth were discussing work that was planned for the Barcelona hotel.

'Problems getting reliable plumbers out there? I think I may be able to help you with that one, Kenneth. After all, we are almost family.'

'And then when he was fifteen he did his first deal, selling Betamax videos to all his school friends.

Made hundreds of pounds. Of course, we did lose some friends over that – some people just don't understand that you can't predict the success of new technology. But anyway, we knew then that our Clark would always make us proud,' his mother warbled. At least with her at the table there was never the risk of an uncomfortable silence.

'Mum, Dad, Kenneth, Jilly,' Clark commanded their attention. 'You know how I hate to make a fuss, but I just wanted to say a few words.' This was it. His big chance to get right in there with Kenneth Kent.

'I'd like to thank you all for coming tonight to share Polly's and my happiness.' They all beamed back at him. Great start, he congratulated himself. Keep it going.

He turned and took Polly's hand. OK, here we go. *Jerry Maguire*. He'd watched it again specially the night before.

'Polly, I love you so much. You're everything I could ever want and the happiest moment of my life was when you agreed to marry me.'

They were all entranced now. His mother was sniffing and Jilly's eyes were definitely filling up. He had them in the palm of his hand. God, he was good. Here it was. It was coming. The big finish. Go Jerry.

'Polly, you complete me.'

With that he pushed the gold circle inlaid with the ten tubit-whatevers onto her finger. He must remember to bung Tam an extra tenner – the ring was fucking sensational. And so was the Tiffany's box he'd managed to snaffle from his mother's jewellery box to present it in. She had loads of them (one for every affair his father ever had – jewellery had always been Dad's way of dissipating any inkling of guilt), so she'd never notice one was missing.

Everyone burst into a round of applause as Polly leaned over and kissed him. So what if the motion of doing that had forced her to immediately sprint to the loos to relieve herself of her curry? The deed was done. Kenneth shook his hand vigorously and welcomed him to the Kent family.

He was the master. He'd fallen in a pile of crap and managed to turn it around and officially come up smelling of money. Lots of it.

He replaced the dental floss and reached for the shaving foam. Better get a move on. He'd told Pol that he was going to be in conference with a party of Eastern Europeans who were considering kitting out the entire population of their previously Russian state with PCs. She'd never ask him to give up a potential deal of that magnitude just to go see a hazy picture of what looked like a Teletubby stuck in outer space. He'd managed to avoid every one of her scans so far and he'd no intention of bucking the trend now. Another job for Fiz. Might as well get some use out of the noxious cow.

He checked his watch again. Shit, he was going to be late. Tee-off time was half past eight.

Polly let out a yelp as the water soaked through to her legs. Fiz grabbed a towel from the kitchen and dived over to her.

'What the feck happened there, Smarm Man? Bottle slip right through your fingers?'

Fortunately, from her position behind him she hadn't seen that the water had actually originated from his mouth. Unfortunately, Polly had.

'Clark, are you OK?' She swatted Fiz's towel away. 'I'm fine, Fiz. It's only water. Clark? Clark?'

He barely registered her above the drums that were

crashing in his head. Cassandra. Sandra. Pregnant. The same stage as Pol. Oh, fuck. Fuck. Fuck. Fuck. He wanted to be sick. There had to be a mistake. Of course there was. Breathe. Breathe. If Sandra was cheggers to him then he'd have known all about it by now. She'd have been right on the blower to him demanding who knew what? After all, look at the strop she got into over a borderline minor embezzlement on an expenses claim. For something as serious as pregnancy she'd have had him swinging by the balls from a tree on the new SySol Japanese roof garden (one of the perks of his Japanese deal – it had earned him mega brownie points with those who mattered).

Fuck. His breathing slipped below the verge of a heart-attack rhythm. She wasn't pregnant to him. She couldn't be. Pol had made a mistake. When had Pol been there before? Twelve weeks, eighteen weeks and twenty-four weeks? Yeah, Cass must have been there today for one of *those* scans. She must be at a different stage – Pol was confused. She didn't get anything straight these days. Only yesterday he'd found his briefcase in the shower. She was just a bit muddled, the poor bird. But then she had said that she'd seen Cass there before at, what was it, the twelve-week scan? Fuck, this was so confusing. There had to be a mistake. There just had to be . . .

He leaned over and gave Polly a kiss on the cheek. 'Have to dash out, love, won't be long. Just have to pop back into the office. Something I need to check on.'

'But you just got home, Clark. Can't it wait until tomorrow?' she asked, her voice full of disappointment.

'Sorry, hon, it's urgent. The Eastern Europeans. Just need to run a quick credit check on them – make sure that they're all above board. Don't want to be sending our kit behind the Metal Curtain if we're not going to get the dosh for it.'

Fiz tutted and shook her head. 'Iron.'

He turned to her, his face perplexed. He quickly scanned his suit.

'Why? It's not crushed.'

'No, Iron Curtain, you twat. Not that it even exists anymore. Christ, you're not the smartest chip on the circuit board, are you?'

He fought his way through London rush-hour traffic. No matter how many times he told himself that it was all just a bit of confusion on Pol's part, his heart still thundered. Eventually, he reached the SySol building. He checked the clock on the wall of the elevator. Seven o'clock. He just hoped she was still in. She would be. She was a workaholic, wasn't she? But then, if she were up the duff . . .

The lift doors opened on the thirtieth floor and he stepped out onto the monogrammed carpet. He immediately checked to his left. Yes! The light was on under her door. She was in. And if she was still working at this time, there was no way she was cheggers. Sure, Pol had had to cut back to working mornings only because she felt so exhausted all the time.

He opened the door and stepped in. Empty. Her chair was empty. Oh, crap, the light must be on because the cleaners were in or something. Maybe she was pregnant after all. Oh holy fuck no.

Then he registered movement. He turned to see a figure come out of what he presumed to be an en-suite bathroom. Poncey executive floor. What were they – too posh to pee in the communal bogs like all the rest of them?

His presence gave her a start. Sandra! She was there. Fantastic. Pol was wrong. She was in the office so she wasn't cheggers after all. His eyes scanned down her body.

So why did she have a beach ball up her jumper? Oh fuck.

She leaned back against the wall.

'Yes?'

'You're pregnant.'

'No shit, Einstein. And here's me thinking I'd just been overindulging in the Mars Bars.'

But she was flustered, he could tell. He'd seen that kind of bravado stance before – it was the same one he used when his back was up against the wall. Well, not literally against the wall. What was that word for when something wasn't really happening? Metafo . . . Never mind. Oh fuck.

Pause.

'Is it mine?'

'No.'

'Whose is it?'

'None of your damn business.' She looked angry. 'Now, if you don't mind, I've got a lot of work to do.'

'Is it mine?' he asked again.

There was a voice in his head screaming, 'She said no, that's good enough for me, let's get out of here pronto pronto, amigo,' but his feet weren't moving.

The voice started shouting again. 'What the hell's wrong with you – have you got a death wish or what? MOVE! GO! SCRAM!' But still, only his mouth moved.

'Answer me. I want the truth.' He had no idea why he was forcing the issue. He was a life prisoner and the warder had just given him a key to escape his cell, yet he was stopping to have a chat before fleeing. *Was he mad?* He just had to know if there was any potential that the new shiny bright life he was building for himself could come crashing down around him.

'It is yours.'

Crash.

'But I'm only telling you because I promised someone important that I would. Don't take this personally, Clark, but I want nothing to do with you. Nothing. I don't want your money, or your name. I don't want you turning up on a Sunday and trotting off with your offspring for a Happy Meal. This is my baby, Clark. Only mine.'

'How did it happen?' was all he could say.

'What, like you want me to draw you a diagram?'

'Do me a favour, Sandra,' he spat through gritted teeth, 'and stop being a patronising bitch. I don't know what makes you think you're on some kind of moral high ground here being as you were every bit as up for it as I was. You know what I meant. Contraception. Or the lack of it. Not that it matters much now, but humour me. After all, isn't that what you were doing all along?'

Cassandra sighed wearily and sat down behind her desk. Then she obviously thought better of it and moved to a leather sofa that sat against one wall. Clark moved to the matching chair that faced it, separated only by a low glass coffee table.

'Your girlfriend's pregnant too.' It was more of a statement than a question.

Clark nodded his head. He still couldn't believe this was happening to him. He felt like, what was that film? *Sliding Doors*, that was it. He'd slipped into some *Sliding Doors* fucked-up parallel universe.

And he desperately wanted to get out of it.

'OK, Clark, the truth. But you may be sorry you asked.'

It was like a horror movie unfolding before him. As she spoke, the words took a few seconds to enter, unravel and reformat in Clark-speak in his brain, causing a time delay in the conversation. It was like a transatlantic phone call in the eighties.

But slowly, gradually, he understood. She'd done it deliberately. She wanted a baby, her biological clock was thudding, so she picked the first guy she came across and it just happened to be him. Wasn't that just his Donald fucking Duck? He'd been in the wrong place at the wrong time. And he'd been stupid enough to think she actually fancied him. He could, he realised, have been Attila the fucking Hun and she'd still have shagged him. This was a nightmare. A living sodding nightmare.

His stomach churned like a cement mixer on overdrive. Similar to the one Kenneth Kent would use to mix up the concrete for the boots he'd put him in before launching him over Putney Bridge. He wanted to cry.

He noticed that she'd stopped speaking. So where did all this leave them? What would he do now? He couldn't make sense of any of this – couldn't even start to try to function. His brain had shut down and was currently applying for a transplant to another body – one that hadn't made a roaring disaster of his life.

'I'm sorry, Clark. No, that's not true. I'm not sorry that any of this happened.' He watched her smile at her stomach as she rubbed it. That was his baby in there. His *other* baby.

'I'm glad and grateful that I'm pregnant,' she

continued, 'But I am sorry I interfered in your life.'

Sorry? She'd chewed him up, spat him out and she was *sorry*?

'You bitch.' But he didn't say it in anger. It was a resigned, stunned observation.

She nodded her head.

'Leave now. Please.'

He got up. At the door he briefly looked back, words on the tip of his tongue, but refusing to leave it.

He slammed the door. Confrontation over. Just like his life.

Clark Dunhill, Shagmeister. RIP.

In a catatonic trance, he walked out of the SySol building and straight over to the Shaker. Turning corners would have been out of the question in his condition. Besides, he had nowhere else to go. He couldn't go home. He had already given up his flat in anticipation of the move into the Belgravia pad the following day. In the meantime he was staying with Fiz and Pol and three was definitely a crowd.

He couldn't got to Taylor's – he was in the Bahamas. Or Fiji. Or somewhere else with palm trees.

There was definitely no way he was going to his parents. He couldn't get within a mile of his mother without her twittering on about her mother-of-the-groom outfit and how Isa from the bridge club was sick with jealousy – her boy was only a second chef in a high-street restaurant. *And* he was still single. Poor woman, she was having trouble sleeping at nights for the worry of it. Anyway, turquoise or lavender for her shoes?

He ordered a drink at the bar: Jack Daniels, straight, on the rocks. This was no time for bubbles.

Ignoring the wary stares of the scattering of drinkers who had only before seen his manic expression on the face of movie serial killers, he sought out a chair in the back corner of the room.

He knew he should be angry, furious, apop . . . he couldn't remember that one. Just really, really insanely outraged by the whole situation. And he was. So how come he wasn't still over there screaming and shouting? What was the point? She'd only call security, the evil cow.

Two babies. He was going to be the father of two children. This was just too big, too crazy, too unbelievable. And there was absolutely nothing he could do to change it. He thought back to all the nights he and Pol had sat imagining what their baby would be like.

Polly. Christ, what was he going to do? Just carry on like before? Just pretend that none of this had happened? Go home to Pol and act like he'd made a few phone calls from work, sorted out the Eastern Europeans and everything was hunky-dory? Why not? There was no way he wanted to hurt her. And letting her in on this little fiasco is exactly what that would do. She'd be devastated.

'Hi Pol, meet the female I shagged behind your back. Oops, that's right, you've actually already met when you were comparing baby scan photos. Did the little chaps look alike? Well, they should do – they're related.'

He ordered another Jack Daniels from a passing waitress.

He couldn't do it. He knew he couldn't keep this from her. He'd be waiting his whole life for the tap on the shoulder that would blow the whole thing sky-high. How many other people knew that Sandra's baby was his? If they could bump into each other at the doctor's then who could say where else they'd meet. What if they met after the babies were born? What if the kids looked alike? What if someone who knew Sandra was gossiping to someone who knew Pol and the truth was spilled? What if Pol heard all this from some stupid bastard with a big mouth?

It was ironic, he realised in a unique moment of brutal clarity. All that time he thought he was being Jack the Lad, scoring points against the guys and stacking up his reputation for being the ultimate casual shagmeister, and all the while he was being shafted.

He downed the Jack Daniels before the waitress even got it as far as the table. 'Keep them coming,' he ordered. She checked him out like she was trying to ascertain if he was for real. Only dickheads and guys in movies came out with lines like that. And this wasn't a movie.

He had to hand it to her. Cassandra, that is. She was good. He'd been well and truly stitched up. But then he'd left himself wide open to it. Shagging her without a condom – was he mad? And why did Polly's face keep coming into his head? And why was she crying?

He downed another drink.

He was going to have to tell her. He owed her that. He'd have to tell her everything. It was the least she deserved. She was too nice a person to get all this from someone else.

Another glass clinked down on the table, then slid in front of him.

'Hear we've got a run on Jack Daniels over in this corner.'

He raised his head wearily.

'Oh please, Fiz, don't take this personally, but fuck off. On a scale of one to a million of who I want to bump into tonight you're round about, oh, a million. Goodbye.'

Couldn't a guy even get suicidal in peace? Was there no privacy in this world? And why did she have to be working tonight of all nights? Par for the course, Clarky, par for the shagging course, mate, he told himself in a wallow of self-pity.

'You're going to have to tell her,' Fiz said quietly. Not threateningly, not furiously, just in a calm, succinct tone that begged no contradiction.

'Save it, Fiz, I know. I'd worked that one out for myself. I just hadn't worked out how.'

Just when he thought it couldn't get any worse. How far removed was he from reality that he was sitting here having a civilised conversation with the daughter of Satan? Maybe he was already dead. That was it! He was already dead and it was, like, Patrick Swayze, Demi Moore . . . *Ghost*! That was it. Or maybe he just needed another Jack Daniels. Bottle, not glass.

'How do you know?' he asked wearily. He wasn't even sure that she did, but the way things were going it was a fair bet.

'Your reaction, tonight, in the flat. I already knew you'd got up to no good a while ago with someone from work, behind Pol's back. Don't ask how.'

He didn't. What did it matter?

'When you reacted the way you did tonight it was easy to put two and two together and get one two-timing bastard with two girlfriends up the pole. Are you still seeing her?'

'I never was. She was a one-night stand, more or less. On a business trip months ago.'

'I think I can work out exactly when it was. Pretty much to the day actually.' Fiz pointed out the obvious. 'Here's the deal, Smarm. I've covered up for you until now because Polly loves you. Lord knows, I'll never understand why, but she does. And I love her, so I'd never do anything to hurt her. But she needs to know this. I won't have her humiliated. So you tell her and you tell her soon, or else I'll do it for you. Capeesh?'

The Godfather. Parts 1, 2 and 3.

'Capeesh.'

Polly was lying in bed when he got home reading a book. Marian Keyes. He knew it was her favourite. He stared at her for a minute. She was so beautiful, lying there in her tartan pyjamas that barely covered her stomach.

The Jack Daniels was making him maudlin.

He would miss her. His stomach contracted again and the pain mutated from emotional to acutely physical. When had he started to care about her so much? When had she gone from being just a bit of a challenge to someone that he looked forward to going home to at night? And how could he do what he was about to do to her?

He almost wished her father's heavies would appear now and take him off before he had to face her.

She sensed him there and looked up from her book. She smiled.

'Hey, you,' she said lazily. 'Your baby was missing you. Did you get everything sorted out?'

The question confused him. Sorted out? Did she know already? So why was she still being nice to him? Then he realised, she still thought he'd gone to deal with a work problem. He couldn't speak. He knew that when he did, everything would change forever. And he wasn't quite ready for that yet.

'Clark?' His silence unnerved her. As did his appearance. 'Clark, what's wrong?' More urgently this time.

He went over to the bed and sat down on the edge of it. He lifted her hand.

'Pol, I've got some stuff to tell you. And before I start, you have to know that I'm sorry. I really am, Pol. I'm so sorry.'

He watched as her lip began to tremble and her skin paled. She knew it was bad. And, he realised, however bad she thought it was, the reality was even worse.

He told her everything. The bet. The beauty. The brains. Cannes. Having sex with Cassandra. The proposal being a reaction to Fiz telling him she was pregnant. And then, today's discovery. That Cass was also carrying his child. He didn't bother telling her the circumstances of the seduction. What was the point? Sandra's motivations would be of no interest to her – it was his reaction to them that mattered. He had slept with another woman. And now it had come back and bitten him on the arse.

Interspersed between every episode he recounted was the word 'sorry'.

'I've destroyed everything, Pol. It all just got so out of control. I'm so sorry. I'm just so, so sorry.'

Pol never said a word. She sat like she was cast in stone, her eyes wide with terror, tears pouring from them. Then her body started to shake. And she said one word. No. Over and over again, like she was trying to deny what she knew was the truth. Just no. It was almost a whimper. A whispered exclamation of disbelief.

He reached out to hold her but she pushed him away. She was like a wounded animal lashing out with one last kick at the beast who'd attacked her.

Slowly, she put her hand out in front of her, staring at the ring that he'd slipped onto her finger only a few months before. She inched it off her swollen fingers by rocking it from side to side.

'Keep it, Pol. Please. It's yours.'

She shook her head. 'I want nothing.'

'No, please, keep it. It's not real anyway.' Oh Christ, he hadn't meant to say that. He just wanted her to keep it and thought that if she were under the impression that it was valuable then she'd want to return it. He knew how proud she could be. But now, it just summed up their whole relationship. It was fake.

'I know,' she whispered.

'What?'

Through quiet sobs, she continued. 'I know it's not real. I found out when I tried to insure it. But I didn't care. I just assumed that you couldn't afford a real one. And it didn't matter. All that mattered was that you bought it for me. That you loved me enough to want to marry me.'

She dropped it in his hand.

'Now get out. Leave my baby and me alone. And take your ring with you. Don't ever come near us again. Understand?'

Twice in one night. Twice in one night he'd been ejected by women with large stomachs. He didn't want to leave. He couldn't let her lie here on her own.

Right on cue he heard the door opening then closing again. He turned to see Fiz in the doorway. She immediately sussed out the situation.

'He's told you?' she asked Polly. Pol nodded, then turned back to Clark.

'I said get out.'

Fiz stepped forward. John Wayne. Every movie he was ever in.

'You heard the lady. I think it's time you were leaving.' Followed closely by, 'Why don't you feck off back to that bitch Haven.'

For the first time in his working life, he called in sick to work. You could say what you wanted about Clark Dunhill (and these days he reckoned everyone had something to say about him) but he was a grafter. And look where it had got him.

The seventh floor of an anonymous hotel, full of briefcase-carrying suits in the centre of London, with only the clothes he stood up in. Or rather, lay down in.

He'd been pretty much horizontal since he'd checked in the week before. The only time he pushed himself into a vertical position was to answer the door to room service, sign a receipt for food that he'd only push around his plate and drinks that would vanish within minutes of him closing the door. The minibar had long since been emptied and he hadn't allowed access to the housekeeping staff to refill it. They might try to talk to him and the last thing he felt like was idle chit-chat.

On the second night the porters had obviously tossed a coin to see who had the unfortunate job of asking the weird guy in room 707 for his credit card as the management were getting a bit edgy about the size of his bill. But they needn't have worried. The door opened six inches and an American Express Gold Card was thrust towards them, with a mumbled, 'Just keep it.'

The hotel back-of-house rumour mill was going haywire. He was a stockbroker whose fraudulent deals had just crashed a major bank in the City. No, he was the late Pablo Escobar's second cousin and he was being hunted by a Colombian hit squad for trying to muscle in on the wrong territory. Actually, he was an undercover cop with an alcohol problem who was on a stakeout of a supposed arms stash in the building opposite.

Strangely, no one hit pay dirt: that he was a duplicitous reptile who'd been rumbled and was now swimming in a Jack Daniels-filled pool of self-pity.

His mobile phone had rung incessantly until eventually the battery went dead. He didn't care. Who would possibly be calling that he would want to talk to?

After a couple of days, the alcohol stopped having a numbing effect and against all his wishes his head started to clear. It was what he had been trying to avoid – thinking was right down at the bottom of his Things To Do list. He much preferred oblivion. But it was no use. The brain cells were kicking in. They were sick bastards who were revelling in reliving the events of the last few months. It was torture. And then the dreams had started.

How had his life come to this? He was Clark Dunhill! He was the man! How had he managed to fuck up quite so catastrophically? He'd lost Pol. He'd lost Cass (his slightly demented brain failed to recognise that he'd never actually *had* her to begin with – at least not in anything other than the biblical sense). He'd lost his flat. He'd have to leave his job – both girls worked at SySol so there was no way he could stay there now. He'd lost everything. Everything. It churned over and over in his mind.

He had nothing left. Except probably a contract on his head and a team of East End heavies ready to execute it. Or him.

Everything was gone. On the eighth day, he realised what was hurting him most. If he were honest with himself, he'd probably known it all along. There was only one thing he cared about getting back. And he had to do it now.

He picked up the telephone on the bedside table. The hotel operator came on the line.

'Can I help you?'

'Er, yes. Can you tell me what time it is? I've lost my watch.'

The girl on the other end smiled with glee. She had a tenner on him being a basket case who'd escaped from the Priory. Looked like she was right on the money.

'It's seven forty-five, sir. P.m., that is.'

'Thanks. Can you arrange a cab for me? I'll be down in five minutes.'

He replaced the phone and scrambled upright.

He pulled the cord hanging from the ceiling in the bathroom and squinted as the light went on. For the first time in living history, he didn't even check his reflection. He just grabbed his jacket and shoes from the bath (*why* had he thrown them in there again?) and pulled them on. His left shoe stuck and he reached inside it to investigate the obstruction. His watch. Two thousand pounds' worth of Rado had spent the last week nesting in the insole of a Prada lace-up. He shoved it in his pocket.

As he walked through the foyer, he didn't even notice that the hotel seemed to be incredibly well staffed. And that every member of the staff was staring at him with unbridled curiosity.

As he exited the building, cash began to swap hands – all of it going in the direction of Martha on the switchboard. She was right. He was definitely a Priory escapee.

He alighted from his cab and entered the familiar building. It took only a few seconds to reach the right floor. He thrust open the door, causing the female inside to shriek.

'Clark? Holy shit, you look awful. And you scared the crap out of me. What's going on? Why are you here?'

'I know you don't want to see me, but I had to talk to you. You see, I've been thinking. I've fucked things up so badly, but I need to try to sort everything out. Well, not everything, just the important stuff.'

The woman in front of him still looked horrified at his arrival.

'Will you be getting to the point of this outburst any time soon?'

'I'm getting there. The thing is . . .'

Long pause.

'The thing is, Cass, I've realised we're meant for each other. We're meant to be together.'

Chapter Ten

Cassandra Haven – The Promise

Cass watched her massive stomach lurch from side to side. It looked like two people shagging under a blanket. Or someone getting dressed in a small tent. Or a woman with huge breasts' jumper when she jogs. She still found the visual image and the constant movement in her belly difficult to reconcile with the reality that it was an actual human being in there. A baby.

Her baby. The effect that had on her varied from a warm and bubbly glow to scaring the crap out of her, depending on her hormones, fatigue level and back pain.

That day, the morning of her 35-week scan, it was scaring the crap out of her. And it wasn't just fear of the impending excruciating pain that would come with getting this child from its warm and comfy womb to the outside world, although it had to be said that prospect wasn't exactly filling her with glee (drugs, lots of them, and then some more – that was her birth plan so far), it was more the prospect of coming face to face with the mother of her child's brother or sister. Christ, it was confusing.

Polly. She was filled with dread at encountering

Polly. Or even worse, God forbid, the demon shagger himself would be there. That didn't even bear thinking about. What kind of fucked-up waiting room would that be?

No, hopefully it wouldn't happen. She'd already postponed her appointment twice in two weeks to avoid a meeting. Polly would have had her scan ages ago. There was no way she'd be there. Please God.

The night before she'd had a nightmare so vivid that when she woke she was trembling. It had been horrific. The terrifying scenario played itself back in her head . . .

A white-coated receptionist (blonde backcombed big hair, red lips, scarlet nails, white figure-hugging uniform unbuttoned to the Wonderbra) struts out from the doctor's room, looking dishevelled and guilty. She addresses the room.

'Next, the Dunhill baby please.'

Both Polly and Cass stand up. Polly turns and gasps in horror at Cass. In the middle of them, Clark puts his head in his hands.

'It's my turn. Mine is the Dunhill baby,' Polly spits furiously.

'No, it's MINE,' Cass counters.

Suddenly, a baby's head pops up from under Polly's Laura Ashley smock. Only it isn't strictly speaking a baby. It has Jack Nicholson's face, a twelve-inch cigar in its tiny right hand, and that slow, biting Nicholson drawl.

'Look lady, the tart said "Dunhill". You got wax in your ears? Now sit back down and we'll go easy on you.'

Just at that a tiny head forces its way up through Cass's cashmere Nicole Farhi cardigan. It's another baby. But it bears a terrifying resemblance to Danny DeVito.

'Hey you, watch your mouth. A little respect for the mama here please,' he demands in a broad New York accent. 'Any more than that and I'll have to get The Daddy to sort you out, you hear what I'm saying?'

'Yeah, right,' Baby Jack replies. 'Like, I'm shaking in my fluid over here. I don't care who your dad is, pal, but mine would kick his ass. So put that in your umbilical cord and smoke it.'

DeVito spits his dummy. Literally.

'Why, you wise guy!'

Nicholson's head swivels round to Clark, his head still in his hands like he's trying to make himself invisible.

'Dad, are you going to let him talk to us like that? Get him, Dad, get him, get him.' He screams.

'Hey you, you deranged mutt – you've obviously been smoking too many of those big brown things. That's my dad. Tell him, Dad. Tell him he needs to give up the weed, man.'

'Don't you talk to my dad like that,' Nicholson yells, going purple in the face now.

'Why, you dirty son of a . . .'

At that both babies leap from their mothers' anatomies and charge at each other. When they meet there's a total combustion as they both disappear into a cartoon cloud of smoke, just the occasional limb protruding as they fight it out, accompanied by loud yells of indignation and screamed insults.

The nurse starts to file her nails, obviously bored. Judging by her lack of reaction this evidently happens on a regular basis.

Cass starts to panic. That's her child in there! She

can't be sure but she thinks by the sounds of it that he's winning. No matter. She has to put a stop to it. She grabs the nearest fire extinguisher and pulls out the safety pin. She aims it at the moving cloud of baby boxers and lets rip. A thick fog fills the room and when it eventually clears . . .

She had no idea what happened when it cleared – that was when she woke up. In a sweat, with a heartbeat that could have kept a crowd of ravers going ballistic for hours. She immediately grabbed the phone and desperately punched in numbers.

'Jeff, I had the dream again,' she panted.

'I guessed that,' he answered sleepily. 'Even you wouldn't call at four a.m. just for a chat.'

'Oh, right. Sorry. Didn't look at the clock. Anyway, I think you were right. It's guilt. What if the kids meet? What if they play against each other at football and kick the crap out of each other? Or what if, God forbid, one is a girl and one is a boy and they hook up together? Christ, Jeff, we're not creating babies here, we're creating a fucking Oprah show.'

Silence.

'I'm actually surprised he hasn't come crashing in yet. Maybe Polly didn't recognise me at the clinic last time. She only spoke to Toni and she wouldn't know that Antonia and I were sisters. Or perhaps she did recognise me but didn't tell him. Or maybe she did tell him and he's fled the country. I must check payroll and see if he's done a bunk – we're sure to have stopped his wages if he has. Or perhaps she recognised me, told him and he has just decided that he wants nothing to do with it. I mean, who could blame him? He's probably shitting himself waiting for the CSA to contact him at any minute. No, there's no way he knows. He'd definitely have shown up by now.'

There was a loud yawn at the other end of the line. Obviously her familiar, oft-repeated analysis of the situation wasn't stimulating enough to keep Jeff awake.

'Jeff? What do you think?'

'You know what I think, Cass. You have to tell him. And you have to do it soon. He has a right to know. You promised that you would.'

'I know, I haven't forgotten. I will tell him. I will.' Her voice tailed off.

Even though he couldn't see her, she slowly nodded her head. He was right. She knew it. But doing it was another matter. Just look how she'd reacted to meeting Polly on the day of their twelve-week scans . . .

'Cass, Cass, can you hear me? Wake up, Cass. Come on Cass, wake up.'

The words slowly sank into her brain but in a jumbled formation. She was suffering from dyslexic hearing. She struggled to make sense of it. It was just as confusing as the force ten gale that was wind-blasting her face.

Summoning every ounce of energy, she levered her eyes open just a fraction, to see Antonia frantically waving a handbag in her face (that explained rapid movement of air), chewing her lip and looking panicked.

'Oh, thank Christ! The ambulance is on its way, Cass. I called it from your mobile.'

'Cancel it,' Cass groaned. 'I'm fine. I don't need an ambulance.'

'Cass, you fainted! You're pregnant! You need to be examined to make sure everything is OK. You don't just keel over for no reason.'

Cass didn't want to tell her that there actually had been a reason. A pretty good one too. It had been the shock: the shock of learning that the beautiful female who'd been no more than twenty feet away from her in the clinic waiting room was carrying a baby fathered by the same man as her impending child. Christ Almighty, that had taken the wind out of her sails. And her lungs. Talking of which, she'd kill for a ciggy. Maybe if she lay there long enough a passer-by might cast away a half-smoked Marlboro and she could have a quick suck.

'I just stood up too quickly, that's all. Haven't drunk enough water today. Dehydration. A bottle of Volvic and I'll be doing the Locomotion all the way home.'

Her joviality didn't pacify Florence Nightingale.

'I don't care, Cass. You need to be checked over. We're going to the hospital and that's the end of it.'

Cass's lucidity and power of speech were returning to full strength now. As was her phobic aversion to fuss, drama and being the centre of attention.

'Look Antonia, I'm fine. Perfect. Tip-fucking-top. And I'm not going to hospital.'

And there was no way she was going the two hundred yards back into the clinic either.

Bee-baw-bee-baw-bee-baw.

Cass groaned. What were the chances of that? The press was chock-full of reports about how the NHS was in crisis, the ambulance service was on its knees, response times were down to about a week and a half for a 999 call in central London, and what happens? She has to get the medical equivalent of 'lunch in fifteen minutes or you don't pay the bill' – the paramedic superheroes were charging to her rescue in an unprecedented display of efficiency. Shite.

Two green overalls bolted out of the van and were by her side in seconds. Behind them came two tatty-looking guys, one balancing a camera on his shoulder, the other holding a long stick which appeared to have a badger attached to the end of it. A movie crew. That explained the astounding alacrity of the service.

Antonia gave them the rundown – Cass was too busy dying of embarrassment.

'She fainted, was unconscious for about five minutes and now she's a bit disorientated and very irritable. Actually, she's always irritable so perhaps that's not a symptom . . .'

Cass tuned out. The shame of it. Lying in the middle of a street, in a scene straight out of *Casualty*.

The guy in the green overall who looked like he should actually be changing tyres in Kwik-fit started firing questions at her.

'Are you feeling any pain?'

One big one. In the arse. She shook her head.

'How many fingers am I holding up?'

'Three. Surely in your job you should be able to count that high by yourself.'

'And she's twelve weeks pregnant.' Antonia was still listing the background details.

'Twelve weeks? Have you been experiencing a lot of vomiting?'

Cass nodded. 'Copious amounts.'

The guy from Kwik-fit adopted a pensive expression then fired another dozen questions at her, before sitting back on his heels and checking that the camera crew were getting his best side.

'I think you're just dehydrated,' he said in his best medical authority voice.

Cass turned to Antonia.

'Told you.'

'But we should probably take you in just to have you checked over. We'll just get a stretcher.'

That was it! Cass was not, no way, over her dead, pregnant, dehydrated body, going to get hoisted onto a stretcher and carted away in the back of an ambulance. It didn't get more mortifying than that.

'Stop!' she yelled at the top of her voice, before scrambling to her feet and dusting down her skirt (only Cass would wear a Jaeger navy two-piece suit with coordinating accessories in mauve to a medical appointment on her day off).

'I am FINE! I am perfectly all right. I am NOT going to hospital and if you want to get me on that stretcher you're going to have to kill me first. And I'll sue your ass off if you do that! So please, thank you for your concern. You've been fantastic. I'm cured. Now I just want to go home. Any objections?'

It was said in a tone that suggested that any objections had better be backed up by witness statements, scientific evidence and offered while wearing a crash helmet and a bulletproof vest.

'Well, actually I do think ...'

There was always one, Cass thought. One bloody hero.

'STOP!'

They got the message.

They made her sign a form saying she was a stubborn cow and was completely ignoring their advice and pissing off home. Or something like that.

As she turned to leave the guy with the stick up the badger's botty approached her.

'Excuse me. We're actually making a training video here and we need your permission to include this if we choose to. Could you just sign here, please?'

She gave him an incredulous gaze. This guy wanted to preserve her moment of utter mortification for training purposes? And the worst thing was she knew that they'd include it in the 'How to Deal with Aggressive Patients' section. Either that or it would end up on *You've Been Framed*.

She shook her head in refusal and pushed the clipboard away, then grabbed Antonia's arm. 'Come on Tone, let's get out of here before—'

It almost slipped out: the one thing that had been sitting at the front of her brain since she woke up in the gutter. She had to get away before she bumped into *that* woman again.

'Before I faint again due to embarrassment.'

Too late. As Cass turned she saw the tall dark beauty walking towards them, her arm threaded through her friend's. Cass averted her face in the hope that they wouldn't see her, but she needn't have worried – they were far too deep in conversation to even register the chaotic scene before them. How single-minded must they be to ignore a crowd, an ambulance, a camera crew and a walking wounded? Then she noticed the tears streaming from the girl she now knew was Polly Kent.

'Oh, Fiz, that was so awesome,' she sobbed. 'I just can't wait to tell Clark.' She held up a small square photo in front of her. 'Look at our baby, Fiz. God, Clark is just going to be totally blown away.'

If only they knew, Cass couldn't help thinking. They'd be blown away in more ways than one.

*

Antonia arrived at the flat with plenty of time to spare before they had to leave for the final scan. It astounded her to see her sister clearly agitated. This last few months had been a revelation to her in more ways than one. If anyone had told her a year before that her sister would now be pregnant to a person unknown and that she herself would be employed, financially stable and madly, shaggingly in love with the most incredible guy, she'd have told them to stop taking the drugs and get help. Yet here she was: still smiling at the thought of that morning's activities, eternally grateful to her future niece or nephew for bringing her and her new love together and making herbal tea for her very fat and agitated sibling. It was a crazy world.

'Hey, sis,' she greeted Cass when she finally alighted from the bedroom. 'You look, uh, great.'

Actually, Toni thought her sister had never looked so rough. Her skin was pallid, there were dark circles under her eyes and she was emanating premenstrual-terrorist-type vibes. No mean feat for a tampon-free zone.

'Yeah, well, pregnancy is the new black. I'm a style icon,' Cass replied, her voice dripping with sarcasm. 'Do me a favour, Toni, light a ciggy.'

Antonia was confused. 'I don't smoke.'

'Then do me another favour. Nip down to the newsagent's at the corner and buy ten cigarettes. Either that or just mug a passing thug in a baseball cap and steal his. Either way, could you get back here in less than five minutes, please, with a lit cigarette in you hand.'

'I'm not giving you a cigarette, Cass, you're pregnant. It's not allowed.'

'Look, Tone, don't argue with me, OK? I'm not

going to smoke it myself; I'm just aiming for the reduced guilt of a passive sniff. It's an emergency. It's crucial. And if you don't do it then there'll be stories all round London tonight about a six-foot, twenty-stone thug who was beaten up by a pregnant psychopath for a packet of Benson and Hedges. Understand?'

Toni got up from her chair. She'd seen scenes like this before. In action thriller movies. Just before the good guys got shot.

As she made for the door, she said, 'Won't be long, Cass. And while I'm away, have a word with your hormones before they seriously damage you health.'

Cass sunk onto her sofa and lay along the length of it. Her stomach churned. For a woman who'd made it her vocation to avoid turmoil, trauma and drama, she was drowning in an amniotic pool of them now.

Cass had always thought that she was afraid of no one and nothing. She was indestructible. Fearless. Indomitable. But this time, perhaps, she had to concede that she had bitten off more than she could chew. She'd had seven months to consider it and in hindsight she couldn't believe she'd entered into this so glibly.

Not that she wanted to change the current situation i.e. being in the late stages of pregnancy. Well, maybe she'd just tweak the picture a little. Admittedly, she had slightly underestimated how daunting it would become to do this on her own.

The Cassandra Haven of old who would be quite happy to go a fortnight without a conversation with anyone other than work colleagues and cab drivers (even those were short, authoritative, direct ones) now had the occasional longing for company and reassurance.

And sometimes even, God forbid, a hug.

There: she'd said it. It wasn't that she wanted a partner of the opposite sex, as she knew that her aspirations in that department were pretty much unmatchable (a millionaire husband who would drop his business concerns in the Far East and fly home to be with her, taking charge of every little detail until the baby was born. Immediately after, he'd piss off back to Asia, corresponding only by e-mail and fax, and appearing again only when she summoned him for short visits. That, she decided, would be her perfect marital arrangement).

But if she were entirely honest she did sometimes feel a bit lonely. Another new emotion to her. She'd suddenly think about a name for the baby and want to bounce it off someone. Or have a massive hormonal surge of aggression and want to bounce the nearest lamp off someone.

Antonia, Jeff and Paul had been great, but then they had their own lives to lead and she was reticent to lean on them. Much to their annoyance of course. Especially Jeff's.

Jeff. What an amazing guy he'd turned out to be. Mr Indecision, Mr Bland, Mr Antithesis-of-Everything-That-Was-Spontaneous-and-Dramatic-in-the-World.

When he made his proposition to her on the night he'd discovered her pregnancy, she'd been dumbfounded.

'Cass, your baby can't go through life thinking that its father doesn't exist. Do you know what that thought could do to a child? Or worse, the feeling that its father didn't want it? You have to think about these things, Cass. You've got more than just yourself to consider now.'

It was a variation on the 'you're a selfish bitch' theme that Antonia had so eloquently confronted her with just a short time before.

'So, I have a proposition for you. Cass, we've been friends for the last twenty years. We'll be friends for the next twenty. And then the next.'

Christ, thought Cass, this was like a bad moment on *This Is Your Life*. Any minute now she expected to see her old maths teacher trundled out to do an 'I always knew you'd go far . . .' speech.

'And?'

'Put me on the birth certificate, Cass. Name me as the father. At least that way your child will grow up with me around and I'll always be there for him. Or her. I'm serious about this, Cass. Think about it. We'll just tamper with history a little, say it was a relationship that didn't make it but that we'll always be close.' He gave an ironic laugh. 'After all, that's almost the case, isn't it? Just the timing was about twenty years and a fertilised egg out of synch.'

'But . . .' she immediately retorted, on the verge of bursting into an incredulous tirade about how ridiculous he was being.

'Don't say a word!' He cut her off abruptly. Then softer, 'Think about it, Cass. Really think about it. For all our sakes.'

She had. Uncharacteristically, it had taken her months to decide. But inevitably she had concluded that it would be a mistake. Jeff was right, she hadn't fully considered the impact that not knowing who its father was would have on her child (there was no way on earth she would ever reveal the truth – that can of worms was staying firmly shut), but she did know that she wouldn't lie. She couldn't. She'd rather plead the Fifth Amendment and say nothing than build a child's life on a basis of untruths. Even if that was the easy way out.

Somewhere around her thirtieth week, she'd pressed the 'off' button on the DVD that she and Jeff were watching. It was crap anyway – the fact that it was starring Jean Claude Van Damme should have been a giveaway.

'Jeff, I've decided. About your proposition,' she started hesitantly.

He stared at her for a second. 'I can tell by your face that it's a "no".'

'I'm sorry. I just don't want to lie. Who knows what havoc that could cause later on down the line. What about when you get married and have kids?'

'So they'd have a stepbrother or stepsister. Or maybe I won't get married. Who knows?'

'Jeff, I appreciate what you're doing. I really do. But it wouldn't be right.'

'Well, we could try,' he blurted.

'Try what?'

'A relationship. To be together. To be a family.'

Shite, this was the last thing she expected. She had no idea that Jeff still harboured those kinds of feelings for her.

'Jeff, are you . . . are you in love with me?'

Long pause. Oh, no. He was. He still loved her. After all those years. That explained why he'd never married. Why he never made it past the second date: nobody matched up to her. All those years he'd been waiting for her to realise what was staring her in the face – *him*. This was terrible. A complete nightma—

'No.'

See, she knew it! She'd ruined his life by not recognising how he felt about her. She had been totally blind to . . . *what*? She looked at him quizzically.

'What? No?'

He smiled. 'Sorry, Cass, but I'm not. Never have been. But we are good together – we understand each other, we make each other laugh, we'd be a great balance as parents: you'd be a strict ogre and I'd be a pushover dad. Maybe we could make it work. I've always wanted to get married and have kids, Cass, and this might be my chance.'

Good Lord. She was horrified. Touched, but horrified. He was prepared to marry her, take care of her child as if it were his, and act like it actually *was* his. But then another thought overtook that one. He was settling. He was doing that thing that she read about in *Cosmo* when women in their thirties decide they want kids and marry the postman just to fulfil that need. She was his postman. He was prepared to go through with this just to have the life of domesticity that he craved.

'Jeff, that's absurd. And unfair. The child would grow up in a home where its parents showed no physical affection for each other whatsoever.'

'More unfair than telling a child that you will never reveal who its father is? Or that it was the result of a one-night stand with someone whose name you never caught?'

She shrugged ruefully. 'I don't know, Jeff. But I don't want its whole life to be a lie.'

'Then you have to tell the truth, Cass. You have to tell the baby who its father really is. Let it know where it came from. And that means you have to tell *him* too. He has a right to know if he's going to get a knock on his door in sixteen years' time. It's the least you can do, Cass. For the baby's sake.'

She nodded. He'd vocalised what she'd been mulling over and trying to deny for months. She had to tell Clark the Tosser. She had to. And soon. She slowly nodded.

'You promise you will?' Jeff probed.

Ah, shite, that's right. Pressure the fat lady. Ask her to give her word when you know she'd rather lie through her teeth about the whole thing. Even although she knew he was right.

'I promise.'

Antonia spluttered like she'd just swallowed a fur ball the size of an egg.

'Lordy, Cass, how could you do this to your lungs all those years.'

Cass wasn't listening. She was perched over Antonia's shoulders with her eyes closed, deeply inhaling the thick smoke that Toni was exhaling. It was making her feel slightly giddy. Great.

After a few moments Toni stubbed it out furiously. 'OK, that's it, you sick addict. You've had your fix, my clothes and hair stink and I feel like I've been chewing on dung. Happy now?'

Cass nodded. It had been the most enjoyable few minutes in months and it had somehow reminded her of who she was (an unreasonable cow with a cigarette addiction) and filled her with resolve. She stood up straight and took a deep breath. She could do this. She could go for this scan. Even if the unthinkable happened and Polly was there, she would handle it. She would deal with whatever situation arose. And she would *not* crumble, cry or faint. She was Cassandra Haven. She was unbreakable. She was strong. She was dying for another fag. And besides, there was no way Polly would be there. Surely.

'Hello again. Miss Haven, isn't it?' Polly said, as she exited from the doctor's room, obviously already having completed her consultation. Her sweet open face was flushed with what Cass could only imagine was the joy of impending motherhood. Crumble. Christ, what had she done to this poor girl? Polly was standing there glowing, blooming, radiating, doing all the things that pregnant women were supposed to do, including being friendly to all others in the same fat boat, and Cass harboured a secret that could bring her life crashing about her. Polly was an innocent victim in what could be about to become guerrilla warfare.

Guilt. A crushing weight of it descended on her again. Christ, now she remembered how it felt to be Catholic: feelings of guilt from the moment of birth. Christ died for you so you'd better be a good girl and get that room tidied . . .

She couldn't win. If she said nothing she'd feel guilty every time her child raised the inevitable subject of its father's identity. If she confessed all, she'd trash the girl standing in front of her. It was a lose-lose scenario.

So she had to remain distant. Cold. Polly what's-her-name's happiness was *not* her responsibility. Clark should have thought about that when he was screwing her on the French Riviera. This was his cock-up (metaphorically *and* literally), not hers. The culpability for Polly's life and future was his. Just ignore her, Cass, she told herself. Be polite, but don't encourage any form of further communication. Cut her dead.

So why, as she contemplated Polly's flush of happiness, did she feel responsible for her? Why did she want to sit her down and explain what had happened? Why did she want to try to ease the onslaught of pain that would come her way when and if Clark confessed all to her (although knowing the standard of his morals she did reckon that he might wait a decade or two to do that).

Shite, this was what they called 'maternal' feelings. They were finally kicking in. And they were all currently pointing in Polly's direction.

'Yes. Hi. How did things go?' She nodded to the room from which Polly had just alighted.

'Great. God, it's just SO exciting, isn't it? Look!'

Polly held out a print of her scan. Cass tried to swallow but the obstruction in her throat was too great. That was her baby's sibling. Shite. Shite. And again . . .

She made a play of studying it to buy her more time. Just long enough for her to remember how to form words. Her focus on persuading her mouth to function wasn't helped by the incessant foot-tapping of Polly's red-haired friend who was obviously impatient to move on.

That threw her. Polly was about to walk out of the door and she might never see her again. Antonia had already told her that during one of their chats while Polly hung around reception waiting for a cab, Polly had confessed that she had no plans to return to work after the birth.

Cass couldn't just leave it. She had to say something, find a way of keeping in touch. Control freak that she was, she couldn't bear the thought that she'd have no knowledge of what was going on in Polly's life – if Clark would tell her the truth, if Polly would then hate her, if she would have a psychotic reaction to the news and track her down with a baby over one shoulder and an AK-47 over the other. Like a mistress who is intrigued by every detail of her lover's wife, she suddenly, desperately wanted to know Polly better.

Someone was speaking. She was horrified to discover that it was her.

'Look, I don't know any other pregnant women and I thought that, since we're both at the same stage, it might be good to keep in touch. You know, compare notes.'

Polly's friend rolled her eyes. 'Aw, feck, fat women bonding alert.' Polly dug her in the ribs.

'Ignore her, she's certifiable. And yes, that would be great. Here's my number.'

She scribbled some figures on a piece of paper. Cass removed a business card from her wallet and returned the gesture.

'Great. I'll give you a buzz next week. We can go for a decaf and a slice of something really fattening.'

Polly laughed and rubbed her protruding bump. 'Like it will make a difference! I look forward to it.'

She was absolutely stunning, Cass decided as she watched her go. Just beautiful. She told Jeff that later on when he called her. She was still in the office working overtime to make up for taking the day out and trying to distract her mind from the insanity of the situation. The one that had been made even worse when she'd seen her baby's heartbeat on the screen earlier that day. To her absolute shock and horror she'd burst into tears. Hormones again. And Catholic guilt.

'She's so beautiful, you know, Jeff. Dunhill's girlfriend. It makes it even more incredible that he wanted to shag around behind her back with me.'

Jeff was stuck for an answer. He was totally aware that Cass's mood swings could be sudden, explosive and have catastrophic repercussions these days. A pizza delivery boy who'd got his pineapple and pepperoni mixed up and therefore brought her a rather Italian version of a thin and crispy Hawaiian could testify to that. He'd have had a migraine for a fortnight after the bollocking she'd given him.

And now she'd come out with one of those female trick statements where every answer would evoke a negative and possibly hysterical response. If he agreed with her statement she'd shoot into orbit and accuse him of reinforcing her belief that she wasn't attractive and desirable. If, however, he disagreed with her statement, well, that didn't even bear thinking about. Cass didn't do disagreement.

Sometimes he questioned his sanity when he had made the offer to live with her and raise the baby together. He still wished that she'd agreed to name him as the baby's father: he'd been entirely committed to that idea. But actually trying to co-habit with Cass? That suggestion had been a bit hasty. Much as he adored her, living with her would have pushed the limits of even his easygoing nature. She needed a different breed of man, he recognised. One with a bulletproof vest and a death wish.

He played a safety shot: tried to deflect the need for a response.

'Tell me about her. What's she like?'

Cass described Polly's appearance. She painted a picture of a beautiful, vibrant young woman.

'Even her name is frivolous. Straight out of a nursery rhyme. Polly.'

There was a slight pause. 'Polly what, Cass? What's her surname?'

Jeff's mind went whirring ahead. Well, maybe not exactly whirring, but it did veer slightly to the rapid, away from its normal steady, methodical, measured pace. This was a coincidence. His boss's daughter was pregnant. She was called Polly. The only reference Cass had ever made before to Dunhill's girlfriend was that she worked for SySol. Kenneth Kent's daughter worked in the City too. Jeff wasn't sure where. Ken didn't do social chit-chat. He'd worked for Ken for more than ten years and all he knew about him (other than his business concerns and history) was that he was married with a daughter and that he had almost had a stroke when he found out that she was pregnant.

Still, there had to be countless pregnant Pollys who worked in London. Hundreds. OK, at least several. A few. More than one.

Cass hesitated. 'Essex.'

Jeff derided himself as he exhaled in relief. He knew he'd been ridiculous. It was a small world but not that small. Coincidences like that only happened in soap operas and really bad movies.

'No, it's not. Wrong county. It's Kent. Polly Kent.'

And now. He was dumbstruck. Silence.

'Jeff?' Still silence.

'Aaargh. These fucking mobiles, they're useless.' He heard her banging her phone on the desk.

'It's OK, Cass. We haven't been cut off. I'm still here. Cass, do you realise who she is? Polly Kent?'

'Yeah, she's Dunhill's girlfriend. I've already told you that.'

'No, I mean apart from that. Cass, Polly Kent is Ken Kent's daughter.'

'No! *The* Ken Kent? Your boss, Ken Kent? *Sunday Times* Rich List top ten Ken Kent? What the fuck was his daughter doing working at SySol?' Her voice was getting a touch hysterical now. 'She should be spending her life on a fucking yacht somewhere! And Clark Dunhill? What could she possibly have seen in him? Shite, Jeff, this must be a mistake.'

She couldn't believe it was true. 'There's no way that anyone could be so stupid as to screw around on Ken Kent's daughter. He'd kill them! No one could be that thick. Not even Clark.'

She knew she was right. This was a coincidence. A misunderstanding.

'Oh no – Jeff, sorry but I need to pee for the twentieth time in the last hour. And there's no way you're listening to me do that so I'll call you back in a minute.'

She ran to the loo.

Ken Kent, indeed. Nope, definitely a mistake there.

She sat back down in her chair and picked up her phone to call Jeff back. Before she could press the button, though, she heard a faint noise in the corridor. Strange. She was sure the cleaners had finished on this floor. Must be security. But then, they'd popped their heads in only a few minutes before as they did their rounds. They wouldn't be back for at least another couple of hours.

When she realised who it was, she almost wished it had been a mad mugger. Clark. Polly must have told them about their meeting and the bright spark had finally managed to put two and two together.

There was only one thing for it. Lie. At first she went with her initial plan and denied, denied, denied.

But she underestimated him. She expected that

after the first rebuttal he'd be out of there with sparks coming off his heels, buying drinks all round at the Shaker in an ostentatious gesture of relief.

But he just kept on pushing her to admit the truth. And pushing. And oh, for Christ's sake, would he never let up pushing?

And all the time she knew. She had to admit what had happened. She owed it to Jeff. She'd promised him. And she also owed it to her baby.

'OK, it is yours.' Resigned. Defeated. Surrendered.

And so the nightmare became a reality. She told him everything: that she'd selected him, seduced him and used him as a sperm donor. And the not-so-insignificant point that she wanted nothing further to do with him.

His rage was almost volcanic. She was sure if she hadn't been a pregnant lady he'd have punched her. Cancel that. If she hadn't been pregnant then he'd only have been there with one thought in mind: a quickie on top of her walnut, executive, don't-mess-with-me-because-I'm-lethal corner desk.

Not for the first time, she was thankful for her condition.

His parting words to her were a bitter, 'You bitch.' Said with extra venom, hostility and a portion of abhorrence on the side.

Nice way to talk to the mother of his child. But then, she both expected and deserved it. She'd probably irrevocably changed the course of his life and not for the better. Who could blame him for being furious? Enraged. Freaked out. She was a mite tetchy herself.

'Please leave,' she asked. And he did. There was a moment at the door when he hesitated and she thought he was going to unleash another tirade on her, but mercifully he hadn't.

As the door slammed, she sank into her seat. It looked like she was getting everything she wanted. She was pregnant. She'd fulfilled her promise to Jeff by being honest. And she was pretty sure she'd never see Clark Dunhill again.

Wasn't it great when a plan came together?

Just over a week later the picture was identical: same place, same time of night, same obsessive–compulsive woman with no social life and workaholic tendencies sitting behind the same desk.

Cass looked up at the doorway of her office and gasped. One of the tramps who lived in the alley next to the building had somehow managed to get in. Shit. Where was her panic button? Her heart started to race as she fumbled under the desk, never once taking her eyes off the dishevelled figure in front of her. What a mess. His hair looked like it belonged on Macy Gray and his clothes reflected the grime of the London streets. Although, she admitted, a suit was unusual attire for a down and out. Must have been a very generous philanthropist who gave that one away.

Hold on. Under that beard, it wasn't an old guy. He couldn't have been much more than forty. And there was definitely something familiar about . . . shite, where was that panic button?

He stepped forward into the glow of her desk light and Cass gasped. Clark! Twice in a fortnight he'd appeared out of nowhere in the middle of the night and terrified the life out of her. Didn't he know she was a pregnant woman, for God's sake? Weren't you supposed to tiptoe round them, bringing them banana milk shakes, Gaviscon and benign smiles?

But then, he didn't seem like a guy who had pregnant-woman etiquette at the top of his priority list. He was a mess. He looked like he'd come straight out of rehab.

Her hand froze over the button that she had finally located. She was tempted to press it anyway just to put the wind up him the way he had done to her. Her heart was thumping – he was the last person she wanted to see and she suddenly had a desperate urge to pee again. Her bladder was crap in a drama.

She chided him for scaring her. It was her immediate reaction after deciding not to have him escorted from the premises. Rollick first, talk later.

But then came the immortal line.

'The thing is, Cass, I've realised we're meant for each other. We're meant to be together.'

That's it, she was pressing the button. He was deranged. Mentally unstable. She'd rather amputate a limb than spend the rest of her life with this man. *Wouldn't she?*

The thought distracted her. Good Lord, she couldn't believe it. For a split second there she had actually wondered if he had a point. *Could* they *be* a couple?

Then she realised that his mouth was opening and closing. That must mean he was still speaking. She switched back to what he was saying.

'We'd be great together, Cass. Two peas in a pod. Think about it! We're both self-centred, both ruthless, both act like we don't give a fuck if anyone stands in our way – we just trample right over them.'

She regretted tuning back in. The last thing she felt like doing (the first was still having a pee – it was getting desperate) was listening to a character assassination, no matter how accurate. And for the record, she was proud that she was single-minded and inexorable. These were her biggest strengths.

So how come Clark made it sound like it wasn't a good thing? Besides, if he was trying to persuade her that they should be together, shouldn't he be telling her that the sun shone out of her arse? Nasty thought. Reminded her of the whole peeing business again.

'But the thing is . . .'

Good God, was he *still* talking? Nothing like using a hundred words when ten would do. She definitely preferred him when he was the silent shagging type. This new conversational version of the Clark model was altogether draining.

'. . . Polly's not like that. She's ten times the person either of us will ever be. She'd never screw anyone over the way you did or shaft someone like I did. And that's why, even though you and I are probably meant for each other, it's *her* I want to be with. I have to get her back, Sandra. And you need to help me. It's the least you can do.'

Cass was aghast. 'Why would I possibly want to get involved in this – it's *your* problem.'

'Yeah, and you caused it. Look, I'm not denying I was a prick to shag about behind Polly's back.'

'Agreed.'

'But we hadn't been going out long and I didn't know she was pregnant. You have to admit, if you hadn't been on a mission to get your eggs fertilised then none of this would have happened. I'd have gone home, found out about Polly, we'd have made a go of it and I wouldn't be standing here in week-old clothes, smelling like a fucking skip, with nothing left except a contract on my bollocks.'

Cass nodded again. 'Yeah, I found out last week whose daughter she is. Tough luck there, Clark.'

'Thanks,' he said in an ironic tone. 'That'll be a comfort when I'm hanging upside down with an electric probe attached to my prick in a warehouse in Bethnal Green.' Then softer, 'Help me. I know I don't deserve it, but help me anyway. If you do this then you can call the shots. Not that you weren't already doing that anyway. But I'll agree to whatever you want. With the baby I mean. Just help me with Pol. Please.'

Cass groaned. Christ, he was pitiful. Standing there looking like he'd fallen in a bush then been driven over by a tractor. That pleading expression on his face. At least, the bit you could see behind the week-old stubble. He was a mess. A physical, emotional and utterly complete mess. Yes, he was still an arse, but then nobody was perfect.

She shook her head and watched as his shoulders slumped. Good grief, she had to say something before he burst into tears – that would have her opening the window and contemplating jumping.

'Hold on there, sad case. If I help you, you'll agree to anything I want?'

He nodded.

'And I presume you have some kind of action plan as to what you want me to do?'

He shrugged his shoulders. 'I don't. I just want you to get Polly to talk to us. Tell her the truth about everything. I mean, for all she knows you and I could have been having an affair the whole time she and I were together. Or that I went behind *your* back to sleep with *her*. Who knows what she's thinking? I need to make her understand that I know I fucked up but it was right at the start, it'll never happen again and I'm telling the truth. She'll only believe that if you're there to back me up.'

Cass was horrified. This was worse than being in a soap opera. This was a soap opera crossed with a talk show combined with the worst kind of reality TV. In short, it was her idea of hell. But she did acknowledge that she hadn't been entirely blameless in all this. The only one who held that moral high ground was Polly. The poor girl must be in agony. Oh shite, where did this fucking conscience come from all of a sudden? She much preferred herself when she was a complete bitch.

She sighed as she reached down and pulled the piece of paper from the front of her handbag.

'Prada,' Clark observed.

'Of course,' she replied curtly. Only he would have observed and commented on that in the middle of a life-changing experience, she mused. A man after her own heart. Maybe there was something attractive there after all.

She dialled the number on the paper. It was answered almost immediately.

'Polly?' Pause.

'This is Cassandra Haven. Look, I know that I'm probably the last person you want to speak to right now, but I think we should talk.' Pause.

'No, and I don't know where he is. That's what I want to talk to you about.' Pause.

'But surely you want to know the truth about what happened?

'Come on Polly, please. I know you probably think I don't warrant it, but I really would like a chance to explain.

'OK, fine. I understand. I'm sorry to have bothered you.'

Shit, it was no use. Polly had been very polite but she wasn't interested in raking over the situation. She sounded devastated. She could barely speak. Cass's conscience was pulled again. She had to try to fix this. She had to get Polly here, to talk to her. Not just for Clark's sake but for hers too. After all, she was the mother of the brother or sister of her son or daughter. How dysfunctional was that? But they *were* almost related.

Forgive me, Polly, for what I'm about to do, she prayed silently.

Clark's face contorted with fear and horror as Cass suddenly started to pant really loudly and emitted a loud scream of pain.

'Oh, my God,' she panted furiously. 'Polly! Polly, I think, oh my God, my waters have broken!' she screamed, then almost laughed as Clark's expression turned to something akin to revulsion and he automatically hitched up his trousers so that he wouldn't get the hems of his Armanis soaked in the flood.

'No. I'm. In. My. Office.' Cass panted through clenched teeth. 'Oh, my God,' she yelled, 'I'm . . .'

She pulled the phone from her ear and slammed it down.

She turned to Clark and gave a resigned smile.

'She'll come.'

Clark was three stages behind. She could almost hear his brain galloping to keep up with events. His eyes darted from her to the floor, back to her crotch, then to the phone.

'You mean, you faked all that?'

She nodded her head. 'It was the only way to get her here. She didn't want to talk to me. But you're right, she should know the truth. If she's as nice as you say she is then she'll be on her way here right now to find out if I'm OK.'

Clark gaped at her in wonderment.

'I never stood a chance against you, did I?'

'Nope,' she agreed. 'Not a chance.'

Chapter Eleven
Polly Kent – The F Word

First, he was decapitated. Quickly, brutally, so that he wouldn't feel any pain. Then his feet were amputated so that only stumps remained. He'd never dance again. Then, mercifully, he was put out of his misery – thrust into the abyss, where the crushers clamped down on him and pummelled him again and again until there was no trace of his existence. Nothing. Nothing to show for the pleasure he'd brought . . .

Except another inch on my thighs, thought Polly as she pulled another jelly baby out of the box and this time swallowed it whole. Poor thing.

She rubbed her stomach. Poor baby.

Tears started to form behind her eyes and she reached for the man-size super-strength box of tissues that hadn't been outwith three feet of her for the last week.

'Aw feck, not again.' Fiz spotted the familiar movement. 'What is it this time? Sympathy for the brutal death of yet another jelly baby or rogue thoughts about Smarm Man, the designer Prince of Darkness?'

In spite of herself, Polly managed a grin. She

knew that Fiz wasn't being callous. Sarcasm, insults and disparagement were just her friend's way of trying to prevent her from slipping into a paralysing depression. If she were lavished with sympathy and concern then she'd be finished. It would only fuel the pain to an even more unbearable level.

She blew her nose and popped yet another jelly baby. Fiz brought over a cup of decaf hot chocolate – just one of the components of the weekly care packages that had been Fedex'd over from Kent Castle since the discovery of Polly's pregnancy. God bless mothers – this one had Fiz's mum Patricia written all over it. It was the condoms that gave it away. Jilly would hardly have included those for her daughter, given her present condition.

'When are you going to work?' Polly asked Fiz. She hated it when Fiz left because then there were no distractions at all. Then the only thing she had to think about was the baby. And Clark. And the pain of it.

Nothing, but nothing in Polly's life had equipped her or prepared her in any way for this situation. It was excruciating. In hindsight, perhaps she had been pathetically naive, but she honestly hadn't suspected for one second that Clark was capable of this. Fiz said that that there had been more clues than in an episode of *Poirot*, but she had obviously been blind to them all.

She'd honestly thought that he wanted to keep their relationship quiet because he cared about her image at work. She'd wholeheartedly believed that he wanted to marry her and have their baby. And she'd never questioned where he was when they weren't together because she had complete faith and trust in him and their relationship. He loved her. Or so she'd thought. She swallowed another jelly baby whole. A green one. It was male, he deserved it.

Sure, she knew Clark was egotistical, and a bit on the shallow side and, yes, he did veer into a fantasy world (of the emotional *and* the physical nature she now realised), but she thought that she had seen through that to the real guy. *Her* Clark was funny and spontaneous and underneath the strutting bravado he was tender and even a little bit insecure. That's why he liked to be ostentatious and was so fastidious about his image and appearance. Wasn't it? Or was it really that he had been an arrogant megalo-maniac who would have stood on his granny if it meant he could reach a Dolce and Gabbana sweater on a high shelf?

Obviously, that was the case. She realised now that everything they'd had was a sham from start to finish. How stupid had she been? And how much did it hurt?

According to Fiz, Ray Charles could have seen this coming, so how come she hadn't? Because she'd believed him. About everything. First Giles and now Clark: was she never going to learn?

The strange thing was that she had absolutely no feelings at all towards Cassandra Haven with regards to the affair. Fiz had offered to slash Cassandra's tyres on her behalf (on account of the fact that Polly was now so big that if she squatted then she'd have to stay in that position for the rest of her pregnancy) but she'd declined. Although she had gone along with Fiz's new sobriquet for Cass – Bitch Haven – on account of the fact that Cassandra had obviously committed a crime of terrorism against another member of the female species.

However, Cassandra hadn't betrayed her. Clark Dunhill had.

The only thing that did bother her was the fact that Cassandra must have known that she was Clark's girlfriend and carrying his child (she'd discussed Clark with the receptionist at SySol whom she now knew was Bitch Haven's sister – surely she would have passed that little nugget of gossip on), yet she still tried to befriend her at the clinic. What kind of sick woman was that? Why would she possibly want to be her friend when she had slept with her fiancé on at least one occasion? Repulsive bitch. Even erratic hormones couldn't explain or defend that behaviour.

She wondered how often they had slept together. Had it been going on for years before he and Pol had met? Was it still going on now? Were they at this very moment shacked up and shagging furiously? They were, she decided. They were lying in bed this very minute planning names for their child. Bastards. The mental image made her want to throw up. No change there then.

The worst thing, though, wasn't the hurt for herself but for their baby. She'd had almost eight months of thoughts, plans and fantasies about the life the three of them would lead together. She had pictured the birth, the christening, the baby's first Christmas. First birthday ... and in every image Clark was there laughing and throwing the little bundle up into the air. Now her child would barely know her father. Judging by the way he had disappeared off the face of the earth for the last week, it wouldn't know him at all. How cruel was that?

She blew her nose again. She was devastated. She longed to go home, to sleep in her old bed and let her parents take care of her, but she couldn't run away like that. She was an adult. She was about to be a parent. It was time she stood on her own two feet. They had rushed to see her when she'd called home and sobbed out the whole story. Her father had been apoplectic and wanted to storm right round to Clark's and face him. The only problem was that there was nowhere to storm to. Clark had given up his flat the week before in anticipation of the move to their new home. The one that she'd live in alone now.

Besides, even in her heartbreak she didn't want her father fighting her battles. But her mother holding her close and stroking her hair was allowed. It was the only thing that got her through the first few days. Since they'd reluctantly left to return to the Castle they'd been on the phone at least three times every day. At least her child would have wonderful grand-parents. Even if it didn't have a father.

Only the door buzzer saved the box of sweets in front of her from being drunk down like a shot of tequila in a frantic cross between comfort eating and mass genocide of the jelly baby race.

'I'll get it,' Fiz called. 'Whoever it is will have given up and gone home by the time you manage to get your arse off that sofa.'

Polly reached for the remote control for the television. It wouldn't be anyone for her. She'd been completely reclusive for the last week and anyway none of her friends would dream of dropping in without calling first to make sure she was up to it. Must be a pizza delivery, or the Avon lady, or someone for Fiz, or . . . Miles!

Her boss was standing in front of her, holding a

huge gift-wrapped box and wearing an apprehensive expression.

He took in her appearance in a split second. The bloodshot eyes, the tear-stained, swollen face, the unwashed hair, the old cardigan wrapped round her shoulders. He decided that she had never looked more beautiful.

It was the sweetie boxes that alerted him to the trauma.

'Don't get up,' he insisted.

'Miles, I'm sorry. I'm so embarrassed. I didn't know you were coming.'

'Oh, darn, honey, did I forget to tell you? Well, there you go. Memory like a sieve. That's what I get for drinking vodka during puberty,' Fiz said in the decidedly overbright tone that she always used when she was lying.

God, did no one tell the truth anymore, Polly thought. Does the whole bloody world just revolve around people conspiring to tell lies to me? She knew why Fiz had done it. If Polly had known that Miles was coming over she'd have insisted Fiz cancel him. But even when her friends thought they were doing what was best for her, it was still bloody annoying. Wouldn't anyone let her make her own bloody mind up about things for once? She was a grown woman, for God's sake! Why did everyone want to treat her like an indulged child?

Miles detected her irritation. It wasn't difficult – she was turning purple.

'Look, I'm sorry to have bothered you. I just wanted to drop this off. When your friend called and said you'd be off sick all week we realised that you'd miss the baby bath the girls were throwing for you.'

'Shower. Baby shower,' Fiz hissed as she

appeared with two steaming cups and a jam roll. She deposited them on the coffee table and backed out of the room. This was the first time she'd met Polly's boss, although he did sound lovely on the phone. And if she wasn't much mistaken, she'd seen that adoring look before. He was yet another candidate for the 'We Love Polly' campaign. She turned to glance at Polly. Yep, as she suspected – not a hint of coyness. Polly had absolutely no idea he fancied her. As usual.

Miles leaned over and dropped the present at Polly's feet, then stood to leave. From her vantage point in the hallway, Fiz realised what was happening and realised that she had to stop it. It was for Polly's own good, she decided. Not only did she not want to leave Pol on her own, but this Miles guy seemed genuinely nice so maybe his company would take Polly's mind off Smarm Man for a while. She'd kill that bastard when she got her hands on him.

She burst into the room, throwing on her jacket as she did so. 'Miles, it was really nice of you to come round. Could you possibly do something for me? I need to go to work now, but could you stay with Polly for a while and keep her company? I worry about her so much when I'm out that I just can't function properly. Didn't earn a penny in tips last night because I was so crap.'

Polly gasped in horror. This was the last thing she wanted. It was uncomfortable enough having Miles sitting in her living room without him being coerced into staying any longer than he needed to. God, the humiliation.

She spoke with a false levity in her voice so as not to insult Miles. But she could do nothing about her gritted teeth. The result was that she sounded like an American shop assistant saying 'have a nice day' through braces that had stuck together.

'No, no, I'm fine, honestly. Miles's wife will be wondering where he's got to.' She turned to Fiz, directing her most evil stare at her. 'And besides, you never get any tips, Fiz, you're always crap.'

Miles spoke first. 'Em, it's OK. My wife's not wondering where I am. Because I'm not. Married that is. I'd be happy to stay for a while.'

Polly was genuinely surprised. She'd always assumed that he was hitched. He never discussed his private life and he never socialised outside work. She'd just thought that it was because he was a happy family man who liked to keep his personal life private. Most of the other SySol execs who were single lived lives of unadulterated hedonism fuelled by inflated salaries and even more inflated egos.

God, she thought of Clark again. Her eyes filled and to her embarrassment and dismay big fat tears started to slide down her cheeks.

Three things happened. Polly put her head in her hands. Miles adopted a look of pure terror. And Fiz slipped out of the front door.

It was several minutes before Polly could stop sobbing long enough to speak. During that time, Miles hesitantly put his arm round her and softly patted her back. Was that what he was supposed to do? He was clueless in these situations. Not for the first time he cursed his mother for giving birth to four boys – the whole girl thing was way over his head. His dating history hadn't enlightened him much either. He'd been so career orientated, even since school, that he had never devoted enough time or energy to any of the relationships that he had managed to squeeze in. It was simply a matter of priorities. No one had ever seemed worth it. Before now. Oh crap, he wished she'd stop crying. He didn't know how to respond to this at all.

'I'm . . . so . . . sorry,' Polly eventually spluttered. 'It's just that it's all been rather a disaster.' More sobs.

The mortification. She'd never had more than a five-minute conversation with this guy about anything other than work and now she was pouring snot all over the arm of his jacket. She reluctantly realised that she owed him an explanation. A few tears she could put down to a hormonal blip, but full-scale wailing couldn't be so easily cast aside. As if she hadn't had enough to deal with this week.

She grabbed two tissues. One to blow her nose with and the other to attempt to remove her nasal fluids from Miles's jacket. God, if that was Clark's jacket he'd have hit the roof and the nearest dry-cleaner's by now.

He brushed her away. 'Don't be crazy. It doesn't matter. Are you OK?' Only a man could ask such a stupid question at that moment. Of course she wasn't. If she were she'd be out rollerblading with a puppy, or singing gospel music or whatever else people bloody did when they were OK. But somehow, the absurdity of the question just made him seem so sweet. She stopped dabbing his jacket and dolefully nodded.

'It hasn't been the best of weeks . . .'

'Is it the baby? I've heard pregnancy gets very difficult in the last couple of months. I totally understand. It's the biological changes that are happening to prepare you for the birth. That's why you feel so low. But it *will* be worth it though; you just have to focus on that. And you'll make a fantastic mum.'

He was really proud of that statement. It showed empathy, knowledge, a man who was able to relate to the trials that women endure in the propagation of the human race. It demonstrated that he understood what miracles women were and that he supported them in their pain.

Actually, he wasn't sure whether it was a whole lot of bollocks or not. Maybe it was tough all the way through. Maybe it wasn't worth it. All he knew was that when his brothers' wives were pregnant they spent an inordinate time down the pub in the last few weeks and blamed it entirely on 'the missus' hormones are on a different planet again – lost the plot altogether so she has.'

Polly shook her head. 'If only it was just that. No, it's my boyfriend. Ex-boyfriend, actually. He's run off with another woman. And she's pregnant with his baby too.'

Good grief. If Miles was dumbstruck before, it was nothing compared to how he felt now. It was out before he realised that it was even on its way. 'Not Cassandra Haven?'

Polly's eyes widened. 'How did you know that? Is it the talk of SySol? Am I the laughing stock of the whole company?'

Her voice was getting shrill now and the tears were on the way again. This whole situation continued to plummet to new depths.

'Sssh, ssh, sshh, no, no, Polly, not at all. I think it's only me who knows. It's just that I saw them together briefly in Cannes. But I thought that was just a one-off – a quick fling. I know she's pregnant now but I didn't realise that he was the father because she's, well, she's . . .'

'It's OK, you can say it. She's half the size that I am. Jelly babies,' she added by way of explanation.

'Well, now that you mention it . . . Anyway, so I did suspect that they had a thing but I thought that was long before you two settled down together. Sorry, Polly. I guess I should have realised.'

He was astounded. Who'd have thought it? Cassandra Haven pregnant to one of the sales team. And they all had it down to be a sperm bank and a turkey baster. He shuddered at the thought. Sex with Cassandra was far too scary a prospect for him. Clark Dunhill must be a brave man. And an incredibly stupid one, he reflected, looking at the love of his life (or at the very least, the lust of his life – he was getting a bit carried away with all the emotion that was flying around) in front of him.

'He's nuts, you know,' he whispered.

Polly sniffed. One of those huge sniffs that feels endless, sounds like a fart and strips you of any modicum of dignity. And Miles didn't even flinch. He just leaned over and pushed her hair back off her face. He didn't want it to get to near the danger zone that was her nasal passages.

'What?' she asked quietly.

'I said he's nuts. Crazy. To do anything that would lose you. I never would.'

It wasn't a flippant comment. His tone was intense and soaked in every emotion that he had harboured since Polly came to work for him years before. None of this was planned. Not one of the words that were coming out of his mouth had been run past his brain first. He'd fantasised for so long about what it would be like to be this close to her, to hold her, to tell her how he felt. And it was everything he had anticipated and more (the 'more' being a large round stomach and about two pints of snot). But it still felt wonderful.

It did to Polly too. He was being so gentle and kind. The way Clark used to be before . . . God, why had he waited so long to say these things to her? She had no inkling whatsoever that he even *liked* her before this. And how come it felt so good? Like a warm bath that she could just sink into where her problems would fritter away like the bubbles on the top of the water.

Slowly (through necessity – her body was no longer built for speed) she leaned towards him. Their eyes were at the same level. As were their noses and mouths. Closer. Closer. Then it got to the crucial moment: the one where she could either back away and brush off the proximity of their faces or decide which side her nose was going to in relation to his and go for full lip-lock.

Lock.

Dring, dring!!!!

Shite, Miles thought as he automatically put out his right arm to switch off his alarm clock. He'd known this was all too good to be true! It was the Polly dream again. The one where he snogged her but just as he was about to slip the straps of her velvet bodice down over her shoulders, the bloody alarm clock went off as usual.

His arm was still floundering in mid-air and hitting nothing. And he was still dreaming. He opened one eye. Polly, check. Snogging, check. Yep, it was the dream again. But hold on, she was never that fat in his fantasies before. And he definitely didn't recognise the surrounding so that must mean . . .

'Em, sorry,' she apologised shyly, 'but I'd better get that in case it's my mother. If I don't answer it she'll only worry and have paramedics, Medivac helicopters and an SAS team here in about five minutes.'

She grabbed the phone.

'Hello.'

'Yes, it's Polly. Who's this?'

'Why would I want to talk to you? Is Clark with you?'

Her head was screaming. Her heart was thumping. Clark was missing, Bitch Haven was on the phone and she'd just kissed her boss. And loved it. What the hell was going on? She felt a sudden urge to lie down, eat and throw up. Not necessarily in that order.

She listened again then replied, 'Well, I'm afraid I have no desire to talk to you.'

It was a struggle – her mouth was having trouble forming words. Bitch Haven was still trying to persuade her to meet. Something about 'wanting a chance to explain'. Uh-uh. She'd already been taken for one ride and she'd no desire to repeat the experience. Besides, Miles was there. On her couch. And she'd kissed him.

'No, I won't meet you. I'm sorry.' Polite. Succinct. All she could manage.

The phone was almost back on the cradle when she heard the crystal-shattering, eardrum-splitting, waters-breaking scream.

Her heart began to race again. Bitch Haven was in labour.

'Cassandra, Cassandra! I'll call an ambulance. Are you at home?

'OK, I'll . . . Cassandra? Cassandra?'

The tone that emanated from the earpiece was the loudest noise she'd ever heard. Apart from the one her heart was making. She jumped off the couch. Actually she prised herself up, but it did feel swift compared to all her recent movements.

'Miles, I'm really sorry, but I have to go.'

He had surmised what was going on just by hearing Polly's end of the conversation.

'I'm coming with you. We'll call an ambulance on the way.'

They were at the SySol offices in less than ten minutes. Thank God Dad had insisted on letting her have a flat so close to where she worked. He had always been so conscious of her safety.

When they screeched to their destination Miles grabbed his door handle to follow her inside, but she put her hand out to stop him.

'No, Miles, please. Let me go in alone.'

Having spent months visualising the moment that she would go into labour from every perspective, there was one thing she knew for absolutely sure: she didn't want it to happen surrounded by strangers or people she'd be embarrassed to face again. Maybe Bitch Haven would feel the same. She was well aware that she owed her nothing, but the least she could do was to spare her any unnecessary distress by pitching up with a guy she'd have to face across the boardroom table again in the future.

He started to object, but she raised her hand. 'Don't, please. Here's my mobile, I'll call you if I need you. Just send the ambulance crew up to her office when they get here.'

He stopped protesting. This assertive Polly wasn't one to be argued with. Besides, he knew that you should never argue with a pregnant woman – wasn't that why his brothers all went down the pub instead?

Polly punched her ID code into the door entry system and flew pass the security guard with a wave.

He wasn't concerned. It was unusual to get anyone in at night, but this bird didn't look like trouble. She'd had a code to get in and she was obviously pregnant – she wasn't exactly going to steal the safe then scale down the side of the building.

He went back to watching *NYPD Blue* on his portable.

Polly burst out of the elevator on the thirtieth floor and wobbled at speed down the corridor. She pushed open Bitch Haven's door, consumed with trepidation at what she would find. All the way there she'd had visions of blood and hysterics and having to deliver the baby herself with only a bemused security guard as an assistant. This could be terrible, it could be horrific, it could be . . . Clark!

She didn't understand. The scene before her was repeatedly flying into her brain but someone somewhere was pressing the reject button and it was flying out again before it made any sense. Sitting behind her desk looking anything but in the throes of excruciating labour pains was Bitch Haven. In fact, sitting behind her desk like that she was only clearly visible from the chest up and she didn't even look pregnant.

Sitting on the office sofa to her right-hand side was Clark. At least she thought it was him. He looked terrible. And scared.

'What's going on?'

Clark spoke first. 'I'm really sorry, Pol. It was the only way we could get you here . . . to see you . . . to . . .'

'WHAT?' She swung round to Cassandra. 'You

mean that was all a lie? I nearly killed myself trying to get here to you and it was just some fucking joke! What kind of people are you?' She was yelling now, fury overtaking every other emotion she'd experienced in the last few hours.

The others stared at her, too shocked and frankly too terrified to speak. For the first time in her life, Polly Kent lost her temper.

'All right, so I'm here,' she was still shouting. It was a blessed relief. All the pain, all the hurt, all the snot of the previous week converged and the result was Hurricane Polly: ready to wreck the place and blow away everyone in its path. 'So what do you want? To talk? To tell some more lies? Some kind of fucked-up threesome? Is that it? You're bored now just fucking behind my back so you want to add a bit of a thrill by including me? Well, you can fuck off, you pair of worthless reprobates!'

Aaaaargh! She wanted to scream some more. She was so insanely angry and disgusted and yet at the same time this felt so liberating. She'd never said the F-word more than once or twice in her whole life and now she suddenly sounded like Joe Pesci in *Goodfellas*. It was one of Clark's favourites. The fuckwit.

'Polly, Polly, please. Calm down. The baby . . .'

'Don't you DARE talk to me about the welfare of my baby. You didn't think about that when you were off shagging Bitch Haven there.'

The expression on Clark's face was almost comical. She'd never seen him so shocked and overwhelmed.

'Five minutes, Polly, please. That's all we're asking.' It was Bitch Haven speaking for the first time since Polly had entered the room.

'Aw, just ... fuck off.' She spun round and reached for the door in the same moment as it flew open and two men in green overalls, a confused security guard and a stretcher came bursting through. They lunged towards her.

'No!' she yelled.

No one was safe from this new, improved version of the Polly doll – the one that came complete with an antisocial behaviour program and a great line in profanity.

'It's not me! I mean, sorry, but it was her. Only it isn't. It's a false alarm. You were called for the smug one in the chair over there, but it's a false alarm.' Polly tried her best to explain. She was struggling with rational thought. Perhaps if she threw in the odd F-word it would flow better. She seemed to have done well with that before.

Now all three of the newcomers looked confused. The call had definitely been for a pregnant woman and yet there she was standing in front on them saying that it wasn't for her. What the hell was going on? And they'd cut short their tea break for this.

Suddenly, there was a loud gasp from 'the smug one in the chair'.

'Actually.' Another gasp. 'I don't think it is a false alarm.'

The paramedics moved forward.

'Don't take another step!' Polly roared. 'Don't believe her! She's a compulsive liar. Ignore her.'

The medics stopped. There was some mix-up here. This wasn't a medical emergency; it was a psychiatric one.

There were another two short, sharp pants from Cassandra.

'Get over here now,' Cass panted, pain contorting her face, 'and get me out of here. This baby's coming and I'll be damned if I'm going to have it on this carpet. Do you know how much it cost?'

Chapter Twelve

Not *that* Kind of Threesome

The stretcher slammed through the doors of the Portland Hospital, propelled by two very hungry paramedics and pursued by a man who appeared to have been sleeping in a skip for the last week and a very pregnant woman who was constantly repeating the F-word. Only now it was driven by panic, not anger.

A doctor joined them as Cass was pushed into the labour room that the paramedics had radioed ahead to prepare.

He spoke to Clark and Polly. 'I'm sorry, but I'll need to examine Miss Haven so I'm going to have to ask you to leave.'

'But I'm the father!' Clark blurted it before he realised the consequences. What the hell was he doing? He hated hospitals, the prospect of childbirth terrified him and his pregnant fiancée was in the same room as his pregnant ex-lover. Why would he possibly want to be anywhere near there? This was a living nightmare and the doctor had offered him a reprieve and he'd *objected*? What a bloody hero. How was he going to extricate himself now?

Thankfully, Cass rescued him.

In between grimaces of pain she shouted, 'Look, Clark, no offence. I mean, I know you've been there before, but I really have no desire to reveal any parts of my anatomy to you again so do me a favour and piss off. Please.' She added the last bit out of courtesy. This was the Portland after all – it wouldn't do to forget her manners.

'And please take my bag. My address book is in it. Call Antonia and Jeff.'

There was a loud scream from the bed. It was amazing how much that quickened his step.

He turned to follow Polly, who was already backing out of the room, her face ashen and her hands trembling. As she stepped into the corridor, she stumbled and Clark caught her just in time. He led her to a row of blue plastic chairs that obviously hadn't been designed for comfort and supported her as she lowered herself into one of them.

He wondered if he should get someone to check her over, but she immediately dismissed the idea.

'I'll be fine in a minute, I just need to get my breath. Make Cassandra's calls.'

She realised that it felt a bit strange calling her by her real name, but the fury that had consumed her less than an hour ago had now completely dissipated. Cass was in labour and Clark was about to become a father for the first (as far as she knew!) time – she could suspend her issues with the whole situation for now.

'And while you're at it, could you call my mobile number and tell Miles that I'll make my own way home. Tell him thanks and I'll call him tomorrow. Please.'

Clark's hackles automatically rose. He thought he'd seen Miles Conway in the SySol reception as they rushed from the building to the ambulance, but it hadn't fully registered. Now he knew why: he was with Pol. What was Polly doing with Miles Conway at this time of night? As if that took much working out. He might have known there'd be a queue of guys waiting to muscle in on her, pregnant or not. Had she already moved on from him to pastures new? How could she just sail right into another relationship after what they'd had?'

There was another scream from the room they'd just left. OK, so that *was* another woman having his child. He didn't exactly occupy the moral high ground here.

He whipped out his mobile phone.

'Sorry, sir, no mobile phones inside the hospital. There's a payphone just down the corridor,' a receptionist who looked like she'd trained for this job by working the door of a Bronx nightclub reprimanded him.

Shit! He rummaged in Cass's bag for change. He'd left all his at the hotel as a tip for housekeeping – they deserved it for being the only people who would talk to him for the last week. He found a couple of pound coins.

'Right, I'll be back in a minute. Don't go anywhere, Pol.'

'Yeah, right. And here was me thinking I'd just pop down to the local nightclub or nip out for a jog.' God, this felt great. Being a bitch was coming so naturally to her – she hadn't lived with Fiz all these years without learning a thing or two.

He was back in less than five minutes and slumped into the chair next to her. A week-long alcoholic bender was no training for a night like this. He was shattered. A bit like his life. But, he realised, this was a salesman's dream situation. He had the prospective buyer in front of him, she couldn't go anywhere because her arse was wedged into the seat, and there were no distractions apart from the small matter of what sounded like someone being tortured in the next room. It might be the only chance he got to make his pitch.

'Right Pol, I know you don't want to hear this, but we need to talk . . .'

'Just relax as much as you can. Now, how far on are you, Miss Haven?'

The irony didn't escape her. This man was a stranger, his hand was rummaging somewhere around her cervix and he was telling her in his best patient-reassuring voice to relax. Was he mental?

'Thirty-seven weeks. Is it OK? The baby? Is it OK?'

Dr Dulcet Tones glanced at the monitor attached to the leads that were strapped to her belly. He nodded. 'The baby's fine. You're fine. But you are eight centimetres dilated. This little one will be here within the hour.'

Cass's head buckled up so that her chin was on her chest as another contraction ripped through her body.

'Drugs. I need drugs. Tons of them.'

The doc shook his head matter-of-factly. 'I'm sorry, Cassandra . . .' Since when did they get on to first-name terms – good God, one quick feel of her privates and suddenly they were best friends? 'But it's too late for pain relief. I'm afraid you're going to have to do this on your own.'

She groaned pitifully. Oh, crap, this wasn't going according to plan at all. It was against her religion. She was morally opposed to a natural birth on the grounds that she was sure it would hurt like hell. Trust her child to want to come shooting out in a foetal demonstration of efficiency.

With a sunken heart she scanned the room and realised that the doc was right in more ways than one. She was going to have to do this on her own. And completely alone.

He was halfway through the pitch, deploying every ounce of persuasion he possessed. Think Richard Gere. Think *Officer and a Gentleman*. He couldn't lift Pol up and carry her out without risking permanent back damage, so he was trying to get her back the only way he knew how. Persuasion.

First, he covered the current situation – just to make sure they were singing from the same song sheet (it was obviously a country and western one, full of betrayal and sorrow. All that was missing was a Bible, a dog called Shep and a pickup truck).

It all boiled down to a few key bullet points which he took no pleasure in recapping:

- He'd entered the relationship with Polly under false pretences
- He'd lied vociferously to her
- Cass had needed sperm
- He'd been a complete prick to provide it
- Their relationship, such as it was, had been a one-week thing in Cannes
- Cass was presently in the throes of producing his other baby
- And he'd fucked up beyond imagination.

Progress check. It was going OK so far. Somehow, it didn't seem as bad when he listed it like that. He checked Polly's face for a reaction. She looked like she wanted to jump on his head until it cracked. Maybe it wasn't going that well after all.

Time for the product. The big sell. He took a deep breath. The offer that would solve everyone's problems and leave everyone in a win-win situation. On a level playing field, that is. Within the ball-park. By deploying an effective strategy to move forward. Oh fuck, he was playing for time. And running out of bullshit sales clichés. He had never been more unsure of attaining a deal in his life. Polly's ire had definitely softened – she was no longer searching around for weapons – but she seemed to have slipped into a trance-like state and had been staring at the same spot on the opposite wall since he'd started speaking, her face a mask of aggression. It was the big, bad, omen. No eye contact. He was doomed.

'So, Pol, please, I need you to listen to me . . .' he implored. 'I was trying to prove some stupid point about beautiful females and brainy females and me being the big-shot guy in the middle and I've realised now that I'm a complete prick. You're everything Pol, *everything*: you're beautiful, you're smarter than I'll ever be.'

He considered throwing in that she was great in bed but his new politically correct mentality realised that it wasn't the most opportune time. This was definite progress.

'I love you so much, Pol. Please, please come ba—'

'EXCUSE ME!' A tall blonde with a frantic expression, clutching the hand of a bald black guy who was wider than the doorway, skidded to a halt in front of them. 'Cassandra Haven, do you know where she is? The receptionist isn't at her desk,'

Toni yelled in a panic to the couple who were sitting in front of her. Then she realised who it was. Well, well, well, it was a small world. Polly must have gone into labour too. How shocking then that they'd made her sit in a corridor – they could at least have found the poor girl a bed. Maybe it was a false alarm. She'd had four of those with Ben.

'Polly! I thought you had a couple of weeks to go yet. But then so did Cass.' She spluttered. 'And Clark?' Antonia hadn't recognised him at first. Whenever he'd glided past her at reception he'd always appeared so suave and dapper. She didn't think much of his off-duty style – he looked like a bag-man.

'Yeah, it was me who called you.'

Why would Clark Dunhill have made Cass's phone calls? He must have been here waiting with Polly and stepped in to help when he realised Cass was on her own. That was so nice of him. No wonder Polly had been so thrilled to hook up with him.

'Cassandra is in there, Toni. You'd better hurry,' Polly said quietly.

Did they know? Polly wondered. Did the whole world know that Clark was the father of Cass's baby? The whole world except her, that is.

'OK Cassandra, now push. Come on. Just one more ...'

'Thank God, we're not too late!' Toni and Paul dived to the side of the bed. 'Oh, Cass, we're here, we're here,' Toni squealed.

Cass barely registered their arrival. One more. She could do this. One more. Big breath in ...

Jeff burst into the room and dived to the bottom of the bed. Bad move. It was entirely too much visual information for him – reminded him of a creature from the Black Lagoon. He darted to the same side as Paul. At least the big man would block his view of anything gory. He'd always fainted at the first sight of blood or pain.

'Aaaargh!' Silence.

More silence.

Then a sudden, 'Wahhhhhhh.'

The nurse lifted the tiny, gunky, gooey creature from the bottom of the bed and raised it up to Cass's chest.

'Congratulations. It's a girl!'

Cassandra Haven cried. In public. And she didn't care.

She had her baby.

'Come back to me, Polly, please. I swear I'll never hurt you again. And I'm not saying this for any other reason than I love you. And the baby. I do, Pol. So much. Please. For all our sakes . . .' He was losing it. He knew the signs. Not one gesture of agreement. Defensive body language. No buyer vocalisation.

But he couldn't stop. It was like he was pounding the heart of their relationship, administering CPR, keeping it barely alive, and he knew that when he stopped it would die. It would be over.

Suddenly Polly turned to him. Bingo! She was buying into it. She was open to possibilities. Ready to negotiate. Wanting to clarify the points of what was in it for her.

But then she started to push herself up from her chair. OK. OK. She just needed to pee. It wasn't over yet. It was just a physical interruption. The deal was still on the table. It had to be.

'You know Clark, this isn't like the movies. There

isn't always a happy ending.' She turned to walk away, but then briefly turned back. 'Or maybe it is. Because in the movies the bad guys always lose. And you just lost.'

She waddled away. Not exactly into the sunset, but close. He didn't even try to go after her. It was gone. The best sales person in the world couldn't pull this one back.

His head fell into his hands. It was over. It was all over.

'Excuse me, Mr Dunhill. Miss Haven wondered if you'd like to come and see your daughter.'

Chapter Thirteen

The Threesome and Baby Makes Four

'I still can't believe you're doing this. Even Mother fecking Teresa would have had reservations about this charitable act. She's probably up there right now looking down and saying, "Polly, love, you're off your fecking head. Go for a lie-down with a family-size box of jelly babies until the notion passes."'

Polly ignored her. She pulled her car into the space that was miraculously available right in front of the building. Maybe Mother Teresa was on her side after all.

'Wait here, Fiz,' she commanded when she saw Fiz reaching for the door handle. 'Please,' she added in a gentler tone.

Fiz slumped back into the seat and folded her arms. She wasn't going to argue. Polly had become totally implacable of late and she didn't even want to waste energy by trying. If Smarm Man had served one purpose in this whole affair (apart from the obvious – Polly was now the size of a shed), he'd certainly toughened Pol up. She took no nonsense now from anyone. Fiz liked that thought. Being as soft as she was only set Pol up to get hurt. She was sure that wouldn't happen again. She'd go into everything with her eyes wide open from now on – not blinded by all that love and romance crap.

She pulled a Danielle Steel from her bag and opened it up at the turned-down page. She was desperate to know what happened next.

'You know I still can't believe of all the men in the world you chose Clark Dunhill,' Antonia commented. 'Still, that probably explains why Georgie is so beautiful. She had to get her looks from somewhere. Didn't you darling?' she cooed as she lifted two-week-old Georgie to her mouth and smothered her in kisses.

Cass pulled a face but resisted the urge to sling something at her sister. She might hit the baby by accident. Her baby. A surging, bubbly sensation welled up in her stomach again. She couldn't believe the force of her feelings for the pink bundle in Toni's arms.

She had cried in horror when they took Georgie away to check her over after her birth and then insisted that she spend a few days in the special baby unit due to her being premature. She counted every hour until they brought her up to her for regular breastfeeds.

When they'd finally discharged her a week later, Cass vowed that she wouldn't let her out of her sight again ever. She had already extended her maternity leave and was trying to devise a career move that would allow her to work from home.

She loved to lie on the couch at night with Georgie sleeping on top of her, the top of the baby's head nestled into her neck. That type of physical contact she could definitely handle. Of course, she only wore old T-shirts when she did that. Getting baby vomit out of cashmere was a complete nightmare.

'Has he been around?' Toni asked, snapping Cass out of her thoughts.

'Who?'

Antonia rolled her eyes. Honestly, her sister had the concentration span of a chicken these days. 'Clark!'

'Oh, em, yes. He pops in most days. He's besotted by her. That's what persuaded me to involve him in her life. It would be cruel of me to deprive her of her father. He's actually an OK guy.'

Toni wondered if she detected a hint of something more in her sister's tone. Had she and Clark got it together? What a fantastic ending that would be.

'Don't even go there. I know what you're thinking,' Cass chastised her. 'I just said he's an OK guy, not someone I want to spend twenty-four hours a day with for the rest of my life. I'd never get near the bathroom. Or a mirror.

'But I do see him in a bit of a new light now. It's almost as if since he stopped trying so bloody hard to impress, he's actually become quite impressive. Does that make sense?'

'No.'

'Doesn't surprise me. I struggle with joined-up sentences these days. Something to do with hormonal imbalances and sleep deprivation.

'Anyway, talking about growing old with someone, how're things with you and my friend from childhood who's far too old for you?'

Antonia laughed. Cass had struggled to accept that she and Paul had become an item, since she found out at Georgie's birth. Cass told her twice a day that

Paul was too old for her but she had a stock answer to that. Catherine. Zeta. Jones. Michael. Douglas.

And the age difference between *them* was twenty-five years. The twenty-year gap between her and Paul paled into almost-insignificance compared to that.

Toni refused to let Cass change the subject. She wasn't quite on the phone to Oprah yet begging for a spot on the show to unburden her life history, but with a bit of persuasion Cass was now prepared to at least comment on her personal life. Toni had no intention of allowing her to regress.

'So there's definitely nothing between you and the father of your child then?' Toni probed some more.

'Not at the moment, no.'

Well, well, well. That was definitely not a 'definitely never'. She was right! There was a little spark of possibility.

'And what about Polly? Have you heard how she's doing?'

Cass shook her head. 'I don't know. She's refusing to see Clark, or even speak to him on the phone. He's gutted. I do hope she's OK though. Can you get that, please?'

She nodded in the direction of the door intercom system that had just buzzed.

'If I stop in the middle of preparing these bottles then I'll lose count and have to start all over again.'

Toni laughed at the irony as she laid Georgie down in her crib. Her sister, the one who could calculate multimillion-pound profit and loss accounts in her head while eating her lunch and reading the financial section of *The Times*, was struggling to count to eight. Babies were indeed a great leveller.

'Eh, Cass, you know how you just said that you had no idea how Pol was?'

'Yes. Oh bugger, was that four or five I'd just put in.'

'Well, I think you're about to find out.' She pressed the buzzer on the phone and watched as Polly disappeared from the camera.

She took so long to climb the stairs that Toni was ready to go out with a posse to find her. Eventually, breathless, she staggered to the flat door.

'Come in, come in,' Toni beckoned.

Polly looked questioningly at Cass, who was standing just behind her.

'Please,' Cass reinforced.

'Sorry to bother you, but I just wanted to drop this in. It's for the baby.' She pushed the box she was holding in Cass's direction, then turned to leave.

'No, please. It was good of you to come. Do you want to see Georgie?'

'You had a girl?' Pol asked nervously. She was obviously hugely uncomfortable. 'I'd love to. If that's OK.'

Poor girl, thought Toni. She knew exactly how she felt. Pregnant, alone, lost. Although she realised that Pol did have a several-million-pound trust fund to fall back on so at least she would never run short of Pampers. Still, it *had* been really brave of her to come here.

Cass lifted Georgie and placed her in Pol's arms.

'You know, Polly, in spite of everything, our children are going to be siblings. No pressure, but if you do want to keep in touch then I'd be happy to do that. It would be kind of cool for them to grow up together. I've always wanted to be part of a dysfunctional family,' Cass joked, trying to lighten the atmosphere a bit.

It didn't work. Tears flew down Polly's face as she thrust Georgie back into Toni's arms, turned and fled back through the door.

'I'm sorry, I . . .' They didn't catch the rest. By the time she got halfway down the first flight of stairs she was out of earshot.

Cass and Antonia stared at each other.

'You know, for a fat bird she can't half move at speed,' Toni observed.

'Oh, I fecking knew it,' Fiz exclaimed as Polly climbed back into the car in floods of tears. She'd moved into the driver's seat in case Polly had taken a mad turn and punched Bitch Haven's lights out, therefore necessitating a quick getaway. 'What did Bitch Haven say to you? So help me God I'll kick her ass! As if she hasn't done enough already. That's it! I'm going—'

'Drive, Fiz. Just shut up and drive!'

The ferocity of Pol's order shocked her.

'And don't take me to the flat, Fiz. Take me home. To the Castle. Please. And where's my phone – I have to call Miles.'

Fiz was gobsmacked.

'But I've got to be at work at the Shaker in an hour. I'll never make it.'

'Fiz, they won't miss you. You're crap. Give up the bar work and try to get more fashion gigs. At least there the people you insult are getting paid for it.'

Fiz stuck her chin out in petulance. If that's the way Polly wanted to be, well, that was fine! She'd take her home, but only because she was pregnant.

And she wasn't going to speak to the hormonal cow the whole way there.

'And just look at the skirt I'm wearing, as well,' Fiz muttered. To herself obviously. Not to Polly Sniff-a-lot sitting next to her. 'It's so short that when my ma sees it she'll have me saying Hail fecking Marys for the rest of the week.'

'So where are we off to next, mate? How about going down the Romp Room then?'

Clark downed his glass of champagne in one go. He was out with the boys for the first time in months and he was determined to enjoy it. Or rather, he was out with one of the boys. Nick had still vanished off the face of the earth. Even Taylor hadn't seen him in ages. Must have got himself a bird.

'Eh, nah, not the Romp Room, mate. That place has gone right downhill lately. Prick of a manager there has gone and barred me. Big mistake. He'll never get a decent class of totty in there now.'

'Barred you? For what?'

'Long story. Doesn't matter. The guy just didn't appreciate what I could do for him. Back in a minute.'

Taylor set off in the direction of the Gents. That'll be 'back in thirty minutes' he meant to say then, Clark mused. It took Taylor a quarter of an hour just to go through all the mags in the cubicles.

No problem. He scanned the room. Time to make one lucky girl a happy one. This was his first night back in circulation and he intended to make it one to remember. He ran his fingers through his hair, wondering how the highlights looked. He knew the answer already. Subtle. Sexy. Senfuckingsational. So what if he hadn't had time for a sunbed session – a quick slap of fake tan had given him that 'just stepped off the plane from somewhere outrageously expensive' look.

The Shagmeister was back. And he was open for business.

So who would it be? Who'd be the one to initiate him back into the ways of casual sex? His first outing since the last time he'd been with Po . . . He didn't finish the thought. He refused to go there.

Back to tonight. Sex. With condoms only, of course. Damn right. He'd learned that lesson. Check that they were on the pill, wear extra-strength (he already had to wear extra-large – some guys just *had it*, he thought with a grin) condoms and make a hasty retreat just before it all got explosive. With precautions like that, he'd never get caught out again. Not that he'd change what had happened now. At least not all of it. His Georgie was just different class. He wondered if she was sleeping. Maybe he should just give Cass a quick call and check – Georgie had been a bit colicky earlier. He reached into his inside pocket. Versace. And pulled out his phone. He decided against ringing – if Georgie was sleeping he didn't want to wake her. He sent a quick text. 'Just wntd 2 check G ok & asleep.' The reply came back almost immediately. 'Yes, G snoozing. Thot u were on nite out – go njoy instd of txt us u sad bstrd.' He laughed aloud. Cass was OK when she wanted to be. And she was right. Time to climb back in that saddle. He hadn't had a ride for far too long.

He scanned the room. The blonde in the boob tube? Nah, too brassy. The black-haired chick in the leather corset. No way! He just knew that would end up in the basement of an S&M brothel in Mayfair.

What about the redhead? Mmm. Nice tits. Nice ass. Cute smile. Not Polly.

His best I'm-too-fucking-gorgeous-for-words-but-if-you-play-your-cards-right-you-might-get-lucky-sweetheart grin faded. They weren't Polly. None of them. They weren't even Cass, for God's sake.

A picture of Cass holding Georgie came into focus in his head. She'd been really cool about letting him see the baby. It had come as a total shock to him that he'd even wanted to. But from the first time those little fingers wrapped around his he knew that he couldn't just walk away and leave her. And anyway, what was it Cass said? Yeah, fatherhood was the new black! He was ahead of his time as per usual. Although he did get the feeling that Cass took the piss out of him sometimes. Nah, he was just being paranoid.

Shit, he couldn't concentrate at all. He was well out of practice. Right. Who was it to be? The skinny bird with the red power suit who was knocking back blue things with umbrellas in them like they were going out of fashion? Nah. Nothing to hang on to. He started to get a feeling of unease in the pit of his stomach. He desperately attempted to shrug it off. What about the Oriental babe in the hot pants? Now she was so hot she was singeing her mate's nylon hair extensions. Nah, she'd be high-maintenance. Anyone who came out to play in what was really nothing more than her knickers was going to have issues.

His stomach started to tighten uneasily. What about the . . . Tighter. Nah, too tall. Would do himself an injury snogging that. Tighter. What about . . . nah, too old. She wasn't a day under a facelift and a bus pass. Tighter. Tighter.

'Well, if it isn't Smarm Man himself. Thought we

had a new policy here to stop letting in dickheads. Now feck off home and stop lowering the tone of the place.'

He turned and as he did a massive grin spread across the width of his face. He would never have believed it. His drink must have been spiked. Or that curry at lunchtime must have been off. Something was definitely affecting his mental state. It was a sad day when he was glad to see Fiz O'Connor.

'Fiz, do me a favour . . .'

'Feck off.'

'Come on, Fiz. Just come and sit over there with me for ten minutes.'

'I can't. Not that I would anyway, but I can't because I didn't pitch up to work here last night and Psycho Stan over there will fire my ass if I put one foot out of line the rest of this year.' She gestured to the owner of the bar who was eyeing her with an iniquitous stare.

'Yo, Stan. If I buy two bottles of Krug can I borrow Fiz for ten minutes? It's an emergency.'

'Mate, I'll *give* you two bottles of Krug if you keep her for longer. She's bloody useless,' he retorted, laughing.

'Fantastic. So everyone's a fecking comedian now. OK, Smarm Man, ten minutes,' she said as she climbed over the top of the bar. 'The clock is ticking.'

He pulled out a chair for her at a nearby table. She was so shocked that she nearly missed it and landed on her red-leather-clad arse. She wasn't sure about this skirt now. Maybe red leather should be the sole preserve of hookers and Christine Hamilton.

'OK, Fiz. Talk to me about Pol.'

'What do you want me to say?' she retorted with attitude.

'Anything. Anything at all. Just as long as it's about Polly.'

The Shagmeister was gone. He'd shagged off and disappeared. Only Clark Dunhill remained.

Chapter Fourteen

All Together Now . . .

Polly pushed away the untouched bowl of apple crumble and custard. It joined the sausages and mash and the wedge of melon on the tray. When her mother came in to collect it her dismay was palpable.

'Honey, you have to eat. For the baby's sake as well as yours.'

Polly nodded. She knew that. That's why she'd forced down a bowl of soup and some fruit earlier on that afternoon. It had been an ordeal. It was pea and ham and the colour reminded her of green jelly babies. God, the very thought made her want to retch. She never wanted to see another sweet in human form as long as she lived.

Her mother sat on the side of her bed and ran her fingers through Polly's hair. Pol closed her eyes. Mum used to do this for hours when she was a child. Would she do that to her baby? To *their* baby?

'Heartburn,' she explained. 'It's excruciating.'

Jilly wasn't fooled.

'What are you thinking, honey? We're so worried about you.'

'I'm sorry, Mum. I just can't stop thinking about him. I'm driving myself nuts.'

'Miles?'

'Nice try,' she jibed. Miles had been great to her this last couple of weeks – a shoulder to cry on that she'd certainly needed. One that didn't say 'feck' all the time. But friendship was as far as it went for her. Maybe it would be different after the baby was born. Her baby. Clark's baby. God, why couldn't she erase him from her head? He was there from the minute she woke up until she fell back into a fitful sleep. And the same scene played over and over again in her head. They were in the hospital, sitting in the corridor, and he was begging her to come back to him. He kept repeating that he loved her, that he loved the baby, that he wanted them to be together.

Her mother's sigh cut through her thoughts.

'Look, honey. Don't bite my head off for saying this, but are you absolutely sure it's definitely irredeemable?'

Polly gasped in surprise. 'What?' Had she heard right? Did her mother just allude to the possibility of her and that bastard reconciling? God, had she taken leave of her senses? This was the same mother who had wrapped her in love and sought to protect her from anything that could possibly hurt her and now she was suggesting that she return to the person who'd maltreated her more than anyone else. The world was going mad.

Disbelief and indignation made her voice a couple of notes higher than normal. 'You think I should take him back? After everything he's done? I can't believe you just said that. I'd have thought you'd have been outraged at the very prospect of it!'

Her mother just shrugged her shoulders, her

expression unreadable. 'But he *did* explain everything to you. I'm not defending him. I know what his behaviour was heinous. But at least he was honest with you in the end.'

'How can you know that? The man has made a relationship out of lies and betrayal. Why should I believe what he says now? For all I know it could all be a pack of lies. It probably is. He was probably shacked up with Cassandra the whole time we were together. In fact, on the nights she worked late, he was probably out on the pull behind *both* our backs.'

'He wasn't.'

'He's probably been out with a different woman every night since, too. The man's insatiable! He's—What did you say?'

'I said he wasn't. And he isn't. Everything he told you was the truth.'

Polly was speechless. How did he do it? How had he got to her mother and persuaded her to defend him? That guy could manipulate anyone, but her mother! She was horrified.

'How do you know that?' she asked in astonishment.

Jilly reached over and picked up the phone at the side of Polly's bed. She pressed in a number. 'Henry, could you find Kenneth, please, and ask him to come up to Polly's room as soon as possible.' She replaced the handset. 'Polly, love, I think it's time you heard a few truths.'

'Ah love her, Fizzy. Polly. How'm ah ever gonna get her back? You have to help me.' He grabbed her arm as he slurred in her face. The alcohol on his breath made her want to faint, but that was surpassed by the fact that his presence for the last two hours made her want to kill herself.

She'd tried desperately to return to work behind the bar, but every time she did, the twat had bought another bottle of Krug and begged Psycho Stan for more time. Evil git, Stan. She hoped he met a particularly painful accident on his way home for subjecting her to this. Preferably one that involved the removal of his bollocks.

'Look, Smarm, I need to go. And don't dare ask for another bottle. Clark, phone the fecking Samaritans, they're much cheaper than me.'

'But you know her, Fizzy. My Polly. You know her. Tell me 'gain 'bout the Chrizmaz party. How you met. How she was an angel . . .'

Where was she? Oh yes. She wanted to kill herself.

'A private investigator? What? I can't believe I'm hearing this? Dad, how could you?'

'I'm sorry, love, but I thought I was protecting you. After Giles, I wanted to make sure that never happened to you again.'

'Well, I hate to point out the obvious, but it didn't bloody work, now did it?'

She closed her eyes. This wasn't happening. God, she needed a rewind button. She needed to go back to the time in her life when her parents were a warm soft haven, she didn't have a lying bastard for a boyfriend and the whole damn world wasn't doing things behind her back. This was madness!

So what if the investigator had confirmed that Clark had been telling the truth about his affair with Cass and it had only been that week in Cannes? He was still a bastard for betraying her.

And OK, so Clark had only been with her for a few weeks and he didn't know that she was pregnant, but still . . . she hated him.

Anyway, what about the fact that he'd only asked her out for a bet? And that he'd proposed to her only because she was pregnant and he thought her father would kill him? Spineless prick.

She vocalised the last two thoughts to Dempsey and Makepeace in front of her. Private bloody investigators. Indeed.

Ken couldn't believe that he was party to this discussion. It had taken weeks for his wife to persuade him not to get Clark Dunhill and have him slowly tortured. But as always, Jilly had been the voice of reason. He had Polly's future to think about. And his grandchild's. Jilly had made a pretty convincing argument for encouraging them to give it another go. He'd eventually relented. He just hoped it was the right thing for his Pol. She'd been through enough.

'Do you believe he loves you now?' her dad asked.

She considered that for a few moments, then nodded. She did believe that. Otherwise surely he'd have gone off with Cass or some other female long ago? And why would he constantly be trying to persuade her to return to him? Why would he call her mobile phone every day and leave a message saying that he missed her?

'Yes, I think he does. But I don't care.'

Her dad looked at her mum and raised his eyebrows, as if asking her a psychic question. She subtly nodded an affirmation.

'Pol, love, maybe you should think about giving him another chance – forgetting about the circumstances that brought you together and concentrating on what you've got now. You know, your mother only married me for my money.'

Polly burst out laughing. Trust dad to joke at a time like this. He always knew how to make her smile when she was down.

Her mum put her hand on her arm. 'He's not joking, love, I did. My family had the connections that your father wanted, although, bless him, he really did love me.' She smiled at her husband. 'But we needed his money. So I married him. Simple as that. But there's the thing, Polly, somewhere along the line a few years later I realised that I loved him. I think the same thing has happened to Clark, only he had the sense to realise it much sooner. Not soon enough, though, but then everyone makes mistakes, darling. Everyone.'

Fiz was trying to decide if the tie-backs on the curtains or her tights would make a better noose. Tie-backs. The tights might stretch and she'd bounce off the floor and then she'd be left with two broken legs and no way of escaping this wanker who was STILL droning in her ear. To make matters worse, the Shaker was beginning to empty so there was even less chance of someone distracting him or engaging him in a conversation long enough for her to flee. Even that tosspot Taylor had pissed off with some tart in a skirt the size of a cummerbund.

'Dear God,' she started to pray. 'You don't know me, but my ma, Patricia O'Connor, is a regular visitor. I wonder if we could possibly do a deal, Lord: if I can use up some of my ma's credits – she must have loads, she's verging on sainthood – and you save me from this wanker, pardon the language, in front of me, then I won't say "feck" for a whole week. OK, a month. Feck it, a year. There we go. A whole year.'

'FIZ!' It was Stan. She turned to find out why he was shouting at her. If he wanted her to get the mop out and start cleaning the floors then he could fec—, sorry God, slip of the tongue there, he could piss right off.

'Fiz! I forgot to tell you – Romeo called earlier to say he'll pick you up about . . . never mind, there the poor sod is now.'

Fiz turned to see her boyfriend walk in the door. If he picked her up and swept her away from all this she'd have his babies.

'Nick? Nick! Ye came back to me! Ah knew you would, matey. Ah love you, Nick,' Clark slurred, right before he passed out and his forehead hit the table.

Nick looked accusingly at his girlfriend. 'Shit, Fiz, what did you do to him? Drugging him in public is mental!'

Fiz was outraged. 'I did not! He managed this state all by himself, the moronic twat. And anyway, I couldn't get the strychnine over the Internet. Something about a Customs intervention . . .'

Nick shook his head. It was hard to tell if she were being serious or not. In the months that they'd been together only one thing had been predictable – that Fiz wasn't. At least life would never be dull. And she did look sexy as hell in that red leather skirt.

'Excuse me, is that Clark Dunhill under there? Only I think I'd better take him home.'

Fiz spun round in disbelief. 'Bitch Haven! I fecking knew it! Shit, sorry God.'

Clark started to prise his forehead off the table. It

hurt. But not half as much as the voices in his head. He opened one eye just a fraction and sheer terror made him snap it shut. It wasn't an alcohol-induced hallucination. Fiz and Cass! And they were both furious. It would be a brave man who got in the middle of those two. He put his head back on the table. Bravery had never been his strong point.

Cass put her hands on her hips and her chin up in mid-air. 'Excuse me? You knew what? And mind your tone there, lady!' she spat. She would not be talked to like that by a female who worked in a bar and wore an outfit that resembled a cow with sunburn.

'I *knew* you two were still at it. You should be ashamed of yourself!' Thank God Polly wasn't here to see this, Fiz thought, it would tip her over the edge!

'I beg your pardon!' Cass spat a retort. 'Don't *dare* assume that everyone else lives their lives to your standards! Not that it's any of your damn business, but we are not *at* anything. Come on, Dunhill, let's get out of here.'

'Cass? How'd ye know where ah woz?'

Cass reached into his breast pocket and retrieved his mobile. She checked the screen. Yep, there it was – the message that Clark had sent her earlier. The one that he'd been sending continuously for the last two hours. In his drunken slump he must have been leaning on the 'send' button. After the forty-seventh message, she'd actually started to worry about him. And with due cause, she decided as she stared evilly at Fiz. She was only glad that he'd told her where he was going that night, and that Toni had been with her to babysit Georgie while she rescued him. She didn't fancy Clark's chances much if he'd been left any longer with the bitch in the leather.

She started to hoist Clark up, but he was a dead weight. As opposed to the dead man with the hang-over that he'd be tomorrow morning for dragging her out of the house at this time of night.

'Ah love Pol, Cass,' he slurred. 'Ah love her.'

'I know you do, Clark. Come on now, on your feet. Let's get you home.'

A new voice emanated from the direction of the door. 'God, life never turns out like the movies, does it? I was expecting a big romantic *Sleepless in Seattle* ending and what do I get? An irate best friend, my boyfriend's ex and a man in an alcohol-induced coma.'

'Pol! Mother of God it's like some freaked-out reunion show in here tonight. If Cilla Black walks through that door next I'm making for the back door. What are you doing here?'

'I called her. Hey, Pol, how are you?' Cass asked warmly.

'Fat. Tired. Here. Therefore obviously insane. Thanks for calling me, Cass.'

'No problem. I wasn't sure you'd come though. I'm glad you did. And so will he be when he sobers up.' She gestured towards Clark, still sprawled across the table.

Polly smiled. He'd better be. For the hundredth time since Cass had called her she had the same thought: he'd better be worth it.

'Come on, Clark. You're coming home.'

Cass grabbed one arm and Nick grabbed the other. As they raised him to his feet, his eyes squinted open.

'Pol? POL? Ah luv you, Pol. More than anyfing ...'

Polly grinned as she shook her head.

'That may be so, Clark, but you're still a twat.' She winked at Fiz. '*My fecking twat*.'

Epilogue

And Finally There Were Five

The Shaker hadn't been that full on a Sunday afternoon since the last televised England game. Clark had missed it. He usually took the girls to the park on Sunday afternoons and there'd be hell to pay if he changed his routine. Not that he'd want to, of course.

He searched around the room. It wasn't his first choice of venue for his daughters' joint birthday party, but Polly had begged him to agree to it. Apparently Fiz was on the verge of getting sacked and only an assurance to Stan that she would arrange this party and thereby boost his finances would give her a stay of execution.

Actually, he hadn't agreed to it for Fiz's sake, he'd done it for Nick. If Pol's maniac pal got sacked then she'd be home every night instead of out working and who knew what that would do to Nick's sanity? The poor guy would be damaged for life. Not that he'd admit it though. Fiz had brainwashed him into believing that she was the most wonderful female on the face of the planet and he'd proposed to her fourteen times in the last year. She'd agreed on the thirteenth, but he'd asked again just to double-check. Maybe he could arrange some kind of therapy for him – he was obviously ill.

'Pol, have you got a baby wipe there? Daisy has just thrown up over my shoulder and I don't have a free hand.'

Polly laughed at the sight of him. Georgie on one arm, Daisy on the other, a huge smile on his gorgeous face in the middle.

'It's OK, Pol, I've got it.' Cass jumped up and quickly wiped down the back of Clark's jacket. As always, she came armed with a full range of wipes and stain removers. She wasn't having Georgie getting her Baby Gucci dress dirty – how would that look in her birthday photos?

How time had flown, Cass realised. A whole year. They'd made it without giving up, emigrating or killing each other. It wasn't always perfect, but they knew it was in the best interest of the girls to establish a happy environment so they'd all been forced to put egos and pride to one side. If they coped with the next fifteen years of the inevitable ups, downs, jealousies and teenage hormones with the same attitude then they'd be on course to produce two gorgeous, well-balanced, grounded sisters. They were a family. A modern-day, new-millennium, dysfunctional family They'd be doing a talk show next . . .

'What are you thinking, sis?'

Cass's ultra-sharp cerebral response time was back to its old standard.

'That if you and the old one there don't stop stroking each other's legs I'm going to throw up.'

Antonia chuckled. She didn't care. She couldn't believe how happy she was. She and Ben had moved into Paul's house and now that he'd finally found a manager he could trust, he would be switching to working day shifts. She didn't want to get too excited about it just yet though as this was the fourth manager Paul had employed in a year. Apparently he had some surveillance system in his office that caught every one of his predecessors embroiled in one fiddle or another. The last one had been hilarious. His assistant manager had actually embezzled money from the cash desk at the door to pay some male model to bring glamour models to the club. Then he'd sit in the middle of them in the VIP lounge and ply them with drinks in the hope of pulling one of them. When Paul fired him, he'd buggered off with a Page Three girl called Tropical Storm in the general direction of Milton Keynes. It was a nice little earner for the male model pimp-type guy though. Taylor something or other. Bet he was cursing Paul upside down for blowing his sideline out.

'I knew I recognised him!' Cass exclaimed.

'Who?' said Paul and Antonia simultaneously as they turned in the direction of Cass's stare.

Paul had an instant reaction. 'Shit, that's him. That's that model who was in on the scam in the club.'

Polly had heard the whole exchange. 'Taylor? He's an old friend of Clark's from the days when he used to be allowed out alone,' she laughed. 'What's he been up to?'

'A long story,' Paul groaned, 'but suffice to say I wouldn't mind seeing him fall flat on his face.'

'Too late,' Cass retorted.

'What?'

'I tripped him over once, a long time ago. He went down like a stone.'

The others laughed.

'How sad is it that you get pleasure from that, my love?'

'Yuk, Jeff! What have I told you about all those endearments that you trot out? My name is Cassandra, Cass or if you can't manage that then Miz Haven will do. Understand?'

'I think so. Do you want to repeat it just so that I'm sure?'

Cass rolled her eyes. Just because they now spent every Friday and Saturday night together didn't mean it was open season on the slush stuff. It just meant that they were sad. Pathetically sad. She did like it though.

She was tempted to give him a quick hug, but not here. Not when a fellow board member was in the same room. Much to her surprise, Polly had remained friendly with Miles Conway and invited him today. He'd come with his new girlfriend. Zoë something, from the marketing department. Lumpy thighs, but she seemed nice. For a Sloaney.

'Right Cass, come on – extended family photo,' Polly commanded.

She was so excited. Today was in effect her hen party. She and Clark, Daisy and their parents were leaving straight afterwards for her family's villa in Marbella, where they'd get married the following week.

Clark had wanted to do it long ago, but she'd insisted on waiting. She wanted to be sure, really sure that this time it was for real. And it was. Sure, he still had an ego bigger than some planets, but it was under control now. The fiasco of the year before had brought him crashing down to earth to join the rest of the mere mortals, and he'd discovered he liked it there. Times were good.

'I love you, Clark Dunhill,' she whispered in his ear as they lined up for the photographer.

Flash! The cameraman got the shot – the one of the biggest grin witnessed outside an advert for toothpaste.

Polly just had that effect on him, Clark acknowledged. Thank God, she'd taken him back.

He was suddenly struck by the situation around him. He was in the Shaker. He had a girl on each arm. Two girls in fact. Cass and Georgie on one side and Polly and Daisy on the other. And he was leaving later that day for Marbella.

He'd done it. He'd won the bet. And he would never, ever gamble anything again.

'Right, Smarm Man, stop standing there with that stupid grin and order the celebration champagne, before Stan changes his mind and fires me again.'

'Only if you give me a kiss first.'

Fiz was horrified. Euchhhhhhhh! She'd rather unblock a sink with her bare lips than kiss the Smarm Man. But she did need her job. She had a honeymoon to save for.

'Oh, feck.' She stood on her toes and pecked him on the cheek before rubbing her mouth with her sleeve. 'Anyone got some spare mouthwash?'